Jon shook his head, closed his eyes. But when he opened them, it was still there.

Slowly it moved forward as if it was testing his reactions, and when it finally emerged into the open space his shock forced him to take a step back. Its eyes were as red as car brake lights, demonic in their intensity, and when it opened its mouth slightly to make a rough sound in its throat, he saw distinctly a row of sharply pointed teeth. What startled him most of all was the long, gnarled horn in the middle of its forehead.

Unicorn, he mouthed silently, only it was like no unicorn he had ever seen in any fairy-tale book.

MARK CHADBOURN
SCISSORMAN

VISTA

First published in Great Britain 1997
by Victor Gollancz

This Vista edition published 1998
Vista is an imprint of the Cassell Group
Wellington House, 125 Strand, London WC2R 0BB

A catalogue record for this book is
available from the British Library.

ISBN 0 575 60224 4

Printed and bound in Great Britain by
Caledonian International Book Manufacturing Ltd, Glasgow

98 99   10 9 8 7 6 5 4 3 2 1

For Chris Udall

Acknowledgements:
Frank Mafrici, whose atmospheric artwork
inspired the cover illustration; James Udall
for absolutely legal insider information;
Dale Beeson for legal briefing and an insight
into the arcane world of the Metropolitan
Police; Helen Rollins for computer labour;
and, most of all, Elizabeth for guidance.

Human kind
Cannot bear very much reality.

T. S. Eliot
'Burnt Norton'
Four Quartets

Epilogue: Boxing Day

All of this has happened before and it will all happen again.

The corridor was filled with ghosts. At the sound of leather soles on the linoleum, they ventured out, blinking, into winter sunlight streaming through windows too high to reach. An oriental boy in his late teens stood in the doorway of the darkened TV room, his eyes filled with a dispiriting blankness. Behind him, an older man with a shaved head and doll-like eyes cowered nervously. A teenage girl, her long sandy hair obscuring the right side of her face, Veronica Lake-style, hiding imaginary scars, stared implacably for a moment and then approached the two men.

'They took my baby away,' she said in a voice like crystal. 'Do you know, he was wonderful? But they wouldn't let me keep him.' She beamed beatifically. 'He was the baby Jesus. Yes. The baby Jesus.'

Culver smiled patronizingly, but kept walking; he refused to get trapped in a conversation with one of *them*. With his short, silver hair and serious, lined face, he supposed they considered him one of the hospital's authority figures, a calming influence in a dangerously unpredictable world. His ability to read ordinary people made him secure, but he couldn't read *them* at all; they might as well have been creatures from another world.

Beside him, the younger detective bristled like a cornered cat, casting thin-limbed, angular shadows on the stained white walls. Culver caught a glimpse of a defensive sneer beneath Miles' bowed head as he projected his beacon of ginger hair to the world.

'Fuckin' nutters,' he said under his breath.

'Very liberated of you, Ryan. Very nineties.'

'Well, they are, aren't they? What would *you* call them?'

'Sanity-challenged?'

Miles thought about it for a second, then sniggered. 'I had an auntie who went doolally. She used to talk to my grandad all the time.'

'What's wrong with that?'

'He was fuckin' dead, wasn't he? She used to make him a cup of tea like he'd just dropped round to see her or something.'

'Maybe he had.'

'Don't start. I just told you – he was dead. And you know what really used to piss me off? She always saved the chocolate biscuits for him. All I got was Rich Tea. Like eating sand, that shit.'

They paused at a junction with another corridor while Culver scanned the signs on the wall. He guessed left. 'Bloody maze, this place. They must do it on purpose – trying to put the visitors on a par with the inmates.'

'My auntie couldn't find her way to the fuckin' bog. And I tell you, Charlie, you could get there by your nose. I reckon it only got flushed when the home help came round.'

'The point I was making, Ryan, is who's to say who's a nutter and who's not? Those poor bastards you and I think are off their heads probably just see the world a little better than us. Do you get what I'm saying?'

'Yes. But it sounds like bollocks to me, Chief. I remember what the home help said about my old aunt: "She's just got skewed perception." I said, "No, she fucking well hasn't. Her brain's turned to jelly, that's what it is."'

'So what happened to the chocolate biscuits?'

'What do you mean?'

'I mean, if she was saving them for your grandad, did she have one packet that went green and mouldy, or did they pile up in the corner like some EEC biscuit mountain?'

'I dunno. I suppose she ate them when I went home.'

'Or maybe he did.'

'Who?'

'Your grandad.'

'Don't wind me up, Chief.' Miles flicked his hair back from his face distractedly. 'Charlie?'

'Yes?'

'What kind of person could do this sort of stuff? Those bodies—'

Culver paused at another junction. 'Fucking hell,' he hissed, checking both ways, then choosing left again.

'It was like they were just pieces of meat, not people. You couldn't see them as people and do that to them.'

'Will you stop going on about it,' Culver snapped. 'Jesus Christ, Ryan, it's bad enough without you wittering on about it in my ear constantly!'

'Sorry, Chief,' Miles replied, chastened.

Culver felt a twinge of guilt. It wasn't Ryan's fault he felt so helpless and frustrated, it was the thought of what lay ahead. Examining photos that made him think of abattoirs. Trying to make sense of something that hinted there was no goodness anywhere in life. He hoped his wife was up to it; he wouldn't be much of a laugh for the foreseeable future.

'What is it about Christmas that sets all the nuts off?' he muttered. 'Most people are content just to stuff themselves stupid and lie in front of the TV. We're living in a sick society, Ryan, and it's getting worse. I'm used to getting called out on my day off, but at Christmas, for a case like this . . .' He paused to moisten his arid mouth. 'Some lunatic who's been creating his own bloodbath, that's the end of the fucking line.'

There were too many mysteries. When he first started to examine the big picture he had the vertiginous feeling of looking through a hole in space on to an alien world. It made him feel small and pathetic and, for the first time in his life, terribly frightened.

The door and its police officer guard presented themselves suddenly. Room five, no name. A dirty smear above the handle looked like blood. The officer nodded to them impassively. Culver shifted uncomfortably, feeling Miles' stare heavy on his back, then knocked once and walked in.

The room was spartan: a desk, a filing cabinet, a pot plant with browning leaves. A door led off on either side. No windows; they had selected it for the security. The doctor, a woman in her late forties with greying hair pulled back in a pony tail, sat perched on the end of the desk, biting her nails anxiously as she studied a heavy folder. It took a second or two for her to register Culver and Miles had entered.

She nodded. 'CID?' The two policemen introduced themselves. 'I'm Dr Lansing. I'm glad you're here.' She looked like she wanted to say more, but caught herself at the last moment.

'How's the patient?' Culver asked.

'Patient X,' she replied. 'That's his designated title until we do a positive ID. He's in a bad way.'

She went to the left-hand door and opened it a crack. In the bright, white room, Culver and Miles could see what looked like an Egyptian mummy lying on a bed surrounded by monitoring machines. Two small black eye-slits had been cut into the bandages that swathed his face, and a longer one near his mouth where two tubes snaked in.

'Jesus, he *is* in a bad way,' Miles whispered. 'The bastard got what he deserved. But who did it to him? Was it self-inflicted?'

'I want to question him,' Culver said firmly.

'There's no point. You won't get anything out of him.'

'Has he said anything since he was brought in?'

She shook her head. 'His injuries are so appalling, it's

possible his mind has simply switched off to cope with the pain. There isn't a single square inch of his skin which wasn't cut. We stitched the deepest as best we could, but the rest . . .' Her voice trailed off. 'I don't know how much longer he can last. The trauma alone—'

'He's the only chance we've got to find out what happened.' Lansing made to protest, but Culver pushed past her into the room, regretting it a second later. There was a feeling of electricity in the air which made him queasy. The smell of antiseptic was almost overpowering; Culver guessed they had soaked Patient X with it before applying the bandages, out of desperation more than anything else. Up close he could see the white bandages turning pink at too many points.

He pulled up a chair and leaned forward, trying not to gag. 'Can you hear me? It's Detective Culver.'

If not for the machines bleeping, he might have been dead. Culver couldn't find any room in him for pity.

'I need some answers. You must have been a witness to what happened.' He paused. 'At *least* a witness.'

Culver waited for several heartbeats, then sighed. He should have known better than to expect any easy answers. The case had been a nightmare of conundrums from the very first murder.

Patient X moved his head almost imperceptibly towards Culver and tried to raise it. Anxiously, Culver leaned forward and caught a glimpse of the eyes through the ragged slits; what he saw in them almost drove him from the room.

There was a barely audible sound. Culver lowered his ear close to the mouth and felt the patient's breath on his lobe like a blast of air from a long-sealed room. It took him almost a minute to force out the brief message and then Patient X rolled back and refused to acknowledge Culver any more.

Miles and Lansing watched him curiously as he exited.

'You did well. I didn't even think he *could* speak any more,' Lansing said.

'What did he say?' Miles asked.

Culver pushed past him. 'Can I see the kid now?'

'Thankfully, he's in much better shape,' Lansing said, leading them to the other door. 'Physically, at least.'

The room was in darkness. She switched on the fluorescent striplamp, which flickered on and off with a noisy crackle of electricity, refusing to settle down in either light or dark; after the atmosphere of the other room, it made Culver feel even more nauseous. 'I'll have to get maintenance round,' Lansing sighed. 'Bloody cutbacks.'

In the intermittent illumination, Culver glimpsed a boy of about six standing erect like a sentry in the corner of the room, his hands smartly behind his back. He was like a doll, with skin so clear and white it seemed to have a pearly lustre, eyes that were pools of shadow and black hair which flopped lusciously across his brow. No emotion was visible in his face. Culver couldn't tell if the boy was frightened or traumatized; for a moment he even thought the child was watching them with the cold, dispassionate eye of someone much older.

'Is this how he was found?' Culver asked.

'He's not spoken either,' Lansing replied. 'And those clothes . . .' He was wearing pale breeches, a dark blue frock coat and a frilled shirt.

'Maybe he was on his way to a fancy dress party,' Culver muttered. 'The report said he was standing next to your man, just watching him.'

Lansing took a step back and whispered so the child couldn't hear. 'It's quite the strangest thing. He looks like a little Victorian boy, don't you think? And his eyes could just suck you up. They're so big and dark, like a wise, sensitive old man's.'

'Hang on a minute,' Miles barked. 'He's got something in his mouth.'

The light flashed off, on, off. Culver peered, but could see nothing.

'Just an illusion,' Lansing said.

'No. I can see his cheeks moving.' Miles squatted down in front of the boy. 'You have, haven't you? Come on, sonny, spit it out!'

Culver could see it now. The boy's cheek was bulging as if it contained an enormous gobstopper. 'Leave him alone, Miles. He's having you on.'

Miles put his fingers to the boy's lips, but they remained clamped tightly shut. 'You'd better do what I say,' Miles muttered. 'You don't want to get in trouble, do you?'

Futilely, he tried to prise the lips apart until the weight in the boy's mouth shifted. The child pursed his lips and Culver saw a glint of white teeth. His senses, honed during a lifetime of difficult situations, started to jangle. 'Leave it be, Ryan,' he said curtly.

'Hang on, I can just see something poking through his teeth—'

'Leave it be!'

The boy suddenly opened his mouth with a roar.

Frozen in the flashing light, Culver saw what erupted out as it slammed into Miles' face before disappearing into the shadows under the small bed.

Miles pitched backwards, scrabbling to wipe stinging slime from his face. 'Jesus!' he gasped. 'A toad! He had a fucking toad in his mouth!'

Lansing stared in horror. 'Ridiculous,' she said hopefully. But she had seen it too.

Miles coughed and choked, then scrambled upright, searching for his composure.

Culver pulled Lansing out roughly. 'Shut the damn door,' he hissed.

They stared at each other for a long moment before Culver said to her, 'What *is* going on here?' as if it were her fault.

'There's no way he could have got a toad in here. Unless . . .' She shook her head.

Miles finished for her. 'Unless it was inside him.'

Culver and Miles left soon after. As they stumbled around the corridors trying to find the exit, Miles asked suddenly, 'What did that bastard say to you?'

Culver shook his head. 'Just rambling.'

'But what did he say?'

Culver sighed, then spotted the exit and brightened perceptibly. 'Just one word. Scissorman.'

There was so much to do, but Culver was determined to finish it all before the wintry darkness closed in; that seemed important. The body was already in place for the autopsy when they arrived. Ryan stayed for just twenty seconds before he made his excuses and left. Culver pictured Vivien Leigh to keep his gorge from rising.

'Not pretty, is it?' Markham snapped on his rubber gloves. His aftershave was almost overpowering. Culver wondered if the stink of too many bodies had destroyed the pathologist's sense of smell, or if it was simply the same bad taste that forced him to wear yellow polka-dot bow ties with chalk-stripe suits.

'That's the understatement of the year. What have we got?'

'Caucasian female, aged early thirties. No preliminary identification.'

Culver couldn't resist one brief glance at the body and regretted it instantly. 'You're sure it's a woman?' he asked bitterly.

Markham finished laying out his tools.

'How do you cope with all this cutting people up, Markham? Doesn't it make you think of your friends and family as pieces of meat and bone?'

'On the contrary. It's made me a firm believer in God. When I look inside a body I see miracles, Culver. I see more than evolution at work.'

'I'm glad you've maintained your sense of wonder. After all my years on the murder squad, atheism's about the most I can hope for. It's a bleak, horrible world out there filled with people trying to get one over on each other. When I see something like this, I think, if God made man, what does that make God?'

'Still like Christmas, though, don't you?'

'Yes, I do.'

Markham clicked on his mini-cassette. 'Time,' he checked his watch, 'two thirty-five p.m., December twenty-six. Commencing preliminary examination of alpha fourteen stroke five.' He cast a cursory eye up and down the body. 'Deep cuts in the torso, head and upper limbs suggest the deceased is the victim of a severe attack with a long cutting tool, possibly a machete or a sword. More delicate incisions indicate the use of . . . ahm . . . a smaller tool, possibly a scalpel. Some of these cuts are quite precise, suggesting some medical knowledge. It seems from the angle and placement of these smaller incisions that they were made after the initial assault, suggesting the attacker incapacitated his victim with a furious frontal flurry before moving in to continue with the smaller tool.'

Markham placed the cassette on the metal tray next to the table and gripped the head with both hands. There was a sucking noise as he twisted. 'Head almost completely severed with one clean cut, suggesting a very strong, full-grown male assailant.'

'Jesus!' Culver backed off a few paces.

Markham moved down the body, probing its secret places, prising apart flesh that should have remained sealed.

Culver leaned over and clicked off the cassette. 'I haven't got much time, Markham. Give me the short form.'

'It's another one, all right. I mean, you can tell that by looking at it. But see here,' he delved into the gashes that had hacked through the ribcage, 'there's the trophy. Or

17

rather, there it isn't. No liver. Very carefully removed. If I didn't know better I'd say he was a surgeon.'

'Maybe it was his hobby.'

'Have you got him?'

'We're pretty sure. He's in a bad way. Might have a partner who did it to him, but I'm not convinced.'

'Self-inflicted?' Markham asked with puzzlement.

'He's capable of anything.'

'The body was laid out in a ritual position, wasn't it?' Markham asked. Culver nodded. 'So there's an occult angle?'

'We figure—'

'Hang on a minute.' Markham probed into the liver cavity and fished something out.

'What is it?' Culver felt his nerves tingle; he knew the answer before Markham replied.

'It's a piece of paper.' Markham used the scalpel to unfold the sodden, red scrap. 'It's been torn from a book. Same pattern.'

'Can you read it?'

'No. You'll need to get the forensic guys to clean it up.'

'What the fuck was this bastard up to?' Culver hissed through his teeth. And this was only the beginning. He dreaded what other mysteries lay ahead.

The snow was still thick on the ground and there seemed little prospect of a thaw as Culver and Miles trudged against the biting wind to the house. It lay dark and heavy against the grey sky, an oppressive, threatening presence amongst the surrounding neatly tended homes. Its Victorian architecture was too imposing, its bricks too smoke-stained. Culver couldn't understand why anyone would want to live there.

'I know forensics have been over the place like dogs in a dustbin, but give it another go, Miles. I'm off to talk to the neighbours.' He could tell Miles felt the same way about the house and wondered if he was being fair sending him in there.

Culver slipped through the gate of the house next door and hammered on the brass knocker. The last time he saw Miles before he entered, the younger detective was standing on the path looking up at the first-floor windows as if someone had spoken to him.

A woman with silver hair and flushed cheeks answered the door. Culver smelled the alcohol instantly. He was glad someone was enjoying a little Christmas cheer.

'I'm Detective Culver, CID,' he said, flashing his warrant card.

She stared at him intently for a long moment, then tears sprang to the corners of her eyes and slowly began to trickle down her cheeks. 'They wouldn't listen,' she said bleakly. 'When people are in a dream, they never do, do they?'

'I've come about your neighbours,' Culver continued tentatively. 'Did you have much to do with them?'

She looked past him, towards the house. Her jaw began to tremble with suppressed emotion and after one sudden, racking sob she pressed a knuckle into her teeth to contain herself.

Culver followed her gaze into the growing gloom. A deep wave of despair swept up inside him and he felt tears come to his own eyes, although he couldn't explain the feeling at all.

'Can I come in?' he asked.

'He loved her, you know. I could see it in his eyes the first time I met him in the garden. When you see that kind of love, you never forget it. He came here to recover. I tried to tell him.'

Culver tried to work out if she was more drunk than he thought or if she'd slipped through the net of the Mental Health Act. Her eyes gave nothing away, apart from the pain.

'I've been trying to escape from here for years,' she

continued. 'Putting the house on the market. Writing to friends to see if they'll allow me to stay. It won't let me go. I'll die here, in its shadow, as I've lived. It watches me. Sometimes I see white horses in the garden – you wouldn't think that'd be allowed, would you? And music in the night. Not *nice* music. It makes me feel sick, like I'm getting a migraine.' She looked at him properly for the first time. 'Don't trust the cats.'

Culver pretended to search for something in his notebook, attempting to earn some space away from her jumbled thoughts. Then he said, 'Did you hear something yesterday? Early?'

Her gaze drifted away from him to the house and then, slowly, she began to close the door.

'I haven't finished my questioning, Mrs—'

She silenced him with a shake of her head. 'No. No more.'

Culver waited in the car for Miles for half an hour. When he got bored and irritable in the cold, he headed back up to the house, but all the doors were locked and Miles had the key. He spent five minutes peering through windows and cursing him, then he kicked the gate so hard it almost flew off its hinges. He stormed back to the car and drove off at speed. Miles could make his own way back to the office.

Night fell quickly at that time of year. Culver sat at his desk in the deserted CID room, looking out at the lights of the city. His anger had subsided, leaving a deep-seated despair and a weariness that cut to the bone. In a city like London, brutality was endemic. He had seen it as a young beat cop in the sixties, when the gangs of the east and the south were chopping, stabbing and shooting each other over paltry plots of land. And in the grey seventies, when the violence hadn't been quite so stylish, but more painfully effective.

But in the eighties something had gone wrong; with

London, with the country. A sourness had taken over. Any innocence that still rippled on from the swinging sixties was swept away. The crimes worsened – paedophiliac killings, drug-addled young men raping housebound old women, things that had never been seen before. It was as if all the stops and checks of society had been disabled, allowing anyone to do anything for their own gratification, however sick or depraved. Sometimes, in his bleaker moments, he could see no end to it. And now this, culminating on Christmas Day as if to emphasize that goodness had finally been choked out of all their lives.

Patient X, The Pinstripe Slayings, all that blood and butchery. Yet his anxiety wasn't simply due to the horror of what one man could do; it was the fact that nothing connected to the case seemed *right*. He had investigated plenty of sick, bizarre cases, but this was so twisted from reality he couldn't even find a frame of reference. It disturbed him on some level he couldn't explain, like the time he had gone to a spiritualist meeting and seen an elderly woman break down at a message that could only have come from her long-dead husband.

On his desk, the crimson cover of the journal glowed incarnadine in the pooling light of his desk lamp. In the centre was a sticky label with *Jonathan Marshall Summers, Personal Assessment* typed by some faceless administration official who hadn't embraced new technology. Over the top, someone, presumably Summers, had scrawled *CRAZED RAMBLINGS!* in black felt tip. It was another artefact, heavy with potential meaning about the inexplicable, troubling mystery, in a pile of artefacts that promised illumination yet were as indecipherable as alien relics. A shattered hand mirror. Scraps torn from a book. Handcuffs. Antique children's toys. A message on a dressing-table mirror: *Love crosses all boundaries*. Fragments of lives lived on the flipside of the real world. Culver, used to mysteries, felt sick and disorientated.

He picked up the phone and bleeped Miles once more. Still no reply. The thought of bollocking his wayward assistant the following morning distracted him enough to give him some comfort.

'Still here, Charlie?'

Culver started at the voice, then felt angry with himself. Across the room, the duty sergeant's head was silhouetted against the corridor light filtering through the half-open door.

'Fine, Jack. I'm just going to tidy up here a bit before I call it a night.'

'Don't stick at it too long, Charlie. They're not paying you for it.' A long pause, then, 'Crazy case, eh, Charlie?'

Culver tried to find the words to answer him, but nothing came. 'Have a quiet night, Jack.'

He would have liked to go home and examine the journal in the light of a new day. But he had to go over it all again, find some way to impose order on the churning chaos which troubled him so; otherwise, he wouldn't sleep.

He picked up the journal, put it down, placed it in geometrical alignment with his blotter. It was time to start.

Then, faintly, he heard what sounded like a door opening somewhere nearby. He looked curiously into the dark, but, hearing nothing more, returned to the journal with reluctant determination. It would be a long night.

1

All of this has happened before . . .

The day was like a bad hangover – grey sheen, bad-tempered clouds, sour odours rising from the churning Thames, polluted on its weary journey from its sparkling source by chemicals, plastic and paper and the odd sub-merged body or two. A barge filled with rubbish chugged relentlessly through Docklands while seagulls swooped and dived, plucking morsels from the detritus. In a gleaming tower of glass and steel visible across London, like a needle stitching the sky, Jonathan Summers tried to recall who he was and how he came to be there.

'Don't jump – think of the wife.' A comic pause. 'OK, jump.'

Jon pulled his focus back to see the reflection in the glass. Richard Beeson stood just behind his left shoulder, a mass of muscle-merging-to-fat topped by long, wavy hair which he described as red and the rest of the world called ginger.

'I wouldn't give them the pleasure.' Jon let his gaze fall back to the skyline, seeing London in a light he hadn't experienced since he had first moved to the capital as a child: the Tower of London, St Paul's, Nelson's Column, Buckingham Palace; a boy's city, a place where anything could happen.

'It's not the end of the world, old chap. So what—?'

'So what if I'm working from dawn to dusk, five days a

week, and then spending my weekends keeping my contacts sweet? So what if I never get a lunch break? Now they want me to stay even later each night to finish this report that's got Gilmore so hot under the collar.'

'You'd only be hanging around street corners with the other rent boys. Face it, Jonathan – your looks are going. You'll have to find another way to pay your mortgage.' Richard placed a shovel-sized hand on Jon's shoulder and shook it gently. When he didn't get a response, he added seriously, 'They've turned the screw because of the second quarter losses, you know that. It's only short term. After the big bonuses last year, the unmentionable self-abusers of the dealing room have been too busy playing with themselves to do any work. Certainly, the last quarter results look like a bad day in Bosnia, but you know it will sort itself out.'

Richard's voice was almost lost in the thunder of blood in Jon's brain; it sounded like a steam press, pounding things smaller and smaller until they disappeared completely. He pushed both palms against the thick glass and took a deep breath to control himself.

'It's not just having to work late, don't you see? That's just the latest sign of the malaise.'

'I know you've not been happy for a while, Jon—'

Jon snorted ironic laughter.

'—but much as I loathe polluting my mind with philosophical discussions, I have to tell you to take a step back. Get some perspective. You're top dog here, BSD. Think of all that dosh you've made for yourself in your diligent employ at the very wonderful Steelguard. Everyone gets a little burned out every now and then – that's the nature of the job. Take a holiday. Mexico. The Caribbean. When you come back, the old buzz will be there. You were born to compete, Jon. You were made to succeed. It's who you are.'

'No, it's not.' The thunder was drawing closer. 'That's not the person my parents made.'

Richard rapped Jon's head with his knuckles. 'Hello? Is Jonathan Summers coming out to play? Please don't indulge in all that nineties ka-ka, Jon. That attitude is ruining the fucking City. Remember the eighties: *He who dies with the most toys, wins.* Now *that's* quality of life.'

'You know, the first time I heard that aphorism I was amused. And then I sat down and thought about it and I realized how pathetic and sad and dismal it really was.'

'You really *are* in a bad way. When did all this start?'

That was the question. When did he suddenly open his eyes and realize he'd been sleepwalking for the last ten years? When did he notice the ties that bound him to his youth had been broken? When did he become a different person?

'What's gone wrong with this country, Richard? Work never used to be the most important thing in people's lives. There used to be excitement out there, real excitement in day-to-day existence. Debate, arguments, wild ideas, values. Where are they now? Not in my life, Richard, and it's driving me mad. I feel like I've been dead for years and only just realized it.'

Richard checked over his shoulder to make sure no company weasels were in earshot. 'What you need is a good spliff. In the toilets. That'll calm you down.'

The thunder became the deafening sound of tanks clanking across a battlefield; Richard wasn't listening to a word he was saying. 'No more drugs. Anyway, I'm wired—'

'Again?' There was a new note in Richard's voice. 'How much did you do last night? Two grams? I like the old marching powder, Jon, but I prefer to give myself a day or two off after a binge.'

'I had a headache this morning—'

'Well, that would be the brandy, wouldn't it? The whole *bottle* of brandy. You were shit-faced when I left you, you and Sarah.'

'Now *you're* going to start preaching to *me*?'

'Everybody does it, Jon. You've simply got to remember to stay on top of it.'

Jon looked back at the landmarks. The transcendental feeling had gone. He was locked back in his body, in a room with windows that didn't open, in a tower that cost more to build than the GDP of a Third World country, in a region where people spoke a strange, incomprehensible language.

'Richard,' he began quietly, 'sometimes I think I'm losing it.'

The small heap of desiccated white crystals on the toilet lid was all he had left to tide him over until he got to the club after work, but he felt in urgent need of a pick-me-up beyond the norm. He'd left his razor blade in his desk drawer – forgetfulness seemed to be a constant these days – so he used his platinum Amex to chop and draw the lines; they looked comically long, like some government warning film about a drug abuser's white road to hell. He snorted with a rolled-up fifty he kept specifically for the purpose and then waited for his throat to numb. The insectile buzz in his ears grew all-encompassing; he barely heard Richard yell something from the toilet door.

'What?'

'I said get your bony posterior out of the cubicle. Gilmore wants to see you.'

Jon emerged, flushed and sweating, rubbing his nostrils clean of evidence.

'Not *more*—'

'Give it a rest, Richard. If I could face a few more hours of this fucking job without filling my head full of shit, I would do. End of conversation.'

He regretted being so obnoxious as he was pushing past Richard, but it was too late. He could identify the person he wanted to return to being, recognize how he should act, but like some late-developing autism, all his best efforts failed to connect.

The dealing room was sound and fury. Sunlight breaking through the floor-to-ceiling windows illuminated the motivators that lined one wall: *Do it to them before they do it to you. Act fast, be a hero – hesitation is for zeros.* And, finally, a lifestyle justification from *Wall Street*, for all those who had no concept of irony: *Greed is good.*

Jon saw Gilmore pacing his glass-fronted office like a caged panther before he had crossed the dealing room. He was down to his bespoke shirt-sleeves, tie yanked loose in studied rakishness; Jon wondered how long he had spent in front of the mirror to get the knot *just* right. He kicked the door shut noisily as soon as Jon entered.

'Where the fuck have you been?'

'I was—'

'It doesn't matter. Shut up. Have you started on that report yet?'

'No.'

'What do you fucking mean, "No"? What kind of answer is that? I distinctly remember telling you this morning it was urgent. Do you know what urgent means?'

Yes, it means you've just had your arse kicked by someone in the boardroom and now you're going to make my life hell, Jon thought.

'You'd better lift your fucking game, Summers. Some people might think you're king bunny on the dealing floor, but that means fuck all to me. You've got an attitude problem. You sneer every time someone tells you to do something. You're a fucking liability waiting to happen.'

Jon noted the sweat patches under Gilmore's armpits; it must have been an epic dressing-down. They were obviously more worried about the second quarter results than they were letting on.

Gilmore was ranting again, waving his arms, kicking out at his chair, desk, wastepaper basket; Jon was surfing on crystal foam, listening to the tide in his ears, grinding his teeth, swallowing coke-flavoured snot. For an instant he was a million miles up in space, looking down with his telescopic vision at meaningless ants that had no influence over his life whatsoever. It passed too quickly and the tension in his chest and spine returned; these days it always seemed to be there, throbbing when he woke, constricting when he went to sleep.

'Are you fucking listening to me?' Gilmore thrust his face so close to Jon's that beads of sweat from his forehead splattered Jon's cheek. Gilmore stank of expensive after-shave. His face was florid, deformed by senseless rage and fear. He had embraced the City culture of bullying because it was the only way he knew how to cope with his own weaknesses, but that didn't mean Jon had to take it; at that moment, he wanted to punch him out.

'Well, fucking listen to this,' Gilmore continued. 'All leave is cancelled for three months until that fucking report is finished. Got that? *All* leave.'

It took a second or two for Gilmore's words to worm their way through Jon's cocaine buzz. Gilmore seemed relieved, almost happy, when he saw the realization creep over Jon's face.

'That's right, you fucking wanker. No Christmas holiday. I want you in here on Christmas Eve, Christmas Day *and* Boxing Day. Not even a fucking virgin birth is going to keep you away. Book your turkey and stuffing now – you'll be eating it at your desk.'

'That's not fair—' A pathetic thing to say, but it was a natural response to Gilmore's playground brutality. Christmas had already been planned in his mind: a sanctuary where he would attempt to return to the values of his childhood, spend quiet time with Sarah on Christmas Eve, forget the life that made him feel like he spent each day swimming in a sewer. If he admitted it to himself, it was even more important than that; Christmas was his *one* chance to turn the clock back and escape. If he missed it, he was lost.

Gilmore was sniggering, gearing up for more abuse. Jon knew there was no point in arguing. He turned and marched out, slamming the door so hard the glass frosted. He heard Gilmore's animal bellow of rage as he headed back to his desk.

Richard caught his arm before he could sit down. 'What the fuck was that all about?' he hissed.

'I hate this job!' He pulled his chair out so forcibly it crashed over backwards. Heads all around turned and stared.

Richard righted it and pushed him down before kneeling beside him nervously. 'Calm down, for God's sake,' he whispered. 'You may be a winner here, but you're not indispensable. You know they don't like prima donnas.'

'I don't care if they sack me tomorrow.' His head felt like it was being crushed in a vice and his chest seemed too small to contain all the air he needed.

'Are you OK?' Richard asked, suddenly concerned.

'Just an anxiety attack. Rage does that sometimes.' Jon closed his eyes and focused on his breathing until he just about managed to control it. Eventually he said, 'This job is destroying me! All the hours I'm sitting here in this office . . . think of the things I could be doing! Life's so short, but I waste my time doing nothing to make my life, or anybody's life, any better. Just amassing vast amounts of digital money and shifting it around the globe. We kid ourselves it's important to get through the day, but it's not, Richard. Not at all. There's got to be more to life than this.'

'You're just going through a bad—'

'No! It's more than that. I wanted to be a writer, did you know that? This job was just going to be a stop-gap, give me a little cash, buy me some time so I could do what I wanted to do. But somewhere down the line, the job polluted my mind like a computer virus. Turned me into

29

somebody else. I haven't written a word since I started here. I haven't done anything except become the kind of person the job wants me to be. While I was staring at this computer screen, my values and ethics slipped away without me realizing. We've done some questionable things, Richard.' He paused, recalling the worst of the crimes.

'We've done what was required of us, old chap. You're just getting maudlin because of all this hassle with Gilmore.'

There was a numbness in Jon's arms which seemed to be spreading in a tightening swathe across his chest. He was sweating profusely. Everything was thunder and light. 'I've been weak, Richard, that's all, but now my eyes have opened. I don't see the point in all this any more—'

'The point is the expensive car, the large house, the best restaurants. The point is not being an insect like all the others swarming to their petty little jobs out there.' Richard's eyes were incandescent.

'I'm not attacking you, Richard. This is about *me*, about being so pathetic that I gave up the person I used to be for something I never really wanted. It's true what they say: on a death-bed, nobody says they wished they'd spent more time at the office. This whole work-till-you-drop culture is *wrong*—'

'Jon—'

'The ethics of this business are wrong—'

'Jon—' Richard grabbed his arm tightly.

'And you know the funny thing? Although I've been feeling like this for months, it took something as ridiculous as missing Christmas to make me realize what a fucking hole I'm in.'

'They'll give you time off in lieu, old chap, and what would you be doing if you weren't in here? Stuffing yourself with food you don't need and entertaining relations you don't like. They're doing you a favour!'

Jon broke through the tension strangling him and saw that Richard would never grasp what he was saying.

Richard wasn't troubled by ethical questions, had no interest in doing anything else. And somehow that made it all seem worse.

'Have you got any coke left?'

Richard shook his head in weary disbelief. 'Come on, Jon. You've done more than enough today.'

'I'm going to blast myself. I've had enough of all this bollocks. I want some time off in my head.'

Richard considered the request for a second, then, still shaking his head, he palmed the tiny paper envelope from his pocket and slipped it into Jon's hand. 'Sort yourself out, old chap,' he said resignedly.

Time came and went. The thunder was rolling all around Jon, in his head and out across the dealing room, and he was at the eye of the storm, floating in total calm; he was immaculate, apart from reality. The dealing room was filled with a hundred monkeys in Cerruti suits and silk ties, shouting, laughing, waving their arms in antediluvian gestures of the jungle. It was like Trafalgar Square on New Year's Eve, the same mix of misery and euphoria, heady conversations punctuated by four-letter words. The computer terminals were plastic Aladdin's lamps, fuelled by wishes, promising wealth beyond measure, riches without responsibility, just as easily disappointing through the trickery of words.

Jon scrubbed at his nostrils to clear away any stray coke; it was the fifth time he had done it that day, but he couldn't seem to stop himself. The last of the gram had been snorted ten minutes ago, but the effect was minimal; he was full to the brim.

He chewed a nail, thought about answering the phone which had been flashing at him waspishly for a while now, and then looked up, past the Steelguard logo to the grey light filtering through the windows. He imagined briefly the sensation of skydiving through them and then falling through the mist into the Thames far below.

A scarlet speckle dappled the window. Jon stared at it curiously. Another burst nearby, and another. It was raining. Red rain. The drops came faster, smearing the window, obscuring the skyline. He thought: *it's blood*.

Dazed, he glanced around the dealing room; no one else had seen it. Slowly, he felt the familiar constriction creeping around his chest as if a belt was being pulled tighter and tighter. His throat seemed to be closing up.

The droplets of blood began to merge together in a crimson wave that surged inexorably down; almost the whole window was covered. He wondered if it was some sign that the world, his world, was coming to an end. With a tremendous effort, he tried to yell out a warning, but all he could muster was a pathetic gargling sound. When he raised his arm to point, it crashed limply on to the desk. The pain in his chest was excruciating.

Dan Vickers saw where Jon was staring, gaped for a moment, then brayed with laughter. Someone else joined in. They were laughing at the blood, laughing at him. Jon grabbed at his chest and rubbed furiously, but the pain wouldn't stop; it was his heart. He was dying.

Suddenly a swathe of the blood was swept away, then another. Through it appeared the angry face of a window cleaner, and as he scrubbed ferociously at the glass, his partner's face loomed, mouth roaring silently, Keystone Cops style. They pointed at the glass, at the blood, argued some more, then scrubbed again. And still the blood fell.

'Cleaning fluid,' someone yelled, then shrieked with laughter.

No, Jon thought. *Blood*.

He gripped the edge of the desk, marvelling at the translucence of the skin on his hand while at the same time feeling the rising horror as his chest crushed inwards. No one was coming to help him; they glanced over, saw the panic in his face, then returned to their computer screens or their phones. He couldn't breathe at all; darkness closed around his vision until he was looking through a bottle at distorted images, mythological creatures, naiads and dryads, fauns and centaurs, half-beasts, half-men, a world of wonder and madness.

Jon plunged his head between his knees, trying to fight it, forcing his lungs to inhale, exhale, rhythmically, calmly. After a few seconds, the pressure eased enough for him to raise his head and in that instant the swirling cacophony of shouting and ringing came roaring back. As he glanced around the room, Jon experienced a piercing moment of clarity that transcended all his previous visions.

He *knew*.

This was it; only one tremendous effort of will would keep damnation at bay.

Leaning forward, he wrapped his arms around his computer terminal as if he was holding a lover, a hug to mark the end of an affair, and then, when the pressure was just right, he braced himself and heaved.

There were tiny kisses of sound as snaking wires burst from the back and then he had it in his arms, close to his chest. The room fell suddenly silent, faces gaping with simian stupidity. Jon marched down the aisle until he reached the window, eyeing the soaring sheet of red and grey curiously. He rocked back and forth twice and after one final, vertiginous instant, he hurled the terminal with all his strength.

The glass erupted outwards in a glimmering, beautiful explosion. Jon gaped in wonder at the jewelled shards turning slowly in the air, catching the glorious light before following the terminal down, through the wisps of cloud, to the murky grey far below.

2

'I suppose you'll call this a confession when you hear it. Well, I don't like the word confession. I just want to set you right about something you couldn't see because it was smack up against your nose.' Tough words from a tough man in a tough film a long time ago. Relevant, though, in an abstract kind of way.

Write it all down, they said. Write it all down in this beautiful red book with its creamy white Winston Smith pages. All part of the 'recovery process'. The theory is that if I dig deep in that sewer flowing through my head, I'll manage to sift out all the ordure to leave the sparkling, pure water of my thoughts. That's the theory. The truth is a little more prosaic: they think I'll simply give them enough rope to hang me higher. The rational, sane thing to do would be to write a few platitudes, a few clichés, nothing too threatening. Show I'm back to normal.

Ha fucking ha.

Rehabilitation is a funny word. It implies you want to get back to the state you were in before. Get back to wrestling for space with commuters every morning, sitting in a room without fresh air or sunshine, staring at a computer screen, counting figures, yelling down a phone, getting bullied by superiors, counting more figures, feeling the tension rise, dealing with office politics, all the people trying to stab you in the back, being stuck in that artificial place until the sun has gone down, then wrestling for space with commuters on the way back home where you crash straight into bed because you're too exhausted to do anything else. Now *that's* insane.

There are more meaningful things with which to trouble oneself. For instance: what's more important – the fantasy of artists or the reality of bank managers? Ethical poverty or financial poverty? Should you protect your innocence and wonder at all costs or trade it for material success?

I have this horrible feeling that the meaning of life can be boiled down to a few twee phrases: hold on to your childhood values; money and power seduce and destroy and make you vulnerable and unhappy on every level; focus on people – love and relationships are more important than possessions; keep the magic in your life. Sounds sickening, doesn't it? But is it really so bad?

What's important in my life right now? Well, Sarah is certainly at the top of my list. I'd try to describe how I feel about her, but I know it would come out like a verse in a card you might find in one of those specialist card shops. You know, Cards R Us or something. They're all pink and lemon with large plastic animals covered in fur that feels like the stuff you put in lofts. They're actually the cause of more murders around the country than drugs. On Valentine's Day, soppy boys turn up with them only to be bludgeoned to death with their present by Doc Martened girlfriends who know a wanker with no taste when they see one. Somewhere there's a police warehouse stuffed with blood-stained, life-size, electric blue sheepdogs and teddy bears. Sorry, I'm rambling again. A sure sign . . .

So: Sarah. I'd do anything for her. She's one of the few things of value in my life right now. My mother always used to say you know when you've found the right person because you'd lay down your life for them. Well, I would. Then again, my mother always used to say, *Every time you tell a lie, a fairy has to die*, which means that with the job

I've been doing there's a Bosnian war grave-size pixie atrocity at the bottom of my garden.

Richard's right up there too. He falls firmly into the good bloke category despite his wholehearted embrace of the ways of Mammon. We've been best mates ever since he started at Steelguard. Plenty of outrageous fun, a few bad times. I trust him and that's not the kind of thing I'd normally say about someone who works in the City. I hope he never gets to see this or he'll use it to tell everyone in the office I've got latent homosexual tendencies. Bastard. I hate him.

And, apart from my great parents who have retired to the wilds of Norfolk, that's the sum total of the things that matter in my life. I'm changing my name by deed poll to Sad Pathetic Bastard.

Oh yes, and films. Movies are great because they cast life in a true light; on film, everything is fantastic. The first flick I remember seeing, the one that started my fascination bordering on obsession, is *It's A Wonderful Life*. Nothing unusual about that – everyone knows it and loves it. Frank Capra tugging at the heart strings, Jimmy Stewart as the truly good man wounded by circumstance, that Christmas Eve ending which ensures there isn't a dry eye in the house. There's one aspect of it that's always concerned me, though. George Bailey was only saved from suicide because heaven sent down the wannabe angel Clarence to show him what a terrible place Bedford Falls would be without his do-gooding. But we all know angels don't exist. So in the real world, George Bailey would be fish food. And the message is, *ta-daa*, being good isn't good enough. You've got to be a nasty bastard to get what you deserve in this world.

At least, that's the cynical adult perspective which life seems to have been trying to get me to see, but for the most part I think I've resisted it. As a child, *It's A Wonderful Life* was the most magical film I'd ever seen, but it remains forever tied up with possibly the worst experience in my life to date. Pay attention, all you psychologists, psychiatrists and psychoanalysts. Negative and positive influences colliding – surely this is your territory.

The film was on one Sunday afternoon just before Christmas. I remember the cold outside, the hiss of the fire as I curled up on the hearthrug, rapt. The smell of my mother's baking drifting through from the kitchen. The muffled drone of my father talking on the telephone in the hall. The moment the final credits rolled up, I suddenly felt I had to run and tell someone about this amazing new discovery of mine. But before I could make a move, there was a crash, a bang and repeated tiny explosions like miniature fireworks going off. I ran out into the hall where I saw my father lying across the Christmas tree, a real one, mind you, which must have been at least ten feet high. Broken glass decorations littered the floor. It was one of those horrible moments that make you feel sick to see, yet you have to stifle a laugh because they're inherently funny. Let's face it, it looked like the aftermath of a Three Stooges sketch.

At first I thought my dad must have tripped and stumbled into it, until I saw he wasn't moving. I was only ten – I couldn't understand what was happening. But then my mother came hurrying through and she screamed so loud I burst into tears.

It turned out Dad had suffered a heart attack. The ambulance arrived quickly enough to prevent any lasting damage, but it was probably as much to do with my mum's clumsy attempt at heart massage. She looked like she was beating a minute steak in the kitchen. I always reckoned Dad suffered more from that than anything. That sight really instilled in me my belief in what marriage is all about – fighting against the odds to save your loved one. Challenging the Grim Reaper face to face.

So, thanks to Mum, his heart started beating again, but for some reason he didn't regain consciousness. I remember the first time I saw him in hospital, lying in his bed with his eyes shut, pale, hollow-cheeked, looking like an old man. I kept screaming to Mum, 'That's not my dad! Where's Dad?' It took me a few visits to come to terms with it, but I never quite accepted that feeling inside like somebody had cut out a major organ without anaesthetic. Every night I'd pray for Dad to wake up, and every morning I'd get ready to visit him with the kind of optimism you can never quite muster as an adult.

One day the doctor took my mum out into the corridor to tell her something and I sneaked out to listen. Through the fog of his bedside manner, I made out he was telling Mum if Dad wasn't out of his coma by Christmas Day, he wouldn't come out at all. Mum just crumpled up like a paper bag. You never see someone really cry until the threat of death is close.

I had to do something, but what? I was ten. That Christmas Eve, Mum put all the presents under the tree as usual. She was determined I wasn't going to miss out; Mum always did have that blitz spirit. While she was on the phone to Auntie Eileen, I collected all my presents in a sack and went down to the tube station where I got a cab – I had all my savings ready to pay. He took me to the hospital – didn't charge me either, after I told him where I was going. I went up to Dad's ward and sat on the end of his bed with the presents. And then I made a deal. I said, 'Dad, all these presents are yours if you wake up. I really, really want them. But I want you more.' I opened them one at a time, saying a little prayer as I unwrapped the paper and put them on the bed around him. An Action Man with French Resistance outfit. A board game – Risk, I think it was. A book, *Grimbold's Other World* by Nicholas Stuart Gray. A selection pack of chocolates. Then I sat and waited. At some point I must have fallen asleep because the nurse woke me to say my mum had rung – she was frantic. But I remember having this dream that my dad had been talking to me.

And the next morning he woke up.

Now tell me there's no magic in the world.

He's still got the Action Man. I saw it on the dresser in his bedroom the last time I went up to Norfolk. Sentimental old fool. He made a full recovery and I like to think I had something to do with it. But imagine what it was like for me. When you're ten you always think your dad is indestructible. Then you witness something like that. It turns your world on its head, I can tell you. I was screwed up for a long time until I started searching for answers to explain *why*. It seems Dad had just received a phone call from work. On a Sunday. To tell him they were giving him the bullet. Now remember – this was back in the sixties. They didn't have words like 'downsizing' then to soften the blow. It was just, 'You're out, matey. Get on with your life.'

We'd moved down to the Smoke from the sticks when Dad landed a good job with a City company, thanks to somebody he had known at university. Dad had put his all into that company. He worked long hours, weekends. He thought they respected him for it. They didn't. Companies never do. My dad was never the same afterwards. To get back in the saddle, he had to take a junior's job. As a manager, he'd had respect, responsibilities, all the things he'd earned with the minutes of his life, and there he was working with spotty-faced oiks who treated him like the office idiot.

I always thought I'd learned a great lesson from that. (I'm very big on learning lessons.) Then somehow I found myself in the same situation, working for a faceless corporation that was sucking the life out of me, ready to spit me out when it had drained me dry. That was the worst thing for me over the last few months and years, that sticky realization that I'd cheated myself. And, in a way, my dad.

For what? Instant financial gratification. It's true what they say – money is the biggest drug of all.

I've always been the kind of person who lives in their head. Dreams, they're the thing that make us human. Not cash, power or possessions. I always wanted to be a writer, living in dreams constantly, so waking up one day and finding myself in the City like being hit with a shovel. I can't even remember how I got myself trapped in it. It started as a stop-gap solution to a financial fallow period and ended up as a career. I found myself doing things I would never have dreamed of doing before. Morally suspect, possibly even reprehensible things. And suddenly I woke up with no idea how I'd mutated into this loathsome thing. Gregor Samsa had nothing on me.

Looking back, I wasn't the only one who experienced that corruption. The country as a whole followed the same path, although that doesn't make it any better. Oh, we had our problems in the seventies, but we were still basically decent. Then a virus spread out from the City and Westminster, infecting, corrupting, transforming. The Big Bang, financial deregulation, capitalism gone mad. Its ripples turned us into a society of 'I Wants'. I thought I was just playing a game while keeping my values safe. Sure. So safe I lost them. During the latter part of the eighties, the whole country went clinically insane and I was there screeching with laughter along with the rest of them.

Here on the brink of the millennium we're a different society – sour, grasping, ethically suspect. Slowly we're waking up to it, wondering what went wrong, wondering if it's too late to go back to innocent childhood. And I, always the last to open my eyes, realized I'd been perverted too. Is it too late to change, for me, for everybody? Well, at least I'm trying.

So, to round off, here are a few random thoughts, the kind of things concerning me right at this moment as I sit and wait for Sarah to arrive.

We are all living in a concentration camp, only through some arcane act of magic we are blind to the barbed wire and sentry towers and oblivious to the scent of death. The midnight knock on the door comes the night after school has ended, when we are trooped to the cattle trains, glimpsing what we have lost only through the slots of the carriage as it rattles along relentlessly to its bleak destination. Our brutalization begins on arrival; it is so complete that soon all memory of what we had before is eradicated.

Somehow I've broken free of the process. Maybe it was the drugs or the drink or the endless drip-drip-drip water torture of working life. Whatever, I've been given the chance to glance back to see how it all went horribly wrong, and while it's nice to have clear vision for the first time in years, it's also painful to the point of despair because I'm suddenly burdened with the awful knowledge that what's gone is gone forever. There's a terrible conundrum for the human condition: should we choose blind ignorance for security and happiness, or knowledge and sophistication when it only brings disquiet and pain? That's a tough one, boys and girls. Think about it for a while.

I don't have a choice in the matter. My outer persona, through which I interact with the world, has been stripped away. That's doctor-speak, not me. It's funny – you think people are either sane or crazy, but when you're in that strange little world doctors inhabit, they tell you there's a whole shifting scale with markers which say 'breakdown' or 'psychosis'. You can creep into madness without knowing it, like driving through Barnet and suddenly finding yourself in London. So they say.

I personally think they're the crazy ones. And they're not alone. Here are the other enemies – a scorecard so you can keep on top of the game: scientists – the people who build better video recorders while the death rate from diseases grows higher; anyone who calls themself an executive; businessmen who think in terms of profit and not people;

insurance salesmen; building company bosses who look for greenfield sites for maximum financial gain. There are more, I'm sure, but I'll get around to them when they come to mind. They're not bad *per se*. They're the guards in the towers, shining the searchlights into no man's land beyond the wire. Just doing their job. They're the people who tell us that this is the way the world is – dull and oppressive, structured, grey, with boundaries of cinder block that cannot be changed. When really it's a playground of infinite possibilities, the Land Where Anything Can Happen. Tell me that isn't a particularly heinous war crime.

I'm fighting for a new Dark Age. Belief, faith, wonder – they're the important things in life. Not high interest savings accounts, the latest Renault model or flat-packed furniture.

I think that should have placed me firmly in their not-so-elaborate trap once this little document is unveiled at my next 'assessment'. Oh, well. Honesty is the best policy, *que sera sera* and all that.

I've finally found out where the real me went, and there's no going back once the body has been dug up.

3

The cold had come a few days earlier, bitter even for December. Along the traffic-clogged North London streets, shoppers braved the chill to stare into windows cluttered with gold tinsel, red and green plastic and fake snow, wishing they had more money, dreading the journey home through the crowds cluttering the pavements. Jon watched them curiously through the passenger window as the car inched along at the speed of a funeral cortège.

'What's on your mind?' Sarah glanced at him askance as she fumbled to click in the cigarette lighter on the dashboard.

'Morecambe and Wise. *Bugs Bunny's Christmas Movie.* The smell of cooking ham on Christmas Eve.'

As he turned to look at his wife, Jon had a sudden flash of the night they met. It was at some party in the City, Mason Freeman or another of those brash new American banks. People were drinking champagne like it was beer and the dimly lit cellar bar was filled with a November fog of smoke. He'd been listening to one of Richard's filthy jokes when he had seen her across the room like some clichéd moment from a forties movie. Her blonde hair had been a tumble of curls back then, not the sleek, efficiently straight style it was now. He was impressed by the confident, almost arrogant way she was conducting herself at the centre of a circle of men, flirting one moment, flinty and sparking the next. Much to Richard's annoyance, Jon broke away before the punchline and manoeuvred himself across the room and into her circle. She was wearing a sharply cut charcoal suit with a skirt so short she seemed all legs; her cheekbones were razors, her eyes ice-blue. It didn't take him long to pick up she was in PR, just starting out in the business. At the time, he was just beginning to make a name for himself at Steelguard, the Boy Most Likely To. The stars were aligned; there was a comet in the heavens.

Love at first sight? Probably not, but after they split a gram of coke in the toilets, they couldn't wait to get their hands on each other.

Sarah lit a cigarette and offered it to him. He shook his head. 'I've given up.'

She raised her eyebrows in mild surprise, slipping the cigarette between her red lips and sucking deeply. 'You'll regret it.' The smoke clouded around her face and stung her eyes. 'You know a couple of lines won't buzz the same without a long drag to wash them down.'

'No more coke.'

'No, of course not. Not now, not straight away. The doctors were right – you should have a good break from it to get back on your feet. You prob . . . *we* probably were doing too much of it.'

'No more coke, ever. No more Es, no more whizz, hash or grass. And no bottles of brandy in one sitting.' Jon smiled at her easily, but she was looking at him as if he was crazier than when she had picked him up from security at Steelguard after the incident with the computer terminal. For a moment, he thought she was going to spin the car round and drive him straight back to the 'recovery centre', which the white coats laughingly called their funny farm. Jon thought he ought to try to explain a little more. 'We . . . everybody . . . only do drugs for one reason – because we want to be children again. When you finally get out into the cold, grey, real world – and you might be as young as twelve or as old as thirty – you suddenly get this vague feeling that you've lost something important. And you have: freedom, a sense of wonder, the ability to fly. It's the human condition not to accept boundaries, but the world builds walls around us all. Drugs are an easy way to touch what we had. But they're not the right way.'

'Did those doctors tell you all this?' she asked with unconcealed disgust.

'No. I've done a lot of thinking over the last few weeks.'

She sighed wearily and then hammered the horn as she forced her way into the traffic filtering to the right. 'What are you talking about? Drugs are for grown-ups, not children.'

'I'm not getting preachy, Sarah,' he added hastily. 'I'm not one of those reformed users who ruins everyone else's fun. This is right for *me*.'

She wasn't listening to him; Jon could read the expression instantly. They had always been so in tune, a synchronization of ambition, humour, sex and intellect so close that at times Jon had the strange feeling he was walking and eating and sleeping beside himself. Now he had the even more disorientating sensation that he was talking to her through a glass wall.

'"I've seen things you people wouldn't believe. Attack ships on fire off the shoulder of Orion. I watched C-beams glitter in the dark near the Tanhauser Gate."'

Her head snapped round, her eyes flashing with a mixture of irritation and deeply buried anger. 'And I think we should get this out of the way now if we don't want to fall out later on. This newly found conceit of yours for speaking in quotations from your favourite movies whenever you get stressed out is fucking irritating, to say the least. I know you love films, Jon. I know they've always been your stress release, but, Jesus . . . Just talk straight – you're not going to get better until you do.'

A life-size plastic Father Christmas waved its mechanical arm at Jon from a shop window, its jaw dropping eerily with laughter he couldn't hear as it rocked back and forth. Where were they? The street names were unfamiliar; he knew they had passed through Tottenham, and this looked vaguely like Crouch End, but North London had never been his playground. Not for a long time, anyway.

'Are we visiting someone?'

'I told you, it's a secret.' Sarah flicked the hair back from her face and Jon was struck again by how attractive she was, the hardness of her features containing a dangerous sexuality. Beautiful like a diamond.

'I don't want to go back to the house . . .'

'We're not going back to the house.'

'Only the doctors thought I should make a fresh start without anything to remind me of the old lifestyle. And while I don't agree with them on many things, this—'

'We're not going back to the house.'

The anxiety which had been nibbling at his guts since he left the hospital took a larger bite; he calmed himself by searching for other signs of Christmas along the grey streets, as if they were beacons guiding him home.

It was only when they were a couple of streets from their destination that Jon recognized the smart signs of Highgate. Sharp suits and designer dresses on the street. Bistros instead of take-aways. Houses like City gents off to the Beefsteak Club. The view as they crested a hill took his breath away; the panorama of London from east to west, grey and dingy in the winter light, yet still beautiful, its vibrancy and history only sleeping behind the mask. It was an awe-inspiring view he hadn't seen since he was a child.

A tingle of excitement burst to life in his limbs as he recognized the familiar landmarks, igniting a bright awareness of a destination which couldn't be true. They couldn't be going *there*, going back. Only when Sarah pulled up outside did he allow himself to believe, and then the memories broke through and swamped all other thoughts.

Arcadia.

'Recognize it?' Sarah was smiling at his gaping expression.

'Here?' he asked, still fighting a few doubts.

She nodded.

'Here?' Almost a whisper.

The Victorian mansion loomed in smoky brick between the two sentinel trees which stood in the small front garden. Dark, enormous windows looked down at him, summoning memories of the last time he had been there. But of course it had changed; the paintwork on the window frames and the claret-coloured front door needed attention, and there was an abundance of long yellow grass on either side of the path which led up from the small iron gate. Over the door, however, the sign was still clear; black letters on a brass plate.

'Arcadia,' he murmured.

'It's ours for six months. At least six months,' Sarah said as she scanned the double-front and tried to see some sign of whatever Jon saw. 'When I first had the idea after talking to Dr McKenzie, I thought it would be a bitch to get, but it was remarkably easy. The company that owns the freehold had been trying to rent it out for the last eight months without any luck. The secretary told me they'd also tried to sell it a few times over the years, but even during the eighties they couldn't find a buyer. You'd think someone would see the investment potential, a property like this on a prime site in Highgate.'

Jon wasn't listening. All he could think was how right it was, to be returning, at this particular point in his life, to the house where he had spent the best years of his childhood. It was almost as if the Hand of Fate had put the two elements together and said, 'Heal yourself. Learn. Remember.'

'Inside—'

'Is just how you recall. Oh, they might have

47

re-upholstered a sofa or an armchair here or there, but everything else is original. I couldn't believe it when I went on the guided tour. It's a time warp, stuffed with antiques that must be worth a fortune. The secretary told me they like to keep the Victorian charm because it helps attract the right sort of tenant. You know, rich Americans looking for somewhere to stay in the summer.'

'It was never expensive when my parents rented it out. Back then they left in all the Victorian furniture and fittings for cheapness.'

'That was in the sixties and they didn't recognize the value of things back then, did they?' She lit another cigarette from the end of the previous one. 'Look, I've got some things to do. Are you going to be OK here on your own for a while? I guess you'll want to poke around a bit, pull up a few old memories.'

'Can't you take the rest of the day off? It would be nice to settle in together.'

Sarah laughed. 'Time off from work? You *have* changed, haven't you!' When he didn't laugh too, she added, 'Come on, Jon, you know my business. I've got a blue-chip client list. They expect personal attention from the boss if they need it. You'll be fine. And if things do start getting bad – they won't of course, but if they do – just pick up the phone and I'll be round in an instant.'

She dipped into her unfeasibly small handbag, where she kept the make-up compact filled with coke, and pulled out a key on a dirty string with a tattered, browning tag.

'To your dreams.' She dropped it into his palm and then folded his fingers around it. 'Relax, get better, and then we'll be shaking the world again.'

'This is the best thing you've ever done for me, Sarah. I won't forget it.' He looked up at the big, old house and was sure for a second it was calling to him. This was his last chance, a serendipitous opportunity to prove the lost things weren't gone for good.

He opened the car door and stepped out to face the future and the past.

As the front door closed behind him, Jon was instantly aware of Arcadia's peculiar scent: warm wood and beeswax, leather and the smoke of long-dead fires, sunshine on old furniture, and behind it all, the dusty, fruity, but not unpleasant aroma of great age. Like people, every building smells different, and this house was an aged, immaculately turned-out gentleman who loved books, fine wines and good food. Jon breathed deeply with his eyes shut. There were his father and mother acting the fool, dancing around the hall on the day they moved in. His father, tall as a skyscraper, thin as a pin, his spectacles teetering on the end of his nose. His mother, like a young Elizabeth Taylor, her floral dress floating out as she twirled. An odd concoction of joy and sadness filled him.

'Don't cry.' His voice jarred in the stillness of the hall. 'Christ, my emotions are shot after the last few weeks.' A pause. 'Last few fucking years.' A longer pause as the reverberations died away, then an embarrassed laugh. 'Fucking talking to myself now. I really *am* crazy.'

The floor tiles with their odd geometric design in cream and black seemed to pull him on towards the back of the house, but he turned left and stepped into the study. He felt a giddy sense of disorientation as he crossed the threshold; it didn't appear to have changed since that glorious summer in 1967. The walls were lined with the same collection of Victorian books he had delved into as a seven-year-old, and the leather, high-backed chair still sat comfortingly close to the fireplace. It was as if it had been sealed up on the day they moved out for their new, far less grand home in Clapham when the house in Norfolk had finally sold.

He selected a book at random. *Alice's Adventures in Wonderland*, a first edition from 1865. He wondered if Arcadia's owners were aware of the value of the contents;

he certainly wouldn't tell them. The company would only sell them off and replace them with a collection of Reader's Digest abridged classics.

Flipping the book open, he read a few paragraphs and felt his shoulders instantly start to unknot. A sudden urge to see the rest of the house overcame him and he hurried through to the drawing room, the memories igniting with each step, as colourful as the pictures and ancient photographs that lined the walls. The sofa where his mother read *The Times* and the escritoire in the corner where his father used to write his letters. That first Christmas in Arcadia, the family gathering from all over Britain, marvelling at how old Roger had managed to land himself such a wonderful residence. 'Only rented,' his father said apologetically what must have been a hundred times. Across the hall, the butler's pantry, the old servant's room where his mother had painted and made dresses. Past the cellar door, sealed shut with an enormous, rusty padlock for as long as he could remember. The kitchen, the only room so far that had been modernized, but the old black range still sat lumpenly in the corner. Forgotten smells returning: roast chicken, chocolate and walnut cake, that boiling ham and herbs on Christmas Eve.

He sprinted up the stairs like a child, pausing briefly next to the window as tall as two men which overlooked the street, before dashing up the last few steps to the landing. He threw open the bedroom doors one after another until he reached the one that had been his own all those years ago. Where he had read *The Wind in the Willows* and *The Moon of Gomrath*, visited Narnia and Middle Earth, swung across the New York skyline with Peter Parker and felt the wonder of Ben Grimm as he gazed on the face of Galactus.

As he paused on the threshold, lost to time, a sound suddenly disturbed him. It was so distant that it could have come from memory, but it unnerved him nonetheless. It had been many years before he had been able to sleep without fearing the cry of a child. A mystery from thirty years away, still haunting him if he let it, and it had started in the only room he hadn't visited.

The moment he stepped into the nursery, all sour thoughts were forgotten. The heavy atmosphere of great age which characterized Arcadia didn't seem to exist there; everything felt fresh and new. There were windows in two walls, and even though it was a dreary day, a light and airy feel filled the room. Jon walked to the centre of the room and breathed deeply; the air tasted oddly fresh and charged as if he was next to the sea or on a mountaintop. It was a peculiar characteristic of that room which he remembered from the moment he had first entered it.

There wasn't much in the way of furniture – an old rocking chair, a giant maple wardrobe and a fading Persian carpet which left bare boards showing round the edge – yet it was filled to bursting with wondrous toys from different ages, as if the children of a Victorian statesman and a Summer of Love hippie had played side by side: a doll, its porcelain face spiderwebbed by minute cracks, dressed in a red velvet clown's outfit before his grandparents had been born; a Johnny Seven rifle with grenades and missiles attached; a train set lapping the room with a few feet of track missing; a doll's house replica of Arcadia filled with minute Victorian furniture; more dolls, an embarrassment of teddy bears, magnificent clockwork boats and carriages that looked too sophisticated to be more than a hundred years old.

Jon had a sudden aching regret that he and Sarah had not had children. They had discussed it – twice, if memory served – but they both agreed the time wasn't right. Kids would get in the way of their jobs; they were up and out of the house before six, back at nine or ten at night, often working weekends. There was no way children could be squeezed into the equation. That was then. Perhaps when he got around to telling Sarah he would never be returning to Steelguard, the time might be right to broach the subject once more.

He gave a gentle push to a dappled rocking horse with paintwork so chipped it looked like it had been in a salvo of gunfire. As it creaked backwards and forwards noisily, his gaze fell on two items tucked away behind it. Excitedly, he pulled them out and blew the dust from them.

The first was a magic lantern, its brass body dulled by age, the glass smeared by fingerprints. With it was a box of hand-coloured slides: Samson and Delilah, Cinderella, Icarus, myths and romances, still bright, still enticing. The second object had fascinated him for weeks during that first, hot summer in Arcadia. The zoetrope, the first clumsy attempt at creating moving pictures, a wooden base with a spindle on which was placed a tin bowl with slits cut into the side to allow light to enter. With it were strips of paper featuring repeated images, slightly different each time. One had a horse galloping, jumping over a fence, landing on the other side. When the paper was wrapped around the interior of the bowl and the zoetrope whirled on its spindle, the images flashed by giving the impression of movement. Kids used to the frenzy of arcade games would sneer, but Jon tried to imagine how amazing it must have been to children not raised on television and cinema.

He placed both toys in the centre of the room and resolved to have a go with them later, for old time's sake. At the door, he turned and looked back around the room before whispering, ' "Memory, Agent Starling, is what I have instead of a view." '

The garden had its own special delights, despite the chill. Jon and Richard stood beneath the twisted, ancient apple tree as twilight fell, watching the shadows pool and then run among the shrubs, ash and elm until they lapped at their feet. It was a garden of the imagination where a young boy could skip in and out of dreams at will. From any vantage point, much of it was hidden by banks of foliage; the path wound around, presenting private places to the careful explorer: the white stone fountain, the sunhouse, the seat near the herb garden. And at the far end was an eight-foot wall of salt-crusted brick, separating the magic world from the mundane.

Right then, all Jon could smell was wet soil and rotting vegetation, but in summer it was clouded with the scent of honeysuckle, lavender, wistaria, rose. He recalled himself running through it as a boy, finding those hidden places for the first time, realizing in one exuberant moment they had come to live in the best place on earth.

'Thanks for coming,' Jon said after his long period of reflection.

'I wanted to welcome you back into the real world, old boy.' He grinned and fingered the lapel of Jon's leather jacket. 'Getting used to ones that don't fasten at the back, I see.'

'Fuck off, Ginger.' Jon turned to him and grinned back, challenging him to continue the verbal sparring.

'Nice language. Remind me ... you went to a, what do you call them, comprehensive, didn't you?'

'At least I didn't spend my nights getting buggered by the prefects.'

Richard laughed heartily. 'I'm glad to see you're fully recovered, old boy. So, when can we expect you back in the saddle at Steelguard?'

Jon's grin slipped away; he couldn't say anything until he had told Sarah, but the thought of returning to work brought him out in a cold sweat. As he struggled to think of some reply that wasn't a lie, the sound came again as it had outside the nursery, this time carried by the breeze.

Jon stiffened, glanced round nervously. The cry of a child, a lost, mournful sound. 'Did you hear that?'

'Hear what, old boy?'

'A child ... crying ...'

'Just a spot of good old parental abuse. Have to keep the sprogs in line, you know.'

Richard was probably right, but Jon couldn't stop himself looking up into the dark face of the house. In an instant he was back in the sixties, with all the irrational fears of a seven-year-old. The wonder of Arcadia had a dark side, like all magical places, but the fear it generated wasn't an adult terror, that black, depressive shut-down tied up with disease and crime; it was a fear of unknown possibilities that attracted as much as it repelled.

'You look spooked, old boy. What's wrong?'

'When I was a kid I was convinced the place was haunted.'

Richard followed his gaze up into the shadows. 'Only natural for an old place like this. It's rather creepy now. I don't think I'd like to stay here, but each to their own.'

'It was in that first summer soon after we moved in. I was playing on my own because I didn't know anyone else in the area, and I heard a boy's voice. I swear it, clear as day, like he was next to me, but invisible. When I told my father, he listened to what I said carefully and then we tried to find a rational explanation together. We wondered if it was the creak of a floorboard which I imagined as a voice, or my mother's singing carrying up the flues of these huge chimneys. A bird cooing in the eaves. We found nothing to explain it, Richard. If it had only happened once, I could have forgotten it. But it didn't. Three times I heard him. In the end I just decided that it was a friendly local ghost, just another part of the furniture. Kids accept things like that easily.'

Richard chuckled dismissively. 'Ghosts? Didn't anyone tell you you're not allowed to have an imagination in the City?'

'I don't know if it was imagination – it's certainly stayed with me to this day. Looking back on those few years I spent here, it's so hard to tell the difference between what was real and what was just in my head. It's like here in Arcadia, the boundaries seem to blur.'

'So what did this *voice* say to you?'

'I can't seem to remember. I know I knew at the time, but—'

Richard started to laugh, but Jon waved him quiet. There *was* something there. Edgily, he listened again, eliminating the sound of the wind in the trees, the distant drone of traffic, the rumble of a train, until other, hidden noises surfaced, strange vibrations, weird rhythms; he could almost hear the house breathing.

His concentration was so deep that when the cry came again it was like ice water down his spine; instantly he knew the source.

'There!' he said triumphantly. Richard stared at him blankly. 'You must have heard that!' Jon felt anxiety start to knot his stomach. 'I'm *not* hearing things.'

Without checking if Richard was following him, he ran back into the kitchen, along the hall and up the stairs. Memories are strange things, he thought; some swim around in the head constantly, others sink into the silt of the mind like fossils. When everything shifts and they are discovered years later, all one can do is marvel that they had ever been forgotten in the first place.

He had heard the voice in the same room every time and it had spoken the same two words. He flung open the door to the nursery.

The toys eyed him curiously. The room was still and silent. He searched the corners of the room futilely and then felt the familiar buzz of panic in the pit of his stomach. The nursery fractured like a dropped mirror as he clutched on to the door jamb.

'Are you all right, old man? Maybe you should sit down for a while.' Richard's voice sounded a million miles away.

The doctors had been wrong. He wasn't going to get better. His mind was going to continue fragmenting under the stresses until it finally broke up and drifted off into the ether. He wished Sarah was there.

He looked back at his friend. Richard's eyes were heavy on him and they were saying, You really are crazy. 'I'm not imagining it,' Jon said again.

For that brief instant, the voice had seemed so real. He could still hear the same words in his head that he had heard as a boy.

Help me.

Sarah came back early and they enjoyed a pleasant dinner together, although it didn't erase the jangling worries which pervaded Jon's thoughts. He feared that if he spoke about them Sarah would see it as another sign of his listing mental state, and the last thing he wanted to do was burden her with more of his problems. She had been so good during his hiatus from the real world: visiting every day despite the hike from the Smoke, offering the kind of encouragement and support that could only come from deep affection, keeping everything ticking over ready for his return. His quick recovery . . . his *desire* for a quick recovery . . . had been inspired by Sarah.

'Thanks,' he said as she toyed with the last of her tiramisu.

She eyed him curiously. 'What for?'

'I daren't say in case you think I'm a soppy git.'

'It's a bit late to start worrying about that.'

'I know it must have been hard for you over the last few weeks. I just want you to know I appreciate everything you've done.'

'A girl's got to protect her investment.' She smiled, allowing Jon access to that carefully protected part of her persona that he loved. He wished she would open up more, but even though they were close she found it difficult to lay bare her vulnerabilities.

'Do you trust me?' he asked.

'What kind of question is that?'

'Which word don't you understand?' He laughed with faint embarrassment.

'Have you been saving up all these stupid conversations for the last few weeks?'

'Well?'

'Yes, I trust you. Implicitly. Why do you ask?'

'Just wondered.' He wished other people could see the glimpses of the real Sarah only he caught; then so many of them wouldn't think she was such a hard-faced bitch.

'If we're on that tack, do you trust me?' Her smile became mischievous.

'Of course I do.'

'Because you've been out of circulation for a long time. I could have been out every night having a fling with the dustbin-man. Hmm, that aroma of carpet dust and rotting food is so appealing.'

The truth was, he didn't doubt her for an instant. In Steelguard's culture of deceit, he suspected almost everyone, but Sarah bypassed all his natural defences. He *knew* in a way he couldn't explain that she was one of the few people in the world he could rely on; that's why he loved her.

'It's going to take a while to get back on my feet,' he said apologetically as the weight of his situation fell on him.

Sarah nodded understandingly, her gaze unflinching. 'I'm not unaware of what it's going to take. Now you really do have to trust me. There's no need for apologies or doubt or recriminations. You just have to understand I'm going to do everything in my power to help you get back on your feet. I'm not going to be there all the time – work's a nightmare at the moment . . .'

'I don't expect you to let the company slide. You're the boss. Everything relies on you.'

'. . . There could be a lot of late nights. I've got some new accounts I need to keep sweet . . .'

'Don't worry. I understand.'

'The bottom line is I'm thinking of you all the time, even if I can't be by your side.' She sat on his knee and gave him a hug. 'We'll work it out together.'

Her touch was soothing, her kiss a balm to the anxiety that was beginning to swamp him. He was glad she was there to help him through.

That night they made love hesitantly, reacquainting themselves after so long apart, but afterwards, in the quiet of the room with Sarah dozing beside him, all Jon's deep fears resurfaced. He lay awake for too long, trying to calm his rapid, shallow breathing, and when sleep came, it hit him hard.

Jon is in bed sleeping. Jon is on the landing, walking. Jon is in the nursery, staring at the blank wall next to the wardrobe. And then ...

Thick-boled trees, misshapen with age, cluster round on all sides. Sharp-thorned briars and ferns tangle the ground. Vines and bushes flourish alongside strange blooms with remarkable, almost alien, colour schemes. A pungent, choking aroma of greenery, bracken and the scent of flowers fills the air. Yet none of it seems fast in reality; each frond and branch and petal has an inner light constantly changing across the spectrum, the edges of objects falling in and out of focus. There is a ground mist. Jon advances. Away to his right, something monstrous crashes through the undergrowth, trailing in its wake a sound like the keening of a bird. There is a flapping near his face, buzzing, droning, then a muttering of incomprehensible words.

He is on a thin, winding trail, plunging into the darkness. Ahead of him, a flash of white crosses the path. A unicorn, but not quite right somehow, gone too quickly for him to see what is wrong. He glimpses fabulous creatures away in the forest.

The trees twist and fold back upon themselves and suddenly he is on a rocky path, moving upwards towards a snow-capped summit, and he can smell smoke in the chill air; everything is fluid.

There is a strange sound, which becomes a whistling of pan pipes. Seated on a boulder is a red-headed boy; his mouth is stained with blood. He points upwards and grins.

'We are not your brothers,' he says. 'Look! I am missing a finger!' He holds up his right hand, then laughs terribly.

Jon is overcome with a monstrous fear and he hurries past without looking back; the laughter and the sound of the pipes seem to follow him. The path winds upward. He flaps his arms around him to keep out the bitter chill, but it pervades his bones and he shivers as if he has an ague. He senses a presence just behind his left ear, but he knows he will be damned if he looks around. 'Do not stray from the path,' a creaking voice says. The presence disappears, but the atmosphere of foreboding remains, almost too strong to bear.

Jon continues, listening to the cries in the night, across deserts and marshes, beaches and wastelands; and then he is in the primordial forest once more.

There is a disturbance among the trees far off to his left, just shadows against the greater darkness, and a dim sound like chattering and chewing. Jon feels a sudden pull. 'Do not stray from the path,' a lost voice says again. But Jon knows his life revolves around whatever is happening away in the gloom. The pounding of his heart obscures the voice and he strides out among the bracken and curling brambles.

Closer now and closer still. The chattering becomes excited voices, the chewing sounds wet and sticky. Soon he sees hunched shapes, kneeling figures crowded in a circle like animals around a water hole. Jon is fearful of disturbing them, but he can only move forward.

And then the figures raise their heads with sickly smiles, as if they had known he was there all along. Blood is smeared around their mouths, dripping from their caked teeth. One of them, with a white face and a matted mane of black hair, stretches out an arm over the fifteen feet separating them and Jon is drawn inexorably forward. Jon protests, yells, prays, but his captor simply smiles.

And then Jon is close enough to see what they are eating. A figure, pale skin torn and bloody, the stomach cavity gaping. A flash of blonde hair, of perfect lips, and Jon thinks, *It's Sarah!*

And Jon screams and screams, but no sound comes from his mouth, and his captor continues to smile. The predator shakes his black hair and droplets of blood fly. His eyes widen and then he says emphatically: 'The Queen! Look! We have her heart!' And then: 'This *will* happen.'

And then . . .

4

All Jon could remember was the blood. Shiny droplets spurting high, then falling like rain, like his vision in the dealing room when the windows turned bright red. It hinted at prophecy, hooked his subconscious, made him feel queasy. On waking, he wanted to believe it was a dream, but it had been too realistic; he had never experienced anything like it before. And then, in one instant of arctic horror, he rolled over to find Sarah was not by his side. Sprinting downstairs, he discovered her making an early breakfast in the kitchen, listening to the radio, happy in her thoughts. It didn't make him feel any better.

His time in the clinic had left him with a terrifying belief in the fragility of sanity. When he went in, he was confident he had merely suffered burn-out; shattering, but requiring no further treatment than a recharging of the batteries. The change that came over him within days of being quizzed, coddled and sedated was like a blanket slowly being pulled over the head of a corpse, and by the time he left he feared something had been broken that could never be put back together again. It was a fear very close to dread; the space between madness and death was tissue-paper thin. He was terrified where it would end.

Slumped at the kitchen table, he could barely find the words to express the claustrophobic fears he felt strangling him. 'I don't want to go back to that place,' was all he could manage in a hoarse whisper. Oblivious to the despair in his eyes or the weight of his terror, Sarah smiled as if it could never happen, and the gulf between them became uncrossable; he felt alone in a crumbling world.

After Sarah left for work he moved out to the garden to try to dispel his troubled thoughts with the crispness of a winter morning, but it was a futile exercise. The day had a brutality about it which he found almost unbearable. Despite the frost which scattered pinpricks of light across the lawn and trees, any pleasure was excised by the scything wind and the insipid grey of the sky, which seemed to leech everything of colour. Nothing suggested the nearness of Christmas, and he found himself yearning for the epic weather of childhood.

'You're the new ones, then?'

It took Jon a few seconds to find the source of the voice. Between two overgrown bushes, a woman peered over the garden fence, her grey hair falling lank and ratty around her face. Jon smelled the cloud of booze surrounding her from three feet away. Her face had the ravaged appearance of long-time alcoholism, marked out in burst capillaries and sagging muscles.

'Hello, I'm Jon Summers.' He held his hand over the fence, but she shied away from it uncomfortably and then looked past him to the rear of the house.

Her bottom lip began to shake, and then a single tear squeezed out of the corner of her eye. 'I've wanted to get out of its shadow for forty years,' she said. 'It won't let me go.'

Jon turned to follow her gaze, but he couldn't guess what she saw. 'Oh? I've always loved the old place.'

'Different eyes.' She glared at him. 'You've been here before. I remember you. See. It won't leave you alone either.'

'I was here as a boy, just for a short time.' Jon smiled.

'I don't see anything funny,' she snapped. 'I've lived here since I was a girl. Watched my mother die in the upstairs bedroom. Seen my father drink himself to death. And I always said to myself, "Wendy, you have to get away from here if you want a life of your own. If you want to forget the past and look to the future." Now the past is all I have.' Inexplicably, her hand, resting on top of the fence, started to tremble violently. She snatched it back and buried it in the folds of her cardigan. 'I've seen them all come and go. No one stays for long. They can't come to terms with how different it is, not at all what they expected. It never quite looks how they think it should look. You must know what I mean.' She looked past him with an emotion he couldn't read. 'You should get out soon. It will suck the life right out of you.'

She began to shake her head vehemently as if answering some invisible spirit guide. Jon couldn't help glancing behind him again. 'We plan to stay for a while,' he said as lightly as he could.

'Who is "we"?' Her voice was suddenly insistent. Jon heard her breathing grow ragged.

'Me and my wife, Sarah.'

'No children. Please, no children,' she said in a whisper so insubstantial Jon barely caught it before it was snatched away by the wind.

'Just the two of us.'

She closed her eyes in relief and another tear eased out. 'Sometimes, in the night, I hear things,' she said, disconnectedly.

'What kind of things?'

'Just things.' She backed away from the fence. 'Watch out now. It'll all change soon. You'll find you won't know where you are at all.'

And then she turned and walked away unsteadily, leaving an oppressive air of suffering and despair that was almost tangible.

*

'So how's he bearing up?' Richard cradled the phone against his shoulder and scanned the figures scrolling across the screen. Around him, the buzz of the Steelguard office almost drowned out Sarah's voice.

There was a long pause before she said, 'He's not the same. I don't know what it is ... something seems to be missing ...'

'You're saying he's still off his rocker?'

'No ... maybe ... I can't put my finger on it. I just know he's not the same Jon Summers that went into that place.'

'Well you of all people should know. Perhaps we should get him out for a night on the town. We'll have the old boy back to normal in no time.'

'I don't think so, Richard. He doesn't seem to want to leave the house. He's sworn off drugs, won't have a drink ...'

'Jonathan Summers, no drugs, no drink. Sorry, doesn't compute.' He laughed as he tapped at his keyboard.

'I'm serious, Richard.'

'Sorry, old girl. I'll try to control my flippancy. What do you suggest we do?'

'I'll meet you after work. We need to sit down and really talk about it if we're going to agree on the right way forward.'

'He's lucky to have you for a wife.'

She laughed. 'And you for a friend.'

'You don't think there's any chance he might end up back inside, do you?'

Her silence told him all he needed to know.

The chiming of the old grandfather clock in the hall woke Jon with a start. It was 1 a.m. He had fallen asleep in the study two hours earlier, lulled by the flickering of the gas fire as he dipped into a musty, worn copy of *A Christmas Carol*.

He had been dreaming about Sarah and the life they had

before. He feared the loneliness he felt would only trigger more anxious thoughts about his state of mind, and that he couldn't bear. In the hospital, the anxiety had always been the worst thing, like a rat in his gut. He knew his escape from Steelguard was right, but he couldn't help feeling that by knocking down one wall which separated him from his happiness, he was only building another one behind him. After spending so long with Sarah going in the same direction, with the same thrills, the same aims, he had suddenly peeled off down a side road. Was he being selfish, if not stupid, in expecting her to follow him? The rat began to gnaw; he needed something to distract him.

The book skidded off his lap and thudded to the ground as he hauled himself to his feet. The hall was in darkness. He dismissed the thought of a late snack. There was no TV, no booze, no drugs. What else was left? Feeling out of sorts, he switched on the light and absently climbed the stairs, shivering from the chill in the air. Half-way up, he paused to look out of the window at the large snowflakes drifting down under the light of a crisp winter moon; there was already a thin covering on the road and parked cars, transforming the grubby reality into something magical. The view triggered his imagination and he continued to the top of the stairs with sudden determination.

In the nursery, among the scattered memories of summers past, he realized the time and mood was perfect; he *had* to do it. So what if he was too old to play with toys? There was no one there to berate him; he could do exactly what he wanted.

There was an aroma in the room which he struggled to identify. It smelled like pine, smoky fires, cold nights. It smelled like Christmas. He let it seep into his system, overwhelming his senses until he felt almost drunk. With a measured tread, he circumnavigated the room three times, each circuit stripping away a layer of time until he was filled with images of his childhood and a yearning to return to simpler, innocent days; it drove him on with almost mechanical force. He had been truly happy, lost in dreams and books with his mother and father just a call away. Nothing had matched up to that since. Not his job, which provided a buzz but was relentless and suffocating. Not even his marriage, although he had hoped it would. Perhaps he simply hadn't tried hard enough.

For a flickering instant, reality intruded and he thought: *What's happening to me? I feel off my head.* But then it was gone, and his thoughts burst like bubbles as the warm blanket descended once again

Almost in a daze, he located the items he wanted and placed them in the correct position. He turned to the magic lantern first, feeling drawn to one particular slide, igniting the wick in the brass casing with the lighter he always kept on him for joints. A second later, a blurred, colourful picture projected on to the white wall. Hurriedly, he switched off the main light and the image fell into crisp relief. A scene from Greek mythology. Lush grasslands, a small white temple, a centaur swigging from a wine sac.

Satisfied, he turned to the zoetrope. From its accompanying box, he selected a string of pictures of a bizarrely long-limbed man leaping over a giant ball, which he wrapped around the inside of the toy. Crouching down for a better view, he peered through one of the long slits in the cylinder and then he spun it with a deft flick. It whirled on its base with a rapid, insectile clicking. The long-limbed man leaped into life.

Jon lost himself in its hypnotic whirl, unaware of time passing. The man running-jumping-running-jumping, on his way from there to here. As he watched, a creeping uneasiness worked its way through his drugged enthusiasm until he realized what was bothering him: the zoetrope wasn't slowing down; the toy seemed to have developed a life of its own, rattling away as if it was motor-driven.

And that wasn't all that was wrong. Turning his head felt

like swimming through mud. The colours of the magic
lantern picture looked brighter, almost glowing with an
inner light, and there was a detail he had never noticed
before. In one corner, a goat-legged thing playing pan pipes
leered out at him. Something about its expression made him
shiver.

A great ocean sluiced around between his ears, pounding
against the back of his eyeballs. The zoetrope, rat-tat-tat,
faster now, and faster still. The projected image, seemingly
changing every time he looked at it; not a picture, a
window. His skin tingled, his tongue felt fat and dry. There
was a faint tang in the air, as if a generator had come to
life.

A door slammed far off in the house. *Sarah's home*, he
thought with relief. Then another one, slightly closer. And
another and another, progressing quickly towards him,
louder each time until they sounded like giant iron gates in
a city wall.

What's coming? he wondered queasily.

Then a slam so near and so loud a clockwork doll fell
over and began to walk on its back. And he realized the
thunderous sound wasn't coming from outside the room; it
seemed to emanate from behind the wardrobe. Jon stared
at it, his breath frozen in his throat. There was one final
slam, the wardrobe quivered and Jon slumped to the floor,
unconscious.

When he awoke what must have been a few minutes later,
toys were strewn across the room in disarray and the door
was wide open.

With a foggy head, he staggered to the top of the stairs.
Slipping into the hall beneath him, he thought he glimpsed
a figure so unnaturally long-limbed it seemed a product of
distorted shadows.

He clattered down two steps at a time in pursuit, almost
collapsing in a heap on the monochrome-tiled hall floor.

There was a sound like the cry of angry birds, followed by doors banging at the back of the house. Jon picked himself up again and ran through to the kitchen where the back door stood open on to the sparkling, white garden and the dreamily falling flakes. Despite what he had heard, the snow was unmarked by footprints.

Glancing over his shoulder, Jon reassured himself there was no hiding place in the dark kitchen, and when he looked back he caught a hint of movement further down the garden. Without considering the logic of his actions, he launched himself outside, raising mushroom clouds of snow with each step along the path. Away from the house, the trees and bushes appeared menacing despite the light provided by the snow's glare; the branches seemed to be moving with a life of their own. Nearby, he heard strange sounds which he couldn't attribute to the wind.

Running faster, he followed the path into its secret places until he lost sight of the house. Finally, as he passed the shuttered sunhouse, he caught sight of a shape vaulting the eight-foot garden wall, black against the lighter sky. And then it was gone – if it had ever been there in the first place; the snow beneath was undisturbed.

Breathlessly, he crashed against the bricks and then slumped into the thickening snow on the marble seat near the herb garden. Listening to his ragged breathing helped calm his swimming head, and then he became aware of the cold with such force that he couldn't understand why he had not felt it before. With shivers racking his body, he pulled himself to his feet, determined to hurry back to the study to consider what had happened in front of the blazing gas fire.

But before he could take a step, he was brought up sharply. Among the clustered trees beyond the vegetable patch was a horse, partially obscured by the trunks and shadow. It was as white as the snow that surrounded it.

The anxiety knots gave Jon's stomach a sadistic twist; a hallucination of such intensity was too much of a blow.

But he could see the plume of condensation as it floated up, hear the rasp of its hot breath in the stillness, and the sound of its hooves, slightly muffled by the snow, as it advanced.

Jon shook his head, closed his eyes. But when he opened them, it was still there.

Slowly it moved forward as if it was testing his reactions, and when it finally emerged into the open space his shock forced him to take a step back. Its eyes were as red as car brake lights, demonic in their intensity, and when it opened its mouth slightly to make a rough sound in its throat, he saw distinctly a row of sharply pointed teeth. What startled him most of all was the long, gnarled horn in the middle of its forehead.

Unicorn, he mouthed silently, only it was like no unicorn he had ever seen in any fairytale book.

It took a few more steps before pausing to scratch the earth threateningly with one of its front hooves. Those hideous red eyes never left him. Jon sensed something malign and alien. Its razor-teeth clacked together and a spark fizzed out into the air.

He looked from right to left in search of escape, but before he could move it reared up suddenly on its hind legs and let out a terrifying sound like the roar of a jungle cat. The gleaming embers of its eyes swelled up and filled Jon's vision, and then he was falling backwards into the snow as TV static crackled through his mind.

5

'Wake up, Little Boy Blue.'

Jon's eyelids flickered open. Sarah was bending over him, her eyes glittering with the diamond sheen of a night on the coke. He could smell booze on her breath, mingling with fresh perfume and sweat. Glancing around, he was at first disorientated and then despairing to see he was lying in the nursery among the strewn toys. His memory of the chase through the house and the unicorn was clear, but it was as if he had never left.

The thought of what that meant droned from the dark depths of his mind until it was screaming behind his eyes. He put his face in his hands and shook with a convulsion of despair. A hallucination.

'Bad dream?' Sarah shook his shoulder gently.

With a swimming head, he pushed himself up on his elbows and asked, 'What time is it?'

'Late. You know, most people prefer a bed. Or is this a new habit you learned in the home?' She pronounced the last word with undue emphasis, then looked around the nursery and smirked. 'Playing with your toys, Little Boy Blue?'

Desperately, he turned away from thoughts of what had or hadn't happened and focused on Sarah's face. 'I expected you back earlier,' he muttered. All his joints ached, as though he had spent a night sleeping in a field.

'I got delayed. Richard sends his love. He wants to know when you two boys can go out on the town again.'

Jon wandered over to the window and searched the dark sky for some sign of dawn. A movement caught his eye down in the road, on the edge of a circle of light cast by a streetlamp. A tall, thin man was looking up at the house. He melted into the darkness an instant later.

Sarah's arms folded around his chest and he felt the hot touch of her lips on the nape of his neck. 'Come on, my brooding little bunny. Let's go to bed.' These days he could never tell when she was being ironic. She took his hand and led him along the landing to the bedroom at the front with its unique scent of lavender and old furniture.

'We should start making plans for Christmas Day. Or have you done that already?' He forced the words out, suddenly feeling exhausted.

Sarah placed both her hands on his chest and pushed sharply so he fell back on the bed. The old springs groaned and then sank back alarmingly. 'You talk too much,' she said, undoing her silk blouse. 'I'm not sleepy. Too much coke. But you know how coke makes me feel.' She slipped off her blouse and dropped her skirt like a professional stripper. Underneath she was wearing what she called her 'seduction gear' – black Wonderbra, black lacy knickers, black hold-up stockings. With feline grace, she crawled on top of him. 'Let's christen our new bed and our new house properly,' she purred.

Jon raised his head to kiss her, but she pressed a finger against his nose and pushed him back with a laugh. Jon refused to allow his fears to pollute the moment. 'I feel like doing something dirty,' she said hungrily. Rolling off him, she fumbled around in the bedside table drawer.

Jon knew the kind of things going through her head. The coke deadened emotions so effectively that the love-free coupling had to be enhanced to hit home. 'There's no need for that. Not tonight,' he said. 'Let's just—'

Sarah hauled herself back on top, holding aloft a pair of handcuffs, her favourite sex aid, the same pair she had surprised him with on their first night together. 'We don't want any of that kissy-kissy stuff,' she said breathlessly, snapping one cuff around her left wrist. 'Hot and hard.'

Her other hand was holding out her black silk blindfold. 'Come on, Little Boy Blue. If you do the honours, I'll blow your horn.'

'I'd rather see your eyes,' Jon protested, but he knew there was no arguing with her. Reluctantly, he took the blindfold and tied it tightly. Satisfied, she lay back and allowed him to thread the cuff around a wooden rail in the bedhead. As he snapped it on her right wrist, she rubbed the toe of her shoe over his groin and said, 'That's right. You remember how to do it. We'll have you back to normal soon.'

Everything about the situation screamed *sex*, but Jon couldn't connect. He removed her underwear mechanically and entered her, desperately trying to remember what the man he had been would have done, what he had felt before, but most of all, what it was about everything they had that seemed so special.

He tried to kiss her mouth, but it was hard and tight.

The morning smelled like fog, petrol fumes and wet leaves. Shivering, Jon left the empty bed and closed the window. The city lowered beneath a heavy white sky that mirrored the blanket of snow across the rooftops and roads. Down in the street someone was trying to start a Fiesta that sounded like it was dying of a smoking disease. Jon had a fleeting memory of being in the nursery the night before, then in the garden, but it was soon lost to the memory of what happened after. He had to pull himself together, for Sarah's sake.

There was no sign Sarah had ever been in the bedroom; no handcuffs, no blindfold, no underwear. Downstairs, he discovered the kitchen was spotless too; she hadn't breakfasted. He made himself a cup of coffee and headed to the bathroom where he listened to the bass-beat of the pipes until the water reached a temperature that would keep the December chill at bay.

As he stripped off his pyjama top, he noticed a curious mark on the soft, pale underside of his forearm. At first glance it appeared to be a tattoo, although he had never had one. It was black and about the size of a ten pence piece. It looked like a crescent moon encompassing a smaller circle.

Dumping the towel on the floor next to the bath, he slipped in and attacked the patch with a scrubbing brush and soap until the skin around it was red and sore, but whatever ink had been used was indelible. He tried to find some explanation – a practical joke by Sarah while he was sleeping? – but nothing made sense. His brain was already scrambled enough, and he felt the anxiety rising with his confusion. He forced himself to switch off his thoughts as they had taught him in the clinic until he could drift in the anaesthesia of a blank mind, and after a few moments he was relaxed enough to allow a few bland thoughts to creep back in.

At times it felt like he was struggling to recall the memories of another person, as if the life he had before and the man he was now had been joined by a thin thread which had broken during his hospitalization. The doctors repeatedly stressed that he could face his problems. His 'awareness of self' had been disrupted, they said, during one of their many spiels of jargon; every routine in his life which had built up naturally over the years was now being observed with new eyes, so each seemed strange and discomfiting. He had to grow back into an ease with himself, and until that happened, nothing would seem right.

A jarring thought crept in with the others. None of them had mentioned terrifyingly real hallucinations and fainting fits. Had they been pulling their punches about his true state of mind?

Gradually he slid down under the water like he was paralysed, drowning. He held his breath and counted, listening to the shush-shush womb echoes of the water merging with the beat of his heart in his head. He held it for as long as he could, wondering what it would be like to just slip away, and then he surfaced with a rush and a shuddering gasp of life. Leaning over the side of the bath, he fumbled for the towel to dry his face, couldn't find it, moved down the bath, fumbled around again without any luck. Finally he wiped the water away with his hands and looked on the floor. The towel wasn't there. Glancing around, he discovered it screwed up on a chair in the corner, nowhere near where he had left it. For a moment he tried to grasp what had happened as the goosebumps rippled over his back.

What was it doing on the chair?

He ran through the memory of dumping it next to the bath, the texture of it slipping through his fingers, the soft bump as it hit the floorboards. He *remembered*. There were only two possibilities. Either his mind really was crumbling like a sandcastle as the tide washed in.

Or someone had been in the bathroom with him.

He stared at the towel for twenty minutes while the water grew cold around him.

As he dressed in the chill of the bedroom, Jon felt he was floating somewhere above his body. His emotions were like a turbulent sea, sucking him under, killing him. He felt like crying. He wanted to shout, then laugh at the ridiculousness of it all. He felt nothing; a needle in his arm would gain no reaction. The fractured faces of the other people he had seen in the clinic at meal times pressed against his back. He bit his lip to savour the pain. The way forward seemed inevitable.

At the foot of the stairs, he was confronted by a large grey cat with a white chin and chest staring at him coldly.

The intelligence cats displayed in their eyes always disturbed him; they looked smarter than most people he knew.

'Sarah is full of surprises,' he said, glad out of all proportion for the distraction. He sat on the bottom step, rubbing a thumb and forefinger towards it enticingly. It came forward slowly with its tail in the air and then stopped about a foot away. 'Choosy, eh? Don't blame you. *I'd* think twice about selecting me for company. No collar or tag. What's your name, then?'

Its supercilious expression made him laugh, which seemed the cat's cue to depart. It sashayed away, following the odd, geometric pattern on the hall floor until it darted into the study.

'It'll be nice to have someone to talk to,' Jon said ironically. His voice created the same timbre of echoes off the wood panelling he had first heard more than two decades before.

The phone at the end of the hall rang, another time-lost sound. It was the black Bakelite model he remembered from childhood with a discordant bell that sounded like an irritated old man. It calmed him more than he could have hoped.

'It's me.' Sarah sounded distracted; Jon guessed she was typing into her computer with her other hand. 'Lots to do, sorry, hon. I was just calling to let you know I'll be late tonight. It's The Python Club. They want me to put in an appearance down there, and you know it's my biggest account so I can't—'

'Don't worry about it. Lunch?'

'I really am sorry, but I haven't got a second free today. I've got a working lunch down at L'Escargot with some dodgy stand-up who wants her profile raising. For that, read the chance of a Channel 4 series. We'll make up for it at the weekend.'

'OK.' He didn't want to let her know how desperate he felt. 'By the way, what's the cat called?'

'What cat?'

'Oh. He must have come with the house.'

'You know I don't like cats, Jon.'

'This one's really cute and I'm not a cat person by any means. Grey, a bit chubby, looks like Sydney Greenstreet. Only with fur.'

'I don't care if it looks like Brad Pitt. Make sure it stays outside. I don't know how it got inside in the first place. None of the doors or windows were left open.'

'We can't shut him out in this weather, Sarah. It's freezing outside.'

'I'm not in the mood for dealing with waifs and strays, Jon—'

'OK, OK, I'll see what I can do.' He replaced the receiver, then added, 'After Christmas. Or maybe Easter.'

The brass door knocker crashed three times. Jon thought twice about answering; anxiety about facing the outside world twisted a knot in his stomach. After two more crashes, he relented. Amid a blast of cold air and a flurry of snow, Richard was stamping his feet on the step, his hands forced deep into the pockets of his overcoat.

'Let me in, old chap. You know I'm a fair-weather person.' As Richard led a trail of dripping footprints into the hall, Jon felt a tightening across his chest at all the associations that trooped behind. 'Settled in yet? Can't understand the attractions of these draughty old Victorian places. How was your night?'

'"I think this situation absolutely requires a really futile and stupid gesture to be done on somebody's part,"' Jon muttered to himself.

'Don't recognize that quote, old chap,' Richard said warily. 'How about a coffee? A good burst of caffeine to the brain is just what I need.'

They made their way to the kitchen and Jon brewed up a fresh pot. Richard took a seat at the table and made to admire the Victorian decor, but Jon could tell his mind was elsewhere.

'I'm surprised you're not at work,' Jon said, trying to fight back the irritation he felt at being reminded of his old life, although he knew it wasn't Richard's fault. 'It's not like you to miss the chance to make a million before lunch.'

'Ah.' He grimaced as his first sip of coffee burnt his lips. 'There's a reason why I'm here. Another reason. I mean, it's not just so I can check on your welfare, like a good friend should. Jon, there's a bit of a flap at the office.'

'What kind of a flap?'

'Apparently, they've found some kind of irregularities. Someone's been playing a bit fast and loose with company information. Top secret information, including next year's strategic plan. Rumours are circulating that it was sold off for large sums ... very large sums. Except the plan that was sold was a bogus one they created to fool any would-be spies. You'd think they'd let it drop as no harm's been done.'

Jon nodded uninterestedly. He had a sudden flash of the unicorn and felt sick that the hallucination wouldn't leave him alone.

'You and I both know the rules are there to be treated with contempt, but you know how it is these days. Nick Leeson has a lot to answer for. With this sickening new mood of honesty sweeping through the City, they're talking about an investigation.' Jon shrugged, marvelling at the patterns the snow made on the branches outside the window. 'Jon, I heard your name mentioned. I came here to warn you. This investigation isn't a joke – it's jail for whoever gets caught.'

'I never did anything like that, Richard. You know me. You used to take the piss because I wanted to do everything above board.'

'We both know that, Jon, but they don't.'

'If I'm innocent I've got nothing to worry about.'

'Oh, tell that to the Birmingham Six! Think of it from Steelguard's perspective – they don't want to lose face over this. They don't want it to be an insider, their latest golden boy, some company man who's been tipped for the top in the *FT*. After what happened, you'd seem a very attractive option to them.'

'Because I quit?'

'Because in their eyes you cracked up. Couldn't take the strain. Damaged goods. They're all saying it, Jon, all rewriting history. "He was never one of us! Never had what it takes." It would be great for them if they could blame it on a rogue, a loose cannon. A nut.'

'A nut?'

Richard was suddenly contrite. 'I'm sorry. But you know what I mean.'

'"Greed, in all of its forms – greed for life, for money, for love, knowledge – has marked the upward surge of mankind."'

'You're lucky you've got me on the inside, old man. I'll be able to find out information early, feed it to you. If the balloon does go up, you can have your defence already prepared so they won't catch you on the hop.'

Jon sat down at the table and nursed his mug with both hands. After a few seconds, he said, 'We've got a great cat here, you know. Must be a stray—'

'Jon, you've got to take this seriously,' Richard said with exasperation. 'You stand to lose everything here.'

'Grey. Big eyes—'

'Forget the fucking cat!' In his anger, Richard clipped his mug and sent hot black coffee flooding across the table. 'Now look what you've made me do.' He fetched a cloth from the sink and began to mop it up distastefully, wringing it back into his mug. 'I'm your best friend, Jon. Sarah's your best friend and your wife. We're going to stand firm and get you through this nightmare, but we need your help.'

Jon shook his head vehemently, unable to meet his eyes.

The combination of anger and anxiety made his hand tremble. 'I want to forget it all, Richard. That fucking job ... Steelguard ... It's part of everything that was wrong with my life and it doesn't mean anything to me now. I don't want to think about it.'

'You're being a child now. You can't bury your head in the sand and hope it will all go away.' He suddenly examined the cloth as if it was some alien life form and then threw it across the kitchen into the sink. 'I can understand why you're acting this way, I suppose. The breakdown ... the hospital ... it was a shock. It's only natural you don't want to be reminded about all that. But it's a passing phase, Jon. Soon you'll start thinking about all the cash you made and what that meant. You'll remember the kudos you had for being the best of your generation. And if you can beat those bastards at Steelguard you can have all that back. It's in your blood, Jon, that hunger to win. You can't simply pretend it's not there.'

'That's not me you're talking about, Richard. Not the real me.'

'And how do you think Sarah would feel if you turned your back on the City for good? She's a high-flyer. She's hooked on the stresses of the whole shebang, and on the rewards, too. Do you think she'll settle for you in some cosy no-job with a common man's wage?'

'We love each other.'

'Of course you do. But that doesn't mean you can take things for granted.' He checked his watch. 'I've got to go. I've got a lunchtime meeting and I want to earn some dosh before then.'

Jon showed him to the door, hoping he was masking his emotions. Reminders of Steelguard were another weight on his shoulders when he was already on his knees. He hated Richard for bringing it back to him, then hated himself for thinking it. 'Come round again soon, Richard,' he said blandly. 'We can talk ... have a laugh ...'

'Why don't you meet me after work one night? We can hit some of the old haunts.'

The snow swirled in on another cold blast; Jon shivered and took a step back. 'I'm not ready for that yet. To be honest, I don't feel up to venturing out much at all.'

Richard shrugged, then slapped Jon on the shoulder. 'You take care of yourself. And remember what I said. You've got to stand and fight or you'll get trampled underfoot. You can't run away.'

Jon smiled falsely, thinking that was exactly what he wanted to do.

Jon hovered on the threshold for an hour while the snow fell thick and crisp on the front garden. On two occasions he tried to propel himself out in the hope that the engaging of muscles would break the grip of the anxiety. Once he tried to close his eyes and step out, but it felt like teetering on the edge of a chasm. Three times he tried a hop, step and jump from the middle of the hall, and once he even tried to crawl, but he had a sudden vision of how pathetic he must have looked to any passing neighbour and quickly clawed himself to his feet. Nascent agoraphobia had infected him since he had stepped into the clinic, but he had never felt it so strongly; it was a reaction to the stresses of watching himself break down, another signpost on the road. But he knew if he gave in then, he might as well give in completely.

Eventually he hit on the solution. He walked backwards along the hall until he tumbled down the steps and landed on his behind in the snow. It had no dignity, but at least he was out.

All he could remember of his journey through the snow-storm was a fight against hyperventilation and the tightening across his chest that felt at times as if he was having a heart attack. He didn't know where he was going, but when the Cross Keys pub loomed out of the blizzard it seemed like it had always been his destination. It was a stone's throw from Highgate Cemetery, with a combined bar and lounge so tiny that a handful of people would have made it seem crowded. The claustrophobic atmosphere was emphasized by the subdued lighting and the mountain of bric-a-brac which cluttered the walls and ceiling, everything from ploughshares and miners' lamps to theatre programmes and a clown's costume. The only other customer was an old man in a drab suit at a table near the door. He nodded and winked when Jon passed by on his way to a seat at the end of the bar.

The barmaid entered from the back, humping a crate of Pils which she dumped on the floor with a too-loud curse. Her skin had the cappuccino tone of mixed-race parentage which only emphasized the darkness of her eyes. She was wearing a skinny, white T-shirt with the words *Sex Machine* emblazoned on the front. The legend drew attention to her breasts, but as Jon looked hastily into her face in case she mistook his staring, he was immediately struck by some quality that reminded him of Sarah. It was a hardness that added an unapproachable veneer to her good looks, but in her it seemed defensive where in Sarah it had always had the opposite effect.

'What'll it be?' Her accent was southern Irish, with a touch of the East End. Jon felt a crackle of something he couldn't explain, as if he had known her well and then mysteriously forgotten her. A shiver ran through him as he searched her face for answers, but all he saw was a faint, disconcerting glimmer, as though she felt it too.

'Mineral water and lime.' He resisted the urge to order a Jack Daniels and Coke. There was no reason why he shouldn't drink – he wasn't an alcoholic – but he didn't want to risk anything which might wreck his chances of getting back on his feet.

'You look like you'd prefer something harder.' Through

her hard smile, Jon had the disturbing feeling she had read his mind.

'"You see a lot, Doctor. But are you strong enough to point that high-powered perception at yourself?"'

'*Silence of the Lambs*,' she noted as she flipped open the water bottle. 'I saw it last week at college. You've got a good memory.'

'It's a gift. I hear things, I remember them. Not a great deal of use in the real world.'

'Breaks the ice at parties.' Her smile lost some of its hardness. 'I haven't seen you in here before.'

'I moved into a house over the way a couple of days ago. Thought I'd check out my new local.'

She glanced around the empty bar. 'Good choice.'

'Well, there's you.'

'Sure there's me.' She held out a slim hand in mock-formality. 'Lisa Donlon. And yourself?'

'Jon Summers. Pleased to meet you. Is it always this popular?'

'Not much trade during the day. This is a local pub, and I guess most people are out at work. Lucky so-and-sos. Have you taken some time off to move in?'

'I'm taking it easy for a few weeks. Recuperating.'

'So what do you do? No, let me guess. Artist? Writer?'

'Foreign exchange dealer.'

Her nose twitched like she smelled rotten eggs. 'Oh.'

'At least I was. I'm looking for a new career.'

'Fired?'

'Walked out. I suddenly realized it wasn't the job for me. It only took me ten years,' he added sourly.

'Don't blame you. They're a bunch of leeches, if you ask me. Cash first, people last. Lots of power and no responsibility.'

'That's dangerous revolutionary talk,' he said ironically. 'The priests of Mammon will have you crucified.'

She shrugged while she rinsed a glass to put in the

washer, her opinions unchanged, implacable. Jon considered telling her she was generalizing about the people if not the job, but he felt uncomfortable offering defences for something he no longer believed in himself. 'What are you studying at college?' he asked, changing the subject.

'Media, Communications and Film Studies. I needed something to get me out of a rut and that seemed more interesting than Economic History. It's perfect – you get to see films and call it work.'

'Sounds like heaven.'

'The only drawback is the whole course is filled with kids. Nineteen-year-olds who want to be the next Tarantino or produce *The Big Breakfast*. They've not lived – they've got nothing to say.' As Jon tried to guess her age, she again seemed to sense what he was thinking. 'I'm twenty-eight. Mature student.' She smiled coldly. 'Don't mind me. I'm just bitter about my responsibilities and having to work here to make ends meet. I wish I'd done the course when I was eighteen.'

'So,' Jon motioned round the room, 'this isn't a career move, then?'

She laughed quietly and shook her head. 'A friend got me the job. It's easy to get to in my lunch break from college and after classes in the evening. A bitch to get home, though.'

'You're not local?'

'You're joking. I can't afford the rents round here. I live in Spitalfields. A real-life East Ender.'

A group of pin-striped young businessmen tumbled in, stamping snow off their shoes and tossing their floppy fringes like thoroughbreds as they brayed with laughter. Jon guessed estate agents; Lisa didn't seem enamoured.

'Better deal with this shower,' she grumbled. She gave him one glance from the other end of the bar which suggested a connection had been made, but more people came in as lunchtime approached and they didn't get the chance to talk again. For a while he couldn't take his eyes off her; it wasn't lust, or any kind of physical attraction, although he was quite aware of her good looks. Jon felt a bond which was almost psychic, as though they could read each other's thoughts, moods, hopes and fears. She was a complete stranger, but at that moment she seemed the only person in the city who really knew him. The mechanics of it baffled him, yet when he took his leave half an hour later, his anxiety oddly seemed to have disappeared.

The biting wind had whipped the snow up into a blizzard. Jon bowed his head into the gale, but the flakes burned his face like fiery sparks; it was almost impossible to see more than a few yards ahead. No one else was stupid enough to walk, and only a couple of cars ground cautiously past. Absently, he started to sing 'White Christmas' until he realized he had taken a wrong turn in the confusion of the weather. He backtracked as best he could, but all the streets looked the same in the snow and soon he was trekking past houses he didn't recognize.

The wind seemed to be blowing stronger, and at one point he heard a strange ringing in the air which he attributed to the sound of the breeze on the telephone wires; it unnerved him for some reason he couldn't explain.

He struggled on in search of a familiar landmark, gradually losing the feeling in his toes while his ears and cheeks burned. At last, through the flurries, he sighted the imposing entrance to Highgate Cemetery. He had been walking away from the house, but if he turned right at the gates he would be able to wend his way back to Arcadia from the north.

As he closed on the cemetery, a figure seemed to detach itself from the pillar at the side of the gates and lurch towards him, black against the swirling white. The man looked like a biker, but his boyish face and wide grin gave him an appearance of indeterminate age. He wore a sleeve-less, faded denim vest over a leather motorcycle jacket, grey

T-shirt, well-worn blue jeans and engineer boots. His brown hair was wild and long and he had a gypsy earring in each ear. His grin reminded Jon of the fixed expression on the faces of fundamentalist Christians who preyed on weary travellers at American airports. Jon tried to sidestep him and head on his way, but he moved with surprising speed and clutched the upper portion of Jon's left arm.

'This world is filled with thunder. The light changes, slightly, turning slowly towards grey.' The biker seemed oblivious to the snowstorm. 'And what can you do when the dance begins? Listen. I hear it now.'

Jon tried to pull away; the grip grew tighter.

'Where he walks, no flowers grow,' the biker continued eagerly. 'Do you ken? The language of light is hard to show. The glamour makes the lie. Know this: five trees will fall to the feller's blade, too soon the light will start to fade. The winds will howl, the gate will fall. Judgement Day. Heed this call.'

Jon's attempts to break free were weakening, as if the biker was sucking the energy out of him.

'Know him by the fallen ones.' His eyes were fixed on Jon's face. Jon had the odd impression he was looking at a mask which covered something horrific. Gradually, he became aware that the biker's lips were moving but the words appeared a split-second later, like a film and sound-track running out of sync. 'Know him by his call: blood and punishment, hearts reach out.'

His hand fell away from Jon's arm as he retreated slowly. The blizzard's gusts snatched him, sweeping him away until he was snowflakes and then nothing. His voice hung in the air for a scant second longer.

'Blood and punishment, hearts reach out.' And then he was gone.

Jon sank slowly to his knees. His head seemed to be filled with luminous bursts, and there was a queasy pitching in his stomach. The peace he had found briefly in the pub was lost, and in its place was a discordant rumble that disturbed the edges of his consciousness.

'Do you always come here to pray?'

Lisa was grinning a few feet away, almost lost in a too-large leather jacket and a thick plaid scarf. She came over and slid a hand under his armpit to help him to his feet. 'What happened? Did you slip?'

'No . . . I don't know . . . I met someone . . .' Through his daze, Jon realized how stupid he sounded.

'A mugger?'

Jon shook his head.

'You *are* in a bad way. Come on, I'll help you home. You need to get a change of clothes before you catch your death.'

'You don't have to—'

'No problem. I'm on a short shift, no lectures today and I've got a couple of hours before I have to pick up Jamie.'

'Your boyfriend?'

'My son.'

Jon was still a little shaky, so she slipped her arm through his for support and together they made their way through the worsening weather towards Arcadia.

'I can't remember the first film I ever saw, but I can remember the first one to really affect me.' Jon cupped his hands round his coffee mug, revelling in the seductive warmth of the kitchen. 'And from then on, every film was special. *Double Indemnity* – now there's a movie. Fred MacMurray, Barbara Stanwyck, Edward G. Robinson. It changed my life. I was only a kid, too young for it really, I suppose, but I was hooked from that opening narration with Walter Neff, "Thirty-five years old, unmarried, no visible scars", confessing to murder. It told me life wasn't boring, that there was romance even in the darkest corners and that emotions were stronger than anything. Does that sound stupid?' Lisa just smiled. 'I owe Billy Wilder and

Raymond Chandler a lot. After that, movies became my life. I saw everything. Even the really bad ones had something to offer. Fantasy's . . .'

'. . . so much better than reality.' Lisa laughed. 'Tell me about it. I spent my earliest years in a cinema. My mum used to run this tiny place at the back of King's Cross, away from the main drag so there was hardly any passing trade. *That* was a good investment,' she said sarcastically. 'I can remember the smell of it even now. Mould and cigarette smoke. The clientele normally comprised a couple of tramps my mum used to let in when it was raining, some sad old buffers with nothing else to do and students who got in cheap-rate, usually so stoned they didn't know which film we were showing. It never did much business, probably because after my da walked out, Mum only showed the movies she liked. Lana Turner, Bette Davis . . .'

'Veronica Lake?'

'Yeah, you've got her measure. Who wants that when they can see *Rocky IV* at the Odeon?'

'Still, must have been great. Your own movie house.' Jon tried to read the past in her face; her relaxed expression was naturally troubled, making her seem aloof.

'I used to creep in and peer over the back row to watch the films. Great films, great stars.' Her face darkened briefly. 'Life outside wasn't too good, especially after my da left, the bastard.'

'How old were you?'

'Seven. The business ground to a halt. My mum had to sell up, go out to work in an office. She's never been the same since.' She fixed an accusatory eye on him. 'Men, eh?'

He shrugged, smiled, couldn't really think what to say.

'So, nice place you've got here,' she said, changing the subject without embarrassment.

'Rented. My folks found it when we first moved to London in the sixties. It hasn't changed at all since then. Can you believe it?'

'Getting back to your roots?'

'Something like that.'

'It's funny. People spend the first ten years after they leave school trying to escape from their childhood and the rest of their lives trying to get back to it. It's like at twenty-six we all suddenly realize that's as good as it gets. We fritter away our innocence and then find out that's the only thing of value that we ever have.'

Jon couldn't bring himself to look at her. 'That's a little depressing,' he said eventually.

Lisa drained her coffee as she examined the kitchen with a cold, perceptive eye. 'The Victorians understood. They worshipped childhood and celebrated death because that was the only way to get back to that state of innocence. What's in between? A daily struggle to fill the void. Work, sex, drink, drugs. Nothing does it.'

'Nothing?'

She shifted uncomfortably. 'Maybe nothing. I don't know.'

'I don't believe that.' Jon took her mug and dumped it in the sink with his own. 'There's got to be a way back to that . . . goodness. That uncorrupted view of the world.'

'If there is, I bet there's a big price to pay. You can't get out of the swamp of everyday life without finding some way to wash off the shit.'

'And I've been in that swamp up to my neck,' Jon muttered.

'There's always a price to pay,' Lisa continued as if she hadn't heard him.

The front door slammed and Sarah's querying voice echoed through the house.

'I'm here,' Jon shouted.

'What a fucking day I've—' The words caught in her throat when she saw Lisa. 'I'm sorry. I didn't know you had company.'

'Some lunatic grabbed me in the street. Lisa dusted me

down and brought me home.' He felt his cheeks redden inexplicably. 'This is Sarah, my wife,' he added hastily.

Lisa greeted her and then stood up. 'I'd better be going—'

'Oh, don't go on my behalf.' Sarah's voice was filled with the frigidity she used to put down menials.

'I've got to pick up my son—'

Sarah raised one eyebrow. 'A son. Really?' Jon wanted to shout at her not to be so aggressively defensive of what she saw as hers, but he knew it was futile; Sarah did whatever Sarah wanted.

If Lisa was offended by the frostiness, she didn't show it. 'Don't go falling over in the snow now,' she said to Jon with a warm smile. It seemed like she didn't want to leave; perhaps it was just the weather. 'And get better.'

'I'll show you out,' Sarah said.

When she returned, Jon could see the questions mounting up in her eyes, but he knew her pride would not let her say anything. Jealousy. Pride. Lust. Gluttony for drugs. Wrath. Sarah loved her deadly sins.

'You're back early,' he said.

'Hmmm.' She managed to pull herself away from whatever she wanted to say. 'I left the Carmell file here. I tried to call so I could send a bike round . . .'

'I went out, for a walk. I thought it would do me good.'

'I think I'm going to have to get an answerphone,' she moaned. 'There's one lying around at work I can bring home.'

A gust of wind rattled the panes and he said excitedly, 'Have you seen the snow? I can't remember the last time we had a fall like this in London. I thought all the pollution had put paid to that.'

Briefly he considered asking her to come into the garden for a snowball fight, but the tautness of her features told him she was trapped in work mode. For an instant, he had an odd, disconnected impression of what she might have been like as a young girl, but the image was indistinct and he couldn't draw it into focus.

'Have you seen that cat around?' Her nose twitched with distaste. 'I can't stand cats.'

He remembered her saying something similiar in New York shortly after they were married, when the heat was unbearable and there was danger in the air. An uncontrollable urge to connect with her swept through him and he threw his arms around her and kissed her passionately. She was startled at first, but then the iron cracked and she folded into him.

'All this will be over soon,' he said hopefully, 'and we'll be able to get on with our lives. I feel more optimistic than I have done in years. We've got good times ahead of us.' A note of desperation slipped through.

She pulled back and looked searchingly into his eyes. 'You just get better, honey. That's the important thing.'

'Why don't you stay here? Give work a miss for the rest of the afternoon?' The moment the words had left his lips, he knew it was the wrong thing to say.

She pulled away from him, smoothing the front of her blouse mechanically. 'You know I can't do that. It's unprofessional. There's so much to do.'

'Important things? More important than having fun? You're the boss . . .'

'It would be unprofessional.'

The brief moment of connection fizzled out as Jon felt the cold rush into the vacuum that lay between them. The disentanglement felt worse than the moment deserved, and Jon knew that if he didn't do something he would be set adrift. But he was unable to go back, terrified of moving forward, and in that instant of stasis Sarah smiled without any particular sign of happiness, muttered something he forgot instantly and slipped slowly out of the room.

*

Jon wanted to talk, but there was no one who could understand what he had to say. He couldn't even comprehend it himself. Nervously, he turned his arm and examined the unfading black mark beneath. He recalled the chase in the snow and the unicorn. The transmigrating towel. What did it all mean? What was happening to him?

Resignedly, he had to accept one of the final things the doctors had told him: in the difficult times ahead, the only person he could truly rely on was himself. Bitterly, he stalked up to the bedroom and pulled his blood-red journal from its hiding place at the bottom of his underwear drawer. He hated giving in to the doctors' regime, but there was no one to talk to but himself.

Yet when he flicked the book open, he was disturbed to see several pages were missing. He examined their tiny remnants near the binding; they had been very precisely cut out with something sharp, like a Stanley knife.

Sarah was the only one who could possibly have had access to it, yet there was no reason for her to commit such a mindless act of vandalism. Unless, he thought giddily, he had done it himself during another period of disequilibrium.

Nauseated, he sat down on the bed and examined the crisp white pages that counted off his future. They came to an end on Christmas Day.

6

Somewhere inside everyone is a place the world can't reach.
I firmly believe that. When the humiliations of the work
environment are being heaped on our shoulders, when the
degradations are dealt out by so-called loved ones, when
we are brutalized and beaten and driven to the point of
extinction, it still remains untouched. Pure. The only way
I'm going to survive what's happening to me and prevent
my quicksilver sanity running through my fingers is to find
it. It's my sanctuary, this quiet place, the pure essence of
me. When I walked out of Steelguard I took the first few
steps towards locating it, but it's been like the collapse of
the Communist regimes in Eastern Europe. First you get the
hopes of freedom, then you see the chaos that erupts as all
the repressed bitterness and ethnic rivalry comes flooding
out and you realize it's going to be a long slog through a
bloody battlefield to get anywhere close to the high ground
you'd hoped for.

I know exactly what I'm trying to find – the purity of
emotion and belief that I experienced as a child. But trying
to listen for the faint heartbeat with all the background
noise of your life crashing down is bloody difficult. Almost
impossible.

What's going wrong? I'll tell you. The rules of my life
seem to have been blown away. I keep plunging from real
life to staggeringly real hallucinations via dreams that I can
touch, taste and smell, and I can't tell what's what any

more. It's like living in a virtual reality world. If it were that simple I'd just sit back and enjoy the ride, but it's what it stands for that scares me. It means the hard disk of my mind has been corrupted, bits of data are flaking off, infecting other programs. It means my burn-out at Steelguard was just the start. I can feel things running away from me, out of control, getting faster and faster. I try to hold on to myself, but nothing seems to work, and I'm so desperately afraid of losing all the good things, Sarah, *me*. And sometimes I feel my heart is going to burst out of my body and my head is spinning so much and my emotions are all over the place – everything seems on the verge of shutting down. Breaking down. How much longer can I go on like this? How do I help myself?

I suppose I should turn to all you doctors, but I'm afraid if I do you'll take me back inside and that will be the end of it. If you ever do sort me out there'll be nothing left when I come back to my life.

What terrifies me the most is looking into Sarah's eyes. It's like she doesn't know me any more. Sometimes I'm even afraid I see pity and that's always the beginning of the end. I don't want to lose her, but everything seems beyond my control. By trying to achieve my own state of grace, have I soured everything of value that I had? Why are there so many questions? Before all this happened, everything was certainties.

When I think of Sarah, I always think of the good times – not the drug times or the drunk times – but the good times of two people enjoying life. I remember our honeymoon in the States, New York, and then LA. Going to a tiny retro cinema in Westwood to see *Some Like It Hot*, then heading down to Santa Monica to look at the sea.

I remember a wake at a dive in the City after one of our friends had topped himself because of money problems. We'd both known Matt for a long time. He was gay, flamboyant, a high-roller. But then he lost his job over some political stuff when a new boss came in and everything seemed to go wrong for him. Anyway, he'd always been close to Sarah and me. Sarah loved him.

Some time into the wake I realized Sarah had been missing for a long while. I wandered around and then found her outside in the rain. She looked frightened, like some trapped animal, and when I took her hand she just folded into me. I remember feeling her heart beating like a triphammer against my chest. I asked her what was wrong and I was surprised to see tears in her eyes. She told me she didn't want to lose me. That if she did, she would die. The weight of emotion I saw in her face was so powerful, it cut me up. Sarah keeps her emotions close to her – that's why so many people think she's cold. I wish everyone could have seen her at that moment – filled with love, filled with so many emotions I couldn't even begin to comprehend them.

We stood in the rain for half an hour, talking about everything, stupid things, important things, watching the lights of the Tower of London, and I remember thinking, The two of us, together, for all time, and feeling so happy I thought I was going to die. It was one of those stupid romantic moments that sound ridiculous when you tell someone else, but which can change your life on some deep level you can't normally reach.

When you're young you think old people know everything, as if at some particular age you pass into a state of awareness and wisdom. One of the worst things about growing up is waiting for that moment of transcendence, and waiting, and waiting, and starting to feel terrible and guilty, as you grasp that it's not going to happen to you. The next stage is a feeling of bitterness and anger when you realize you've been fooled; it never happens to anyone. All the old people, your parents, the politicians on the TV, were lying. They weren't wise; the only thing they were good at was pretending that they were.

When you get past thirty, you realize what a frightening

place the world is. All those people running countries, corporations, fighting wars, are just like you. They're all kids, trying to hide the fact, pretending they know what they're doing. The first lesson they should teach us in school is this: you never grow up. Then there'd be no lies, no disappointments, no trust in hopeless causes. And maybe then we'd be able to focus on the things that really matter instead of wasting our time trying to put on masks for each other.

At a point in my life when I was sure I was used to the idea of never being wise, I suddenly find myself wishing I was. All I can do is dwell on my childhood and wish I was there again. Pathetic. I hate myself.

Some strange biker molested me in the street today. That sounds well on the way to a *News of the World* headline. When I say molest, with my penchant for hyperbole, I mean he grabbed my arm and spouted gibberish. He was probably drunk, or perhaps he simply recognized a kindred nut. Maybe there's a secret society of crazies with their own symbols and hidden gestures like the Masons. A dog on a string means you've just started out. A pair of piss-stained trousers, two sizes too big, means you've attained the mystical thirty-third degree Crazy. *Arrglfeckoff* with a wave of the hand at an imaginary fly means, 'Welcome, fellow traveller.' I haven't reached that level yet. I only see and hear things that aren't there and spend all day burying my head in the sand, trying to remember how to communicate with normal people. But maybe soon.

Perhaps I've always been unbalanced. When I first ran to Dad to tell him about the disembodied voice of a crying child, he should have called the men in white coats straight away. Then I probably wouldn't be in this hole. And what does it mean – crying children? Lost innocence? I'm not very good with symbols.

I met a woman called Lisa today. A barmaid, though it's wrong to define her with just that word. She's nice, and isn't that just as pathetic a description? She seems to have values, which is an odd thing in this day and age, and that's the biggest compliment I can give her. A human being in a world of robots. I might make that pub my local. The one thing it seemed to be missing in its decor was the sad, rambling drunk at the end of the bar. Maybe the brewery will sponsor me. Lisa. Strange, that's the only barmaid's name I've ever remembered. It's funny how some people make an instant impact on you. Whatever I saw in her had to be on some kind of subconscious level. I mean, we barely spoke. As this is my forum for brutal honesty, I suppose I ought to note that I'd really like to see her again. Just to talk, understand. Nothing more.

There's one thing that keeps bothering me, though. I can't seem to get what the biker said out of my head. If he was just a nut, why do his words seem to contain such hidden meaning for me? *Blood and punishment, hearts reach out.*

Or in the words of another great man of celluloid: 'It seems to me if they ain't got you one way they got you another. So what's the answer? That's what I keep asking myself. What's it all about? Know what I mean?'

7

Sarah called at 7 p.m. to tell Jon she had a rearranged dinner meeting with clients and wouldn't be back until late. With incipient fatalism, he had half-expected it, but that didn't prevent it sapping the energy from him. Suddenly he couldn't bring himself to cook a full meal; all his limp, weary arms could muster was a little toast.

Looking out of the study window, the street seemed filled with a dreary light as if the lamps were operating at half-power. Occasionally a car crawled through the thick grey slush, each driver hunched over the wheel, looking hunted. The houses across the road were dark and empty, apart from one, lit only by the depressing glow of a TV.

By the time he had walked along the hall to the kitchen, it was snowing again. The huge, floating flakes seemed almost surreally incandescent as they drifted past the window to the purity of the garden's blanketing whiteness. The harshness of the trees was softened by this dusting of crystals, and through their branches he could see the Pole Star shining brightly.

The snowfall entranced him for almost five minutes until he drew himself back to the task at hand and popped two slices of bread in the toaster. The Marmite jar continued to irk him; however careful he was at withdrawing his knife, a deposit always seemed to find its way on to the rim, gluing the lid tight. He hammered it on the table, then held it under the hot water tap before placing it next to the toaster while he went in search of a tea towel to give him a better grip. Sarah had stored them in a bottom drawer next to the fridge, all obsessively folded and piled so that no edge stuck out. He took great pleasure in pulling one out and crumpling it.

When he returned to the toaster, he did a double-take; the Marmite jar was gone. His thoughts flashed like interference on a TV.

There was a jarring moment of destabilization which conjured up conflicting thoughts of his own mental weakness and the sense that reality had done a sudden flip, but he knew in his heart which was the most likely. Feeling the depression creep up on him, he was almost afraid to look round although he knew the only answer was to confront his failure; the doctor-speak came second nature.

It was in the centre of the table.

The self-loathing hit him with full force and all he could do was grab the jar and hurl it into the corner of the room where it exploded in a cascade of brown glass, leaving a smear like excrement on the white wall.

The weight of his emotions proved too much and he slumped into a chair with his head in his hands. He was glad Sarah wasn't there to see him: she had always said she admired his resilience in the face of any problem, like the time in the early days of her business when she thought it was going under, and he had sat her down, talked through all the options, and, she claimed, given her the strength to find a way out. What would she think of him now?

A noise somewhere nearby jolted him alert. Through the daze of his thoughts, it had sounded almost like laughter. His fear of appearing even more stupid and weak was almost overpowering, but he held his breath and listened nonetheless. Naturally he heard nothing; what did he expect?

With a weary acceptance, he prised himself to his feet, his attention falling unconsciously on to the Marmite smear. It hadn't trickled down to the floor like he would have expected. Its sticky mass resembled the shape of a face, like a Halloween pumpkin, with the white wall showing through the gunk to form the eyes and the mouth. Closer inspection added to the unnatural image. There were furrows on the outline as if it had been shaped by small fingers. It disturbed him out of all proportion and he hurried away without cleaning it off.

He spent the remaining hours before bed in front of the relaxingly hissing fire in the study, working his way through *A Christmas Carol*, hoping Sarah would be home before midnight so they could spend some time together. He found it hard to settle, despite the tranquillity, and in one shuddering moment of awareness, he realized he still had much of his old self to eradicate; his body's time clock was reminding him he should be contacting Wall Street, preparing for the opening of the Asian markets.

It was more than he could bear. Bitterly, he went to replace the book on the shelf, but was caught midway across the room by an overwhelming feeling of being watched. He turned suddenly and in the dazzle of the standard lamp thought he saw a shape in one corner, like a fading retinal imprint of something resembling a smile of glittering teeth; it disappeared when he blinked.

At that moment, the house seemed too big and too old, without the welcoming drone of a TV to make it more hospitable. He decided the most comforting place to wait for Sarah was the bedroom.

He shivered as he peeled off his clothes, his breath misty in the chill; the radiator didn't appear to be working. He slid under the sheets so hastily he forgot to draw the curtains, but the room was too cold to get out again. Instead, he watched the falling snowflakes, thinking of Sarah enjoying herself in a world he no longer understood.

He awoke some time later, suddenly aware there was something on the bed. In what little light filtered through the window, his first sight was of a pair of yellow-green eyes staring at him. The cat sat at the foot of the bed, bolt upright as if it had been waiting for him to wake; its white chin and chest looked ghostly in the half-light.

'What are you doing here?' he said sleepily. 'Sarah will kill you if she finds you.' He flopped out an arm searchingly and was depressed to find she still wasn't home.

The cat's eyes were filled with that unnerving intelligence he had noted the first time he encountered it.

'I'm not feeding you now, if that's what you want,' he continued. 'It's too cold.' Instantly, he realized it wasn't. The air was filled with a summery warmth.

The cat broke off its stare and jumped from the bed. Half-way to the door, it turned and looked back at him. *Waiting*, he thought. The door was closed, and he half-wondered how the cat had got inside in the first place, but he was already slipping out of bed to let it out. It darted sinuously along the landing.

An odd glow was emanating from the nursery. The door was slightly ajar and shadows shimmered along the wall. As the cat slipped in, Jon hurried curiously behind it, untroubled by anxiety or fear. When he pushed the door open to look inside, he was hit by a waft of spices.

The nursery had been transformed: mistletoe, holly with gleaming red berries and trailing ivy festooned the walls and ceiling, so thick and vibrant it appeared to be growing there, while in the open hearth a fire roared, although Jon knew the chimney had been blocked long ago. At the centre of the greenery sat two people. The most prominent was a giant of a man with muscular arms and a rotund belly, dressed in long green robes trimmed with fur. At first glance his clothes looked like velvet, but when he moved they shifted and crackled into what appeared to be thousands of interlocking leaves; his long, russet beard and hair, too, were interwoven with leaves and ivy.

At his feet sprawled a small body which suggested a boy,

although his eyes seemed old beyond his years. He was also dressed in green, and his flowing hair was a lustrous red. Jon thought: *I've seen him before*. He was cleaning under his fingernails with a small dagger while eyeing Jon warily.

'This is a dream,' Jon said to himself.

'There are no dreams,' the Giant replied. 'Merely different views from a single window.'

'Sometimes,' the boy added, 'I can hear the sound of chickens crying.'

'I know you. You're the Ghost of Christmas Present,' Jon said. The Giant put his head on one side enigmatically. 'If I'd eaten recently, I'd say you were an undigested bit of beef or a fragment of an underdone potato, but as I haven't I can only put you down to my own mind. And there lurks a very sorry story.' He turned to the boy. 'I don't know who you are, but you look familiar. What this scene is missing, though, is the cornucopia of food – the turkeys, the hams, the sausages, the geese, you know, the whole Christmas schtick.'

'But there *is* a cornucopia of food,' the Giant replied. Jon saw all his teeth had been filed to points. At his prompting, Jon looked around and noticed new details which put a chill in his spine. Poking out from under the greenery, hanging from the trailing ivy like hideous, pale fruit, was a collection of human heads – young children, old men, women, their eyes open but rolled up, their expressions running the spectrum from blank surprise to screaming horror at the presentation of their death. Under the aroma of the spices, Jon could smell the butcher's shop odour of them.

Jon backed towards the wall, glanced at the door, now mysteriously closed; he felt a sudden wave of panic, but his legs wouldn't respond to his urging. The Giant and the boy seemed a little less human, their eyes too staring, their smiles too fixed, as though he had only just noticed they were wearing masks over their real faces.

Jon closed his eyes. 'I could wake up,' he said loudly.

'And return to a world without colour?'

'The Ghost of Christmas Past seems to have passed me by for some reason.'

'There are no ghosts. I am all of them. Do you know my true name?' The Giant's words echoed a split-second after his mouth moved; Jon knew he had experienced the effect before. 'There are some upon this earth of yours,' the Giant continued, with a strange, threatening smile, 'who claim to know us.'

The boy jumped to his feet. Jon noticed his ears were pointed like some fairytale sprite's, but his expression seemed more malicious than mischievous.

'Do you have something to show me?' Jon asked. 'Something to illustrate the heartless and money-obsessed way I have spent the last ten years? If that's the case, you've come too late.'

'I can show you many things,' the Giant replied. 'Grab hold of my robe.'

Jon felt an urge to turn away; instead he found himself moving forward as if he was wading through treacle. As he passed, the boy whispered, 'Blood and punishment, hearts reach out.'

There was a flicker and a jolt as the room disappeared and an instant later Jon stood next to the Giant on a summer-warm street smelling of smoke and gaslights. There was a movement above his head; the boy was rising up towards the rooftops.

'Still following the same script?' Jon said. He felt detached, like he was coked-up; any emotions he might have been experiencing were beyond his reach. 'I feel like a ghost myself,' he said. 'Where are we now? What am I supposed to be seeing?'

Jon stepped out into the middle of the street and searched for landmarks. He could just glimpse the dome of St Paul's about a mile distant. A grimy sign plugged to the wall above a shuttered shop said *Buck's Row*, and although he didn't recognize the name he had an idea where he was. 'The East End?' He sniffed the air again, sampling the unfamiliar scents. 'Summer, a long time ago.'

'Time is as meaningless as length, breadth and depth,' the Giant said. 'For you, all is illusion.'

'Even you?'

The Giant smiled. 'Nothing is as it seems.'

Jon imagined those pointed teeth tearing through meat; he didn't want to turn his back on the figure. 'You're not quite how Dickens described you.'

'Tales are often told to comfort infants, the truth obscured by honeyed words.' He made a strange smacking sound with his mouth. 'Look, you.'

The boy swooped down through the soot-scented air trailing a patch of glitter in his wake. He pointed to a pile of rags lying on the cobbles in the gutter.

Jon moved closer with a sudden feeling of dread. The rags took shape from the shadows, coalescing into a human form with white face and hands, lying in a pool of congealing black. Drawn by the sight, Jon stepped in the puddle, but no ripples formed. It was a woman. She had been virtually disembowelled, her ragged, filthy, voluminous skirts thrown up to reveal a butchering of her belly carried out with a surgeon's precision.

Jon's stomach turned, and he leaped backwards in shock as a shriek erupted from a nearby doorway. A pockmarked woman in a dirty bonnet and long Victorian skirts scrambled towards the corpse, slipped in the blood, then righted herself.

'Polly!' she screamed, looking round, at Jon, staring right through him. 'Polly! She's been done in! Murder! Lor', murder!'

Her cries were echoed by the blast of a whistle nearby. Jon jumped again as the Giant's hand fell on his shoulder and dragged him slowly back into the shadows.

'What am I supposed to learn from this?' Jon asked queasily.

'It is too late to learn,' the Giant said.

There was another instant of darkness and vertigo, and when Jon next opened his eyes the summery heat had been replaced by winter chill. Snow lay all around a shadowy street. From somewhere nearby, the thrum of traffic came to him, muffled, as if through water.

'I feel sick,' Jon said. 'I don't know what any of this means! Are we back? There's supposed to be a reason, isn't there? There *has* to be a reason.'

The Giant's waxen face drew closer until it filled Jon's whole vision; in his eyes, Jon could see something incomprehensible and terrifying. 'Across the worlds we dance,' the Giant began. 'Once we were close to you, now, made distant by walls and doors not of our making. Soon we may be back.' He smiled his pointed-tooth smile. 'For the feast of Christmas and Christmases to come.'

The boy pushed his face up close to the Giant's. 'Did you ever look in a mirror and wonder why?'

'You're not making any sense,' Jon murmured, looking from one face to the other.

'The price expected is too high,' the Giant continued. 'Vengeance is not our way, but it is his, and all things fall before him if he so desires. Look, you.'

He stretched out a trembling arm, and as Jon followed the pointed finger his gaze fell upon another corpse, face down in the snow.

'Blood echoes down the years,' the Giant said. 'What was then, is now.'

Jon had the awful feeling he knew the figure, even though its face was obscured. 'Who is it?' he asked.

'Turn him over,' the boy said gleefully. 'Look! Look!'

The Giant gripped Jon's arm tightly as he tried to back away. There was too much blood staining the snow, hinting at the butchery he had seen before. He was afraid, in some irrational way, that if he turned the body over he would see his own face looking back at him.

The boy pulled away, giggling, and did a little dance in the snow. Suddenly he stopped and looked up at Jon. In his eyes was the mischief of barely remembered childhood fairy-tales; of lost children and clocks that wouldn't stop ticking, counting out the seconds to the horrors of adulthood.

'Who did this?' Jon whispered.

The boy put his hand to his mouth and mumbled something before continuing his gleeful dance.

'Don't play with me,' Jon said. 'What are you saying?'

The boy stopped, mumbled behind his hand again; his eyes glittered cruelly.

'Stop it!' Jon yelled. 'Tell me!'

This time the boy took his hand away. His lips moved slowly, dangerously, and an instant later the sound crept out.

'The Scissorman is out.'

8

Jon woke in the drawing room to a morning that was so cold his fingers and feet ached. He noticed with some surprise he was barefoot, his skin a translucent bluey-white, the turn-ups of his jeans sopping wet.

Before he could wonder why he wasn't in bed, the front door banged. Sarah stuttered to a halt in passing the open doorway when she saw him, and a split-second after, Richard crashed into the back of her.

'You're up early,' she said in an odd tone. 'Out on the tiles last night?'

'What do you mean?'

'I must have rung ten times to tell you I was staying over at Sally's. Richard and I met her in Trackers. By the end of the evening she was drunk as a skunk and I had to take her home – you know how she gets.' She narrowed her eyes questioningly. 'When I didn't get a reply, I presumed you'd changed your mind about going out.'

'I was here.' Jon tried to convince himself, but his disorientation was overpowering. 'I've been sleeping pretty heavily recently.'

'I think those carpet slippers I got you last Christmas will come in handy, old chap,' Richard chirped mockingly over Sarah's shoulder. 'Barefoot and wet-trousered? You must be having a flashback to your student days.'

Jon checked his watch. 'Shouldn't you two be on your way to work?'

'I met Richard at the top of the road – we'd both had the same idea after talking about you last night,' Sarah said. She crossed the room and kneeled in front of him, taking his cold hands in her own. 'We're both going to help you through this. We're going to give you the support you need to get you back on your feet. The first thing we have to do is get you out of the house. It's not doing you any good staying here brooding all day long.'

'I don't know if I'm quite—'

'No excuses, old chap. It's a done deal. We're going to brave the Christmas throngs, have morning coffee in that nice little place off Piccadilly, do a little shopping, wave the old platinum card under the noses of the paupers. Then a spot of lunch—'

'Richard—'

'Jon, no. You're doing what we say.' Sarah's eyes flashed. 'We're worried about you.'

'What about work?'

'It won't hurt to take a day off. This is more important.' Her fingers closed tightly round his own. '*You're* the most important thing to us, Jon. To see you like this . . . You seem like a ghost floating through life when you used to be so passionate about everything. It tears us up to see it.' It was the first time in years he had heard her speak with such open emotion. 'We're not going to shirk our responsibilities to you, but you've got to meet us half-way.'

Richard shifted uncomfortably in the doorway and moved on to the kitchen. Once he had passed, Sarah pulled Jon's head down and kissed him deeply.

When he pulled away, the memory of the dream had almost drifted away. 'OK,' he said. 'I'll do what you say.'

It was easier to leave the house than Jon had expected, and after a short time in the West End he felt like much of his old equilibrium had returned, fired by glimpses of the better parts of his old life: Richard clowning with one of the

Harrod's doormen, Sarah's acid-tongued monologue on the hidden perils of minicab drivers, lunch in the Savoy Grill, jokes, meandering discourses and old times remembered.

The snow started dusting the bumper-to-bumper traffic on Regent Street just after lunch. It seemed to ignite some forgotten race memory of optimism in the shoppers jostling for position at the crossings as they waited for the traffic wardens' megaphone release. London spent most of the year sleeping, bloated and indolent, but it came alive at Christmas when it remembered its innocent youth. The streets swarmed like a Third World bus station, making it as difficult to cross the pavement as it was to dodge through traffic. A giant golden angel hovered over Oxford Circus, eyeing the red and green streamers that dressed up Oxford Street's tattered rags. And every shop had Bing Crosby and Frank Sinatra crooning about old times, better times, days of people and emotions, not cash on demand.

Jon desperately wanted to be a part of it, but he felt detached, like a ghost, and that recognition triggered the anxiety which was always nearby. By the time they reached the Christmas Past window display at Selfridges, it felt like a weasel was burrowing its way through his intestine.

'Are you OK, old chap?' Richard asked. 'You look like someone asked you to give to charity.'

'Just a little tension,' Jon mumbled.

'It's probably the crowds,' Sarah said. 'We should go in here for a break.' She herded them through the department store's swing doors, and they eventually found a zone of relative calmness in a basement area filled with glassware, silver ornaments and porcelain. Jon located an abandoned chair and rested with his head between his knees while Richard lurked uncomfortably near a precarious display of Cumbrian crystal.

After a few minutes, Jon looked up to see Sarah transfixed by a hand mirror with a delicate frame of moulded silver. Beatific in her dreaminess, Jon found himself remembering the night he had proposed to her after an evening of cocktails at the American Bar in the Savoy, when he had pressed her hand around the ring box and the already-primed pianist had launched into a tinkling version of 'Love and Marriage'.

In the plangent swell of emotion, he remembered he had yet to buy her a Christmas present. The mirror had obviously captivated her in the same way she had snared him; it would make the perfect gift. However hard it would be for him to venture into the West End alone, he would do it. She deserved it.

'How are you feeling, old chap?' Richard flopped a large hand on to Jon's shoulder.

'Better,' Jon lied. 'We should move on.'

'My sentiments exactly. So many experiences, so little time.'

'Sarah looks good, doesn't she?'

'When does Sarah not look good? God knows how you managed to land someone like her. I always saw you with someone a little more proletarian – you know, child-bearing hips, broad shoulders. Russian peasant stock, maybe.'

'You're letting your fantasies run away with you now, Richard.'

'Ah, you've caught me out. My love of dirty-fingernailed girls with chip shop complexions and unconventional perms is obviously too strong to hide.'

'You know, I really am sorry for what happened,' Jon said suddenly. 'I know I must be a bloody burden for you both right now. The last thing I wanted was to unload my problems on Sarah and you.'

'If you can't rely on your friends in times of crisis, what use are they?' Richard said. 'You'll have to dampen down your ego and put yourself in our hands for a while.'

'What are you two boys talking about?' Sarah slipped her arm around Jon's waist and gave him a squeeze.

'I was trying to convince him to take some nude photos

of you for me,' Richard answered wryly. 'Do you want to hear my latest joke? An Irishman goes to a building site looking for work. The foreman says, "We'll take you on if you can tell the difference between joists and girders." "Easy," the Mick replies. "Joyce wrote *Ulysses* and Goethe wrote *Faust*." My first PC joke.'

'Apart from calling him a Mick,' Jon noted.

'You're in the wrong profession,' Sarah sighed.

'Roof-felting would be good,' Jon mocked. 'I don't know where you get your jokes from, but—' His attention was caught by a flurry of movement on the escalator. Someone was forcing their way down the up-side, bowling over shoppers, sending parcels and bags raining down all around as the curses and shouts grew louder. As the figure emerged at the bottom, stepping over a sprawling old woman, Jon recognized the biker who had grabbed him in the snow outside Highgate Cemetery.

Richard and Sarah seemed oblivious as they made their way across the department, but Jon was rooted, his stomach knotting, sweat seeping out all over his body. Suddenly he couldn't stop thinking about his dream of the Giant and the boy. Relentlessly, the biker rammed his way through the shoppers towards Jon, shouting something which Jon couldn't make out above the din.

With inexplicable panic, Jon half-turned, started to run, couldn't resist looking back.

The biker stumbled against a display of glass which crashed to the floor in an explosion of sound and light. Richard and Sarah were staring now, at the biker, then at Jon. Richard was saying something, but Jon couldn't hear it; he felt he was suspended in syrup, the biker his only focus.

Another display collapsed, a silver service, tumbling, catching the light, a percussive retort. The biker shouted again; Jon was hypnotized by his lips, trying to make sense of it all.

'It's starting . . .'

Jon began to break free.

'You must turn away . . .'

Moving away, still backwards. The biker, flailing arms, yelling, yet face impassive.

'It's still not too late . . .'

And then somehow Jon came alive, his feet slipping and sliding around the displays until he had managed to lose the biker in the crowds. He didn't rest until he was out in the street, back pressed against the window, in the glowering gloom amid the smell of roasting chestnuts and the relentless drone of the crowds.

Gradually, he was able to control his panic, without even beginning to comprehend why he had been affected so deeply. Further down the street, a news-seller barked into the twilight, his pitch illuminated by Selfridges Christmas lights. Jon's attention fell on the *Evening Standard* headline scrawled on the flapping paper pinned to the side of the newsman's box.

CITY BOSS MURDERED.

Jon weighed each word carefully until the meaning seeped through the soup surrounding his brain, triggering connections which he couldn't explain but which terrified him nonetheless. CITY. BOSS. MURDERED.

Fumbling for his change, he snatched a copy from the news-seller and read the front page feverishly by the light of the window display.

City Boss Murdered
by CHARLES HUNT
Crime Reporter

Sir Ronald Whittington, one of the City's most respected speculators, was brutally slain in a back street stabbing attack last night. The body of the 62-year-old head of Roche Kamarg was discovered at 2 a.m. by a mini-cab driver, not far from Christ Church, Spitalfields. Murder squad detectives refused to release any details of the killing while forensic tests were being carried out. A Scotland Yard spokesman added: 'So far, no motive has been established. However, the sheer ferocity of the attack suggests this was not a simple mugging gone wrong.'

The story was filled out with biographical details: Whittington's rapid rise to become a pillar of the City; details about his wife, children and grandchildren; his Surrey home; his collection of classic cars and vintage wines. A life defined in mundanities.

'What in heaven's name happened to you?' Richard was at his shoulder, concern and irritation interchanging on his face.

Sarah hurried up behind. 'Jesus Christ, Jon—'

Jon held out the paper. Distracted, Richard glanced half-heartedly at the lead story. 'Whittington, eh? Poor bastard,' he said dismissively.

'He gave me my first break when he was at Steelguard,' Jon said. 'He took a chance on me when all I'd shown was an aptitude for writing. He interviewed you as well, didn't he?'

'Jon, what happened down there?' Sarah pushed the paper to one side so she could stand in front of him.

'It was nothing. Just a panic attack.'

'Don't ruin it all, Jon. You've got to work with us if we're going to get you back to normal.'

He nodded in agreement, caught on the barb of her cold, grey eyes.

'You've got to put yourself in our hands,' she continued. 'Do everything we say, no questions asked. No running off, trying to sort things out for yourself. Do you understand?'

He nodded again, but his thoughts were already turning to a body in an East End street, and a dream that seemed too real to be fantasy.

*

Sarah and Richard both had to tie up loose ends at work before the day was out, so the taxi dropped him at Arcadia alone. After the chill of the late afternoon, the house seemed almost unbearably hot, but within minutes he found the atmosphere oddly comforting. He made himself scrambled eggs on toast and smoothed out the crumpled *Standard* on the kitchen table to read the story again while he was eating.

His abiding memory of Sir Ronald was of him leaning across the polished table in the walnut-panelled Steelguard boardroom and intoning dramatically, 'In life, there are many crossroads, Jonathan. One simple decision will affect all your tomorrows, leading to other choices, other paths. One must select carefully because once a path has been walked, there is never any going back. You must accept the future choices presented to you, good or bad. This is one of those crossroads, Jonathan.'

Whittington had been attempting to convince him to take the job with Steelguard, but now Jon saw it more as a warning. He had wanted to be a writer. His parents, in their infinite wisdom, had convinced him it would be better to have a *proper* job to fall back on – just in case the writing didn't work out, of course. A friend of his father's was Something In The City, and had landed Jon the interview at Steelguard. He had a good degree to back him up, but Whittington claimed to have recognized something in him at that interview which the dull-as-dishwater, pinstripe toff claimed made Jon prime City material. It had always been Jon's nightmare that Whittington was right.

For a long time, that had seemed to be the case. Seduced by Whittington's honeyed words, he had accepted the job. 'Just a stop-gap,' he told everyone. 'It will give me the financial security to write in my spare time.' He never wrote another word. The job dominated his waking hours and, like a computer virus, its peculiar, ethic-free philosophies changed the way he thought. He became very good at making money, the best his superiors had seen in a long time, they told him. He became what he hated.

The child's cry echoed through the house so loudly Jon dropped his fork, clattering, to the floor. It had come from almost overhead – the nursery. This time there could be no doubt of its existence.

Anxiously, he stalked into the hall, listening breathlessly between each measured footstep. Although he could hear nothing, he knew he would have to go further; its resonance down the years was too strong. As he reached the foot of the stairs, a flash of grey shot out from beneath his feet, eliciting a cry of repressed tension. The cat stopped to examine him from the darkness of the drawing room. In the gloom, the ghost of its outline seemed unfeasibly large, like a small dog; its eyes were huge and staring, and the white patch on its chin gave the illusion that it was grinning at him mockingly. That disembodied grin, fading away into the shadows, stayed with him as he climbed to the landing.

The nursery was deserted – he had expected no less – but there was an odd odour hanging in the air, like the smoke of a coal fire. The marks on the wall next to the wardrobe caught his eye a second later. Examining them askance, they seemed merely abstract smudges, but head-on he could see the truth.

They were two tiny handprints, fingers splayed, as if the child who had made them had been pushing with all his strength. He brushed them with the side of his thumb. The flaking plaster was slightly raised as though caused by pressure from the other side of the wall where there was only night air high above the garden. The tension started to twist its way around Jon's body. Here was something tangible, but it was as incomprehensible as any of his hallucinations. He backed away slowly, then slipped out and closed the door firmly behind him.

*

'You don't want to come round here. This isn't the kind of place for your sort.' The drunk's florid complexion glowed in the light of the tube station entrance as he swayed haggardly in front of Jon. His clothes were filthy, his hair a tangled mess of grease. His uncompromising stare forced Jon to look down at his own Hugo Boss overcoat.

'You come poking your fucking nose in here where you don't belong. This is our place,' the drunk continued. 'You've got to pay the price if you want to come in here.' His hacking cough rattled in his chest as he held out a trembling hand. 'Come on, pay up, you fucking bastard.'

Stunned by the sudden confrontation after emerging from the stale warmth of the Underground, Jon palmed a fiver from the roll in his pocket and handed it over. The drunk stared at it in shock. Then, as a hungry gleam came to his eye, he spat contemptuously at Jon's feet and shuffled off through the snow, laughing.

Jon still didn't know why he had travelled to that bleak hinterland in the shadow of the City's shining towers. Certainly, he had felt unable to stay in Arcadia after his inexplicable discovery in the nursery. But the drive that had propelled him from Highgate to the East End to see where Ronald Whittington had died came from somewhere much deeper than conscious thought.

He double-checked the location in the *Standard*, and after cross-referencing it with his *A to Z*, got his bearings and set off into the dark. The night was brutally cold, the snow glittering under the streetlights, but his destination was only a few minutes' walk from Shoreditch tube.

The murder scene was hard to miss. Yellow police warning tape fastened to makeshift poles crackled in the wind around a snow-cleared patch of pavement. Jon surveyed it cautiously until he was sure there was no one around before advancing. Six feet from the tape, as he became more aware of his surroundings, a chilling *frisson* overcame him. It was just as he had imagined it in his dream: the cluster of squat, brick buildings, the interplay of shadows and light. How could he have seen so clearly a place he had never visited before?

A wind moaned gently above his head as the image of Whittington's body flashed through his mind. A premonition? Something crawled in his gut at the thought of what might have brought him to this moment.

He grabbed hold of the plastic tape, then ducked underneath. He had no idea what he was doing any more; his instinct ruled. Standing on the spot where Whittington had died, the image of his corpse became even stronger; it had been lying in an awkward position, with the right leg bent under the left at right angles, and the left and right arms stretched out away from the body. It was too exact for Whittington to have fallen that way by accident.

He kneeled down and touched the icy kerb. The police team had done a good job of washing the blood away, but Jon could still see dark signs of it in the cracks and crevices. He recalled the huge pool that surrounded the corpse in his dream.

As he turned, a small pile of dust at the foot of the wall caught his eye. There was no reason for it to stand out, but his already frayed senses were crackling. He brushed it with his fingers. Powdered cement. Slowly, he raised his gaze up the wall until he saw a small hole scraped out between two bricks. Something had been pushed inside.

Anxiously, he took out the small penknife on his key-ring and probed around in the hole until he managed to extricate a carefully folded piece of paper. It was part of a page torn from a book. Jon quickly folded it back up and slipped it into his pocket. It could have been stuffed into the hole by a child, he supposed, but in his heart he knew it was connected in some way to Whittington's death. The smart thing would have been to go straight to the police, but something prevented him. He was sensing a disturbing element of ritual about the murder which spoke of higher powers, deeper meaning; it seemed to be speaking directly to him.

'Such a terrible thing to happen on your doorstep.'

Jon started at the sound of the voice. A short man with a balding head and silver stubble was standing with his hands in his overcoat pockets on the other side of the police cordon.

'You know, I don't think you should be in there,' he continued thoughtfully. 'The police said they'd finished, but you know how they are, always ferreting around looking for clues.'

'I knew him,' Jon said, as if that explained why he was breaching a crime scene under cover of night.

'Ah. I'm sorry. It's bad enough for such an atrocity to happen to a stranger, but to someone you knew . . . Were you close?'

'Not really. Not at all, but still . . .'

The man nodded sagely. 'I understand. When I came out to investigate all that shouting and screaming in the middle of the night, I was sickened by what I saw. I said to my lady wife—'

'You saw the body?' Jon interjected. The man nodded. 'Was it as bad as the paper said?'

'It looked like he'd been carved up by a master butcher. I've seen some monstrous things in my days – around here life isn't pretty – but that . . .' He shook his head in disgust. 'The killer had gone into the stomach – with a razor-sharp blade, the police said. They could tell from the cuts. The organs had been snipped out and built up into a little pile. Like offal, it was, in an abattoir.' He coughed and brought his hand to his mouth. 'And then the body was thrown over the top. The minicab driver didn't know, you see. He thought your man had stumbled, drunk, and cracked his head on the kerb. He rolled him over to see what he could do. Horrible, so horrible. It was him making all the noise.

He was sitting against the wall there, yelling and crying. The doctors had to take him away, God help him.'

Jon stared at the kerb and fought the pictures which flashed across his mind.

'It never ceases to amaze me what man can do to man. The lunatic who committed that awful murder couldn't have seen his victim as a human being, rather as a thing, an object. That's the only way to explain it.'

Jon slipped out under the cordon. 'Did you hear if the police had any idea who might have done it?'

The man shook his head sadly. 'They were just worried it might be the first.'

'Why?'

'I was standing over there in the shadows where they couldn't see me and I heard them talking. The detective said the kind of person who kills like this doesn't normally stop at one. He said the biggest give-away was that the killer had taken a trophy. He could be building up a collection, that was how he described it.'

'What kind of trophy?'

The man leaned forward conspiratorially. 'The police weren't releasing that information. They said if there were any more murders, it would help identify which ones he had done. *Modus operandi*, you know.' He smiled tightly. 'But you won't go telling the world and his wife, will you? It was a finger.'

'A finger!'

The man extended the index finger on his right hand and waggled it in front of Jon's nose. 'This finger. Now what do you think of that?'

The tube journey home was a blur. Jon felt unduly queasy, as if he had eaten spoiled food, and there were corresponding bouts of sweating which left him uncomfortably clammy despite the oppressive warmth of the carriage. He couldn't shake the image of Whittington's face, looming large in his thoughts, accompanied by an inexplicable guilt that he was somehow complicit in the murder.

The walk back from Highgate station was cold and lonely, and not even the dark hulk of Arcadia rising up against the clear night sky could raise his spirits. In the gloom of the hall, the red light on the answerphone Sarah had brought home from work was flashing anxiously. Jon pressed the play button.

'Jon, honey, are you there? Jon? If you're there, pick up.' Jon recognized the coke-buzz in Sarah's voice and the long drawn-out pause that followed. 'Look, I hate to say this, but I've got to entertain some clients again tonight and it could drag on late so I'm going to stay over at Sally's again so I won't come in late and disturb you,' she babbled. 'I really am sorry about this, hon, but I promise I'll sort things out so we can spend some time together at home. Love you.'

Before the machine had rewound, Jon picked up the receiver and dialled Richard's number. The phone felt hard against his ear after the grace of the old Bakelite model, and he wondered why Sarah had seen fit to get an answerphone. Probably for nights like this, he concluded.

'Yes?' Richard answered with an edge of irritation.

'It's Jon. Is this a bad time?'

'Sorry, old chap. I was just getting set for an early night. I'm finding work a bit knackering in my old age.'

'I've been to where Whittington was murdered.' Jon's mouth went dry. He couldn't quite express his stumbling thoughts. 'He was butchered, Richard. It wasn't just a mugging. Somebody set out to carve him up. I mean, I don't know if he was the intended victim or just in the wrong place at the wrong time, but Jesus . . . What must his family think? I met his wife once, you know, just after I started out. She was nice. She didn't take any of the Steelguard stuff seriously. "Just a job," she said. "Don't ever lose sleep over it."'

Richard yawned. 'Serves him right for venturing into the East End. God-forsaken place. Everyone has tattoos out there, you know. Men, women, infants in the pram. There should be a law against it, but I suppose it means we can recognize them when we see them in the street.' He laughed to himself, then added, 'Jon, why are you calling me at midnight to tell me about Whittington?'

'I think it just shocked me when I heard how he'd been killed. There's probably some guilt mixed up in there as well. The last time I thought about him I suppose I wasn't being too charitable. In a way, I blamed him for getting me into this soul-destroying career.'

'I wouldn't beat yourself up over it, old chap. Naturally you're feeling a little depressed after everything you've been through, but don't fixate on it. Feel sorry for the poor bastard, then move on. There are plenty of other things to get worked up about.' A long pause. 'Like what's happening at Steelguard.'

'What do you mean?'

'I tried to call you earlier, but that damned answerphone was on.' For the first time since Jon had known him, Richard seemed to be struggling for words. 'They've appointed an outside investigator to look into those irregularities I mentioned yesterday. Harry Smallthorn.'

'Smallthorn?'

'That's right. The Bastard of Bunhill Row. Even in the loathsome ranks of management troubleshooters, he's a particularly despicable individual. You know what he did to those poor sods at Rivers Blenheim. Jon, some human dung beetle has sent him an anonymous report which identifies you as the culprit. Obviously I haven't seen it, but apparently there's some damning *evidence* in there.'

'It's a set-up.'

'Of course it's a bloody set-up. You weren't always Mr Clean, but you certainly weren't a cheat and a traitor. If Smallthorn has anything about him he'll recognize it as a con, but I'm warning you so you can pre-empt any complications which might arise from that so-called evidence. You can be sure whoever has embarked on such a low-down course of action will have done their homework. You'll have to pick your way through the lies to prove your innocence.'

'Do you have any idea who might have done it?' Jon wanted to scream: *I don't want to know!*

'Yes,' Richard began tentatively, 'but I don't think I should mention any names at the present. Not without evidence.'

'Come on, Richard! This is me you're talking to! You never had any qualms about coming out with the most scurrilous rumours about people's sex lives in the office.'

'If you're going to push me . . . Rodney Self.'

'Rod? He's barely got the intelligence to use the swing doors in the canteen.'

'Believe me, Jon, he hides his light under a bushel. And he has a particularly nasty disposition as you saw in that rugger match with Bounds Bros last year. I have several good but unsubstantiated reasons why I think it's him, but it's early days yet. I'll turn up something concrete soon, you can count on it.'

'I'm not sure, Richard.'

'Jon, I'm your best friend. Trust me. If you're not concerned about clearing your name, I am.'

'OK,' Jon said morosely. 'I'll try to think of the best way to deal with it.'

'You do that, old chap. And in the meantime, don't waste too much mental energy on Whittington. He wouldn't have thought twice about you if the situation had been reversed.'

Jon replaced the receiver and headed into the study. He pulled out the piece of paper he had rescued from the crack in the wall and examined it beneath the standard lamp. It was precisely cut out of a book, a hardback, Jon guessed from the texture of the paper. And it said:

'But of course he cared very much; and he was so full of wrath against grown-ups, who, as usual, were spoiling everything, that as soon as he got inside his tree he breathed intentionally quick short breaths at the rate of about five to a second.'

Jon read it through twice more, trying to make sense of it. The word *wrath* kept leaping out at him and he knew, on some instinctive level, it was a message from the killer. A shiver ran through him. He ought to take it to the police. It was probably important. Vital.

Carefully, he folded the clipping and slipped it inside the front cover of his copy of *A Christmas Carol*.

Events had disturbed him so much he knew he wouldn't be able to sleep. He spent a brief time searching for the cat – he still had no idea how it got in and out of the house – and an equal length of time musing outside the locked cellar door, wondering what Victorian secrets lay hidden down in the dark.

It wasn't so much a noise that disturbed him, more a subtle awareness that prickled along his spine, manifesting itself as an insistence, like hunger, that he should visit the nursery. He had always trusted his intuition while working in the City, but this time he was held back by a deep, insistent fear. He wondered obliquely if he had half-heard the child crying again, but not registered the fact, yet that didn't seem likely.

He tried to pretend the conflict wasn't happening and busied himself with an examination of the old lock on the cellar door, but after his gaze had been drawn to the foot of the stairs for the fourth or fifth time he knew he would have to respond.

Slowly he climbed up to the landing, blanking his mind to any apprehension of what might lie ahead. The nursery door was shut, as he had left it. He stood outside for a full minute, holding his breath and listening, and then he carefully swung the door open. At first, the room seemed untouched. Then he saw it.

On a chipped saucer painted with pink flowers, which he had seen earlier in the kitchen, lay a severed finger pointing ominously at the wall next to the wardrobe.

9

The first pink tinges of dawn broke through the clouds and dappled the grey buildings of central London with a faint splash of incongruous colour. From the offices of Steelguard, high above Canary Wharf, the effect was breathtaking, but none of the four men seated around the polished oak table in the boardroom were aware of it. All eyes were on Harry Smallthorn, an unremarkable man of average height and build, rattily unattractive but not unbearably so, whose starkly conventional haircut added a decade to his forty-two years. In another life he would have been a middle manager in a mundane company producing forgettable, unnecessary products, but in the City he was a god. He knew instinctively the secrets that made the financial world turn: that abstracts were unimportant – values, ethics, emotions; that to wield true power, one struck at job security and thereby unbalanced the things people held dear – prospects for possessions, money, comfort and pleasure, and the well-being of the family. He knew this kind of destabilization needed to be subtle to be effective, and he sliced into the fear organs with all the skill of a master surgeon.

Smallthorn had assembled the four, and the fifth they still awaited, from all ranks of the company; such was the power vested in him by the board, which feared another Barings debacle if the secret workings of their operations continued to leak out into the real world. No one knew why they had been chosen, but they all knew about Smallthorn's investigation and so they presumed they were under suspicion. Smallthorn did not dissuade them of this notion.

There was a rap at the door which burst open an instant later. Richard's hulking figure surged through and slipped into a chair. 'Sorry I'm late, old chaps. The motor doesn't respond well to the cold.' He smiled tightly at Smallthorn to show he was not afraid.

'Out late womanizing again, Beeson?' Crawley hissed next to him.

'Now we're all here we can start,' Smallthorn began. Richard was surprised at the calmness of his voice; he had expected all the bluster and expletives of Gilmore. 'You're all intelligent people or you wouldn't be working here, so I won't try to pretend; the situation is dire. The rules have been flaunted, rules which hold the financial establishment together and allow us to progress with the freedom we have enjoyed for decades. Other companies, indeed the integrity of the City, will be threatened if this becomes public. So you see, the stakes are high – this problem reaches beyond Steelguard. It's bigger than individual personalities, jobs and careers. It is, quite simply, about the way we work. The management is insistent this problem is brought to a speedy resolution, for everyone's sake. A culprit must be identified and dealt with so that we can all get on with the job of making money. Without this threat hanging over all our . . . your . . . heads.'

Smallthorn chose his words carefully. He kept his eyes firmly on the open report in front of him; he didn't have to look up to know what he would see flickering across the faces before him.

'I will get to the details of how the sale of company secrets was discovered later. First, I would like to bring your attention to a document I received yesterday. I am not aware of its author, but it suggests we already have a suspect. One Jonathan Summers. Does anyone have any views on that?'

Richard felt all eyes turn towards him. The heat rose under his collar and he tried to stop the flush spreading to his face. One of those staring at him was Rodney Self; Richard allowed his gaze to wander to Self's implacable face. He couldn't read what he saw there.

'Well, Jon has been my friend for almost ten years. He was already established as a great success when I arrived, and in all that time I have never known him to be anything less than upstanding and honourable,' Richard stated firmly.

Smallthorn smiled condescendingly. 'Well, you would say that, wouldn't you? After all, you have just told us you are the best of friends. Anyone else?'

Rodney Self raised his hand like the class swot.

10

When the Cross Keys landlord unlocked the front door at
11 a.m., Jon had been waiting on the step in the fresh snow
for fifteen minutes. Shivering, he bounded into the gloomy
interior and headed to the bar with what must have
appeared unseemly haste. Lisa was resting her elbows next
to the beer pumps.

'Jayzus, you're desperate,' she said jovially before she
saw his hunted expression. Then, 'Are you OK?'

'Actually,' he began, and then watched from the corner
of his eye until the landlord disappeared into the back
room, 'I came to see you.'

Lisa looked both puzzled and flattered. 'I'm honoured.'

'You'd better give me a drink or the landlord will get
suspicious.'

'Very clandestine. Mineral water?'

'Jack Daniels, double, straight.' He took the drink without a flicker of guilt at his lost good intentions. Without
raising his eyes from the glass, he said, 'I don't want to
sound too pathetic, but I really didn't know who else to
talk to.'

'This sounds serious,' Lisa said. She leaned close to him
so their voices didn't travel. 'Still, part of a barmaid's
job—'

'I can't tell Sarah or Richard, my friend,' he said distantly,
chewing on a nail. 'I don't want them thinking badly of
me.'

'And you don't really care what I think.'

'To be honest, no. You don't know me from Adam. There's no baggage, so I'll get a fair hearing. And in the short time we've spoken to each other, I recognized someone I can trust. And I think you saw the same in me.'

'Arrogant little bleeder, aren't you?' She smiled to take the edge off the barb.

'I simply know my own worth.' Jon forced a smile in return. 'It's been bred into me over the last ten years.'

'So? Who did you kill?'

Her words brought a cold shadow rushing through him and the façade collapsed. He shook his head a little too forcibly, ran his fingers through his hair as if that would stop the anxiety crashing around inside his skull. He was falling apart, and when he looked into Lisa's concerned face he knew she could see it too.

'This is ridiculous! I'm trying to spill my guts to someone I barely know. What a sad loser—'

He turned to go, but Lisa reached over and caught his shirt. 'Don't be such an eejit. You're right – you only need five minutes to know if you're in tune with someone. Go on. Tell me what's on your mind.'

Jon finished his drink, composed himself, then began in barely more than a whisper. She listened intently as he told her about the work stresses, the drink and drugs, all the problems that pushed him into the clinic. 'I thought that was the end of it – everything would be fine and dandy and I could set about making a new life for myself. Except now I'm sure what happened before the clinic was only the start and I'm slowly going crazy.'

'And what makes you think that?' She rested her arms on the bar and looked deep into his eyes.

He chewed his lip, barely able to bring himself to talk about it. 'Hallucinations, more real than the real world. Dreams that tell me things. Hearing things. Voices . . .' His words trailed off as the anxiety twisted the knife in his belly.

Lisa shrugged. 'Chemical imbalances in the brain. Too many drugs can cause it, sometimes it's just natural. It happens to lots of people. I know some—'

'It's worse than that. Worse than you can imagine.'

'If you're really worried, there are plenty of people who can help.' She looked at him closely. 'There's more, isn't there?'

He closed his eyes and nodded. 'You read about the Whittington murder? I saw the body, the exact murder site, in one of my dreams. Before it happened. Or maybe during.'

'My nan on my mother's side had the sight. Back in the old country they used to see it as a gift, but when she moved here as a girl she had to hide it. When I was young she used to tell me stories of all the things she'd *seen* – you know, precognition. Aberfan, the Coronation – right down to the Queen's dress and who was watching. But she couldn't let anyone outside the family find out because she knew they'd drag her off to the funny farm. It must have been hard on her.' She gave Jon's arm a shake. 'All I'm saying is, don't worry. Go with it. To some people, it's normal.'

Jon had never felt such desolation. He heard what she was saying, recognized her attempts to comfort him, but the gulf was unbridgeable. How could he explain to her how he had spent his morning – wrapping a severed finger in an old rag and burying it in a snowdrift in the garden? At the time he hadn't known what else to do; it seemed like a good way to preserve it, but what disturbed him more was that he felt he *had* to do it, an insistence so deep in his subconscious he had been like a dog burying a bone. What did it all mean?

Lisa must have seen some sign of his thoughts in his face for the touch on his hand was unusually tender for someone who was almost a stranger. 'I think you need to talk,' she said.

'It's not fair to burden you.'

'Jayzus, I'm used to it. I help out at a drop-in centre for addicts, recovering and otherwise. They need to talk and I'm there to listen. It helps them. I'm not saying it's easy, mind. You haven't heard talk until you've listened to a speed freak on a three-day bender.'

Jon smiled. 'How do you find the time? With a child, and this job, and a college course?'

'I don't sleep.'

'I wish I didn't have to . . .'

'Stop being so maudlin.' She pinched the back of his hand sharply.

'Ow!' He rubbed it, but couldn't help smiling at her gently teasing face.

'Believe me, it hurts more on the outside.'

'I get the picture.'

'Sorry for taking liberties and all, but—'

The landlord poked his head out of the back room. 'Oi! Turn it down, will ya? We don't allow fun in the Cross Keys. This is a No-Fun pub.' He winked at Jon and withdrew.

'He needs a good sense of humour with the lack of custom he gets here,' Lisa said. She poured Jon another drink without asking and added thoughtfully, 'I shouldn't worry too much about what's going on in your head – you seem fine to me, for whatever my views are worth. But you've got to get all your worries out or they'll eat you up.'

Jon enjoyed the numbness in his lips from the drink. His instinctive trust in Lisa made it surprisingly easy to unburden himself in a way he wouldn't have dared in the City.

'Something was left at my house which had been taken from the murder site,' he said. 'The fact that I know the victim makes it too much of a coincidence for my house to have been chosen at random. That would suggest, I think, that the killer knows me.'

'Then you have to go to the police.'

'Believe me, I know that's exactly what I should do, but for some reason I can't bring myself to go. Every time I think about it I feel like my heart is going to burst.'

There were a hundred things Lisa could have said, all of them damning, but she gave him the benefit of the doubt with a simple nod of acceptance.

'I don't know what to do,' he continued.

'You're asking for my advice?'

'Any help you can give.'

She chewed on her lip for a moment, transparent in her contemplation. 'My mother always warned me about getting tangled up with men like you.'

'What, married?'

'No, trouble magnets.' She took his glass from him and drained it herself. 'Ah, Jayzus, I suppose it'll pass the time.'

The journey into the West End had been like an attempt on Everest. Each step was agonizingly slow, almost painful, and the anxiety that swelled through Jon left his stomach painfully knotted, a slick sweat growing cold on his skin. It would have been easier to spend the afternoon at Arcadia, but he wasn't doing this for himself. He was determined to get Sarah a Christmas present before his neuroses made him a prisoner in the house, or before something worse happened. Above all else, he wanted Sarah to be happy, and the ornate, silver hand mirror he had caught her examining in Selfridges seemed the perfect way to achieve it. When she had picked it up, he recognized a flicker of simple pleasure, either in her stance or the way she held her head, but that chink in her hard persona had shown him the part of Sarah he loved, the part he knew lay buried deep within. And it wouldn't be Christmas if he didn't have something to give her.

The tube was a claustrophobic nightmare of heat and noise and by the time he exited at Regent Street he almost vomited with the tension. Breathlessly, he clutched at a wall, doubled up like some drunk as the stream of shoppers gave him a wide berth. He had never suffered so much, but the image of Sarah's face as she opened the gift on Christmas morning made it all worthwhile.

His state of mind continued to trouble him. Sometimes he felt as healthy as when he was working at Steelguard. Other times he felt like an invalid. The anxiety came and went without rhyme or reason.

As he forced his way along Oxford Street, he tried to distract himself from his irrational fears. Oddly, his first thought was of Lisa, working away in the pub. She had invited him to her flat for tea after her shift to talk about his problems. Her good nature and desire to help had staggered him at first, and then it had brought home how much his time in the City had changed him. Where did the cynicism and mistrust come from? Did it go with the job? More importantly, would he be able to purge it from his system?

He liked Lisa a lot because she was everything the City was not, everything that he aspired to be once again. And he wanted her to like him, but knew there was little chance of that when he couldn't even like himself.

Relief flooded through him as he made it to the door into Selfridges, and, despite the crowds inside, he felt instant respite. In his mind, the store always epitomized Christmas, that mix of commercialism and celebration, with its traditional decoration and heady aroma of winter spices and perfume, cards and chatter; every December that he had ventured in, he always saw himself as a child, hanging off his parents' hands, bedazzled.

To his relief, the hand mirror was still there. He examined it closely. It reminded him of some trinket in a fairytale, with its exquisitely decorated handle and frame glittering in the display lights. He looked into it at his pale, drawn face and thought he looked ten years older. He tried to imagine Sarah's face staring back; it was just right for her, beautiful and delicate. In a way, he felt it was more than a Christmas present; it was a ritual gift symbolizing their transition into a new phase of life, a happier time for both of them. A gift of hope that had been worth every blast of pain he had felt on the journey to buy it.

The Christmas decorations in the office overlooking Covent Garden were muted – a touch of silver tinsel, a sprig of holly, a minimalist Christmas tree – but Sarah had never had much time for the festive season. It seemed a dull, unnatural break in the good business of earning money and having fun. How could anyone opt for a quiet meal with a bunch of bitter, jaded relatives when they could be out clubbing, consuming vast quantities of marching powder and dazzling all-comers with wit and repartee?

Outside it was already dark. It was the dead time between businesses closing and the tourists and good-time crowds descending on the pubs and restaurants. From the window, Sarah could make out only a few stragglers winding their way across the piazza.

Everyone else in the building had left long ago and there was really nothing else for her to do, but she was loath to pack up the clients' files scattered across her desk. Work made her feel alive, and with Jon's current disinclination for hedonism, home was a stultifying alternative.

Reluctantly, she left a message on the answerphone to tell Jon she was on her way, half-surprised he wasn't there to pick up. All the lights in the outer office and reception had been turned off, but a dull glow filtered from the stairwell. Locating her keys in her handbag, she switched off her desk-top lamp and locked the door behind her.

Distantly, she could make out the strains of 'God Rest Ye Merry Gentlemen' sung by a choir outside the tube station. Nearby a car horn blared and someone yelled abuse in response.

Distracted by thoughts of the evening's entertainment,

Sarah only became aware of the change in the quality of light when she had made it half-way across the floor. There was a faint nimbus of light in one corner, like fireflies coming slowly to life. She watched it for a few moments, puzzled. In the background, the carol singing grew further away until it sounded like she was hearing it through water, the distorted voices no longer human.

Suddenly, the computer screen beneath the pinpricks of light flared into life with a static crackle and a discharge of blue sparks.

'Oh!' Sarah called out, startled. Then, 'Fucking electrics!'

She had complained the building was a death-trap ever since Rebecca had got feedback from a plug socket. She made a mental note to instruct her solicitors to sue the electrical contractors who had been ordered to make the building safe.

As she started towards the far corner to switch off the terminal which was now flashing on and off like a warning strobe, she caught a whiff of an alien smell, thick with spices, and with it a tingling awareness that there was someone in the room with her.

Her breath caught in her throat. 'Who's there?' she said hoarsely.

No one should have been able to bypass the electronic lock on the front door without calling her on the entry-phone. The room looked empty, but she felt a presence there in the same way she knew when a man was staring at her on a late-night tube platform. Casting glances all around, she began to back towards the door to reception, but the flashing of the computer screen made it difficult to focus.

'Who's there?' Her voice was much harder this time; no one was going to intimidate her. Cautiously, she fumbled around in her bag until her fingers closed on the anti-rape spray.

There was a sound like metal being dragged up a desk

leg, then a *chink* as it slapped on the surface. Sarah moved backwards quickly, her hip slamming into the sharp edge of a table; she stifled a cry, then cursed under her breath. In that instant, in the fading glare of the computer flash, she glimpsed something that could have been a distorted shadow looming up the far wall. A shadow, because it was too inhuman to be a silhouette: long-limbed, incredibly thin, hunched over like a praying mantis.

It brought a shock of fear that fired her into action. She crashed through the doors into reception and then out on to the well-lit stairwell. The lift was on the ground floor. As the odd metallic scraping began to draw closer, Sarah propelled herself frantically down the stairs, pausing just long enough to notice something which made her shiver with terror.

At the bottom, she tore open the front door and tumbled out into the icy night, not stopping until she reached the other side of the piazza where she pulled out her mobile phone and dialled 999. In that short time, there was no way anyone could have exited the building after her.

'I've got you now, you bastard,' she muttered, wiping away a tear of frustration and rage.

But all she could think about as she waited for the police to arrive was what she had seen in reception. Above the desk was the company logo, *Frost PR* – her maiden name immortalized – and a blown-up head-and-shoulders portrait of herself, which she considered a strong company image and all her employees thought a monument to her ego.

Running across that beautiful monochrome picture were two deep slash marks, as if it had been attacked with a machete.

'You're a big softie at heart, aren't you?' Lisa said after Jon told her about Sarah's present. 'I don't think my da ever bought my mum a thing. Not after I was born, anyway. He didn't respond well to losing his freedom, the bastard. All men are the same, just kids who want to stay in the playground.'

Jon picked his way carefully over the treacherous, packed snow, feeling lighter of step than he had all day. 'Do you ever hear from him?' he added.

'He went to the Caribbean "to find his roots", or so the one postcard we received from him said. Good riddance.' She looked away, still hurt by the memory. 'I could have put that down to a one-off experience,' she continued coldly, 'but then when I got pregnant my so-called partner did the same thing. And suddenly it started to look like a trend.'

'We're not all like that.'

She glanced at him, abashed. 'No, of course not. Sorry, I was letting my bitter, twisted inner self show.'

Obliquely, Jon was aware events were happening against expectations – Lisa barely knew him, yet there she was inviting him back to her home – but somehow it seemed right. Natural. He had no idea what was going on in her head, although he was sure it wasn't the kind of thing she did readily. Perhaps kindred spirits really did recognize each other, despite everything. He certainly wasn't going to question it. For the first time in years he felt truly at peace, notwithstanding the unnerving rumblings of everything else he had experienced in recent times.

Lisa's flat was in a converted Victorian mansion on a grim backstreet of Spitalfields, with a view of grey rooftops and bricks crusted black by two centuries of pollution. It was disturbingly close to the scene of Whittington's murder, a coincidence which re-ignited Jon's overall unease.

Lisa lived on the second floor, just an all-purpose living room with a tiny kitchen off and a bedroom she shared with her son. Despite its cramped interior, it was light and clean and smelled of lime and flowers.

'I've been here for about a year,' she said. 'It's cheap, that's the main thing, but the neighbours are great, and that's something you rich folk are only just starting to learn – you can't buy community. There's a gay couple downstairs, Ralph and Michael, living just like they're married, all rows about who does the washing-up and who walks the dog. Mr Velikovsky, he's this old Jewish intellectual, lives across the hall. He always gives me flowers. Sweet. And upstairs there's an Indian family, the Ilyases. They're always polite and friendly.'

'It sounds like a liberal cliché.' Jon sat on the worn sofa and watched her move around the kitchen, making the tea.

'What do you mean?'

'You know. You're a single mum with a multi-racial background. Gays downstairs, Jews and . . . Muslims, are they? . . . living in harmony.'

'I never really thought about it. That's the way it is round here.'

'Not much money in these parts, I suppose.' He glanced out of the window where he was surprised to see the gleaming white of Hawksmoor's proud church.

'It's not been colonized by yuppies, if that's what you mean, so we've got something to be thankful for. But it's not as bad as it was. They've stopped the decay. There are a lot of local societies working hard to protect the good things.' She placed his mug on the stained coffee table in front of him and perched in an armchair where she watched him intently. 'Not your kind of place, I suppose.'

'I wasn't born into money – my parents never had much of it. I just got sucked into wicked ways.'

'Don't get me wrong. I'm not anti-wealth. Just—'

'Anti-no-values?'

'Right.'

There was a sharp knock at the door. Lisa opened it to a man in his late sixties with silver hair and a close-clipped beard. He had a pleasant, thoughtful face which seemed wrinkled beyond his years, and the most piercing grey eyes Jon had ever seen.

He nodded curtly. 'You have company. I will come back at a better time—'

'Come in and say hello, Mr Velikovsky.' Lisa grabbed his arm and led him over the threshold. 'This is Jon Summers. A friend.'

'Such a good-looking and well-dressed friend too. Young Lisa could do with more acquaintances of this kind,' he said with a secret wink to Jon.

Velikovsky obviously had the wrong idea about their *friendship*, but Jon didn't want to draw attention to it by putting him right. As Jon shook the old man's hand firmly, he felt Velikovsky's grip grow tighter and his face darkened.

Velikovsky moved away quickly before Jon could ask him what was wrong, but as he started to tell Lisa about the intense police presence throughout the East End, he threw occasional worried glances in Jon's direction. Eventually he broke off the conversation to return to Jon.

'May I?' he said, taking Jon's hand once more. Velikovsky's fingers were rigid as he insistently turned Jon's arm over.

'Where did you get this?' he asked sharply, bending forward to examine the strange mark on Jon's forearm.

'I don't know,' Jon replied, taken aback by his brusqueness. 'It was there one morning. I can't seem to get rid of it.'

Velikovsky nodded slowly and in his pale eyes, Jon saw a sudden fear. 'It is known as the Kiss of the Devil. It means The Adversary has condemned you to die.'

Velikovsky's flat smelled of musty leather, old paper, candles and incense. There were only two small lamps to hold back the pervading gloom, but it was enough for Jon to see the walls were lined with shelves of books. Journals scribbled in Velikovsky's illegible handwriting lay open on the table next to a pile of volumes, while others were heaped at various sites around the floor.

He made no excuse for the mess as he led Jon in and pushed him down on to the sofa; Lisa trailed in behind, looking bemused. Velikovsky muttered to himself as he moved quickly along the shelves like a predatory bird. He eventually plucked out an immense leather volume which he riffled through animatedly before laying it on the sofa next to Jon.

'This is the *Maleficium*, a tome of great importance to those who would study the occult in medieval times. Not the original, of course. Far too rare, far too expensive. A copy, but a rare copy nonetheless, one of a very small run privately printed at the dawn of the Victorian age. Aleister Crowley owned one, so I am told. You are aware of Crowley?'

Jon nodded, but his attention was already fixed on the open book. On the left-hand page was the symbol on his arm; the accompanying text was in Latin.

His heartbeat speeded up. 'What does it say?'

Velikovsky picked up the volume and shadowed the words with his index finger as he translated. '"When the Devil selects his victim, for sacrifice, or out of malice, he marks him so all will know his fate and turn their faces away. The sigil of damnation can be found on the face or neck, but most times it will be burned into the soft flesh of the arm. No amount of scouring can remove it. And from the moment of inscribing, the victim's days shall be numbered to no more than twenty."'

Velikovsky closed the book slowly and looked to Jon for a response. Lisa laughed. 'Come on, you're not taking this seriously?'

'Many people do,' Velikovsky replied obliquely. 'The sigil is well-known amongst occultists. They attest to its power.'

'What exactly do you do?' Jon asked.

'For many years I held a professorship in anthropology in the university at Tel Aviv, but I found the constraints of my post too irritating for the growing breadth of my studies.

Now I simply delve into life's little mysteries. And the big ones, also.'

Jon scratched at the black symbol. Outside the window there was a crashing as if someone had dropped a crate full of bottles.

'Do you believe in the Devil, Jon?' Velikovsky leaned forward until he invaded Jon's personal space.

'I've never really been one for religion—'

'In evil? As a force?'

'Bad things happen, certainly. But evil . . . I don't know.'

Jon continued to rub at the sigil; it felt like hot pins were being stabbed into his arm. 'Perhaps it's psychosomatic or something. I've read of people who bleed from wounds like Christ's on the cross when they get into a religious state. The mind can do strange things.'

'I don't think it's very fair to put such fatalistic thoughts into his head,' Lisa said curtly to Velikovsky. 'How's he going to forget all that? It'll make a fine Christmas for him.'

'Forewarned is forearmed,' Velikovsky replied. Then he softened a little and clapped a hand on Jon's shoulder. 'I am sorry, my friend. Like all scholars, I lose track of common courtesy when I discover something which intrigues me. Perhaps this is, as you say, all caused by the mind. Old superstitions may be just that. But still, it wouldn't hurt to think about it, about what was happening in your life when it appeared,' he added with a little more weight. 'Then perhaps we can talk.'

Jon thought about the pages missing from his journal. The coincidence chilled him.

'Come on,' Lisa said, grabbing his arm. 'Jamie will be here soon.'

Back in her flat, she sighed irritatedly. 'Don't take what he said to heart. Sometimes he likes to frighten people with all that rubbish in his old books. It's one of his little games, you know. A power thing. It's all a load of bollocks.'

Jon slumped into the sofa; his stomach was beginning to cramp.

'Ah, look what he's done to you. It's just superstition, Jon.'

He rubbed a weary hand across his face; it didn't remove the confusion. 'I just want things to be normal again. Is that too much to ask?'

There was a knock at the door and a woman with a Jamaican accent ushered in a boy of about seven. Jamie's skin was a shade darker than Lisa's, but his mother was evident in his serious features and thoughtful, dark eyes.

'Jamie, this is a friend of mine. Say hello to Jon,' Lisa said after the woman had left.

'Hello.' Jamie eyed Jon as if he had just discovered an unusual, potentially dangerous species.

'Hello, Jamie.' Jon shook his hand. 'Have you had a nice time today?'

'Yes. I've been reading.'

'You like books, do you?'

'He can't get enough of them,' Lisa interjected. 'Fantasy books, fairytales . . . it's all he does.' As the boy scampered away to his bedroom, concern flickered across Lisa's face. 'What am I going to do with him? He doesn't seem to have any friends, never wants to go out to play. It's like his books are a substitute. There are so many things to worry about when you've got kids. I wonder if he's been affected by not having a father around? By my working and studying. Jayzus. Sometimes you wonder if everything you do could be making another serial killer, you know what I mean?'

'Don't worry, I was the same when I was his age. And look how I've turned out.' He laughed ironically. 'I'd better be going. You'll want to spend some time with Jamie and I've got a few things to think about.'

'We didn't get any time to talk about your problems.'

'There'll be other times. To be honest, I'm happy to have

someone to be normal with. I really appreciate what you're doing. You know, being a friend.' The words came out wrong and he blushed.

'Get away with you, you soppy eejit!' She laughed and slapped his arm heartily. 'You're welcome here any time you want to talk. Don't worry about anything. You'll sort it out.'

Out in the street, the warm, peaceful feeling faded too quickly. He thought of the finger buried in the snowdrift, waiting for the thaw, and he wondered why he couldn't bring himself to go to the police. And he thought of the sigil on his arm which could have been caused by his own troubled mind screaming out a warning. And all he could hear was Velikovsky's quiet voice reading from the book: *The victim's days shall be numbered to no more than twenty.*

At 8 p.m., the door slammed and Jon heard the clatter of Sarah's heels in the hall. He met her at the kitchen door where she crashed into his arms.

'You're in a—'

'Jesus, Jon, if you knew what I've been through!'

'What's happened?'

'There was some intruder in the office. God knows how he got in . . . or out. There was no way he could have left – I was watching the door. If not for the slashed picture, the cops would think I was making it all up like some stupid bimbo. Jesus!'

Jon made her tell him what had happened from the beginning. By the time she had finished she was calm but quietly seething.

'So how did he get out, Jon?' she said finally.

'Maybe on to the roof? Who knows? Those are old buildings. I bet the security's not as great as you think. Get some consultants in to give it a going over tomorrow.'

As he finished speaking, he noticed the cat peering between the banisters through the gloom on the stairs.

'Look, there's our friend,' he said. But as he turned Sarah so she would see the cat for the first time, it retreated into the shadows until all he could see was the faint glint of its sharp teeth.

Sarah looked at him, puzzled. 'What are you talking about?'

Jon sighed. Even the cat was making him feel like he was hallucinating.

That night, Jon woke suddenly, dreams and reality merging uncomfortably. For a few seconds he struggled to guess what had disturbed him, until he heard the thin, pathetic cry of a child echoing jarringly along the landing from the nursery.

Under other circumstances he would have investigated, but in that cry he heard torment and terror merging into an unspeakable sound which chilled him to the bone. He rolled on to his side and covered his ears, praying that it would go away, but even when silence returned there was no respite.

11

'What in heaven's name are you doing?'

Jon had to blink the snowflakes from his eyelashes before he could see Richard wandering up the garden path wearing an expression of comical incomprehension, his overcoat swirling around him like a black fog.

'How long have you been sitting out here?'

Jon looked down. The snow had frosted him so completely he resembled a statue perched on the edge of the garden seat.

'It's minus five and you're taking the air. Any longer and we wouldn't have found you until the spring. Good Lord, man, what possessed you . . .' Richard shook his head wearily and hauled Jon to his feet, brushing him down a little too roughly.

'I was looking at the snowdrift—'

'And a very nice snowdrift it is too. I don't quite think it will win the Turner Prize, but each to his own. Now come inside and warm up, for God's sake.'

As the arrhythmia which had paralysed his consciousness allowed itself to be forced into a regular beat, Jon became acutely aware of his failing state of mind with a choking sense of despair. His fingers were slipping from the ledge. Fingers . . . In the snowdrift . . .

In the kitchen, Richard noisily made a pot of coffee before slamming a mug on the table. 'You've got to sort yourself out, Jon.'

'I know. I—'

'You've got to sort yourself out or you're going to lose everything. You'll be hearing from Steelguard over the next few days. They're going for the jugular, just as I said. They want you to appear before the Investigation Committee. Answer the charges.'

Jon shrugged. 'I've done nothing wrong—'

'It doesn't matter. They want a scapegoat. The Committee's findings are a foregone conclusion. The moment they've gone through the mechanics, the rozzers are coming in. They want you to go down for this one, Jon.'

Jon shook his head. 'I was top man there, Richard. I made the company millions—'

'How can you have worked there for so long and be so blind to how the system works? Loyalty is *not* a concept that is understood. You're a cog, not a person. A part of the machine that did its job and is now obsolete. The future prosperity of the company is the only thing that matters.'

'Surely—'

'Surely nothing. Learn the rules of the game or you're dead meat.' Richard rolled his eyes incredulously. 'You are so *not* City, I can't believe you survived there for so long. It's every man for himself. *That's* the rule. The one rule. The only one that counts.'

Jon slouched back in his chair. The cold inside him seemed unshakeable. 'What do you suggest?' he asked without enthusiasm.

'I'm coming over later and we're going to go out to a little party.'

Jon found his gaze drawn out of the window to the snowdrift. What would he do when the thaw came? 'Whatever you say, Richard,' he muttered disspiritedly. 'I'm in your hands.'

Jamie had finally gone to sleep after a protracted battle which brought into play every delaying tactic he could imagine: arguments over TV, pyjamas, the bedtime story, how wide the bedroom door should be left open. Lisa remembered her mother telling her how bringing up a child was a sixteen-year war, each day, each hour, filled with minor skirmishes and all-out assaults. There was never any respite.

As she lay exhaustedly on the sofa staring at the damp patches on the ceiling, she wondered briefly how she carried on, but the thought was dismissed almost as soon as it appeared; she knew the score when she decided to have Jamie – there was no point moaning about it. Sometimes, though, she hated Gideon for leaving her to face the fight alone. She'd known he was an irresponsible child within weeks of meeting him, so she shouldn't have been surprised or hurt by his sudden departure; but she was.

Her thoughts jumped suddenly to the strange man from the pub. Jon, too, seemed to be regressing to his childhood, shucking off responsibilities with each passing day. It should have annoyed her, yet she found herself thinking of him fondly. Her feelings were a mystery to her; she barely knew anything about him, but her instincts told her he was decent. They had led her into trouble before, of course, but this time she felt they were right. It was a surprise and a relief; she had long since given up trying to find someone who was just like her, who looked in the same direction and responded to life's twists and turns in the same way, but she could see it in Jon like she was looking in the mirror. They could be good friends. And, if she allowed herself to think it, she knew they could be much more than that, but it was wrong to even give the thought time to harden, and she wiped it instantly.

You think you know yourself, but you never do, she reflected sadly.

The knock at the door was light but insistent.

'Go away,' she said grumpily.

The visitor knocked again, forcing her to answer before

Jamie was woken. Velikovsky stood on the landing in a thick woollen overcoat dusted with snow.

'I hope I'm not disturbing you,' he said.

'I was just working out how many days off I would get in the next decade. I haven't run out of fingers yet.'

She invited him in and hung his coat on the pegs above the storage heater which she clicked on reluctantly; these days everything cost too much. When she caught up with him by the sofa, it was obvious he hadn't come in for a friendly chat. His eyes seemed more sunken, his face drawn, as if he had received a sudden shock.

'What is it?' she asked.

'I am concerned about your friend. I think he is in terrible trouble. *Mortal* trouble. I have made some enquiries since our meeting yesterday and it seems the situation is much worse than I feared.'

Velikovsky perched on the edge of the sofa while Lisa curled in a corner with her knees under her chin. 'You mean because of that mark on his arm?'

He nodded gravely. 'As a scholar I have been fascinated by the occult for many years. It began, I suppose, soon after I arrived in this country with my grandparents during the war.' He began to scratch at his bony wrist until Lisa feared he would draw blood; it was a nervous habit that manifested whenever he spoke of the war. 'Life, thoughts, dreams, all are stable until *something* happens. My something was the flight from Warsaw. It changed me forever, in ways I am still discovering. Isn't it awful that innocent people can be transformed into cruel and selfish beings by terrible things beyond their control?' He sighed, then clutched at his wrist, suddenly aware of his obsession. 'The Nazis showed me a side of humanity that even as a child I never dreamed existed. They had power, but no responsibility to humanity. And in their arrogance they thought power self-perpetuating. Ah, if only they had understood there is always a price to pay.'

Lisa watched his face as he slipped into his memories. She realized she thought of him as a grandfather, as the only source of male wisdom still left in her life.

'My father was a scholar and a gentleman, my mother a lady. We fled Warsaw like rabbits with the Nazis beating the bushes behind us. Some of our friends stayed behind – my father knew that would be futile. Twenty of us paid a man to drive us to the border in his lorry. We all had to lie in the back, packed tight like corned beef. A tarpaulin was pulled over us, and then rotten meat heaped on top. We thought if we were stopped the stench would keep the Nazis from investigating too closely. The driver's story was that the meat had been bought for animal feed.

'I remember lying there, in the unbearable heat, choking on the foul smell, barely able to breathe, listening to the occasional whimpering of the old women and feeling their sweating bodies pressed against me. The suffering and the fear were almost too much, but I knew it would be worthwhile once we had reached freedom.

'The truck driver drove around for an hour, then delivered us directly to the Nazis. He took our money, put us through all that torment and then gave us up because he feared we would be uncovered. We were forced to wriggle out through the carcasses at gunpoint.' His eyes grew cold and faraway. 'It was night, chill, the moon was full. We had stopped next to a wood not far from the city. The Nazis gave some of us shovels to dig a pit. They smoked and joked while we laboured. Then, when the pit was deep enough, they lined us up on the edge and raised their guns. My father pushed me into the pit before the first bullet was fired. Then he and the others fell on top of me. The Nazis fired into the pit a few times for good measure, but luckily I was not hit. I say luckily . . .' He choked back the words, then asked for a glass of water.

When he had drained it, he continued. 'I don't know how long I was in hell, but it seemed like an eternity. Before they left, the Nazis shovelled some of the soil on top of the bodies. I was buried alive, with the remains of my family and friends.'

'Oh, Mr Velikovsky. I never knew—'

He leaned forward and dabbed at the tears on her cheeks. 'I went into madness and out the other side as I lay there with my terrible thoughts. I screamed until my throat was raw. At one point I decided there was no God and I roared this revelation as loud as I could. How could there be a God? There was no goodness in the Nazis. There was no point to the suffering, no lesson. Soon after, I heard a voice.'

'Someone else was still alive?'

'They were all dead.'

'Then who . . . ?'

'It was my father's voice. Yet I had seen his face blown apart by the bullets. He said, "Crawl out, little rabbit. The burrow is open." I presumed it was part of my madness, but I crawled nonetheless. I discovered the bodies had fallen in such a way that I could wriggle among them. After an eternity, I reached the soil, but it was not hard-packed, only thinly spread. It did not take long to break through into the daylight.' He removed his glasses and pinched the bridge of his nose. 'I lived like a wolf for days, travelling through the countryside by night until I reached my grandparents' home. They got me out of that hell-hole and away to England.'

Lisa reached over and placed a comforting hand on his knee. Velikovsky jumped as if he had been burned and then smiled weakly in apology. 'I am not the person I was before the experience. Solomon Velikovsky, the boy, died with my father. I was reborn, caked with blood and grave-dirt, enthused with a new, single-minded direction in life. Did my dead father truly talk to me, there in the dark? Or was it the last spark of sanity in a mind struggling for survival? Every day of my life since that moment has been a search for the truth, through numerous religions, through the occult, filling myself with knowledge and other people's thoughts as if somehow that will enable me to grasp that quicksilver essence.'

'Have you found the truth?'

'The only thing I have found is the certain knowledge that we know nothing. Life is filled with mystery. Anything can happen.' Lisa flinched at the power of his stare. 'I told you my story not so you would pity me, but so you would understand that we can dismiss nothing, however strange. Indeed, to dismiss what we are about to discuss could be fatal.'

Lisa looked at him curiously; Velikovsky smiled humourlessly in return. Away in the bedroom, Jamie cried out. Lisa ran to the door and peered in, but he still slept soundly; just a dream. When she returned to the sofa, Velikovsky was swigging deeply from a hip-flask. He proffered it, but she declined.

'Sit,' he said, patting the seat next to him. 'We have much to discuss.'

'Why don't you tell Jon directly? I have his number.'

'Because it is of as much importance to you as to him. I want you to warn your friend, of course, but then I want you to stay as far away from him as possible. Perhaps even as far as out of London.'

Lisa shook her head and looked away, confused and scared by his intensity.

'You recall yesterday when I showed him the *Maleficium*? Written, naturally, from a Christian perspective. What would you say if I told you that mark on his arm and the evil that will follow is also detailed in the Muslim tradition?'

She shrugged. 'I don't know much about religion—'

'And it is present in Native American tradition: The Reaver Spirit Who Cuts Down Wolves. And in Aboriginal culture: The Darkness That Comes From The Dreamtime.

And in African tribal mythology, and Chinese folklore. The same story, the same dire warnings.'

Lisa stared at him blankly.

'All different perspectives on the same phenomenon. Their diverse origins yet similar content suggest something that exists independently, outside of particular religions or cultures.' He leaned forward until she could smell the whisky on his breath. 'Something that *exists*.'

'You're scaring me.' In the distance, the Docklands Light Railway rattled over the bleak wasteland of the new economic quarter.

'I mean to. It will keep your mind concentrated. Your friend is the focus of a great evil.'

'Are you talking about the Devil?'

'I am talking about something which has adopted human form so it can move freely among us. Each culture describes it differently. Perhaps it has no form apart from the one we give it in our deepest fears. But they agree there will be ritual slayings. And that a sacrifice has to be made.'

Lisa plucked at the loose threads on the throw over the sofa. 'Go on,' she muttered.

'It is like a force of nature, unstoppable now it has been released. And it has chosen your friend as the tether that keeps it rooted in this world. Unconsciously, I think, he released it, and he will pay the price for doing so.'

She looked up into his face and what she saw there made her catch her breath.

'It will be driven away by a sacrifice. Every time it is free, there always has to be a sacrifice or something terrible will happen.'

'What?'

Velikovsky shook his head.

'What kind of a sacrifice?'

This time he searched her face. 'The sacrifice of an innocent.'

Her expression of puzzlement didn't change.

'The sacrifice of a child.'

Her eyes flashed to the bedroom door.

'Which is why you must stay away from him. Far, far away.'

Lisa leaned forward so she could peer into his misty, grey eyes. 'You believe this?'

'Yes.'

'Really? Truly?'

'I am a serious man. I think only serious thoughts, of death, and what lies beyond it. I would like to be frivolous, and in my youth I tried, but it seems forever beyond me.' He took another long draught from his hip-flask.

Lisa pulled her legs tight against her, suddenly cold. 'I appreciate you taking the time to give me this advice, Mr Velikovsky, but I don't believe in this kind of thing. It's got nothing to do with my life. Jon certainly has problems, but I don't think it will help him to dwell on this.'

Velikovsky nodded sadly. 'I did not really expect to convince you. But we are agreed on one thing – that your friend has troubles. The kind of young lady you are, Lisa, I know you will be trying to help him. I hope you will allow me to help him in *my* own way.'

Lisa crossed the room to peer through the curtains at the snow-covered rooftops. In the middle distance, the City blazed with light. 'His problems are caused by men, not monsters,' she said softly.

'Sometimes, both go hand in hand.'

'For the sake of argument, say you're right.' She closed the curtains with a shiver. 'Isn't there any way to help him?'

'To oppose the evil is to draw it towards you.'

'And in all your books you can't find something to keep it away?'

Velikovsky shifted uncomfortably. 'I could try. If that is what you wish. Do one thing for me, however. Tell your friend what I have said. Let him make up his own mind.'

Lisa agreed with a sigh. 'If you sit here and watch Jamie, I'll call from the payphone in the hall.'

'At least let me get the phone.'

'There isn't time, Jon.' Sarah hooked one hand under his armpit and propelled him towards the front door.

Outside, the idling cab sent a thick cloud of exhaust smoke into the icy night air. Richard mugged stupidly from the back seat.

'Look, I'm not sure I'm ready for this—' Jon tried to backpedal, but Sarah was like a juggernaut behind him.

'We've already talked about this, Jon,' she sighed. 'Richard's right. You can't hide away here. It doesn't look good. You've got to face your accusers. Show them they're not facing some weakling who will crumple under the least pressure.'

'Yes, but the company Christmas party . . . Jesus, Sarah. Everyone will be there. I'm not ready for crowds. I don't know if—'

'You'll be fine.' She propelled him down the steps with a push.

The DJ seemed too tight, the hard collar an iron band round his throat. There was blood pumping in his ears and he wondered briefly if he was going to vomit.

'"Look, Dave,"' he stuttered. '"I can see you're really upset about this. I honestly think you ought to sit down calmly, take a stress pill and think things over."'

'Shut up, Jon.' She swung open the door and bundled him into the back seat.

'Well, don't you look a picture,' Richard said to her with a grin.

And she did, Jon noted for the first time. Short black dress, long legs, a hint of make-up, a touch of jewellery. 'You do,' he said. 'You look great.'

Sarah smiled and crossed her legs, revelling in the attention.

The taxi lurched away from the kerb with a skid on the compacted snow and headed east. 'You know, I've never known a winter like this since I was a lad,' the cabbie said. 'Last few years you could get a bleedin' sun tan up to Christmas Day. Now look at it. Weather for penguins.'

Richard removed a £50 note from his wallet and held it through the separating window so the cabbie could see it in his peripheral vision.

'What's that?' the driver said.

'A tip,' Richard replied. 'And here's another one: silence is golden.'

Jon saw the contempt on the cabbie's face reflected in the rear view mirror, but he took the money anyway. Jon hoped he had never been so patronizing and arrogant.

Richard settled back in his seat. 'Now that's sorted we can enjoy the ride,' he said unashamedly loudly.

The journey took them in an arc through the wheezing, derelict old man of the East End towards the brash-suited developments of Docklands. From the top of huge glass and steel buildings in the new economic heartland, it had always seemed as though London lay prostrate at their feet, the brave new breed who were going to dominate the next millennium. From the ground, Jon had a different perspective. All humanity had been razed from the area, communities stripped out and discarded. In their place had been erected a film studio soundstage at night, devoid of any of the life that could turn the sham into a reality. The cliché was that it was soulless, but that missed the point. It was meant to be soulless because it stood for just one thing: the pursuit of money. The scale of the buildings was designed to make the human body seem insignificant. What more needed to be said about the financial industry's ethos?

The Britannia Hotel lay across the water from Canary Wharf, *faux* twenties elegance at the front, glass futurism at the rear. Richard and Sarah flanked Jon like secret service men as they led him up the steps and through the revolving doors into the reception. Jon felt he was being thrust into the lion's den to face all the soul-sapping negativity he had convinced himself he had left behind.

Sarah gripped his wrist surreptitiously, then massaged it with the tips of her fingers as if she could sense his rising tension. 'Take it easy,' she hissed out of the corner of her mouth. 'Follow our lead. We'll show those bastards not to mess with us.'

The Steelguard party was in a large room on the first floor. There was a band playing turgid pop-rock numbers, but it was almost drowned out by the whoops and hollers of the already out-of-control dealing room thugs who had turned the dance floor into a rugby scrum.

Sarah was ready to take up position in the most prominent spot in the room, but Jon ushered her into a dark corner so he could compose himself before the inevitable confrontations. Sarah slipped off to get some drinks, leaving Richard to mark the members of the board, the executives involved in the investigation and any other potential troublemakers.

Jon knew it would be impossible to stay in the background for long with Sarah in the room, and before she was half-way back from the bar she had several heads turning, all of them following through with their attention to spot Jon. Even in the half-light, Jon could see this great gossip suddenly spark and light a fire from mouth to mouth. From then it was only a matter of time.

Sarah handed him a double whisky. Jon drained it in one and Richard set off for another. Within half an hour, he had drunk four of the same and after his enforced period of abstinence it went straight to his head. The parading louts from the dealing room had taken on the appearance of the tormenting creatures he had glimpsed just before he tossed his computer from the window; animal instincts mutated faces, voices sounded like the shrieks of beasts. They all seemed to be laughing at him.

As the band launched into a disjointed version of 'Light My Fire', there seemed to be a disturbance on the dance floor. Jon felt like he was watching a storm out at sea; the waves parted and three figures moved through towards him: Gordon Bell, the MD, painfully tall and thin with hollow cheeks, looking like an undertaker; the financial director, Norman Rutherford, his expensively suited bulk in sharp contrast; and another man whom Jon didn't recognize until he got within feet – chief inquisitor Harry Smallthorn.

'Good evening, Summers. We didn't expect to see you here tonight,' Bell said coldly.

I never wanted to see any of you again, Jon thought. He restrained himself and smiled. 'I thought a Christmas party would be a good occasion for reconciliation. After all, I've already apologized for my actions and paid for all the damage I caused.'

Jon heard his words slur and saw the corresponding distaste on Bell's face. He glanced around for Richard and Sarah, acutely needing their support, but it was as if the waves from the dance floor had silently swept in and swallowed them up. Jon's stomach knotted in response.

'I, Mr Bell,' Smallthorn began oleaginously, 'and for that matter, all the other executives of Steelguard, see this more as an insult to their good grace not to pursue you more vehemently for your act of gross vandalism and company destabilization.'

'That's a bit strong. In light of my record—'

'Yes, your record,' Rutherford interjected acidly. 'Things have come to light, Summers.'

'That's why I'm here. I'm not going to hide away—'

'Oh, you'd rather flaunt it, would you?' Smallthorn said. 'From what everyone has told me, that's just what I'd expect of you.'

'That's not what I meant.'

'Your colleagues describe you as insufferably arrogant

and aloof,' Smallthorn continued. 'You thought yourself untouchable, one of them said.' He allowed himself a slight smile. 'Someone who could get away with anything.'

'All your allegations are false!' Jon protested.

'Really,' Bell replied. His merciless stare had not left Jon's face for an instant. 'The documentation suggests otherwise.'

'The simple fact you're here this evening implies, to me, your complete contempt for the company, its institutions and rules,' Smallthorn said. 'And that, in turn, implies a man who would not think twice about betraying his employer. In short, a man who—'

'We're going to see you receive the full measure of punishment for your actions, Summers.' Rutherford leaned forward angrily, a globule of his spittle splattering on Jon's cheek.

'I have always put the company first,' Jon said, wiping his face. 'Always. For the last decade, I've given my life to Steelguard. Can't you see—'

'What I can see is quite obvious deceit.' Smallthorn timed his interruptions perfectly for their show of power and contempt. 'You are obviously an intelligent man, Summers. As you pointed out, you played the game successfully long enough for that to be seen. But an intelligent man – an intelligent, honest man – would have stayed away tonight. Would have realized the seriousness of the allegations of which you are so obviously aware. Would have shown respect for the company, its directors, and its processes. Unless that man was as arrogant and contemptuous as we have already suggested. Unless that man thought he had already got away with it.'

'No.' Jon shook his head vehemently. 'That's not—'

'I think it's time you left,' Bell said, raising his hand to someone near the door.

Two members of the private security team hired for the night ploughed through the crowd and at Bell's nod gripped Jon's arms tightly.

'You don't have to throw me out,' Jon said. 'I'll leave of my own accord.'

Bell smiled tightly, then nodded once more to the dinner-jacketed monkeys. They lifted Jon off the floor in the undignified manner Bell had obviously anticipated, and began to haul him towards the door amid wild laughter from all those around. Jon struggled, then gave up. Anxiously, he searched the crowd for Sarah and Richard, but guessed they were away at the bar.

'At least let me wait for my wife,' he called out.

'Your wife and Mr Beeson are still welcome here,' Bell replied, still smiling.

The bouncers picked up speed, manhandling Jon backwards so quickly his head spun. He caught glimpses of jeering faces and then he was out into the bright lights and heading towards the lifts. Once they were out of sight of the hotel staff, the bouncers threw him to the floor awkwardly.

'Just get a message to my wife,' Jon gasped.

'Right,' the biggest of the bouncers laughed. Then he raised one Doc Marten shoe and kicked Jon forcefully in the face.

Jon blacked out instantly. When he came to, with blood sticky on his face and pain lancing through his skull, there was a shape leaning over him which he at first took to be the bouncer. As his vision cleared, he recognized the flushed, drunken face of Rodney Self.

'Blimey, what's happened to you, Mr S.?' Self enquired in his cod Cockney accent. He swayed dangerously, clutching a three-quarters full bottle of Jack Daniels.

Jon pulled himself to a sitting position, vaguely recalling Richard's allegations of a Self plot to frame him for the shady dealings at Steelguard. Jon felt he should say something, at least show anger, but all he could muster was bleak resignation.

'Nothing like a few beers and a good fight to make a

party, right, matey?' Self said, having obviously been nowhere near anything so working class as a brawl in his life. He helped Jon to his feet, attempting to focus enough to dab the blood on Jon's shirt, then forgetting what he was doing.

'Don't worry, Rodney. It'll be OK.'

'Come on, smile.' Self tugged at Jon's cheek. 'It's Christmas.'

'That's easy for you to say.'

Self wrestled with the unexpected emotions he was sensing, then brightened. 'Oh, that bollocks that Smallthorn is investigating. Don't worry about that. They'll find the bloke who did it.' He gripped Jon's shoulders and squeezed with drunken friendliness. 'Here,' he said, proffering the spirit bottle. 'I've had a skinful already. Happy Christmas!' Then he lurched back in the direction of the party.

Jon found a sheltered spot between two buildings further up the street, where he could watch the hotel entrance. He kept expecting Sarah or Richard to come looking for him, but after an hour he gave up. He guessed they were probably involved in damage limitation with Bell and the others. He didn't care any more. He didn't care about anything.

Only dregs remained in the bottle. He didn't remember drinking it and didn't realize how drunk he was until he attempted to walk; he could barely make it three yards without leaning on something. South Quay station was only a stone's throw away, but it might as well have been five miles. Somehow he made it. The station was raised high above ground level, providing a breathtaking view over the lights of Docklands. The steps up to the platform proved another major obstacle, but at least he could crawl on his hands and knees; through the haze, he was happy there was no one around to see, and, despairingly, he knew it would only get worse as the alcohol filtered into his system.

An icy wind buffeted the platform, but in his drunkenness

the cold didn't bother him. He found a seat and stared at the glittering panorama, his thoughts coming and going like ghost trains.

Some time later there was a commotion on the stairs followed by loud cursing. Dreamily, Jon watched as Father Christmas stumbled on to the platform, adjusted his red, fur-trimmed jacket over his belly, then looked around suspiciously. The manifestation was hazy and bright. At first, Jon thought: *I'm dreaming*. Cautiously, Jon waved. Saint Nick saw him, did a double-take, and advanced.

Gradually, the dreamlike quality faded. Jon saw the still-wet vomit down the jacket and sticky in the beard, the unsure gait, the roving eyes. He plopped down in the seat next to Jon and crashed against him accidentally.

'Sorry, sorry. Too much fucking Christmas cheer.' He checked his gold Rolex. 'How much longer do we have to wait? Fucking public transport. Fucking cabbies wouldn't take me because I chundered a bit in the lobby. Bastards. Bit of sick never hurt anyone.'

Jon suddenly became aware of the stink and shifted uncomfortably; his own nausea was too close.

His movement prompted the Santa Claus impersonator to stare at him intently. 'Bloody hell, it's Summers, isn't it?'

Jon stared back blankly.

Saint Nick pulled away his false beard so Jon could see his face. 'Miles Heath! You remember! I was the one who made you a rich man!'

Jon did remember. In his first few days at Steelguard, when Heath was the rising star and the job seemed beyond him with its labyrinthine rules, Heath took him out to lunch and decided to adopt him. Over a period of weeks, Heath taught Jon all the tricks of the trade, how to lie on the phone yet still sound like a best buddy, how to network and seem like you meant it; a complete make-over.

'That greasy bastard Norman Rutherford called me up to ask if I'd play Santa at your firm's Christmas do,' Heath continued. 'Thought it would be a bit of a wheeze to get a rival's top man to hand out all the festive goodwill. He promised to keep me well-oiled for the night, so why not? Besides, I wanted to see if a couple of his star players were keen on crossing over. Steal them out from under his nose. All's fair in love and war, eh?' He smiled cruelly. 'Would have gone for you, Jonny-boy, if not for that unfortunate business you're wrapped up in. Sorry to say, you're a bit of a liability at present.'

A train eased into the station with barely a sound. Driverless; another example of the elimination of humanity. All three carriages were empty. Heath lurched forward to press the button to open the doors, then came back and took Jon's arm to help him on to the train.

'Tell you what, Summers. You're looking a bit green. You sit here,' he said, pushing Jon into the seat nearest the door. 'I'll go down to the back. Wouldn't want you throwing up on me.'

Heath rolled down the aisle while Jon's head nodded on his chest. The sound of the doors closing stirred him briefly and as his eyes flickered, he thought he saw someone leaping on board at the last moment, just a shadow flashing past, then gone.

The train slipped off smoothly and Jon stirred to look out across the water at Canary Wharf's One Canada Square lit up like a Christmas tree. There was no one at the next station, nor the one beneath the skyscraper, and by the time the train had started its long, slow arc through the East End, Jon was quietly confident he could make it to the terminus without throwing up.

The motion and the passing lights set Jon's head swimming. He thought he heard the squeal of the wheels on the tracks, a loud and piercing sound, but as it broke off, started again, broke off, repeated, he realized it wasn't coming from the wheels, it was inside the carriage. With a tremendous effort, he turned his head and peered towards Heath.

There was a brief instant when he thought he was hallucinating again. At the end of the carriage, the lights were flashing on and off, throwing the scene into stark relief, then whipping it away before he could grasp the full horror. In the bursts of light, all he could see was blood. Streaming down the windows, puddling on the carriage floor. Then he realized someone was attacking Heath in a frenzy of slashing that sent blood gouting into the air. There was a burst of blue sparks from the light. Jon saw unusually long limbs, painfully thin, a blade flashing in the light. Heath's scream ceased abruptly to be replaced by a wheezing-sucking sound. The attacker's face was hidden. Another arc of sparks cast a ghoulish illumination. Bizarrely, the attacker seemed to be wearing a tight, grey Victorian suit topped off by a tall hat.

Suddenly the figure stopped mid-slash, right hand raised high, ready to plunge down with the killing blow. The weapon was not a knife; it was the attacker's hand itself. Twin scissor-blades burst out from the white flesh of its palm beside a spindly thumb. The other hand was the same. Snip-snip-snip, they clicked in the still of the carriage.

Jon remembered his dream that was not a dream. 'The Scissorman,' he whispered.

At the sound of Jon's voice, the attacker turned its head. Whatever face lay beneath the jaunty hat was lost to Jon; he saw darkness, and fire, and flashing blades, but no image that was fixed enough in reality for him to grasp. The Scissorman watched Jon oddly for a moment, and then, fluidly, it turned and swooped into a flurry of snipping as Heath's body melted away beneath the now-baggy Father Christmas suit. And the lights flashed, on-off, on-off.

Through his drunkenness, Jon knew he had to do something. He pulled himself to his feet, but overbalanced as the train rounded a corner, hitting the floor like a sack of potatoes. A second later he vomited up the contents of his stomach, which trickled around him with each rock of the carriage.

Sprawled on the floor like some pathetic alcoholic, Jon could only watch as the thing finished its butchery. With its back to him, it paused, made one final snip, and then bent slowly forward until its face was suspended above Heath's. There was a strange sound like water going down a plughole, and then it raised its head high and turned slowly to face Jon.

Jon tried to push himself backwards, but his hand slipped on the sick-slick floor and his cheek crashed against the wet rubber. With another snip-snip-snip of its hideous hands, the Scissorman began to advance.

Jon rolled over on to his other side until he found a support to lever himself up. His balance shot by the alcohol, each rock of the train threatened to send him to his knees.

By the time he was upright, the Scissorman was only a few feet away. Jon could smell the meaty scent of blood coming off it.

Panic cut through his inebriation. There was no way out of the carriage; the emergency button would leave them stranded on a sixty-foot-high track.

His attention focused on the razor-sharp scissor blades glinting in the flickering carriage lights, and he remembered how easily Heath's body had submitted to their surgery. The carriage rocked again, and blood sluiced down the aisle, mingled with his vomit, and surged around his shoes.

His back was pressed against the door as if he hoped he would melt through it. At the end of the aisle, just two feet away, the Scissorman towered over him, hands raised for attack.

Jon closed his eyes and waited.

With a shudder the train came to a halt at the Tower Gateway terminus and all the doors opened automatically. Jon pitched backwards on to the wet platform. He had one brief impression of blades cleaving air before his instincts took over, and then he was up and lurching towards the handful of people sauntering towards the train. They eyed the vomit- and blood-spattered drunk cautiously, but it was not until he had stumbled off the escalator on to the street opposite the Tower of London that he heard the first piercing scream.

Jon lost himself in the maze of neglected streets that ran into the East End off Cable Street, his drunkenness slipping from him as easily as he shucked his stained, compromising overcoat into a roadside waste bin. As he ran, he listened for the sound of sirens, bleakly aware the rules of reality no longer held sway. When the travellers boarded the train, the Scissorman would have vanished like a nightmare in the sun; he knew that in a way only children and the insane would grasp. All the rail users would have seen was a blood-stained murderer fleeing his crime. Jon Summers, the man who murdered Father Christmas. He laughed pathetically as he whirled off his axis into the night.

The minicab was the kind which would have picked up any passenger, however drunk or drugged. The car was a wreck, but its unlicensed status guaranteed some anonymity and the driver didn't even look at Jon's face when he took his money.

Jon ran to the door and leaned on the bell. It was answered a minute later by an irritated man with a blond crew cut and an acne-scarred face.

'Yes, what *is* it?' he snapped.

'Is Lisa in?' Jon asked. 'I really need to talk to her.'

'She's gone out. Back later.' He went to close the door, then caught sight of something in Jon's face. 'I suppose you can wait,' he sighed. 'We're baby-sitting for her while she goes out to drink her own weight in G & Ts, the lush.'

Jon stepped in, shivering from the shock and the biting cold.

'You do need to warm up,' the man said. 'Are you a good friend of the old tart's?'

'Pretty good.'

'Well, tell me your name then, so I don't have to keep calling you The Big Tall Man Who Smells of Sick,' he said as he led the way up the stairs.

'I'm sorry—'

'Don't worry. You smell like CK One compared to some of Lisa's friends. I'm Ralph.'

'Jonathan. Jon.'

'Jonathan Jon? Weren't you in *The Waltons*?' He sniggered. 'Don't worry, she's told us all about you.'

'Really?' Jon said curiously.

'Yes. Quite smitten, the trollop.' He eyed Jon askance. 'Though God knows why.'

Lounging on Lisa's sofa was a tall, broad-shouldered man with a greasy quiff. Ralph introduced him as Michael. He was softly spoken and at least ten years older than Ralph, a well-preserved mid-forties.

'I think we'd better get you cleaned up before the luscious Ms Donlon gets home,' Ralph said. 'She may not be picky, but she's not *that* not picky.'

'Sobered up would be better.' Jon suddenly felt the full force of what he had experienced. 'Jesus.'

'Look at you, you're shaking.' Ralph pulled a worried face at Michael. 'Coffee would be good, Michael dear.'

'Orange juice works better.'

'This is not the time to come the lord and master.' He sighed. 'Both. I'm not having you say I told you so.' Ralph sat down next to Jon and whispered, 'Are you OK? What happened?'

The image of a flashing silver blade and a shower of scarlet seemed to be imprinted on Jon's eyelids. 'I don't know . . . I think I'm going insane.'

'You're not alone in that town,' Ralph said. He fingered Jon's dinner jacket and winced. 'First thing you need is a change of clothes. I'll get something from downstairs. You look about my size.'

'You wish,' Michael muttered from the kitchen.

Jon peered quizzically into Ralph's face. 'You don't know me. Why are you helping?'

Ralph shrugged. 'Why are we helping, Michael?'

'Because there aren't any stray cats to feed.'

'That's right. Just an old dog like you.' Ralph smiled. 'I'll be right back.'

Jon tucked his hands into his armpits to stop them trembling, but then he noticed the blood on his shoes, and smelled the abattoir odour, and had to dash to the toilet to be sick once more.

By the time Lisa returned, Jon was washed, changed and recovered enough to offer her a smile. She didn't seem in the least surprised by his presence in her flat.

'I've been trying to get hold of you for half the night,' she said, before turning to Ralph and Michael. 'How was Jamie?'

'No trouble,' Michael replied.

'Now if you want trouble . . .' Ralph said, winking at Jon.

'Come on, you.' Michael ushered him to the door. 'These nice people don't want you mincing around them like an old queen while they talk.'

'I do *not* mince,' Ralph protested, but by then Michael had shoved him forcefully out on to the landing.

Lisa gave Michael a peck on the cheek. 'Thanks. You're keeping me sane.'

'You need a man round the house,' he said with a smile as he slipped out.

Concern fell across Lisa's face as she turned back to Jon. 'What's wrong?'

'I'm sorry for coming here. I didn't know where else to go.'

'I'm flattered.' She slipped on to the sofa next to him. 'Do you want to tell me what happened?'

For a moment, Jon thought he wouldn't be able to conjure up the awful memories, but then they came back so powerfully he felt like they were scarring his brain. After fifteen minutes of unbroken rambling, he came to an abrupt halt. He could tell her the hideous mechanics of what he witnessed, but for the first time in his life he had no insight whatsoever; the intensity of the image was terrible, almost religious. His hands were trembling so much she had to hold them tightly together between her cool palms.

'I don't understand.' Behind her shock, Lisa was struggling to comprehend. 'The murderer was dressed like—'

'It wasn't a man, Lisa.' Although the blood and the train and Heath's body were fixed in his memory, the image of the Scissorman seemed to be fading like a dream; Jon only had a hazy remembrance of what he looked like.

Lisa shook her head; it was too much.

'The blades were part of its hands.'

'Prosthetics. Surgeons can do anything these days.'

'It wasn't just that. The whole way it moved . . . It was almost as if he wasn't really there, yet it was.'

'Like a ghost?'

'No. Shit, I can't explain myself.' He bowed his head and shook it forcefully, but his thoughts didn't clear. 'Why me?'

'Jon, it's not—'

'For some reason I've been singled out. It's all directed at me. In one of my dreams, someone told me. About the Scissorman.'

'In your dreams?'

'They were more than dreams. Almost real. These days it's hard to tell the difference.'

There was a bitterness in his voice she hadn't heard before. She put a hand on the back of his neck and pulled his head forward until it rested on her shoulder.

'When you go into one of those clinics, you're told you're

crazy in a thousand different ways every day,' he said. 'At the time I thought I saw it for what it was – that I simply didn't fit into their perceptions of the way I should act. I wasn't crazy – just an outsider. Now I'm starting to think I was wrong.'

'Hush.' She stroked his neck. The weight of his head made her feel at ease. 'Can we believe all this?'

'I've seen it. I have to believe.'

Lisa moved her fingers through his hair until, suddenly, she caught herself. 'Why did you come here?'

'What do you mean?'

'Why didn't you go home and wait for your wife?'

'She wasn't there. I needed to talk—'

'I wasn't here. You waited.'

'Since she realized she married a nut, things haven't been the same. I don't want to give her any more ammunition. You know how this sounds.'

'Don't you think she could see the truth about you?'

He didn't answer.

'Do you love her?'

'Of course. I've always loved her.'

'Would you die for her?'

'Yes.'

'Good. As long as we know where we stand.'

They stayed that way for five minutes until Lisa said, 'Mr Velikovsky wanted me to get in touch with you. He's very worried.' She took his hand and turned his arm over, revealing the brand. 'He did some more research about this. He really thinks it means something terrible is going to happen.'

'He was right.'

'It's so hard to believe—'

'What did he say?'

'That there would be . . . *ritual slayings*, he called them. That all sorts of cultures have a myth about it. He wanted you to look out for yourself, I think.'

'It's a bit late for that. Did he say anything more?'

Lisa considered repeating Velikovsky's information about *the sacrifice of an innocent*, then thought better of it; that would be something to discuss at a later date, when she'd had time to reflect on what it all meant. 'He's making some more enquiries. He wants to help.'

'God knows why.'

'I want to help.'

He looked at her searchingly, then shook his head, as if failing to discern some hidden motivation. Pulling away slowly, he walked to the window to look out over the rooftops. 'Those murders are on my shoulders. If there are any more . . .' His voice trailed away. 'I've got to stop it somehow. Find out what really is going on.'

'How do you propose to do that?'

There was a long pause until she thought he wasn't going to answer. '"You still don't understand what you're dealing with, do you?"' he quoted softly. '"A perfect organism. Its structural perfection is matched only by its hostility."'

'What do you mean?'

'I mean, I don't know if we can stop it.'

Sarah had wrenched the door open before Jon got the key out of the lock.

'Where have you been?' she snapped. There were tears in her eyes and her face was flushed and blotchy. Before he could answer, she threw her arms around him with emotion she had not shown for months. 'I was so worried,' she whispered.

'I drank too much, was sick,' he murmured apologetically. 'I called round a friend's house to get changed.'

'You could have rung,' she said. 'We spent half an hour looking for you around the party. We thought you were hiding in the toilets or something. Then someone told us you'd been thrown out, so we waited for you in the lobby.

Then we came back here, and you weren't here either.' Her voice rose sharply at the end of the sentence.

'I'm sorry.' Jon couldn't think of what else to say. He wanted to tell her everything, but knew it would be a mistake. And he hoped she wouldn't ask which *friend* had supplied him with the clothes; for some reason he felt guilty he'd been at Lisa's, as if it was an act of betrayal.

Sarah led him by the hand into the drawing room. Richard sat by the gas fire nursing a large scotch, looking pale and worried.

'Bloody hell, do you have to give us scares like that?' he exclaimed. 'I thought we were going to have to dredge the river.'

'I'm sorry, I really am.' Jon slumped on to the sofa and rested his face in his hands for a moment. 'Everything went wrong tonight.'

'Don't worry.' Sarah slipped an arm round his shoulders and squeezed him warmly. 'All's not lost. Bell and his cronies have to see reason in the end.'

Jon had forgotten all about the party. 'It's not important any more.'

'Of course it's important! Don't give up on us, Jon. This is your life. Your future, our future. I know it seems too much pressure after all you've been through.' Her voice became shaky. 'I couldn't bear to lose you, Jon. Prison . . .' She buried her face in his shoulder.

Richard stood up uncomfortably. 'Look, I'd better be on my way. I'll sound out the bastards at work, find out how much damage tonight did to our cause. We'll come up with something.'

'Thanks,' Jon said. 'I really appreciate what you're both doing for me. I'm just sorry I've not been more help.'

'Not to worry, old chap. We're playing a long game. This little upset won't hurt you.' He patted Sarah on the shoulder and slipped out.

When he had left, Sarah kissed Jon gently on the cheek

and whispered in his ear, 'Come to bed.' Then she too was gone.

Jon sat for fifteen minutes, steeling himself for what he instinctively knew lay ahead. Then he climbed the stairs and paused outside the bedroom door until he was sure Sarah was asleep before continuing along the landing. The nursery door was closed as he had left it, and briefly he thought he might be wrong.

But then he stepped in and saw the bright red object on the saucer in the centre of the room and all hope for the future died.

It was a tongue. He remembered the Scissorman's hidden final act over Heath's body. Anxiously, he carried the saucer to the back garden and buried the tongue in the snowdrift next to the finger. His instincts told him to destroy both of them, but all rationality had been crushed from him.

He left his secrets where he knew he could find them, then went to bed, hoping he would sleep.

12

I now have a finger *and* a tongue in my little freezer compartment in the garden. If it keeps up at this rate, pretty soon I'll have enough to build me a body. I don't even know why I'm keeping them, but I would guess it's another of my emerging psychoses, a compulsive obsessive disorder, a new entry in the charts. I used to think that mentally I was the healthiest man on the planet. *Now* look at me. I wonder how pathetic I can get?

God knows how I'm even able to write this. The things I've seen are enough to send me screaming to my bedroom, never to emerge. But I've got to force myself; it's the only way I can come to terms with it. At least I've just about guaranteed this journal will never get into the hands of the doctors. I wonder how many crimes I've admitted to in these pages? There are mitigating factors – there always are – but I've got an idea that argument won't hold much water.

So what do I do now? I don't think I've ever felt so impotent. Where do you go looking for something with razor-sharp blades for hands? And when you find it, how do you convince it to beat them into ploughshares? I can't afford to wallow in those doubts and fears now. It would paralyse me, and I have to find the strength to do something before someone else is hurt.

And why *is* this happening to me? I know I haven't been a particularly good boy during the last ten years, but I did nothing to deserve this. Perhaps there doesn't have to be a reason. Perhaps evil just sweeps out of nowhere like a storm in the tropics, randomly destroys a life in its path, then moves on. Wouldn't that be the worst thing – if eternal suffering and damnation happen for no reason apart from someone being in the wrong place at the wrong time?

I still find it hard to accept this idea of a malign, supernatural force. With my memory of the Scissorman fading like a bad dream, I could probably fool myself into thinking it was just a man dressed up. But I know that's not true. What I felt that night is more powerful than what I saw. The Scissorman is something I can't explain, something that terrifies me on a very basic level. Something is out there in the dark, circling my life, waiting to move in for the kill.

We can all have a laugh about tarot cards and ESP, but to be presented with definite proof that the supernatural exists is like having a spike driven into your forehead. Suddenly, anything is possible. There are no certainties, and the world I've been looking at for thirty-odd years is not the world I've been seeing. What are the real rules? Who can I turn to for guidance? It's enough to drive a person crazy.

Thank God for Sarah and Richard, and now Lisa. They're the rocks that keep me anchored, even though I can't tell them the whole truth. After all that time in the City, Lisa has restored my faith in human nature. I still can't believe she's prepared to help someone who's basically a stranger. There's so much about her that reminds me of the way I was before I was dragged down by that stupid job. I wish Sarah would understand how much I've changed. Sometimes I feel like I'm on a boat, waving to her on the dockside. I don't want it to be like that.

And I wish I could talk to Richard. He's always on top of the facts, a good planner, but you couldn't find another person who's more sceptical. He'd have me locked up in record time – for my own good, of course.

I hated him the first time I met him. I was already making a name for myself at Steelguard when this big lump of beef walks in and takes the desk next to me. 'Who do you have to kill to get on in this place?' he asked, in that confrontational way he's made his own. I could have given him a few names, but I just grunted and let him get on with it. Throughout that morning he was like a man possessed on the phone, alternately raging, then cheerily friendly, and while his style irritated the hell out of me, by lunchtime I had a grudging respect for his abilities.

Lunch was sandwiches at the desk, as usual, so it was only a matter of time before we struck up a conversation. He was a bit of a toff, public school background, all that. Nothing unusual in that – the City's full of them. But he wasn't as detached as some of them; he knew what the working man was thinking.

While we were talking, there was an outburst on the other side of the dealing room. At the time the boss was a monster called Smethwick. (When he left, they replaced him with another monster. Steelguard thinks it adds 'creative tension' to the workplace.) Like most managers, Smethwick was a bully who got results through humiliation. This time, though, he'd really overstepped the mark. There was a new woman on the floor, Anita something or other, and she hadn't been 'broken in' by Smethwick – one of his little rituals to ensure the natural order was made known. Most of the time he did it in his office or in a corner of the room where only a few people could see. This time he decided to demolish this bright, optimistic young woman – who happened to be half-Asian – right in the middle of the dealing room. He was screaming and shouting at her and I suppose the adrenalin must have got the better of him, for he suddenly called her 'a Paki whore' before yelling, 'Get back to your corner shop'. He must have realized instantly that he'd gone too far because he bolted back to his office as fast as he could. We'd been watching the scene in horror and

Richard just turned to me and said, 'I think that prat needs to be taught a lesson.'

I didn't think any more of it until two days later, when there was an outcry from Smethwick's office. He came running out of his room covered from head to waist in red dye. Apparently, when he opened his desk drawer he'd set off one of those hidden devices security firms use to stain money to make it unusable if the carrier is opened by thieves. A by-product of this sudden shock was the physical effect it had on Smethwick. He had already ranted around half the room before he noticed the enormous wet patch staining the front of his trousers. With all the directors coming out to investigate the fuss, it was pretty obvious Smethwick's own humiliation would neuter him for-evermore.

After things had died down, Richard leaned over and whispered, 'No one is untouchable.' We went to the toilets to split a gram of coke, laughed about it for the rest of the day, and we've never looked back since. It was good to find a kindred spirit, someone without respect for authority, who liked a good time. We've helped each other through plenty of scrapes and we've both advanced apace. In fact, I'd go so far as to say Richard is the only person I've met in the City who I feel has a deep-rooted goodness at the heart of them. I really wish he was helping me now.

But I suppose it's the same as everything else in life – you can get all the advice you want, but in the dark of the night you're on your own.

13

They were calling them the Pinstripe Slayings. Jon spread the early edition of the *Standard* on the café table and anxiously scanned the lead story. The clink of plates and the restrained chatter of tourists mingled with a steamy atmosphere and the all-pervading smell of frying bacon and coffee.

Serial killer hunted, the strapline said.

The obvious links between the Whittington and Heath murders had been made: the severity of the wounds, the weapon used, the occupations of the victims. Both were 'ritual killings' according to the position of the bodies, the paper said. Police were also examining 'something which could be a note' recovered from the crime scene. *Or which could be a page torn from a book*, Jon thought.

He read on, his anxiety growing. There it was: witnesses had seen the suspected killer fleeing from the train station 'covered in blood'. He was a suspect. The only description was of a smartly dressed white male in his late twenties or early thirties, but the shock turned Jon's stomach nonetheless.

'You're early.' Lisa stood at the end of the table. She was wearing a long leather jacket over a thick pullover, the bulkiness of her winter-wear emphasizing the delicacy of her features.

'I didn't see you come in.'

'Too engrossed.' She tapped the paper, then glanced round before sitting opposite. 'I've already read it.'

Jon rubbed his temples to ease the hangover headache. 'Somehow it seems even worse in black and white. What I remember is hazy, like it never actually happened. This makes it real.'

Lisa ordered a cappuccino; she looked troubled.

'Thanks for coming,' Jon said. 'Have you skipped lectures?'

'It doesn't matter. This is more important. Anyway, the Christmas break starts today so nothing much will get done.'

'Even so—'

She brushed away his thanks with a wave of her hand. 'Did you have any trouble getting here? I know it's hard for you to get out of the house sometimes.'

'The anxiety has bothered me less and less since all this began. I suppose it's given me some perspective.'

'Or a psychological kick in the balls.'

'That too.'

Velikovsky breezed into the café, trailing a long scarf and steaming breath. He was wearing a woollen overcoat which seemed too big for his thin frame. He stamped his feet, then strode up to them with surprising speed for his age. Through the closing door, Jon glimpsed the ornate frontage of the British Museum across the road.

'Good day again,' he said to Jon, his face and voice devoid of all warmth.

'Did you find anything?' Lisa asked.

'Not here,' he said darkly. 'Let us go somewhere a little more comforting.'

They made their way through the bitter cold along Charing Cross Road to the church of St Martin-in-the-Fields. Velikovsky led them away from the tumult of Trafalgar Square down a side street to the entrance of the church's crypt and coffee house. Jon couldn't tell if Velikovsky had chosen the venue for its religious protection or simply because they could get a table which guaranteed privacy; the latter option was more comforting. Velikovsky insisted on sitting with his back to the wall so he could watch the whole room.

'You have seen the force that the legends predict follows the brand?' he began after they had ordered more coffee.

'I saw something that looked like a deformed man,' Jon replied. 'Tall, thin. And with enormous scissor blades where his hands should be.'

'And your dreams informed you of the coming of this entity?'

Jon cupped his hands round his coffee cup for warmth. 'I remember being told, "The Scissorman is out". At the time, I had no idea what it meant.'

'When you came round last night, I knew I'd heard the Scissorman mentioned before,' Lisa interjected. She pulled a battered, pale blue book from her bag. The title said *A Child's Treasury of Stories* in gold lettering above a painting of a little girl in a blue cape holding her hand out to a glowing golden fairy. 'My mother gave me a load of books for Jamie, bless her, and this was one of them.'

She flicked it open to a page marked with a yellow Post-it and spun it round to show them a sketchy line drawing of a long-legged man leaping into a room, brandishing a pair of scissors at a frightened, fleeing boy.

Jon read out the rhyme that lay beneath.

> *The door flew open, in he ran,*
> *The great, long, red-legg'd scissorman.*
> *Oh! children, see! the tailor's come*
> *And caught out little Suck-a-Thumb.*
> *Snip! Snap! Snip! the scissors go;*
> *And Conrad cries out – Oh! Oh! Oh!*
> *Snip! Snap! Snip! They go so fast,*
> *That both his thumbs are off at last.*

Jon glanced back at the drawing and shivered. 'Horrible.'

'Victorian parents used the Scissorman as a bogey-man to frighten their children out of sucking their thumbs,' Lisa explained. She flicked a few more pages and added, 'The small print says it came from something called *Struwwelpeter*, written by Heinrich Hoffman. Like *Grimm's Fairy Tales*, I think.'

'Only more grim.' Jon couldn't bear to look at the illustration any more; the eye of the figure seemed to be watching him. He leaned over and closed the book.

'What can it all mean?' Lisa said.

'Perhaps it's punishing all the naughty little boys who never learned their lessons in the nursery,' Jon said. 'Or maybe it really *is* time I stopped sucking my thumb.'

'I do not think this is an occasion for pathetic jokes,' Velikovsky said coldly. 'Two people have been killed quite horribly.'

'I'm just trying to cope with this as best I can,' Jon said, chastened. 'I still can't fully believe it. There are times when I wonder if everything has happened in my head.'

'Then who killed those men?' Lisa said.

Jon looked away.

'I believe very strongly in another level of existence,' Velikovsky said, 'a medium through which mental connections can be made by people hundreds of miles apart. A medium which is home to whatever energy leaves the body at death, a home for entities which exist fully within its sphere.' He took a sip of his coffee with trembling hands. 'I *believe* in that as much as you believe vast sums of money can be moved around the world without people leaving their desks.'

'I wish I was as confident as you. At the moment, nothing makes sense.'

'Then do not try to *make* sense of it. Simply experience it.'

'Did your friend at the museum help?' Lisa asked.

Velikovsky nodded. 'He allowed me to delve into some of the rare, proscribed books hidden in the basement and we discussed what I found. He is an anthropological scholar who has had many unexplained experiences himself.'

'And is there any hope?' Jon asked.

Velikovsky looked uncomfortable. He drained his coffee, then glanced across the crypt to the cold light filtering through the door. 'The myths are thin stories from old times,' he began. 'Allegories. Steeped in symbolism. There are few hard facts.'

'You're saying there isn't any hope?'

'I am saying that we glean from the myths what we can. As *I* read them, the information I bring back with me is this: that this entity is enacting a dance of death. Like the ritualistic flourishes of mating birds, it is filled with intricacies which carry the weight of meaning; but what this ritual will achieve has never been known, or has never, for some reason, been included in the traditions.' He searched Jon's face, looking for some strength of character which would see Jon through what was to come. 'It is about ritual and numbers,' Velikovsky added.

'What numbers?'

'The mystical number five. Five deaths.' Velikovsky began to say something else, but Lisa glared at him.

There was a crash of smashing crockery from behind the coffee bar and Jon and Lisa jumped. Someone roared with laughter, then shouted, 'That's the way to do it!'

'You're saying five poor bastards are going to be murdered before it's all over?'

'I am saying that is what the traditions suggest. In this field, we are all feeling our way through the dark. There are no facts.'

'Can't we get a priest in?' Lisa interjected. 'Carry out an exorcism or something?'

'This transcends religion,' Velikovsky said. 'You must remember, some of these traditions existed before Christianity. Still, religious faith is a powerful tool. If you feel the need to pray—'

'This isn't about finding comfort for us. It's about trying to stop any more bloodshed,' Jon snapped. He felt the familiar band of anxiety begin to clutch tightly around his chest.

'I will continue to search for a solution—'

'And in the meantime I watch people I know die?'

A woman nearby snorted in horror. Lisa put a hand on his. 'Jon, calm down.'

'You're acting like it's hopeless,' Jon said. 'What happens if the next person to die is someone close to me?'

'I am not—'

Jon jumped up, almost tipping over the table. He was too hot, could barely breathe; the exit seemed too far away.

'Jon, sit down,' Lisa pleaded. 'We're trying to help.'

He shook his head. His thoughts were already spinning out of control. 'No. I have to go.'

'Jon—'

But he was already weaving wildly among the tables. Lisa cursed under her breath.

'He is too excitable,' Velikovsky said. 'He will be no use in this.'

'He's frightened and disorientated, that's all.' Lisa watched as he disappeared out on to the street.

Velikovsky observed her continuing to stare at the empty doorway. 'You would do better to forget about him,' he stressed quietly. 'He will bring you no good.'

London seemed strangely changed as Jon hurried down the street towards Charing Cross tube station. It was snowing again and the traffic had responded by snarling up for no obvious reason. Yet above his head, the age-blackened buildings seemed mutated, a Gothic quality shining through that he had never noticed before, as if the years were rolling back. The quality of light had altered too, and the echoes off the architecture; everything seemed unreal.

A growing paranoia crept over Jon. London was normally

a city of averted eyes, but he passed sly sideways glances and uncomfortable double-takes along his journey. When a siren erupted further along the Strand, Jon started, then ran for the steps that led down to the tube.

He didn't relax until Arcadia's front door had closed behind him. The house was warm and filled with comforting scents. He hurried into the study where he felt safe with the books of his childhood around him and spent the next hour reading *The Wind in the Willows*, driving all thoughts of blood and fear from his mind.

As he reacquainted himself with 'The Piper at the Gates of Dawn', he felt a sudden urge to look up. The cat was watching him intently from the doorway.

'Leave me alone. I'm enjoying myself.'

The cat blinked once. Jon tried to return to his reading, but the insistence of its eyes had broken the mood and he threw the book down with irritation.

'What is it then?' he snapped.

The cat turned and padded into the hall, then stopped and waited for Jon to follow. Reluctantly, he trailed after it through the kitchen to the back door where it pawed incessantly until he let it out. Instantly he noticed something in the garden was different. Oblivious to the cold, he stepped out into the gently falling snow.

The odd detachment he had felt in the West End was there in concentrated form. It was almost as if he was tripping: despite the snowfall, the glaring sun turned the garden into a blaze of white, the hoarfrost transforming every branch into a mass of jewels, and the atmosphere was filled with succulent, alien scents, almost overpowering in their intensity. Jon turned in a full arc, captivated by the wonder of the moment.

When he glanced back up the garden, he saw the cat digging haphazardly in the drift where he had buried the Scissorman's trophies. Panic clutched at his stomach and he kicked up flurries of snow as he ran to frighten the cat away. It stepped lazily out of his way at the last moment and sat to lick its paws, still observing him curiously.

'What are you doing to me?' Jon gasped. He dropped to his haunches and scrubbed the cat's head before adding in a whisper, 'What would the neighbours think if you pulled out those tasty morsels?'

The words triggered all the old fears and slowly he slumped down into the snow. The cat rubbed against him as it crawled into the shelter between his legs.

'What am I going to do?'

As his voice drifted away, he sensed movement on the periphery of his vision. Someone was in the garden with him, hiding among the tangled, skeletal trees and bushes near the bottom. Paranoia flared; they were coming to steal the finger and the tongue, to expose him as a sick, dangerous criminal.

'Who's there?' The echoes of his voice seemed to hang in the air, then drop.

Cautiously, Jon wandered to the edge of the vegetation. There was the sound of someone charging through the undergrowth beyond the next turn in the path.

It would have been wiser to take refuge in the kitchen, but something pulled Jon on. He rounded the bend and the house was lost from view. To his right was a tiny, concealed lawn with the statue of a satyr on a plinth. Odd – the statue had been rotated to face the path.

There was more thrashing in the undergrowth further ahead, like an animal that had broken free from its pen. A jangling sense of dread swept over Jon.

'Who's there?' he called out tentatively.

A dark figure, barely bigger than a child, flitted between the trees and disappeared behind the hydrangea.

The garden's magical atmosphere was darkening rapidly. Clouds had rolled over the sun and a biting wind swirled down from the far wall, replacing the pleasing aromas with the stench of decay.

Jon decided to turn back. Before he could move, a hulking shape erupted from the bushes and clattered into him with the force of a car. He flew through the air, slammed into a tree and slid into a drift, winded and on the edge of consciousness.

Shakily, he pulled himself together and looked up. A few feet away, the unicorn lowered, its eyes blazing like embers, its teeth glinting cruelly.

Jon's head was swimming. The unicorn had been in his dream, but this wasn't a dream. Was it?

Frightened by the noise, a squirrel darted across the clearing between them. Like lightning, the unicorn brought its hoof down sharply, shattering the rodent's spine. While it writhed in its death throes, the unicorn tore at the squirrel's flesh, showering blood over the fabled creature's white hide.

This perversion of every fairybook story held Jon like a hook. As it finished its feed, Jon realized its hunger would not be sated and he slipped off quickly through the undergrowth.

Breathless and aching, he stumbled into the clearing before the sunhouse, wondering if he could reach the kitchen before the unicorn caught up with him. He was startled to see a man barely bigger than a child, yet perfectly formed, sitting on the sunhouse's wooden bench, watching him oddly. He was blinking repeatedly, his lips pursing then opening in a humourless smile like some strange affliction.

'This is no dream,' the man said, as if he had read Jon's thoughts.

'It can't be real.'

'This is not real,' the man added.

Another dream, he told himself. It had to be. He was asleep in the study. Behind him, Jon heard the unicorn snort. He could smell wet vegetation and feel his skin stinging from the cold. He forced himself not to succumb to the rising panic.

Jon made to speak, but the blinking man silenced him with a wave of his hand. 'Who is the Scissorman?' he asked.

Jon read the blinking man's face and realized he was being prompted. 'Who is the Scissorman?' he asked.

'The Scissorman is like me, but now he looks like you. He has a new face.'

'How will I recognize his new face?' There was a hypnotic quality to the blinking man that made Jon feel like he was drifting in and out of sleep.

'You will know him by his actions.'

'Who are you?'

'We come from a place of smoke and water. Your world was once our home from home, but we were cut off, exiled. We still have influence, in thoughts and, at times, in the hard world. But in the main, we watch, and wait.'

'Why are you helping me?'

The blinking man's smile fixed briefly, allowing Jon to glimpse an instant of cruel humour.

'This is the first time this has happened to me when I thought I was awake,' Jon continued dreamily.

The blinking man raised his hands in mocking amazement.

Jon's head began to fill with cotton wool; he shook it forcefully. 'What's happening to me?'

The tiny man was still blinking, still smiling, then not. From somewhere nearby, there came a strange mewling sound. The blinking man appeared not to have heard it. When it started again, Jon was drawn towards it. It seemed to be coming from the stone fountain, but it stopped as Jon neared it. Standing on the edge of the frozen pond, he glanced down and started. Encased in the black ice was a boy of about seven, his dead eyes staring wide, his skin as white as the snow. He had lustrous black hair and was dressed in clothes which, to Jon, looked Victorian in style. Jon kneeled down and peered into the ice in horrified disbelief. The boy's palms were pressed upwards near Jon's own, as if he had been trying to force his way out when the ice closed around him.

The mewling started again and Jon realized it was coming from the boy.

In his shock, Jon stumbled backwards into the snow. The boy couldn't be alive; the ice surrounding him was so thick he must have been in it for days.

There was another wild crashing in the bushes and a second later the unicorn emerged, blood caked round its mouth, dripping from its stained teeth.

'Beware,' the blinking man said, 'the Palatin is hungry.'

Jon backed away a few steps. The unicorn pawed the snow with its cloven hoof, then snorted a steaming, white cloud. Jon knew, even before it lowered its jagged horn, that it was about to charge.

Jon turned and ran. The blinking man sat impassively as Jon sped past him along the winding path. He skidded on the first bend and went down on one knee just as he heard the hooves begin to pound on the frozen ground.

There was no way he could outrun it.

He thought briefly of the horn cracking his spine, piercing his heart in one thrust, and then he was running again, round one bend, then another, on a path that seemed to go on and on, far beyond the length of the garden. Through the trees, he glimpsed the house, unimaginably distant.

The hooves thundered out an incessant beat. When Jon heard another snort, he was convinced he felt the bloom of heat on the back of his neck.

Jon sprinted past the last of the trees, past the drift where his *secret* lay, over the cat licking its paws, hearing death draw closer.

Then, just when he thought he wasn't going to make it, he launched himself with one final leap over the last couple of yards and through the open kitchen door. He skidded wildly across the tiles and came to rest against the far wall.

When he glanced back fearfully, the unicorn was nowhere to be seen.

For the next three hours, he sat in front of the fire in the study, despairing for what had become of him. Finally he mustered the courage to venture into the garden, knowing exactly what he would find.

Only his own set of footprints wound along the path to and from the house. He almost turned back before the pond, but he had to see. The water was frozen, black and empty.

'Who's died?'

Sarah stood in the study doorway, a large cardboard box in her arms. It was 7 p.m. and Jon had not expected her for at least another two hours.

'I was thinking.' He looked back into the fire.

'About?'

'Responsibilities. What I've—'

'If you're about to launch into another movie quote, I'm going to take one of the glass baubles from this box and shove it up your rectum.'

'Now that's what I call a good night out!' Richard's voice floated in with a blast of cold air. It was followed by a series of grunts and a stream of four-letter words before Richard appeared in the doorway, red-faced and irritated, towing an enormous Christmas tree. 'I don't know why you couldn't have bought a small plastic one like they have in poor people's houses,' he said sourly.

'We're decking the halls with boughs of holly tonight,' Sarah said with a smile, before adding with a stage wink, 'and mistletoe.'

'And about bloody time,' Richard added. 'Only days away from the beginning of the season of over-indulgence and this place looks about as festive as a mosque.' He paused. 'They don't celebrate Christmas, do they?'

Sarah nuzzled up to Jon's cheek. 'I thought it would cheer you up. I know how much you love Christmas.'

Jon forced a smile.

Richard snorted. 'Will you two lovebirds give me a hand with this awful manual labour before I get callouses for the first time in my life.'

'For such a big bastard, you're an awful wimp,' Sarah giggled, rising to help.

They hauled in the tree and set it up in the hall where the smell of pine would permeate the house. Sarah had bought new decorations, expensive glass balls, metallic streamers and tasteful ornaments, as well as what seemed to be a carful of holly and mistletoe. It took almost two hours to decorate the place, and afterwards she made mulled wine for them to drink in the drawing room, where the only illumination came from the fire and the Christmas tree lights filtering through the open door.

Richard stretched out his feet and sighed, 'There's nothing like relaxing with a drink after a night's hard work.'

'You wouldn't know hard work if it punched you in the face,' Jon joked. He was surprised to discover he had almost sloughed off his despairing mood during the activity. Sarah and Richard's company was a tremendous comfort, increasingly so as his world fragmented. He really wished he could talk to them.

But then, during a lull in the chat, Richard steeled himself with a draught of wine and said, 'I've been thinking what we can do about the Steelguard problem, matey.'

Jon tensed. 'I don't want to talk about it, Richard. Let's not ruin a good evening.'

'Jon,' Sarah chided, 'you promised me you weren't going to bury your head in the sand.'

'I know, but—'

'Come on, Jon. We *have* had a good time tonight. Imagine how Christmas will feel if we've got the threat of you going to prison hanging over our heads.' She rested a hand on his thigh and Jon felt his resistance melt away.

'Smallthorn has some documents which are supposed to prove your guilt,' Richard continued. 'I don't know what they are, or where he got them from, but the smug little bastard is convinced there's enough there to hang you. Now you and I both know that's a load of old bollocks because you're innocent, which means the documents must be forgeries. Who made them, I don't know, although I have my suspicions. The question is, how good a forgery are they? Smallthorn plans to spring them on you and if you're not prepared, the weight of them, lies or not, could crush you.'

'What are you proposing?' Jon asked reluctantly.

Richard leaned forward animatedly. 'I know where Smallthorn keeps his papers. If you could get a look at them—'

'No.'

'—we could discern how damaging they are and prepare a case to refute them instantly.'

'No way, Richard.'

'Those documents are the cornerstone of Smallthorn's case. Without them, all the lies left are tissue-thin. You'd be off scot-free.'

'And can you imagine what will happen if I get caught breaking into Steelguard to sneak a look . . . read: *destroy* . . . the evidence? They'd crucify me.'

'Jon, this is your only chance.' Sarah squeezed his thigh emphatically.

'Was all this Christmas stuff a set-up so you could push me around?'

'It wasn't that calculating.' Sarah sounded hurt and Jon instantly regretted his tone.

'You must remember we've only got your best interests at heart, old chap,' Richard interjected.

Jon slumped back into the sofa and stared into his wine. 'I just want to leave all this behind and get on with my life.'

'Wishing won't make it happen,' Sarah said. 'If you really want to move on, then do it. I won't stand in your way. But you have to sort this out first. If you go down for it, you're never going to get away.'

Jon weighed her words. 'In my heart I know you're right,' he admitted. 'It's just that when things get too stressful I crawl back into my shell. I can't seem to help myself. I'm glad I've got you two to pull me out.'

'So, will you do it?' Richard asked.

Jon paused. 'I'll think about it.'

'Well don't think too long, old chap. Smallthorn is already building the gallows.'

With Jon's tacit acceptance the conversation turned to lighter subjects. Richard and Sarah got progressively drunk while Jon declined all further attempts to fill his glass. He was excited to see the spark returning between him and Sarah. Perhaps it was the alcohol, but she seemed more flirtatious, almost seductive, in the way she focused her attention on him.

He was revelling in an unexpectedly intimate conversation with her during one of Richard's regular trips to the toilet when they were disturbed by Richard's shout from the hall. He was on his knees examining the rusty old padlock on the cellar door.

'What's down here?' he slurred.

'It's always been locked,' Jon replied, 'even when I was a kid.'

'Thought I heard a cat calling behind there,' Richard muttered.

Sarah looped her arm through Jon's and rested her head against his shoulder. 'Perhaps the owners store all their spare furniture down there.'

'Or perhaps,' Richard said with a lascivious grin, 'it's a secret sex dungeon. Let's take a look.'

'There's no key,' Jon said. 'There never was.'

'Who needs a key? I'll knock it off.'

'Oh, listen to the hairy-chested man,' Sarah mocked.

'The owners might not take too kindly—'

'Bugger the owners.' Richard disappeared through the kitchen and returned with an old brick from the back garden. He swung it down with such force that both the brick and the lock shattered. 'See. You just need a deft touch.'

'Daft, more like,' Jon quipped.

Richard yanked open the door with a flourish and released a blast of cold, musty air. Sarah shivered and Jon slipped an arm round her shoulders. Richard felt round the jamb for the light switch, but when he flicked it there was no response. Jon felt an odd apprehension he couldn't explain.

'Maybe we should leave it till daylight,' he ventured.

'I found some candles in the kitchen the other day,' Sarah said excitedly. 'Let me get them.'

Jon pushed past Richard and peered down into the darkness. For some reason he found himself listening intently. 'Those steps are probably worn,' he noted. 'We could break our necks.'

'Maybe we should stay up here and be boring old tossers,' Richard chided, with a jab in Jon's ribs. 'I tell you what, if you're scared of the dark I'll go first.'

'At least I'll have something soft to fall on,' Jon grunted.

Sarah handed out three candles which Richard lit. 'If I get hot wax on my hand I will not go quietly,' he said.

'Get down those steps, wimp.' Sarah gave him a gentle push.

Muttering theatrically, Richard set off, his candle illuminating the salt-encrusted bare brick. 'Maybe we'll find the remains of your ghost-boy chained to the walls,' he shouted back.

Jon's stomach tightened another notch. Apprehensively,

he followed, steadying himself against the wall; it felt like ice to his touch. There was an overpowering fruity smell of damp, tinged with the odour of wood and cloth.

As they dropped below the ground floor, their candles revealed a cellar as wide as the whole front of the house. Beneath streams of gossamer cobwebs, they saw faded armchairs, a splintered piano with two keys missing, a pile of what appeared to be old curtains, boxes and tables and dressers which would have fetched a fortune at an antiques fair. There were also hundreds of books, stacked in corners, scattered across the furniture; the musty smell of their paper hit Jon in a wave.

'Do you think there are rats?' Sarah asked hesitantly.

Jon didn't know, but there was certainly something down there. The sensation of another presence was palpable, hanging in the air like a sour odour. Jon's heart thumped faster. He knew there was no way any flesh and blood creature could have got into the cellar, but the feeling of being watched made the hairs on his neck prickle erect. It was nothing like he felt when he heard the child crying. Instead, it was cold and dark, almost malign, watching them with a contemptuous superiority. Nervously he turned, and for an instant he thought he glimpsed a pair of luminescent eyes in the dark. His candle flickered and the shadows licked towards them hungrily.

'Steady on, Jon,' Richard laughed. 'You'll have me breaking my neck.'

'Just get a move on,' Jon mumbled.

When they reached the flagged floor, Sarah and Richard investigated in opposite directions; they seemed unaware of the creeping presence Jon felt near at hand. He stayed at the foot of the steps, glancing round anxiously.

Richard called out and he started. 'What is it?' he snapped.

'I think I've found our buried treasure.' Richard was standing over an escritoire examining an old, leather-bound book with creamy pages covered in varying styles of elegant handwriting.

'What is it?' Jon asked again.

'It seems to be a guest book. Something like that, anyway. It's got Arcadia written on the front and a drawing of the house.'

Jon's curiosity overcame his uneasiness. 'Let me see.'

'Hey, you two,' Sarah called out from somewhere on the other side of the cellar. 'I think there *are* rats. I can hear something moving around.'

'Look at this,' Richard said, pointing at a signature beneath a large block of writing.

Jon held his candle high and peered closely. 'Charles Dickens,' he read with gathering astonishment.

'Charles bloody Dickens,' Richard chuckled. 'In his own hand. This will be worth a fortune when we flog it off at Sotheby's.'

'It's not ours to flog, Richard,' Jon said distractedly as he carefully turned the pages.

Sarah let out a shriek and as they turned they saw her hurrying towards them. 'I tell you there're fucking rats down here. We should get out,' she snapped. 'I hate rats. I hate any little squirmy creatures. I saw one. Fuck, it was quick.'

Jon and Richard's attention drifted back to the book.

'I said—'

Richard hushed her with a wave of his hand. Jon smiled to himself; without looking up, he could feel Sarah's fuming temper at the dismissal.

He whistled through his teeth as another signature came up.

'All right, what have you two found?' Sarah said harshly.

Jon traced the name with his fingertip. 'James Matthew Barrie. And here ... Charles Dodgson ... Wilkie Collins ... Herbert George Wells ... Robert Louis Stevenson ... Jesus. All these writers can't have stayed here!'

'Oh shit,' Richard exclaimed with disappointment. 'So it's a forgery.'

'Look, the handwriting's different,' Jon pointed out. 'It would be pretty pointless to get different people to write in the book and then to lock it up down here.'

'Ah,' Richard brightened.

Jon tried to read the scrawled scripts, but in the wavering candlelight it was impossible. 'I can't believe it. Here,' he muttered.

'I think we should take this. At least get it valued,' Richard said.

As he stepped past Jon and made to pick up the book there was a flurry of movement. He recoiled with a yell of pain. 'Jesus, fuck!' he spat as he snatched the back of his hand to his mouth. 'A bastard cat went for me.' When he had sucked at the wound he held it next to the candle so Jon could see the bleeding claw marks. 'Your fucking pet!' he cursed.

'I didn't see a cat,' Sarah said, dumbfounded. 'I didn't see anything.'

But Jon had glimpsed something in the blink of an eye, and although it had vaguely resembled a cat, he had the impression of something *more*. Larger, deformed, feral. *Just a trick of the shadows*, he told himself queasily.

Sarah examined Richard's hand. 'You need some antiseptic cream on that right away. I told you to get rid of that cat, Jon.'

As she led Richard up the steps, Jon turned back to the book; he couldn't bear to leave it behind. Tentatively, he reached out for it. Expecting another flash of claws, his fingers closed around the edge and he snatched it to him.

Something fluttered from the pages and fell to the floor. It was a newspaper article clipped from the 12 November 1888 edition of *The Times*. It detailed the search for a seven-year-old boy, David Saul Cartwright, who had gone missing while visiting his parents in the Whitechapel area of London. There was a suggestion he had been snatched and transported abroad from the docks for some unspecified reason, or that he had been forced into service in one of the East End child pickpocketing gangs, although Jon couldn't see any evidence for either of these theories.

At first glance the clipping seemed an interesting curiosity, but there was something about the tale that set Jon's nerves jangling. He folded the article carefully and slipped it into the front of the book where he could find it easily. Then he slid the book under his shirt with unnecessary secrecy and hurried up the steps towards the light.

14

'You know, this really isn't the best time to go for a walk, old chap,' Richard said worriedly. 'Or the best place, for that matter.'

'These days I like staying up late and sleeping in,' Jon replied. 'Besides, you saw how tired Sarah was. An early night will do her good.'

'She's concerned about you, Jon. We both are.'

'Don't worry. Look, it's only 11 p.m. I need some fresh air in my lungs.'

'All very well, but you didn't tell Sarah you were coming right down here.' Richard put his foot down as they turned into Ludgate Hill. Ahead, St Paul's loomed up in a wash of light.

'I didn't want to worry her. I like it round here. There's plenty of history.' They drove on a little past St Paul's and then Jon said, 'Here will do fine.' Once Richard had driven off he could pick up a cab to Lisa's easily enough. He didn't want Sarah to know his destination, and certainly not at that time of night; Sarah was a jealous person and it was only natural she would get the wrong idea. But he needed to talk and Lisa was his only confidante. He had felt revitalized by the evening with Richard and Sarah, and with his mood lifted he realized how stupid he had been to run off from Lisa and Velikovsky that morning. As Sarah had told him, he couldn't afford to bury his head in the sand any longer. He only wished he could have called ahead.

'Well, it's your funeral, old chap,' Richard sighed, pulling the car over to the kerb. 'How are you getting home?'

'Don't worry. I'll get a cab.'

Jon waved him off, noting Richard's expression of unconcealed concern. The last thing he wanted was to give Richard any more doubts about his sanity, but he had been overcome with urgency. Oddly, it had overwhelmed him while he had been secreting the Arcadia guest book in the drawer with his journal. Richard had been downstairs complaining loudly while Sarah applied Germolene to his scratches. And, in a flash, he knew it was his responsibility to face up to the threat for all their sakes. It was as simple as that.

Bundled up in his overcoat, he decided to take a short cut through Paternoster Row to St Paul's tube station, where he thought he might have a better chance of getting a cab. His thoughts turned sourly to the time he had wasted that day, and how stupid he had been to ignore Velikovsky's help. The memory of the train ride and Heath's murder returned in a nightmarish, disjointed fashion, re-igniting the horror of the moment. It still seemed like a fantasy, but the blades remained real enough in his mind, hard and unrelenting, And the blood coloured his thoughts crimson.

Could he accept it? And the other things he had seen – the apparition in the garden earlier that day who had suggested the Scissorman had taken human form? The thought brought a chilling instant of *frisson*. He had known both victims. Did he know the Scissorman too?

The sound of metal on metal snatched his attention away. Anxiously, he looked round. His wandering had taken him to that maze of ancient streets behind St Paul's where capitalism had thrust up new office blocks to overlook Wren's majesty. With residents driven out by commerce, the winding streets were empty at that time of night, pedestrianization eliminating passing cars.

Jon paused under a streetlamp and listened intently. For

a long minute all he heard was the wind and the thrum of his heart in his ears, but then came the sound of shears closing, echoing among the tall buildings. Jon's breath caught in his throat. Despite the streetlights, there were too many shadows. He glanced across the road into the black hole of an underground car park; up at the summit of a glass and steel office block; into the shadowy alley that peeled off in the direction of the tube station.

Faintly, he heard the jarring screech of metal being drawn across a window.

Slowly, he moved off, keeping his back to the comforting bulk of St Paul's. Far ahead were the bright lights signalling the best-lit route to the tube. A prickling of his nerves drove him to glance back into the gloom and he saw a wildly distorted shadow of a man flickering across the street, the long blades of its fingers playing madly up the walls.

It was as insubstantial as dust particles in a beam of light, yet Jon felt a wave of evil washing out from it that filled him with dread.

He started to run, slipped on the compacted snow and slammed into the gateway of St Paul's Churchyard. As the echoes drifted out across the park, Jon glimpsed a shape within detach itself from the surrounding shadows and move towards him.

'Hello?' A woman's voice; Jon's stomach unclenched. A second later she stepped into the light in a rustle of Chanel coat and suit. Jon recognized the carved features of Steelguard's front office manager, Emma Rexe-Burke.

Once she saw him, her hopeful expression shifted to one of annoyance. 'Jonathan Summers! Is this some kind of joke?'

'What do you mean?' He glanced back down the street but could see nothing.

'You bloody well know,' she snapped. She fumbled irritatedly for a pack of cigarettes in her Vuitton handbag and lit one with a flounce. Only when the cloud of smoke cleared did she see Jon's puzzled expression. 'So it wasn't you?'

'I don't know what you're talking about, Emma,' he said, still flashing glances over his shoulder.

'I got a scrawled message in the post. From one of my contacts, supposedly. It said to meet them here if I wanted to find . . . Oh, I don't know why I'm telling you.'

More insider information, Jon thought.

'Here? Why here?' he said. 'And shouldn't this park be locked?'

'The lock was sliced in two.'

'Look, we can't stay—'

'Get in here.' Emma threw down her cigarette and grabbed him by the lapels of his overcoat so she could haul him into the park. 'You're going to frighten anyone off, hovering there like a great lump. I'm not having you ruining my big break.' She shoved him roughly into the shadows where they couldn't be seen from the road. 'Now listen—'

'No, *you* listen.' Jon snatched her hands away. 'You're in danger—'

'You're just doing this so you can steal my tip, aren't you? I always thought you were a sneaky little oik!'

The fury in her pale, moonlit face ignited a sudden flash of memory: Emma flushed with the adrenaline rush, enthusing the team to ignore ethics, do anything to gain results; Emma ecstatic, then angry, then despairing, making Jon complicit in her numerous petty crimes. She was the one who had taught him about front-running orders, dealing ahead of publication so cash was made at the expense of the client. She was the one who taught him how to slip into the toilets with a mobile phone to call the IG Index and bet on his planned dealing for the day, so every deal put money into his own pocket.

And as he looked at her and around at the bleak, deserted spot, and as he thought about the illicit message she had received, everything fell instantly into place. She had been manipulated into being there, at that time. The sound of the shears was the warning. She was to be the next victim.

'We've got to get out of here,' he said, grabbing her arm.

She knocked his hand away. '*You* get out of here. And do it quick. I don't want—'

'No! Come—'

Something like smoke shifted from the shadows before silver erupted out in an arc. There was a tearing of material as a ragged gash ripped through Emma's voluminous coat. Her eyes widened, but she still hadn't registered what had happened. Another slash and her cheek opened up like an overstuffed paper bag, showering Jon with blood. Her screech of agony tore through the cold night.

Jon grabbed her wrist and yanked her away from the shadows towards the road. He heard a whistling in the air and then the clang of metal striking concrete as a shower of sparks erupted on the edge of his vision. As he ran, he had a fleeting impression of long, long limbs and a terrible face beneath a hat tinted orange by that briefest illumination.

Emma was shrieking and crying, clutching her sagging cheek with her free hand. Droplets of blood splattered the dirty snow. On the pavement, her heels skidded on the ice and she went down on one knee, ripping through her tights and the skin beneath. Jon dragged her four feet or more before she managed to scramble upright.

His aim was to get to the main road at Ludgate Hill where the traffic still passed intermittently, but it seemed so far away. Yelling as loudly as he could in the hope that someone would raise the alarm, he pulled Emma on. Eventually they reached the road where he heard the sound of speeding cars coming from the City; he stepped off the pavement and stood his ground. Emma was flailing and screaming, so he wrapped his arms around her to hold her still.

The first car appeared and slammed on its brakes. The

driver's face turned from anger to concern as he noticed the blood.

Jon let go of Emma. 'Help us! We need the police!' he yelled, running towards the bonnet.

The driver suddenly threw the car into reverse, popped the clutch and hurtled back a few yards before speeding round Jon in a wide arc. The next car passed with a screech of horn; Jon had a fleeting view of a furiously contorted face as the car missed him at speed by only an inch.

He glanced back and saw Emma scrambling wildly along the side of the cathedral, driven by fear and pain. Her drawn-out squealing made him feel queasy; it was like animal sounds.

Breathlessly, Jon pursued her. At the foot of the steps at the south transept, she noticed him and screamed as if he was the aggressor. In her irrational fear, she ran up the steps and into the cathedral.

Jon followed, pausing for an instant to examine the door which he knew was always kept locked. All the bolts and the lock had been neatly sliced through. In the south porch, Jon hurried past the five statues of the apostles, his searching eyes falling on a phoenix and the legend *Resurgam* – I shall rise again; it disturbed him greatly. By the time he entered the vast, echoing building, Emma was nowhere to be seen, and even her cries had subsided.

The cathedral seemed filled with darkness; there were only a few small lamps along the walls, casting puddles of illumination. Beneath the soaring dome he spun round, searching in all directions. When he whispered her name loudly, his voice rustled out like autumn leaves.

His first thought was that she was hiding under the pews or behind one of the towering stone columns, but as he ran back and forth around the cathedral hearing the echoing thunder of his footsteps, he could find no sign of her. Surely it could only be minutes before the cathedral authorities investigated, he thought; security had been stepped up after the last round of IRA bombs. But as he stood and listened, he could hear nothing; it was as if he had been cut off from the world.

Then, in the brittle silence, he heard something less than a whisper and barely more than an exhalation floating along the nave from the main doors at the back of the cathedral. Jon held his body rigid and waited. Nothing. Nothing. And then . . .

Out of the darkness, the Scissorman emerged, appearing and disappearing like a ghost image in a heat haze as it passed from one pool of light to another, advancing relentlessly. Jon fell to the floor, praying he had not been seen, his heart pounding so hard he thought he was going to pass out. Then, as he glanced around, he saw an enormous luminous figure and had to stifle a yell of shock in his throat. It took him a second or two to realize it was simply a trick of the light falling on the cathedral's most famous painting, Holman-Hunt's *The Light of the World*, with Christ promising salvation. But as Jon absently read the words beneath the picture an inexplicable chill rippled through him:

> Behold I stand at the door and knock. If any
> man hear my voice and open the door I will
> come in to him and will sup with him and he
> with me.

With the fear burning in his stomach, he crawled quickly along the stone flags, hearing nothing, wondering when the Scissorman would separate from the shadows and end his life. As he passed between one of the stone columns and the wall, he stopped suddenly. On the floor, flecks of blood pointed the way to Emma's hiding place: the archway that led up to the Whispering Gallery and then to the outside of the dome.

Breathlessly, he launched himself through the opening and on to the stairs. Their dizzying spiral made Jon's head spin as he took the black steps two at a time. Every sound seemed too loud, as if fate was conspiring to make him vulnerable, and as he rose, the faint light dwindled and disappeared until he had the claustrophobic impression of being buried alive. He fumbled for each step with his fingers and propelled himself upwards.

Suddenly the scraping of metal on stone echoed dimly around. Jon froze, his breath catching painfully in his throat; he couldn't tell if the noise had come from below or above. *Get out*, he told himself, but he knew he couldn't leave Emma alone to face those blades. When he progressed to the next step and felt his fingers touch on something wet and sticky, it only reinforced his determination.

Where the stairs opened out on to the Whispering Gallery, he felt relief as the dark was finally dispelled by light filtering up into the colossal dome. Cautiously, he dropped to his knees and crawled out. The gallery continued around the circumference of the dome with only metal railings separating it from a drop of hundreds of feet to the stone floor below. During the day the railings would have provided little cover, but in the gloom he could crawl without anyone on the other side of the dome seeing him.

Quietly, he slid up to the wall, preparing to use the unique acoustics which gave the Whispering Gallery its name – a muttered aside would be carried perfectly audibly around to the other side of the dome. He would be able to communicate with Emma without giving away his position.

But the first thing he heard when he placed his ear to the wall was a merciless, metallic snip-snip-snip, whining to him with the threat of blood and pain.

Anxiously, he flipped one way, then the other. The arc of the dome and the weakness of the light from below made it impossible to see more than a few yards in either direction. He pressed himself into the wall as if he could melt into it and listened against the background of the blood pounding in his head.

Snip-snip-snip.

The acoustics were working against him; he couldn't tell if it was close by or across the dome. Acutely aware of the danger, he began to inch his way along the gallery, hoping he would find Emma first. Then he heard a murmur reverberating around the wall. It sounded like she was whispering a prayer. Jon had barely opened his mouth to speak her name when he became aware of a figure on the edge of his vision.

He whirled round, but it was too late. He felt the cold hardness of a blade-tip against his cheek, an instant of heat, and then excruciating pain as it slid effortlessly through flesh, into his mouth, and then out through the soft skin of his other cheek, pinning his head to the wall.

His yell of agony turned to a choking gargle as his throat filled with blood. He swallowed, heaved for air, and his tongue tasted bitter metal as it slid along the flat blade. Through his pain, Jon had an impression of a tall hat and features like oil on water, until the other hand came into view. There was a faint *snickt* as the blades opened and then levelled with his staring eyes.

In a moment of screaming terror, Jon knew what was to come next.

Slowly, the blades began to move forward until they were all Jon could see. Barbs of fire in his cheeks prevented him yanking his head back; he was held like meat on a skewer. And the blades moved closer. Jon's eyelashes brushed the tip.

He clamped his lids tight and waited for the instant of agony as his eyeballs burst. Suddenly the blades whipped up and scratched his forehead, releasing a flaring instant of pain that turned his muscles to jelly. With excruciating slowness, the blade was withdrawn from his cheek like a red-hot poker dragged through his flesh. As it pulled free, another gout of blood filled his mouth, bubbled out of his lips, and he slumped to the floor, unable to move a limb.

Jon could barely comprehend what the final touch of the blades had done to him. Although he could feel the ringing pain in his head, it was cotton wool-muffled, and his vision had turned black round the edges as though he was looking up from the bottom of a well. Obtusely, he wondered: *Am I dying?*

But he could still hear perfectly. The Whispering Gallery susurrated with Emma's murmured prayers, more desperate now as if she could sense what was coming for her. The insistence in her voice broke through the haze that shrouded Jon, driving him to force his drugged limbs to life, but the most he could do was loll drunkenly to one side. And each new sound that vibrated out of the wall was like the tick of a clock counting out the seconds of Emma's life.

'. . . Dear God, save . . .'

The chink of metal on stone.

Jon pressed against the floor with his foot, but he slid up the wall barely an inch before he fell back.

'Oh God . . .'

Jon heaved again. The black tunnel surrounding his vision began to fracture; he was coming through it.

'. . . It hurts . . .'

A louder clink, then a long scraping noise that set his teeth on edge.

'Who's there?' Emma's voice, a hoarse whisper.

Jon pushed again. This time he rose to his haunches and his muscles supported him. Breathing heavily at the exertion, he pressed his back against the stone.

'Summers?'

Jon felt the world pitch and yaw around him like the worst drug trip he had ever experienced.

'Oh my God . . .' Emma's whisper was drawn in with a sharp intake of breath and then expelled in a short scream of terror that made the entire dome chime.

Snip-snip-snip.

'No!'

Scuffling noises; Emma trying to get away, driving herself backwards across the floor, her head cracking and slipping on the stone.

Another scream. Jon estimated her position and began to heave himself along the wall.

'Emma! I'm coming!' he called out weakly, aware how pathetic it sounded.

Then: 'It's you! Why are you—'

The note of recognition in Emma's voice brought Jon up sharply and before he could move again, the entire wall rang with the sounds of a butcher's shop.

And then he saw them. Somehow Emma managed to free herself and, in a flurry of shadows and silhouettes, launched herself through the door that led to the outside of the dome, with the hideous long-limbed thing in close pursuit.

Jon felt as drunk as he had witnessing Heath's murder, but somehow he managed to weave along the gallery, through the door and up the stairs. He stumbled out into a blast of icy air and a flurry of snow. All around, London sprawled majestically, the heart of the capital lit up like a Christmas tree.

'Emma!' he yelled.

Then he saw them a few yards further on, two black shapes against the white stone of the dome. The Scissorman had her and its blades were whirling in a dance of shimmering light. Jon felt droplets of liquid splatter on his face.

'No!' he shouted, tried to move, held fast in horror.

The blood showered up and was caught by the wind, hurled out across the city and further, a red rain staining the winter beauty.

Finally Jon's legs crumpled and he pitched backwards through the door and down the stairs. Somehow he managed to avoid splitting his skull, but when he came to a stop his body was racked with pain, and blood from his cheek wound was pouring into his mouth with renewed vigour. As he coughed and spluttered, he was blinded by the sudden flaring of lights overhead. In the distance, Emma's brittle screams were punctuated by snipping and chopping sounds.

Then Jon became aware of other anxious voices and the sound of feet on stone. A few seconds later two members of the cathedral staff stumbled across him. He could tell from their expressions that he must have looked a terrible sight, with blood smeared across his face and clothes.

'Good Lord!' one of the men exclaimed. 'Are you—'

'Not me,' Jon croaked. He pointed up the stairs. 'Outside. Save her.'

They were caught up by the urgency in his voice and leaped over him. Jon lay back in relief and allowed the latticework of pain to spread across every square inch of his skin. He thought about closing his eyes, but a drifting voice in the back of his head forced him to sit up.

The two men would not find Emma's assailant, in the same way that the people on the platform had not seen Heath's killer, even though it was against the bounds of reason that he could have escaped. The cathedral staff would think Jon was the attacker.

With a tremendous effort, he hauled himself to his feet and, like a drunk, he began to crash from side to side along the gallery and down the stairs. Above him, cries of alarm echoed through the cathedral.

Jon stumbled, caught himself, stumbled again. He prayed there would be no one else waiting at the bottom. If he was caught it would all be over.

He lurched out of the door at the bottom and glanced anxiously around before hurrying back to the south transept, feeling like Jimmy Cagney ready to go out in a blaze of glory.

'"Top of the world, ma,"' he mumbled.

There was no one outside, but he knew his problems were far from over. Covered in blood, wounded and limping like a killer on the run, he somehow had to make it across the capital to home. In the deserted backstreets that led towards the heart of the City, he heard distant sirens drawing closer, but they were drowned out by his memory of the sound of sharp blades chopping through flesh.

15

It was 3.30 a.m. when Sarah arrived at the doctor's house, her face pale from disturbed sleep but filled with fury. Jon sat in the comfy chair in the lounge, feeling the pain slowly subsiding as the powerful analgesics began to take effect. One of the perks of his former high-flying career was private health insurance and his exorbitant premiums ensured round-the-clock care from his local doctor. It had saved Jon a trip to Accident and Emergency and the kind of questions which would alert the police. Dr Preston was shocked by Jon's blood-covered appearance on his doorstep, but he accepted the cover story of a mugging at face value. Sarah looked like she wasn't going to be so accommodating.

'I told you it was a stupid time to go out for a walk,' she fumed. 'Jesus Christ, Jon, you could have been killed! Did they take anything? Have you reported this to the police?'

'No on both counts. I was just happy to get away.' Jon hated lying, but with Preston hovering in the background he couldn't let his story slip. And any deviation from the account would allow Sarah to prise open the whole can of worms and catch a peek of his sticky, twisted mind.

'I've stitched up the cheek, but I'm afraid there'll be a few weeks of pain and quite severe scarring in that spot,' Preston said to Sarah. 'I did suggest a much more complicated operation at hospital involving stitching each layer of skin to minimize cosmetic damage, but your husband—'

'I wanted it done and dusted.'

'But your husband was lucky. The blade missed the facial muscles and there doesn't appear to be any nerve damage,' Preston added.

'Well that's a relief,' Sarah said sourly. 'He'll still be able to wince when I yell at him for making me tired and irritable for work.'

Preston muttered something, then slipped into the background where he awkwardly shuffled some papers on the table. Jon tried to put his arm round Sarah as they headed out to the car, but she shook him off. Sometimes her temper frightened him.

In a way, he was thankful for her frosty silence on the way home. The dope the doctor had given him had also taken the sting out of the shock that had threatened to tip him over the edge. Too many questions right then would have brought it all back, and he knew if he gave himself up to the terrifying enormity of it, he would be paralysed. Soon he would have to face up to what was happening. But at that moment the night seemed too dark, and too lonely.

Lisa looked tired and drawn when Jon called round just before 10 a.m.; she had been up since the early hours, comforting Jamie who had been plagued by nightmares. Jon had barely slept either. The memories of St Paul's were too horrifying, and by 6 a.m. the drugs had started to wear off, allowing the pain to creep back with a vengeance.

Lisa nodded at the patches on his cheeks. 'That's quite a shaving cut.'

Jon waved to Jamie who was playing with his Action Man in the corner. 'I see you finally got around to putting up the Christmas decorations.'

A two-foot-tall, silver plastic tree stood on the sideboard, dressed up with a few flaking baubles, but the ceiling and walls were festooned with shining streamers and tinsel.

'With college finished, I finally found the time. I'd like to have got a real tree, but have you seen the price of them? We decided to make do with the old favourites.'

'Still looks nice. Mind if I switch on the TV?'

'You've only come round for your fix of Richard and Judy, haven't you?' she said with mock-sternness before slipping into the kitchen to make a pot of tea.

Jon missed a TV for watching movies, but that morning he missed it more for the news. He couldn't wait until the early edition of the *Standard* hit the streets. As expected, the first story on the 10 a.m. bulletin was the attack on Emma, which had already been classified as a third Pinstripe Slaying; the media loved their sobriquets. The relief that swept through him when the newscaster said the unnamed female victim was still alive in intensive care brought him to the verge of tears. There was a brief interview with some harried-looking cop named Culver and then the report cut to a spokesman for the cathedral who appeared both puzzled and sickened.

'I honestly cannot understand how this happened,' he began. 'The cathedral is normally extremely secure. We even have closed circuit television throughout the building.' The incomprehension on the man's face increased. 'Unfortunately, during the incident there was interference throughout the system, which ended the moment the alarm was raised.'

There was a sharp cut back to Culver, who was giving a press conference on the steps outside the cathedral's great west door. 'We are appealing for a man who helped raise the alarm to come forward,' he said.

Jon tensed.

'He was found on the steps above the Whispering Gallery near where the attack took place. It seems he left the scene very quickly soon after. As the victim is in no condition to be questioned, we have been unable to ascertain his connection to the young lady or why they were both in the cathedral.'

'Is he a suspect?' someone shouted.

'We would like to eliminate him from our enquiries,' Culver parried.

'Do you have a description?'

'The details given by the cathedral staff are very sketchy. Apparently the man was himself wounded and there was a substantial amount of blood obscuring his features.'

'Is that why you sounded so concerned on the phone?' Lisa was standing behind him, watching the TV over his shoulder.

'I'm the man they're looking for.'

'You'd better tell me what happened.' She glanced over at Jamie and recognized the pretence of intense play that meant he was listening. 'Jamie, play in your room, will you? I have to talk to Jon for a while.'

The boy departed without argument, but his expression suggested a wealth of deep thoughts and emotions. Children and adults are separate races, Jon thought; he wondered at what age the boundary was crossed.

Lisa slipped on to the sofa next to him; their knees touched, their thighs kissed briefly. Totally innocent, but Jon felt uncomfortable nonetheless. To divert his thoughts, he launched into an account of the previous night. When he reached the point where the blade pierced his cheek, Lisa winced and took his hand. Her fingers felt cool.

When he'd finished, she said simply, 'You know you can't turn your back on it any more?'

Jon looked at the TV, fizzing with the sound down.

'This is about you, Jon. This is your responsibility. You have to face up to it.'

'Whatever the repercussions.'

She gave his hand another squeeze. 'You know I'm with you all the way.'

He turned to her curiously. 'Why are you helping me?'

She looked puzzled. 'Because you're in trouble.'

She couldn't seem to comprehend the question so he left

it. Instead, he told her all the things he had left out in the past – including the truth about the finger and the tongue hidden in the garden – and afterwards he felt a little less alone; she took it much better than he ever could have hoped.

Even though it was morning there was a crepuscular gloom outside. A fog was creeping in from Docklands, as if the City was drawing it in with big, gulping breaths.

'Emma told me she'd received a mysterious message that a contact would meet her near St Paul's to pass on some unspecified information. I think that was a ploy to lure her there for the killing,' Jon continued.

'Why there?'

'The reports said the other two bodies were laid out ritually. Perhaps the place is important.'

'The Scissorman sent her a message?' she said disbelievingly.

'I think the spirit, the Scissorman, has taken the form of somebody in the City. Somebody I know. If I know all his victims, it stands to reason we move in the same circles.'

'What are you going to do? Ring up everybody in your Filofax and ask them?'

'Emma's anally retentive – she's bound to have filed the message away in her desk.'

Lisa's eyes narrowed. 'You big eejit. You're just going to waltz into work, I suppose?'

Jon shook his head. 'My friend's been nagging me to go in there to sort out that business problem I told you about. He can get me in at night and I can kill two birds with one stone.'

'You'd better watch which birds get killed,' she said sharply. Then, 'Look, I think we need to talk about this a bit more. You'd better come with me.'

'Where are we going?'

'To see some drug addicts.'

*

The Spitalfields Centre was in a reclaimed Victorian mansion that reeked of damp and the choking smell of Calor Gas heaters battling futilely against the encroaching cold. The decor was uniform cheap yellow paint, chipped and scuffed along the bottoms of the walls and doors. It had a desperate atmosphere of last chances and lies that fooled no one, and Jon felt his mood deaden. The staff were all smiles, though, and they greeted Lisa with true warmth; it appeared everyone liked her.

'How many victims do you get in here, then?' Jon asked as she found him a quiet corner and a pile of magazines to flick through.

'We prefer not to call them *victims*, Jon,' she said, laughing at his insensitivity. 'But the answer is, a lot. You know how it's got in the inner city. The East End's as deprived as it was a century ago, it's just the problems are different. Lots of crime, prostitution, but drugs are probably the worst. There's a whole generation fading away out here. I really feel like I'm doing something useful.'

Jon felt uncomfortable about how distant all the social problems she mentioned had seemed to him during the last ten years.

'The charity set up the centre here because we're smack in the centre of a ring of streets that are probably the worst in the East End. You saw the graffiti outside. There are whole houses given up to the gangs dealing. Squats filled with users shooting-up. A lot of people think it's too far gone, hopeless, but if anyone wants to turn away, we're here to help. We direct them to all the medical aid and counselling they need to go clean.'

'And does it work?'

'Who knows? But you've got to try.'

Lisa moved off to greet a Goth youth with long, dyed-black hair and a leather pimp's coat. Jon guessed he was in his early twenties, but his skin looked twice that age. He moved painfully slowly, almost bent double, and his gaze ranged so sluggishly from object to object that he seemed bewildered. He appeared to know Lisa and when she gave him a hug, tears sprang quickly to his eyes.

As Jon watched her ministrations, an odd sensation crept over him, which took a while to identify. When he did finally pin it down, he was so swamped with guilt he forced himself to look away, suddenly sick at his own flaws. For the briefest instant, he had imagined her as more than a friend. An image of them kissing flashed through his mind and it triggered a wash of emotion so powerful it made his head spin. He wanted her, not just sexually, but spiritually too. How could he feel that way? Sarah was the only one for him. They were perfect for each other; he had turned that thought over in his head so many times it was one of the rules of his life that could never be broken. Yet against his will his own emotions were attacking that precept, forcing him to betray his wife, his vows and everything he believed in. His love for Sarah was the only thing of value he had left; he couldn't let his own pathetic weaknesses destroy that. In confusion, and with a self-loathing stronger than he could ever have imagined, he desperately drove the thoughts from his mind.

With an effort, Jon settled back with the magazines and a cup of coffee, but his mind wouldn't rest. Now when he closed his eyes, he had a flashing image of a glinting blade inches from his pupil; half-heard sounds were transformed into muffled screams or the sound of scraping metal. And the more he sat and forced himself to relax, the more his anxiety levels rose. He had the jarring feeling that the Scissorman was always nearby, just out of sight.

After twenty minutes wrestling with himself, he knew the only answer was to try to walk it off. The fog had slipped in rapidly during his time in the centre, deadening street sounds, wrapping the buildings in grey; at least it meant there wouldn't be any more snow. Jon shivered inside his thick coat, pushed his hands into his pockets and headed off. Lisa had been right about the area. The damp air smelled of rotting vegetation and burning tyres. Graffiti was splattered across the walls among peeling posters for bands that had long since split up. Every other house had been boarded up, but most of the doors had been kicked in; music that sounded like industrial cleaners floated out of a couple. Occasionally, expensive cars with darkened windows slid by, while huddles of shaven-headed youths hovered menacingly in front of one house whose windows were covered with sheet metal. In comparison, the local residents were almost invisible; they slipped in and out of the fog, hurrying to the shops or back home like frightened mice.

Jon had been out for fifteen minutes when he realized he was lost. All the streets looked the same in the fog. Cursing, he turned round to try to retrace his steps so he would be back before Lisa's shift finished; he didn't want her worrying about him.

He had barely gone a hundred yards when he jumped suddenly at a sound like some unknown animal bellowing away in the murk. With his heart thumping, he paused at the foot of some steps outside another boarded-up house and looked around anxiously. The sound came again, this time high above him, and then again, at ground level, off to his left. He backed up on to the first step. The rest of the street was silent; it was as if it had been closed off from the world.

The next roar came from his right. Jon tried to guess what it could be, but it was like nothing he had heard before. For one split-second, the fog folded upon itself and he had a glimpse of a grey shape rising up two storeys, but it was gone so quickly he had to accept it was just a trick of the light. Still, something wasn't right; the air smelled different and there was a faint metallic taste in his mouth. Despite the biting cold, Jon was sweating. He slipped up to the next step.

Then, through the fog, he saw a figure walking towards

him. The gait was insistent, almost manic. Jon peered, but the fog clung to him, strands trailing off from his hands and head. As the figure drew closer, it seemed to change shape, growing more squat, and when it emerged from the murk Jon recognized the biker he had met outside Highgate Cemetery and who had pursued him through Selfridges basement. His face was contorted in what could have been rage or fear and he appeared to be shouting, although Jon couldn't hear a sound. Terror hit Jon like a sledgehammer and he felt his stomach knot and twist. He sprinted to the top of the steps and pressed his back against the splintered door.

The biker continued marching, his mouth opening and closing, until eventually his voice faded in and out like someone was tuning in a radio.

' . . . Ook . . . Re . . . ook . . . Read . . . k . . . Read . . . book . . . Read the book . . .'

Jon felt as if he was in a dream. The fog rolled around the street, obscuring his view of the rest of reality. All his attention was focused on the biker and his shaky, unreal movements. As in a dream, Jon's fear was inexplicably strong, as if it had nothing to do with what he was seeing, more with something terrible he was sensing behind the scenes.

The biker stopped at the foot of the steps, the muscles on his waxy, mask-like face twitching as if he couldn't quite find the right expression to present.

'Read the book,' he said emphatically.

As Jon tried to perceive some meaning in what was happening, there was another sound away in the fog which he recognized instantly. The scraping of metal, the chiming of a blade, echoing with an otherworldly cadence. The signature of the Scissorman.

To Jon's horror, the biker's head swivelled through 180 degrees, then snapped back with a contorted expression of pure fear.

'Read the book,' he gasped. The head flashed round again, eyes trying to pierce the fog. Then back to Jon again, his face radiating a fear so powerful Jon almost felt it crackling between them.

The blade rang closer.

The head swivelled once more, and when it looked back, Jon was convinced the face was melting like a candle. Before he could be sure, the biker turned and lurched away wildly through the fog, emitting an awful, keening cry as he ran.

Jon had a fleeting impression of a dark shape approaching quickly through the murk and then he turned and wrenched at the handle. The door had been bolted, but the wood was rotten and it burst open with a wet, hollow sound. Jon threw himself inside and slammed what remained of the door behind him.

The house was condemned but obviously in use; there was an anarchist poster on one wall. The hall was littered with torn newspapers, beer cans and bottles and a stench of human excrement and urine hung in the air.

Jon decided to try to find a way out at the back, but as he passed the first open door he was caught by a dismal scene of utter squalor. The room was practically unfurnished, the walls bare, but it contained several young men and women in various states of stupor; some lay prone, others slumped against walls, the paraphernalia of heroin use scattered around. A boy of about three played lazily with a pile of wooden bricks next to a couple who were having sex. At first, Jon thought the woman was dead. Her eyes were wide and unfocused and she didn't register any feeling as the youth on top of her thrust in a bored, languid manner. But then her eyes fell on Jon and she smiled eagerly and beckoned, although her partner seemed oblivious. Jon stepped forward out of habit and she wheezed, 'Spare some change?'

Jon shook his head queasily and began to back out.

Before he reached the hall, a comatose teenager in one corner suddenly groaned as his eyes snapped open mechanically. Blood-flecked spittle bubbled over his lips and he croaked, 'Here.'

A girl lying on her back rolled her head towards Jon and her eyes opened in the same unnatural way; Jon could see no consciousness in them. 'He's here,' she said.

Another drugged youth followed suit, and another, randomly around the room, until they were all staring at Jon without seeing him. There was something incomprehensible and terrifying in their blank eyes which Jon could not bring himself to contemplate. He shook off the dreaminess which had gripped him since he'd stumbled into the street, and ran towards the back of the house, through more rubbish, vile smells, past walls daubed with graffiti which spoke of decay and poverty and no hope or kindness.

The garden was an overgrown mess of yellow grass and bizarre, waist-high weeds which looked like alien flora. He scrambled on to a rusty dustbin and threw himself over the listing fence into the next garden. A black Doberman broke away from the back of the house, snapping and spraying spittle as it barrelled towards him in a wild display of teeth and flaring eyes. Jon barely made the next fence in time and rolled over it into an alley that ran between two streets.

Somehow he found himself back at the centre a half-hour later, after running crazily through fog-bound streets where every shop seemed boarded and every house filled with blank, stupefied people. Lisa was waiting for him at the door, looking concerned and a little afraid. 'Where've you been?' she asked plaintively.

Jon couldn't bring himself to answer. The endemic despair and decay he had witnessed made him feel like he was in hell, with the twisted figure of the Scissorman towering horribly above it all.

On the journey home, though, he managed to tell her

what had happened. 'What did he mean, read the book?' Lisa asked.

'Who knows? He's probably just crazy.'

'You don't think he's linked to all this? That's the third time you've seen him in different parts of the city. He must be pretty keen to give you a message.'

'Nothing makes sense any more,' Jon said irritatedly, but he thought about it for a moment, then added, 'I found a book in the cellar at Arcadia.'

'Maybe—'

She was interrupted by a commotion outside her house as they turned into the street. Ralph was sitting on the step with his face in his hands; he looked like he was crying. An Asian man Jon guessed was Ilyas sat next to him with an arm around his shoulders. A woman, obviously Ilyas' wife, stood behind, wailing uncontrollably.

Lisa sprinted up with Jon close behind. 'What happened?'

Ralph looked up with red eyes. 'They arrested Michael.' He tried to say more, but the emotion choked him and he buried his face in his hands once again.

'The police were round here making some enquiries about those murders. They've been all over the area all day,' Ilyas said. 'One of the detectives came knocking on our door. I was talking to Michael in the hall. Michael answered and told the detective he knew nothing, had seen nothing. I don't know, I don't know ... The detective became very abusive.'

Jon noticed the splashes of blood leading down the steps to the pavement.

'The homophobic bastard!' Ralph cried.

'Michael asked the detective quite kindly to leave,' Ilyas continued, 'and the detective suddenly went wild. He grabbed Michael by the hair and started smashing his head against the wall. I tried to pull him off, but he threw me to one side.'

'His poor face!' Ralph sobbed.

'The detective called in on his radio and others came and dragged Michael away. I don't know what they are charging him with. I don't even know where they've taken him.' Ilyas shook his head dumbfoundedly.

'They can't do that! He hasn't done anything,' Jon said disbelievingly.

'Maybe not in Highgate,' Lisa said. 'They have different rules for people like us.' She sighed. 'The police are rattled. People are scared. They want to know what's being done. Everyone's pointing fingers and putting on pressure and the cops are rounding up the usual suspects.'

'They can't do that,' Jon said, more to himself.

Lisa dropped to her haunches and took Ralph's hand. 'Don't worry, we'll get him back. I'll go to the station now and badger them until I get some answers.'

'I'll come with you,' Jon said.

Lisa pulled him to one side. 'Best not, I think. They might put two and two together with the descriptions they've got.'

'But I want to help.'

She gave his hand a squeeze. 'I know you do. You stay here and keep Ralph company. He tends to get very emotional – you'll have your work cut out.' She gave Ralph a kiss, then set off down the road. Jon heard her mumbling to herself, 'Holy Mary, Mother of God, somebody's going to get a piece of my mind.'

The antiquarian bookshop was hidden down a tiny alley in an undistinguished section of Charing Cross Road. Despite its appearance, the owner, Rourke, was regarded as one of the most knowledgeable and successful dealers in the field, a fact which had been rammed down Jon's throat by Darren Wickes, a dealer who had fallen on the idea of rare editions and obscure publications in his constant search for lucrative investments. 'You don't have to read 'em, Jon, God forbid,' he had said. 'Just bang 'em in a vault and watch 'em appreciate. Best investment you'll ever make.'

The shop's picture window was hung with maps of the world, with only a few art books of the classics to hint at the breadth of its trade. An old-fashioned bell above the door jangled as Jon entered the overpowering atmosphere of paper, dust and age. The interior was gloomy, the wood of the counter, floor and bookcases too dark for the cramped space, the shelves crammed with uniformly leather-bound books.

Rourke emerged after a few seconds, trailing an aroma of fragrant pipe smoke. He was disproportionately short, like some character out of a Disney cartoon, but not a dwarf or a midget. His bald head fringed into straggly grey hair just above his neckline, continuing round into an Amish-style beard. He had a hook nose, and piercing grey eyes which sized Jon up in a flash.

'Can I help you?' Jon didn't recognize the faint accent.

'Jonathan Summers. I called—'

'Ah, yes. Do you have it with you?' Rourke tried to appear uninterested, but Jon caught the gleam of excitement in his eyes.

Jon opened his briefcase and pulled out the ledger they had found in Arcadia's cellar. After returning from Lisa's he had examined it closely, and in just three pages what he had seen had proved so disturbing he knew he couldn't continue reading until he was sure it was real.

Rourke took the ledger from Jon gingerly and laid it on the counter. 'You know this is ninety-nine per cent likely to be a forgery,' Rourke said. 'To find all those authors you mentioned on the phone writing in the same book is too unbelievable. A dream. Of course, it would be *nice* if it was true, but . . . a dream. I cross-referenced the details with the best biographies. There's no mention of Dickens or Barrie ever visiting this house you mention. Which doesn't mean it isn't true. But I've found over the years that wild coincidences are usually fabrications.'

Jon let him babble. What he had read suggested the

writers had been *drawn* to Arcadia by something more than a human impulse; it was no coincidence.

'Well, the paper and binding are certainly from the correct period,' the shop owner mused. 'Look here – you can see the watermark. However, that doesn't mean the rest of it isn't a forgery. There have been plenty of instances of skilful con men buying up old, unused ledgers, filling them with new work and trying to pass them off as the real thing. I will need to get the handwriting of the various authors checked by experts in the field. It will only take forty-eight hours. Twenty-four at a push. May I keep the book until then?'

'It doesn't leave my possession. I've photocopied selected pages.' Jon removed them from his briefcase and held them out.

'I really need the original material itself,' Rourke said hopefully.

'Sorry. This is the only way it can be done. Take it or leave it.'

Reluctantly, Rourke took the photocopies. 'You'll hear from me shortly. Even a forgery could be worth something, though obviously not as much as the true item. If it is real, the value would be – well, we can talk about that when we know for sure. And you found it by accident, you say?'

'I'm not too sure,' Jon said enigmatically.

On the way back to the tube, Jon felt sick with anticipation. If the book was a forgery he would be no closer to finding the answers he needed. But if it was real, he, and everyone else in the world, would never sleep peacefully again.

Culver had barely sat down at his desk before Miles dashed over.

'Forensics have been on the blower, boss. They've cleaned up the paper.'

'About bloody time,' Culver said sourly. He was still

smarting from the rough ride he'd been given by some tabloid reporter at that lunchtime's press conference. The media were hounding him for details of the notes and the ritual elements in the deaths, but he was refusing to release any information; it was too disturbing already. Coming on the back of breaking the details of Miles Heath's gruesome death to his family and dealing with Emma Rexe-Burke's shattered relatives, his nerves seemed permanently frazzled.

Heath's wife had been the worst. There had been that moment of blank shock he had witnessed so many times before; that was bad enough, but familiarity had made it easy for him to deal with it. But then a tremor had started deep within her, which finally erupted in an ear-piercing scream as she tore at her hair and then her clothes before flinging herself on the floor. The last time he had seen her she had been virtually comatose in shock, sedated, eyes staring, cut off from everything around her. The hardest thing was that Culver felt sure she wouldn't be the last to suffer.

'I went over Heath's autopsy report again,' Miles ventured.

Culver winced. 'Worst thing I'd seen in all my years on the force. Even worse than Whittington and that was bad enough. And what he did to that poor girl . . .'

'I can't understand how he managed to make so many cuts in that short space of time between South Quay and Tower Gateway. He must have been going some. I mean . . .' Miles' voice trailed off.

Culver caught his shudder before Miles saw it. He had played Heath's last journey over and over in his mind since seeing the body, and he still came to the conclusion that no one could have sliced him up so terribly, so quickly. The autopsy said there were hardly any bone nicks, so the killer hadn't been slashing wildly; every cut was precise and considered. This was no maniac who, though terrible, could be easily contained in the imagination. It suggested a cold intellect; someone with great skill and an inordinate amount of calmness through such a hideous act of butchery.

'How's the profiling gone, boss?'

Culver led the way from the incident room's gory array of photos to the comforting blandness of the corridor. 'I don't even want to think about that, Ryan.'

'No results?'

'Three different ones, and they all add up to some kind of monster.'

'You told us not to blow him up into something big, Charlie. He's just a man, remember?'

'Right.'

'No news on the prime suspect, then?'

'Come on, Ryan! You know the descriptions were so vague it could have been Charlton fucking Heston.'

Culver almost ran down the stairs, subconsciously trying to leave Miles and his questions behind. The whole business was making him sick to his stomach. It wasn't just the dispassionate hacking that turned a man into barely more than a skeleton in a matter of minutes, it was the little touches; the ritual laying out of the body; the missing tongue; the bloody note they found slipped into a slash in one of the seats. There was meaning he couldn't even begin to comprehend. Like looking on the work of God, he thought, then winced as the religious guilt kicked in. That should shuffle him a few more steps towards the door marked *aitch, ee, double-ell*.

Forensics was an oasis of calm compared to the chaos of the incident room. Culver sought out Simon Reid who was chatting amiably on the phone. He waited patiently for ten seconds, then talked at Reid rudely until the scientist hung up.

'You always want things yesterday, Charlie,' Reid said in his faint Scottish brogue. He went over to the overhead projector and switched it on. An image of the note was thrown up on the screen.

'We've cleaned it up, as you can see,' he said. 'It's torn out of some book. Good paper stock, fifty years old, maybe more.'

Culver read out the words quietly. ' "By all the unwritten laws of savage warfare it is always the redskin who attacks, and with the wiliness of his race he does it just before dawn, at which time he knows the courage of the whites to be at its lowest ebb." '

'What the fuck's that supposed to mean?' Miles said.

'We haven't identified the original text yet,' Reid noted. 'But unless it's completely obscure it's only a matter of time. It could be some cheap western novel, but the paper stock suggests a non-fiction account of the Wild West. The politically incorrect use of *redskin* and the qualities attributed to the race also suggest pre-1960s.'

'Yes, but what's he *getting* at?' Miles stressed. 'He left it behind for a reason. It must mean something.'

Culver rubbed the bridge of his nose thoughtfully as he read the text to himself again. 'It looks like he's identifying himself with the redskins, an outsider attacking an invading force.'

'The noble savage defending his heritage,' Reid elaborated. 'But there was nothing like this at the Whittington scene?'

'I had men back there going over the site again the moment we found this,' Culver replied. 'They couldn't find anything. But the snow and ice are making it doubly difficult to conduct any kind of detailed examination of the scene.'

Reid switched off the projector. 'What's the country coming to, eh?'

'The thing I don't like,' Culver said, turning to leave, 'is that use of the word *warfare*.'

' "But still I have to say, you play with matches, you get burned." '

'We don't have time for any of that bollocks, Jon. Focus on the matter at hand, for God's sake.' Richard glanced around nervously, but the lobby of One Canada Square was as deserted as they had expected at 10 p.m. 'Now you're sure you're all square with the plan?'

'You create a disturbance, I slip in, try to get a look at the report. Any problems, you call me on my mobile. I still think we're taking an unnecessary risk here, Richard. If either of us is caught we won't have a chance of getting out of this mess.'

'Knowing what's in the report is your only chance, old mate. You'd better make sure this works.' He pressed the button to call the lift. 'Here goes nothing.'

'And you're sure the keys will get me into Smallthorn's office and desk?'

'Yes.'

'How did you get hold of them?'

'Don't ask questions like that.'

'And the files are definitely there?'

'For the last time, I saw him put them in the desk before he left for the night.'

The doors opened and they stepped into the lift. 'You really are a shady character.'

'Yes. Lucky you.'

Jon pressed the button for the Steelguard floor for the first time in weeks and felt a corresponding stab in the pit of his stomach. If not for his desire to get the note from Emma's desk he wouldn't be there, however important Richard thought their mission was.

'I appreciate what you're doing,' Jon said. 'You don't have to take these risks for me.'

'Don't mention it.' Richard shifted uncomfortably. Since leaving the train his bonhomie had ebbed away. Now he looked uneasy and dangerous.

They watched the lights climb to their destination until finally Richard said, 'Ready?'

Jon nodded.

There was a ping and the door slid open. Richard had planned well; the angle made it impossible to see who was in the lift from the security desk. Jon kept his finger on the Door Open button while Richard pasted a smile on his face and strode out purposefully. Richard greeted the guard cheerily and asked if he could pick up the briefcase he had left with security earlier that day. Jon waited until he heard them go into the office at the back of reception, then slipped over to the main entrance. A swipe of Richard's keycard and he was inside.

The offices were in darkness, but the floodlights that washed the tower provided enough illumination to see. Above his head, the gold and silver Christmas decorations shimmered as he passed, their promise of human cheer incongruous in the sterile room.

Emma's desk sported its own miniature plastic Christmas tree which lit up in red when he accidentally brushed it. He was relieved to find her drawers weren't locked. Emma was a compulsive keeper of records and her desk was stuffed with neatly arranged pieces of paper. Jon flicked through them quickly, but there seemed nowhere she would obviously store the secret note, and it would take a good hour to go through each paper and file individually.

In frustration, he leaned back in her chair and tried to guess where she would have stored it. As he put his feet on the desk he triggered the motion sensor which lit the tree again. The fiery light illuminated the folded piece of paper on which the tree rested. Jon grinned; Emma had left her present under the tree.

He glanced hastily at the note to make sure and then slipped it into his pocket to examine later. He would have preferred to have left then, but as Richard had put his neck on the line he had to make an attempt on Smallthorn's office.

Like a ghost, he flitted among the silent work stations

until he located the room Richard said Smallthorn had been using; it was right at the end of the room allowing a vista across the entire floor. *So the supplicants would know the eyes of a wrathful god were upon them,* Jon thought.

The key worked as Richard had promised and Jon eased inside, leaving the door open behind him. Nervously he glanced at the digital clock glowing on Smallthorn's desk. How long could Richard keep the guard talking without the conversation becoming stilted? Ten minutes? Fifteen? At least talking was Richard's strong suit.

Jon unlocked Smallthorn's desk and opened the top drawer where Richard said he had seen him place the file. It was empty apart from some expenses forms and a box of staples. Jon yanked open the second drawer which was bare, as was the third. Only a blotter and the clock lay on top of the desk so Jon anxiously rifled the filing cabinet in the corner, but it only contained a few more expenses forms.

Before he could consider what had gone wrong, he heard the familiar creak of the swing doors into the main room. He dropped to his haunches and scurried across the room so he could close the door. Through the crack, he saw the guard playing his torch across the walls. Why hadn't Richard called him on his mobile, as they had planned? It would only have taken him a second to speed-dial a warning.

With his heart thumping, Jon grasped the handle and closed the door a millimetre at a time until it shut with the faintest click. Then he quickly crawled to a hiding place behind the desk.

The torchlight delved in and out of the office as the guard slowly made his progress around the premises. Jon could tell from the dull echoes of his footsteps that he was coming up the central aisle towards Smallthorn's office. As long as he didn't try the door, Jon would be safe. Cursing Richard, he held his breath and hunched down lower.

Suddenly his mobile phone buzzed into life. Jon scrabbled for it and punched the off-button, but by then it had already rung out twice more like a fire alarm in the still of the office. The footsteps had stopped, the torchlight slowly filtering into the room until it blazed a circle on the wall above Jon's head. He leaned back against the desk; he could almost hear the jail door closing.

As the footsteps started again, Jon winced at each thud on the floor. They came to a halt outside the office and the torchlight played around the interior. Hunched up in a foetal position, Jon prayed no part of him could be seen from outside.

Go away, he thought. *Go away, go away, go away.*

The handle creaked, then the door swung open and slammed against the wall. Jon gritted his teeth and waited.

A crackle of electricity echoed loudly from somewhere near the other end of the main room. Jon heard the guard whirl round. 'What the fucking hell was that!' the guard blurted.

Another loud crackle followed and then the guard was sprinting away from the office door. Jon seized the moment, rolling out from behind the desk and running into the main room, bent close to the floor. Pausing behind a work station, he saw the disturbance had been caused by a computer which was spraying blue sparks into the air while flashing on and off like a giant, blinking eye. Nervously, the guard hovered a few feet away wondering if it was about to explode. Jon shared his hesitation; there was no reason why it should act that way.

Explanations could wait. He began to crawl as quickly and silently as he could towards the door. Before he had gone more than a few feet, another computer burst into crackling blue life, and as he speeded up, another, and then another. He had the disturbing feeling the phenomenon was following him, or, bizarrely, that he was triggering it, but whatever, it was drawing the guard's attention in his direction. With his knees burning, he crawled as fast as he could towards the exit, halting at the very last moment when he heard the guard talking into his radio.

'This is Greg at Steelguard calling Tower Security. Over.'

'Go ahead, Greg. Over.'

'I think I've got an intruder on the premises. Can you send some assistance and make sure no one leaves the building? Over.'

'We'll send someone up in the lift and cover the stairs. Out.'

Jon felt instantly deflated; the only exits had been closed off. Miserably, he prised open the swing doors a few inches and slipped through quietly.

In reception, the illuminated switch showed the lift was climbing. As he spun round wildly, searching for an answer, he spotted the door behind the security post, and in the same thought, vaulted the desk and sprinted to it. It was open as he knew it would be. Inside was a tiny cubicle and a metal ladder he had climbed once before when a few of them had played a prank on the *Mirror* newspaper offices several floors below. As Steelguard occupied the top floor, it had access into the roof space used by maintenance. A few of them had used the window cleaners' gantry to lower a weighted banner down to the *Daily Mirror* newsroom which said, 'Socialists go home!' Jon hadn't agreed with the sentiment, but it was worth it to know the paper's management would be tearing their hair out over the message just beyond reach outside the window.

At the top of the ladder he found the switch for the strip lighting in that section. It was freezing cold and there was a smell of oil and charged air caused by the electrical equipment which throbbed relentlessly through the walls. He made his way quickly along the walkway, occasionally cracking his head against the numerous heating ducts crisscrossing the area.

At the door marked DANGER he paused as a tremor of

apprehension rippled through him. When he finally summoned the courage to yank it open, the buffeting, icy winds blasted him a step back. Ahead of him and far below, London lay ablaze with light, beneath the howl of the lofting gale that rang in his ears, promising more snow, more suffering.

Jon stepped on to the tiny balcony and gripped the rail tightly. His stomach pitched as he glimpsed the dizzying drop and then he screwed his eyes tight and considered for an instant giving himself up. He knew it wasn't an option, but it seemed favourable to what lay ahead.

In front of the balcony, the window cleaners' basket swung from side to side in the wind like a boat bobbing on the waves. The ominously creaking cables supporting it were as thick as his arm, but to Jon they seemed like cotton.

It took a tremendous effort to prise his white fingers off the rail and open the gate to reveal a three-inch gap between balcony and basket which yawned like a chasm. Jon stepped over it gingerly and placed one foot in the basket. It swung wildly and he flung himself to its floor, his heart pounding, ready for the drop. With his eyes shut tight, he lay paralysed at the bottom of the basket for five full minutes while it swung back and forth so much he felt nauseous, imagining the huge gulf a fraction of an inch beneath his face.

Eventually he found the strength to roll over and then on to his knees in front of the controls. He had seen the basket in operation enough times to understand the theory of how it worked: one button controlled the motor which moved the gantry arms along the top of the building, taking the basket from side to side; the other buttons raised and lowered the cable at each end of the basket to take it up and down.

Steadying himself against the swinging, Jon steeled his nerves, then pressed the buttons. The basket shot down ten feet in a second and Jon let go of the buttons frantically, slamming into the metal floor so hard he saw stars.

'A little less pressure,' he muttered.

Hauling himself up, he prepared to try again, until he noticed that after the brief fall the left-hand side of the basket was slightly raised. He would have to level it out for a smooth descent. Delicately, he touched the button and the left cable began to lower.

The huge gust came out of the blue from somewhere down the estuary, hurling the basket into the side of the building, and Jon on to the button. The left side went into free fall.

Jon had a fleeting instant of absolute terror and then his stomach flipped as he plummeted down. There was a brief sensation of the spinning lights of the tower, and then nothing until the pain of whiplash snapped through his body.

His fall had been halted by the sleeve of his leather jacket snagging on a hook where the window cleaners hung their tools. Kicking madly, he swung, suspended hundreds of feet above the ground with the basket nearly vertical. The shock almost made him pass out.

And the gale seemed to be worsening, hefting the basket forwards and smashing Jon into the tower. He felt a shift of resistance as the leather sleeve began to tear.

Fighting back the terror, he focused all his attention on the basket. His fingers were so cold he could barely feel them, but somehow he managed to curl them round to grip the wire mesh next to the tool hook. It took some of the pressure off his sleeve, but he knew he wouldn't have the strength to keep holding for long. Swinging his other arm up, he caught hold of the edge of the basket where he hung, trying to catch his breath in the face of the wind while fighting the urge to look down.

His arms felt as if they were being torn from their sockets, and he was glad he had made good use of the Steelguard corporate membership at the City gym, but he didn't know if he had any reserves of strength to pull himself up.

The wind howled louder, tearing at the basket which creaked and groaned under the strain. Jon forced his free arm a few more inches up the wire mesh and clung on once more. To progress, he would have to free his sleeve; then it would be only his arm muscles preventing the long fall into the water below. With a prayer, he drove his hand forward until the leather slipped off the hook.

The fiery pain in his arms began to turn to numbness. Jon realized he couldn't feel his fingers enough to know if they were gripping; they could slip free without him knowing.

Anxiously, Jon began to swing his legs back and forth. The basket rattled terrifyingly, but each upswing allowed him to push his arms further inside. There was a point where he didn't think he would be able to continue, but fear drove him to locate a reserve of determination he never knew he had. When his armpits reached the edge, he realized he could do it. Swinging his feet up, he used his toes to lever himself so his knee slipped over the edge and then he was able to haul himself in.

The basket was still thrashing around so much, Jon was afraid the cables would break. It was like some terrifying amusement park ride, with each second a battle against the fear that threatened to paralyse him. He wasn't aware of crawling up the inside of the basket, but suddenly he was near enough to the controls to reach up a hand and tease the right cable down.

And suddenly the fear was gone. The adrenaline rushed through his system so quickly he felt more vibrant than he ever had done on coke. He operated both release buttons instantly and dropped the basket at breakneck speed until he saw one of the inspection hatches that peppered the outside of the tower. He manoeuvred the basket in front of it and wrenched off the cover. Underneath was a mesh door with four flip-release locks. Jon snapped it open and wriggled inside.

It wasn't until he was ten feet into the tunnel that the shock hit him. For five minutes, he shook like he had a fever, huddling up and hugging his knees. At least it was warm with the hot air circulating through the system from the underfloor heating pipes. The tunnels were like a rabbit warren running through the building, just big enough for an engineer to crawl through with access to all the electrical and heating systems that kept the monster alive. They wouldn't be able to find him in there, and in the morning he could drop discreetly into one of the lavatories and slip out among the multitudes thronging in for work.

An ache had swallowed up the entire right side of his face. He guessed all the grimacing he had been doing had pulled at the stitches in his cheek wound. But eventually he drifted into a disturbed sleep which eased into a dream memory of his first Christmas in Arcadia. By noon the house had been full to bursting with relatives and friends of his parents who had travelled from all over the country. His job was to take the coats and pile them on his parents' bed, and he remembered giggling as the Everest of garments grew until it was way above his head.

The turkey was so big his father had had trouble forcing it into the oven, and there were some anxious moments in the kitchen during the morning, but when everyone was sitting round the table in Arcadia's refined dining room, all the strain had been worthwhile. For Jon that meal was a golden event. It was only as an adult he could comprehend his feelings that day; the security that came from being surrounded by people who at their heart were good and decent and cared for each other; the feeling of belonging.

After the Christmas pudding, his father made a speech which Jon had never forgotten. 'This world makes us lose sight of the important things in this life,' he said, with a faint slur from too much wine. 'Like ... what we do for others is more important than what we do for ourselves. Achievements in life are more important than achievements in work. And magic means more than money. There's magic here today, as there always is at Christmas, so I know we won't forget. Here's to the magic.'

When Jon woke as the dawn light eked into the tunnel, he felt sadness as the vibrancy of the dream slipped away. 'Here's to the magic,' he whispered.

Absently, he pulled from his pocket the note he had lifted from Emma's desk and laid it on the floor of the tunnel, rolling on to his stomach to examine it in the growing light. But the moment he laid eyes on the few scrawled lines, a chill ran through him. It was in his own hand, yet he knew he had not written the note. For five minutes, Jon wrestled with the questions it threw up and then put the note away, refusing to accept it as the final proof of the insanity he had sought to dismiss since the Scissorman's attack upon him.

Queasily, he watched the sun rise past the tunnel's opening and prayed for illumination.

'What the hell happened to you?' Confronted with Richard and Sarah drinking coffee together in Arcadia's kitchen, Jon couldn't control his anger.

'Jesus, Jon! Where have you been?' Richard jumped to his feet; Sarah seemed to be on the brink of bursting into tears.

'You're sitting here taking it easy while I could have been banged up in some police cell!'

'Jon, you know it's not like that—'

'Well that's what it looks like to me.'

'Don't blame Richard,' Sarah pleaded. 'He's been tearing himself apart about what could have happened to you.'

'So where was the warning then, Richard?' Jon seethed. 'When it did finally come, it was so late it actually told the guard where I was. I might as well have jumped up and waved to him.'

'God, I'm sorry, Jon. It's that bastard phone of mine. It's been playing up for days, but you know I checked it just before we went in. When the guard went on his rounds I couldn't get a blasted signal. Then suddenly I could. I had to do something to let you know.'

Jon shook his head and turned away.

Sarah came up behind him and put her arms around his waist. 'It was just bad luck, Jon. It could have been terrible, but it wasn't. You got out.' She kissed the back of his neck. 'How did you get out?'

'That's not important now.' Jon slipped free of her and turned back to Richard. 'The report wasn't even in the fucking desk. It was all for nothing. I thought you saw Smallthorn put it there.'

'I did.'

'Well, what happened?'

'I don't know,' Richard snapped. His neck and cheeks were flushed; Jon was pushing him too far.

'I know you're only trying to help me, but I've had enough of all these machinations. I'm going to fight Steelguard on my own terms, make my arguments with honesty and integrity.'

'Do you think that's wise?' Sarah ventured.

'It's the only way.'

'But—'

'No more, Sarah. My mind's made up.'

Sarah and Richard looked at each other. They said nothing, but their faces told the whole story; they didn't believe in him or his abilities; they thought he was doomed. And suddenly Jon felt totally and completely alone.

16

Although it was only 3 p.m., evening already appeared to be falling. London seemed to be in the grip of an omnipresent gloom that was leaching light from the city. Jon felt it most in the quiet streets away from the main drags, but there in Trafalgar Square it was held at bay, with the lights from the towering Christmas tree burning brightly and the Salvation Army choir singing 'Once in Royal David's City' with a life-affirming gusto.

He saw Lisa long before she saw him. She sat alone on a bench, a delicate figure wrapped in a too-large coat and scarf, watching Jamie and a friend play around the base of Nelson's Column. Jon felt the urge to watch her for a while, feeling the soft play of affection begin to build in him as the conflict rampaged through his mind. He couldn't deny it any longer; he had fallen in love with her. It was a thought that should have filled him with joy, yet it only made him feel sick. He loved Sarah. How could he love Lisa? The worst thing was, he knew Lisa felt the same way about him. It was there in the way she touched his arm or his shoulder unselfconsciously, in the movements of her body near him, and the way she held his eyes when they spoke. He guessed the sparks had been there from that first meeting in the Cross Keys, but he had subconsciously tried to deny it to himself. They had always been in tune; in hindsight, the result had never been in doubt. Rationally, he knew he should break off all contact with her; that was the only chance both of them had for salvation. But he couldn't do it. He was in a car with his foot to the floor and his arms pinned to his side. Only heartbreak lay ahead.

Eventually she saw him and waved. He hurried over, pretending he had only just arrived.

'You could have picked a warmer place to meet,' he said as lightly as he could muster.

'Jamie and his friend wanted to see the lights. Oxford Street was heaving and I needed a place to rest my poor old feet.'

'You're a sucker for punishment.'

'I don't mind the crowds really. It wouldn't be Christmas without a few people bumping into you. So how did your commando raid on your old office go?'

Jon told her the whole story and watched the dismay creep across her face.

After a few seconds filled with a long, deep sigh, she turned to him and there was thunder in her features. 'And you say this man's a friend of yours? How many friends leave you in the lurch like that?'

'What could he do? There's no point—'

'He ran off to save his own skin,' she said firmly, before giving him a sideways glance to size him up. 'You should know by now that I like to speak my mind, so I hope you won't take offence at what I'm going to say.'

'Go on.'

'What's your wife doing in all this? It seems to me like she's too concerned with herself and not enough with you.'

Jon was taken aback. 'I don't understand. Sarah's been behind me all the way.'

Lisa's eyes blazed. 'Well, if I was your wife I'd do things differently. When you came out of that clinic, I'd have taken time off from my own job so I could help you get back on your feet. That's a terrible thing to have to do on your own.'

'She couldn't leave her work like that. It's—'

'It's her company, isn't it? And I wouldn't be out galli-vanting on my own every night. I'd be spending my evenings with you, having fun together, helping you forget all that shit that got you down.'

'It's not as simple as that.'

'And I'd be at your side in all this trouble with your old bosses. Not just giving lip service. It drives me mad to hear what's going on.' She bit her lip, then looked at him. 'And if I was your wife you'd have told me about the Scissorman.'

There was a long silence while Jon looked slowly up the Christmas tree to the star at the top. Then he said tartly, 'Well, you're not my wife, are you?'

'No,' she replied. 'I'm not.'

The uncomfortable atmosphere remained between them for a few minutes while they watched Jamie and his friend play. Inexplicably, Jon felt a hard lump of emotion rise up in his throat.

Out of the corner of his eye he saw Lisa glance at him. 'I'm sorry. I overstepped the mark. I'm so wound up by everything that's happening . . .' Her voice trailed off when she saw no change in Jon's stony face, and she looked back at her son.

The words came to Jon's lips unbidden. '"I love your wide eyes, the way you smile, and your shyness, and the way you laugh at my jokes."'

After a long pause, Lisa said, '*Brief Encounter.*'

'I can't catch you out, can I?'

The choir slipped into 'Silent Night' and a hush seemed to descend on the crowds hurrying across the square. Almost absently, Jon slipped his hand into his pocket, pulled out a sheet of paper and handed it to Lisa.

'What's this?'

'The note I took from Emma's desk.'

'"Meet me at St Paul's Churchyard midnight tomorrow to hear some top secret information which you could use to your (financial) advantage. A friend."' She looked up incredulously. 'I wouldn't respond to a note like that. It could be from anyone!'

'Emma always kept her eye on the doughnut. The potential for gain was too attractive to turn down.'

'So does it give you any clues?'

Jon continued looking ahead impassively. 'I think it's my handwriting.'

Lisa's mouth gaped as she glanced back at the note. 'You think?'

'It could be a forgery, I suppose. It's printed, easy to do. But I'm ninety-nine per cent sure.'

'But you didn't write it?'

'I don't *remember* writing it. I was really coming to terms with the fact that all this stuff wasn't just a product of a crazy mind.' He broke off sharply.

'Jon, don't go down that road.'

'What can I do, Lisa?' he said passionately. 'I can't trust myself. There are two options and they both fill me with horror. Either I'm mad and the world is sane, or I'm sane and the world is unbearably crazy.' Jon bowed his head and massaged the back of his neck.

'Jon? Are you OK?'

Jamie was looking at Jon with his mother's wide, concerned eyes.

'I'm fine, Jamie. Are you having a good time?'

The boy nodded, still watching Jon strangely. 'Matt's worn out so we're having a rest. Are you coming for Christmas lunch?'

'I'd love to Jamie, but I've got my own family to be with.'

'You could bring them too.'

Jon smiled weakly, imagining Sarah in the Spitalfields flat. 'I'll call round on Christmas Eve with your present.'

'You're getting me a present?' Jon thought Jamie's eyes were going to burst from his head.

'If you look after your mum for me.'

'I will!' Jamie nodded eagerly, then turned and ran with a whoop.

'He likes you,' Lisa said.

'He always seems to be giving me the cold shoulder.'

Lisa laughed. 'He keeps it all inside. He's never known a dad so he's always drawn to any male presence in the house. But he's been badly disappointed in the past.'

'I'm deeply honoured.'

They watched the boys running around for a while until Lisa said, 'So what are you going to do?'

'Up in St Paul's I heard Emma shout something when the Scissorman was attacking her. I can't be sure . . . it's all hazy . . . but she seemed to know him.'

'How?'

'I don't know, but I've got to find out, Lisa. I've got to talk to her.'

'You're mad!' Lisa said, before she could stop herself. Sheepishly she continued, 'She's in intensive care and she's probably got a police guard. It's too risky.'

The choir and band decided to take a breather and suddenly the square seemed darker without the music.

'I have to find out for my own peace of mind,' Jon said quietly. 'Not trusting myself like this is hell.'

Lisa could tell from his face there was no point in arguing. She took his hand unselfconsciously. 'You take care,' she said. 'I have a very bad feeling about this.'

The first thing Jon saw in the dark of the house was the red light flashing on the answerphone. He guessed it was Sarah presaging another night out, so when he pressed the button and heard an excited male voice, he was thrown enough to miss the start of the message and had to rewind. It was the antiquarian book shop owner sounding like he'd just won the lottery.

'It's Mr Rourke here, Mr Summers. I've received the results of the handwriting tests I ordered on your book and they are very, very promising. Oh, let's not beat about the bush. It's quite remarkable. All the samples you gave me are bona fide, Mr Summers. No doubt about it. You have a quite wonderful item there, unique. I think I could negotiate a *very* lucrative deal with a private collector on your behalf, for a small commission, of course. Please call me back as soon as you get in, it doesn't matter how late, and we can discuss the way forward.'

Rourke's voice echoed in the still hall as the tape rewound. Jon stood there for a full five minutes, letting the implications of the message sink in, and then he bounded up the stairs two steps at a time. He was almost afraid to remove the ledger from his drawer; the weight of what he guessed it contained was too much. The answers he sought to all the problems that assailed him, the truth – and fears and horrors undreamed of.

The vodka bottle had long been emptied and Wendy had slipped gratefully into her nightly stupor in the house next to Arcadia. She normally slept until dawn, in her chair in front of the gas fire, secure in the knowledge that the alcohol had destroyed her ability to dream, or at least her memory of dreams. Yet that night she woke early, at midnight, as the carriage clock on the mantelpiece chimed the hours. She shivered despite the fire's heat, checked the bottle for dregs, then realized she was still drunk.

But not enough, she thought. The nap had taken the edge off it and she could feel the uncomfortable notions already wriggling in the back of her head. Why had the system failed her? she wondered, with the faint desperation that came from knowing there was no more booze in the house.

Clutching and kneading her bony fingers, she heaved herself to her feet and lurched around the room.

Don't do it, she thought. *For God's sake let it lie.*

She resisted the powerful forces tugging at her for almost three minutes, a major success, but then her resolve caved in, like a card house crumpling in a sudden breeze. Her breath clouded as she stepped into the chill hall and scurried towards the kitchen.

There was a sense of dread as she opened the back door a crack and slipped into the garden, making sure to keep close enough to bolt back if necessary. Steeling herself with a sharp intake of cold air, she turned and looked up at the damnable residence next door.

At first all she could see was its looming bulk black against the clear, star-speckled sky, and that irritated her because she *knew* it had called to her. But then her subtle senses took over and the jarring signs made themselves evident.

From the garden there came a sound like telegraph wires singing in the wind, yet the timbre and rhythm changed constantly in the patterns of speech or song. A twinkle of light like a golden firefly darted among the stark branches before swooping down behind the fence. There was a snort and whinny of a horse, and then came the voices Wendy had heard many times over the years, not human, rumbling so deeply they were barely audible to human range; in them she heard something so malign she almost dropped to her knees in dread.

The spirits were more active than Wendy had ever heard them. It frightened her, made her wonder *what* had disturbed them.

Something, she thought coldly, *is going to happen.*

Obliquely, she wondered if she should warn the young couple living in there, but it seemed a futile act; no one ever believed her. The batty old woman at number twenty-one; she had long since given up trying to change her neighbours' perception of her.

Her thoughts were disturbed by a scrambling noise between the two houses. Anxiously, she pressed herself back against the wall and held her breath. In the light of the moon she saw a young man with a scarf wrapped across his mouth heave himself over the entry door and drop to his haunches on the other side of the fence. Someone was trying to break in.

Rather than call the police, Wendy's first thought was to warn the intruder, who had no idea of what lay ahead. She wanted to scream out for him to run away, but she was so afraid for herself, all that came out was a choked whisper. She knew instantly that she had doomed him and her eyes filled with tears of self-disgust.

The burglar made no sound, but Wendy could picture his every movement: he was creeping along to the end of the house; he was in the back garden; now he was approaching the rear windows.

The night was filled with a sound like a long-closed door slowly opening with a protest of rusted hinges. Wendy heard the burglar start to shout, but his cry was choked off before an intense light flared into the sky and disappeared in the twinkling of an eye.

Wendy could contain herself no longer. She ran forward and threw herself at the fence to peer over.

The garden was empty. In the spot where the flare had originated, there was a slight shimmering in the air which disappeared like mist before her eyes.

The despairing sobs racked her body in an instant, and that seemed to trigger a response.

From the other garden came a child's voice filled with a nerve-jangling horror, screaming, 'No! No! No! No! NO!'

'When are you coming home?'

Culver felt a pang of guilt at his wife's understanding tone; she had every right to be furious. He checked his watch and mouthed a curse while switching the phone to his other ear.

'Soon, love. I've just been sifting through the calls that came in on the hotline. The usual mixture of nuts and vague, so-called sightings, but I've got to check everything just in case.'

He wished he was back at home with her, with a glass of wine in front of the TV. Sometimes, when he accidentally caught sight of the autopsy photos, he thought he'd been spoiled for home for good, tainted so much by the sheer horror that he would never again be able to mix with normal people.

'Charlie?' There was a note in her voice he didn't like.

'What is it, love?'

'I've heard some things about these murders.'

'What kind of things?'

'What's done to the bodies. I wanted to know if it's true. If it's as bad—'

'I don't really want to talk about it now, Shirley.' He felt suddenly sick that she even had an inkling of what had happened. He couldn't pretend to her the terrible things he saw in the world didn't exist, but he knew he had to protect her from the worst horrors; he couldn't bear it if she became tainted too. 'There are a lot of rumours flying around at the moment. It doesn't pay to give too much heed to all the wild talk.'

'How's that poor girl?'

Culver sighed; why wouldn't she let it drop? 'To be honest, Shirl, she's in a bad way, but the docs reckon there's a chance she'll pull through. We're guarding the hospital just in case the nut gets it into his head to go back and finish the job.'

'Charlie?'

'Yes?'

'You take care.'

'I'll be home soon, love.'

Culver replaced the receiver before rubbing his tired eyes to try to dispel the thoughts suspended like lung shadows on an X-ray. He wasn't the only one unusually disturbed by the killings. Shock waves seemed to have rippled out across the country, touching everyone. The lunatics were out in force, howling at the moon; eight people had already confessed to the killings, way above average; three in London, one in Manchester, others in Norwich, Glasgow, Leeds and one from some hayseed village in the Lake District. There'd been a spate of attempted copycats, although luckily nobody had been badly hurt. Someone went wild with a pair of scissors in a shopping centre in Tyneside. Knife crimes generally were up thirty per cent.

Even *regular* people had been touched by it. The Samaritans had been forced to take on more volunteers to help their increasingly overworked operators. Churches were reporting rising congregations. Some middle-manager from Bridlington had given up a well-paid job to move his entire family to a croft in the Scottish Highlands because he thought it was the only way to keep them safe. The papers were filled with edgy discussions about the malaise that was gripping society, the words apocalyptic in flavour, far beyond the response one would expect to two murders, however brutal and inhuman.

Culver couldn't put his finger on what it was, but he felt it himself like subsonic rumblings; it made him sick to his stomach. He didn't dare think where it was all going.

Miles wandered in and slumped behind his desk, whistling off-key. Culver watched him for a moment, then asked, 'Why do you want to do this job, Ryan?'

Miles gave him the kind of look that suggested the young detective thought he had suddenly gone senile. 'Keeps me in beer and pizzas.'

'I'm serious, Ryan. We both know there are plenty of other jobs that pay more. Yet you choose to come in here and look at the kind of things we've seen over the last few days, and think the kind of thoughts that causes.'

Ryan's sigh suggested a weary acceptance that he couldn't get out of the conversation. 'It's *because* I see those things.

Somebody's got to try to stop them happening and I know I can help.'

'You really think you can make a difference?'

''Course.'

'That's a bit idealistic for a copper, isn't it?'

Miles shrugged. 'That's what I think.'

The phone rang and Miles snatched it up as a respite from Culver's ramblings. Culver smiled sadly and glanced around at the darkened incident room. Anita was still working away in the corner, her desk lamp illuminating a pile of files. She had a thankless task, Culver thought, establishing all the connections among the victims. Like most closed environments, people in the City knew each other almost incestuously, working together, playing together, sleeping together.

The obvious links suggested the killer came from the same world. But what kind of City bod would have the surgical knowledge necessary to perform the exquisite butchery evident in these murders? And could someone intelligent and sophisticated enough to work in the City really have another side so monstrous they could commit such atrocities? That last thought made his stomach shift queasily.

He glanced back at Miles, hoping for some lighter thoughts, but the expression on his colleague's face only added to his uneasiness. With a growing hollowness Culver kept his eyes on Miles as he listened intently to what the caller was telling him; a muscle beneath his right eye was taut, the slackness gone from his shoulders.

Miles replaced the receiver, but Culver heard the words before they were uttered.

'There's been another one.'

Arcadia was quiet and tranquil. With an almost ritual reverence, he removed the silver mirror from its hiding place in his drawer and wrapped it lovingly. Then he took the fountain pen his father had given him when he started work, and wrote on the gift card, *To Sarah, with all my heart, Jon.*

Before he left the bedroom, he found one of Sarah's old lipsticks and inscribed on the dressing-table mirror: *Love crosses all boundaries*, as if the act would eradicate any feelings he had for Lisa. Then he slipped downstairs, laid the present carefully under the tree and left the house with a whispered prayer that he would return to see Sarah unwrap her gift on Christmas Day.

'Jesus, Mary and Joseph, Jon, do you know what time it is?'

Jon looked up to see Lisa hanging out of the window. He'd been banging on the front door for ten minutes. It was bitterly cold and the snow had started again in force, but he had been determined not to give up. She let him in a minute later, wrapped in an old terry towelling robe, her hair sleep-tousled around her face. Despite everything, his first thought was how appealing she looked, but he dismissed the notion immediately.

'I'm sorry, but you said call round anytime,' he said as they climbed the stairs.

'Any *reasonable* time.'

'This is important.'

She stopped and glanced back at him curiously before leading him into her flat. Jon sat on the sofa with the ledger in his lap while she closed the bedroom door so they wouldn't disturb Jamie. When she curled up on the sofa next to him, Jon had a flash of creamy-brown thigh before she pulled her robe over her legs.

She yawned and said, 'This had better be good.'

'The book checked out,' he said. 'The authors' handwriting is genuine.'

'I'm still waiting to be impressed.'

Jon flicked open the cover, desperately trying to put into

words exactly what he had read during the last few hours. 'There's something special about Arcadia,' he began. 'I always thought it was just me, my memories of the place, all my emotions and beliefs tied up in what I felt during those three great years I spent there as a kid. I always believed it was somewhere magical.' He tapped the book for emphasis. 'But these writers felt the same way.'

'It is magical. I expect the garden looks great in summer, and those big, old rooms—'

'It's more than that. The names in here read like a *Who's Who* of Victorian literature. Dickens, Stevenson, Barrie, Carroll, Collins, others I barely know. And they all spent some time at Arcadia during their lives. Sometimes just a day, others stayed for a week or more. They were all drawn there.'

'By what?'

Jon flicked backwards and forwards until he found the right page. Then he began to read. '"This damnable house has crawled under my skin. On several occasions I found myself diverting the carriage from its intended journey into town, just so I could pass by its door. Sometimes I would ask the driver to pause awhile so I could climb out to spend some moments surveying its façade. Each driver must have thought me consumed by some strange mental obsession, for it is an unremarkable residence by anyone's tastes and certainly not worthy of the attention I was lavishing upon it. Indeed, if they had asked me of my interest I would not have been able to explain it myself. My actions concerned me so greatly that on every journey I attempted to withhold my interest, but I always found myself outside the house.

'"Two weeks ago, I could contain myself no longer and I enquired of the owner. I discovered the house was empty – for rent, in fact. The letters required only a few pounds, which I considered a small price to pay to satiate my curiosity, and so I took rent of heaven – Arcadia – for a weekend, and told my family and friends I was seeking isolation to dream up a new idea for my writing."' Jon moistened his lips. 'Arthur Conan Doyle.'

Lisa shrugged, still unimpressed.

'That story is repeated by all the writers, in one form or another. They felt that something was calling them. That they *had* to spend some time in Arcadia.'

Lisa's eyes narrowed. 'What are you getting at?'

Jon smiled and opened the book again. ' "The days I have spent in Arcadia have been quite delightful. I almost feel like a child again, which is quite remarkable when one considers how many years separate me from that golden age. The nights, though. Ah, the nights! Sometimes I fear for myself. Last night I dreamed of the flying boy again. He was cruel, as all children are, and he told me the most terrible things. I wish I could not remember them. I say 'dreams', but that is not how it is. Those who have written before me are correct. In Arcadia, dreams are something more – a medium of communication between here and there." J. M. Barrie.'

Lisa looked puzzled; her interest had been piqued. 'He dreamed of a flying boy. Is this before he wrote *Peter Pan*?' Then, 'What does he mean by a *medium of communication*?'

Jon could see Lisa going through the same process he had experienced when he first read the book. Bewilderment was only the start.

'Are they writing these things in all seriousness?' she continued.

Jon nodded.

'Because it could be some kind of game. Each writer continuing . . .'

He shook his head emphatically. 'Imagine if every supernatural thing we're frightened of, every wild, terrifying fantasy, was real.' Jon looked deeply into her eyes, not wishing to scare her, knowing there was no alternative. 'All these writers were drawn to Arcadia by some strange force.

An empathy, if you will. They felt in tune with whatever was happening there. Maybe their imaginations made them more open to it, I don't know. But while they were there they all had strange dreams which coloured the books they subsequently wrote. Some of them even saw or heard things while awake around the house and garden.'

'What kind of things?'

'Do you want to know where *The Hound of the Baskervilles* came from? Dickens' ghosts? The Queen of Hearts screaming, "Off with their heads!"'

'Dreams?' Her bewilderment was turning to something darker.

'Listen to this.' Jon opened the book to a page marked by the old newspaper clipping. '"My time in Arcadia has been one of transformation. I am not the same fellow who stepped through its claret door on that cold winter day two weeks ago, replete in the knowledge that I had served my apprenticeship to Life. Oh, how foolish I was then! To say I am a wiser man now is certainly true. A better one, debatable. A more fearful one, certainly. Arcadia, in its infinite glory, has shown me wonders aplenty, yet it has also cast a pall over the remainder of my short, weary life."'

Jon paused to moisten his lips; Lisa was rapt. There was a stillness in the air, as if the entire house was listening.

'Who's writing?' Lisa asked.

'Dickens.'

She nodded, looked at the window to check the curtains were closed.

Jon moved ahead a few paragraphs. '"There is no longer any doubt the following is true: there is another world as diverse from ours as hell from heaven. It impacts upon our own at certain points, sensitive, fluid spots where existence is not fast, and which allow carriage between the two. This house, Arcadia, is one of those loose fields, and it has allowed me to peek through that dark doorway on four occasions. I can barely lay down what I have seen for fear of my hand trembling so much my writing becomes unreadable!

' "This world next to ours is filled with creatures so unimaginably terrible we can barely describe them with reference to the frame of our own poor existence. The best we can do is mould them into kinder shapes, to say they are 'like this' or 'like that', but never truly to say 'they are', for that would be too much for our poor minds to comprehend. These creatures are, I believe, the source of all our deepest fears from the time when we first stepped out of Eden. The bogles, spectres, ghouls, fairies, little people, fauns and satyrs of our myths and fairy tales. It is my assumption that poor folk witnessed them passing between worlds on dark nights and wove fantastic tales to transmit to their family and friends the true terror of their experience. More, it is my belief that these creatures have an abiding interest in our own realm. During my first glimpse through the portal, I witnessed ghastly, suffering people in dress not seen for a hundred years or more, prisoners, I aver, of these creatures who snatched them from their hearths to torment them for all eternity. I recently attended a meeting of a group which aims to cure society's ills, and part of the discussion concerned the vast number of common folk who simply disappear each year as if they had fallen through the cracks in the pavement. The talk was of those poor individuals being the victims of crime or spirited away by unscrupulous traders to foreign climes; but what if the missing had been pulled through to this other place, like those unfortunates who were lured into the mounds of the little folk in the fairy tales of our youth?" '

Jon took a deep breath. In the bedroom, Jamie stirred and called out from the depths of a nightmare.

'Dickens saw things in Arcadia which changed his life,' Jon continued. 'There's a biography of him on the shelves in the study and it talks about the dark aspect that came over him in the latter stages of his life, yet he never spoke about why he changed.'

'It's so hard to accept.' Lisa chewed on a knuckle anxiously. 'It's like some elaborate game.'

'All the writers were aware of what was written in the book before them, and they all come to the same conclusion while adding anecdotes of their own. They all talk about doors opening or ... here in Dickens ... "the creak of hidden doors". Dickens himself saw something which he used in toned-down form as the basis for the Ghost of Christmas Present.' Jon shuddered at the memory of his dream that was not a dream. 'I saw it too.'

'But what is this *other place* that Dickens talks about?'

'Wonderland. Neverland. Narnia. Faerie. Another dimension. A spiritual realm.' Jon shrugged. 'The source of all myth. It's a world slightly out of sync with ours, but at certain points you can cross over. And vice versa.'

'And these things ... ?'

'So alien, so utterly incomprehensible that our own minds have to give them shape to understand them.'

'You say.'

'Several of these writers say. Lisa, do you know how many people go missing from their homes each year? Thousands. From all walks of life, from all parts of the country. Happy, contented people as well as depressed, suicidal ones. They occasionally make little snippets in the local paper, but nobody stands back and sees the big picture.'

'And they're all being dragged through to this other place? Why?'

'Food. Sport. Who knows? Imagine ... you could be heading to the launderette or coming back from the pub on your own and a door opens in space. Whoosh! You're gone. No reason for it apart from you being in the wrong place at the wrong time, and nobody the wiser.'

'That's horrible. Why didn't all these writers talk about what they believed?'

'Well, would you? I know exactly what happens to people who give a view outside the accepted wisdom. In a way, though, they did try to warn people, through coded messages in their books and short stories.'

Jamie called out again and Lisa jumped.

'We see them in our dreams,' Jon continued. 'And if we're very unlucky, we meet them in our waking lives.'

Lisa stood up and paced across the room, hugging herself tightly. 'And the Scissorman is one of them.'

'For some reason, I was the catalyst. My return to Arcadia allowed it to slip through into our world. And now it's roaming the city doing the kind of things that it does to people in its own place.'

'You make it sound like an accident. You don't think there could be a *reason* why he's out?'

'Like what?'

'I don't know.'

'Now I feel it's even more urgent to find out what Emma saw. I have to get into the hospital to see her. If she can give us something that could help track it down . . .' He took a deep breath. 'The answer must be to try to find a way to send it back before any more lives are lost. But how do we do that?'

Lisa glanced at Jon and then at the bedroom door, an arctic coldness creeping through her body.

'You seem remarkably upbeat about discovering we're all at risk of a hideous fate every second of our lives.'

At her words, Jon seemed to catch himself. 'I'm sorry. It's not really like that. The first time I read through the book the implications of it terrified me: we think we know all about our world, but we don't know *anything*. But what I've been through made it easier for me to cope with that. Despite it all, I felt a real . . . I don't know, calmness, to discover I wasn't crazy. All the things that have been troubling me can be explained by this.' He tapped the book.

'You don't think you're being too . . .'

'Gullible?'

She shrugged. 'Because of our circumstances, it's easier to think . . .' She swallowed her words and left an uncomfortable silence.

Jon didn't seem unduly concerned by the implications of her unspoken thought. He handed her the book. 'Read it, then try telling me it's a fantasy.'

Lisa went to take it, then drew back her hand. 'Now what?' she asked reluctantly.

Culver stamped through the thickening snow to the nexus of the activity. Big, white flakes drifted down, giving the impression of a dream, but Culver only had to glance at the pooling stain across the white pavement to see the reality. Reid from forensics was already at the heart of the chaos, freshly scrubbed, but his eyes were still heavy with sleep.

'What have we got?' Culver didn't even glance at the body.

The rotating lights of the patrol cars turned Reid's face into a fluid mass of shadows and colours. 'White male, early twenties. Same pattern of incisions, some deep, some minor, all precise. Right hand and lower left leg almost severed. Rib cage pulled apart.'

'Any idea what's missing?'

'Can't tell at first glance. It's impossible to do anything in these conditions.'

Culver nodded and turned to DI Anscomb who was waiting patiently with his notebook out. 'Did we get an ID?'

'He still had his wallet. No signs of any robbery,' Anscomb said. 'His driving licence says Gary Finch of Brentwood, Essex. There was a security swipe card for Steelguard.'

'Emma Rexe-Burke's company,' Culver noted. 'Two from the same place. We're getting closer to him.' He glanced up and down the plush Highgate street at the big Victorian houses. 'Any witnesses yet? The neighbours must have heard something with this kind of butchery on the doorstep.'

'Nothing so far, Guv'nor, and we've knocked up the nearest ten houses on either side. Regular, quiet night, they say.'

'You're joking!'

'The killer could have subdued the victim from behind with this incision here,' Reid said. Culver forced himself to look down at the steaming corpse for the first time. Reid was pointing to a deep gash that had severed the windpipe. 'The angle and severity of the cut would have disabled the victim and prevented him calling out.'

'Still warm,' Culver noted. 'When did it happen?'

'Within the hour,' Reid said.

Anscomb chipped in before Culver could question him. 'It's already gone out, Guv'nor. We've got three cars in the immediate vicinity and everyone else has been alerted. I called for the chopper, but they can't take it out in this weather. Still, with all this blood they shouldn't have any trouble spotting him against the snow.'

'Unless he went home to change.' Culver looked back at the looming, old houses. 'If Finch is from Brentwood, what's he doing round here? Girlfriend?'

'We'll check it out, Guv'nor.'

As Anscomb turned away, Miles trudged up muttering something about the cold. 'The weather centre says we're going to have snow right through Christmas.'

'Bad news for the bookies,' Reid said wryly.

Culver cursed. 'Get a tent in, Ryan. We'll bung in some heaters and thaw the scene out. I don't fucking believe this weather.' He looked down at the corpse again. 'There's not going to be much Christmas cheer for this poor bastard's family.' Culver felt sick at the thought of relating the brutal details of the death to more grieving relatives; the despair that came off them was like a poison; it was all becoming too much. 'You know, I used to worry about getting numb to all the human suffering,' he said softly.

'I know what you mean. It's dehumanizing to see it on a daily basis,' Reid replied.

'But somewhere down the line, events turned a corner. Every day seemed to have something worse and it was coming at me like shit off a shovel so I didn't have a chance to get numb. Is it just me?'

Reid hunched his shoulders against the wind. 'It's been getting worse since the eighties. The things people do to each other now, you'd never have seen in the past. There's no personal responsibility, no discipline, no respect.'

'Every man for himself.'

'Sometimes I think the way society's breaking up faster and faster, it's a sign we're all rushing towards the apocalypse.' He shivered. 'So much for the age of reason.'

'You sound like two old men at a funeral,' Miles said sourly. ' "It was all fields round here when I was a lad." '

'Fuck off, Ryan.'

'Over here!' The cry went up from one of the forensics team who was examining an ornamental hedge bordering the pavement next to the body.

'What is it?' Reid called out.

'Found something. Take a look.'

His latex-gloved hand held up a tiny bag containing a wad of paper.

Culver smiled. 'Good work.'

'It was buried in the soil under the hedge. I spotted the mound. It was the only patch not frozen.' He grinned proudly.

'He's still talking to us then,' Reid said. 'Looks like it's cut from the same book.'

Culver read it aloud: ' "The unexplored patches arose in

it and spread; black shadows moved about in them; the roar of the beasts of prey was quite different now, and above all, you lost the certainty that you would win. You were quite glad that the nightlights were in."'

There was a yawning moment of silence as Culver's voice trailed away and then it was filled by the shriek of the wind rushing between the houses.

'I thought we were looking for a western?' Miles said. 'That's no Zane Grey.'

Culver turned to Reid. 'Like to comment on his state of mind?'

Reid chewed his lip for a second. 'Why couldn't it have been someone stupid?'

'You think they're easier to catch?'

'No, because then you can believe they're not someone like you.'

Culver looked at Miles. 'Here's a longshot. Get on to Steelguard first thing. Find out if any of their other employees live in this area. Maybe our man Finch was on his way to see the killer.'

Miles grumbled under his breath as he walked away.

'I said it was a longshot, Ryan,' Culver called after him.

Reid brushed away the snow that was frosting his brow. 'You used to pray for weather like this when you were a kid.'

'Then you grow up and find out it's God's way of punishing you.'

'You're an old cynic, Culver.'

'Realist.' He shivered with a cold that seemed to go deep into his bones. 'It's a tough month, December,' he said, pulling his collar up. 'Thank God for Christmas.'

After Jon left for the hospital, Lisa tried to get back to sleep but the things he had told her charged around in her head mercilessly. She would pause suddenly as she moved about the flat. Was that the sound of a door opening? In the glint of light from polished surfaces she would see twin blades raised high, ready to plunge. But most of all she thought of Jamie and his role in the unfolding events. She couldn't help but check on him sleeping every hour, which became every half-hour, every ten minutes. As time passed, her resolve gelled: come morning she would make arrangements for him to go on holiday for a few days, perhaps with her aunt in Poole, somewhere far away. She could easily join them for Christmas Day. The best thing would have been for her to go with him, but she couldn't abandon Jon; her heart wouldn't let her.

During her aimless roaming, the book lay where Jon had left it, like a body before a wake. She glanced at it each time she passed, but couldn't face up to the thoughts and emotions it conjured. But as the night wore on, she slowly came to realize she would not be able to put it behind her or learn to deal with it until she took a peek.

She was, she admitted to herself, a little afraid; Jon had hinted at things in there even darker than what he had expressed. At present, she was detached enough from the information to fan the small doubt she maintained and keep herself warm. To read the book would give her no hope of an escape.

Reluctantly, she dropped on to the sofa, stared at it for a moment, then opened it to the page Jon had marked where Dickens' writings began. His spidery style was difficult to decipher at first, but she gradually became accustomed to its flourishes and soon she was reading easily.

When she reached the end, she stared at Dickens' signature in puzzlement for a while, then returned to the beginning of the entry and scanned it again just to be sure. Finally, she flicked through the pages trying to find another entry by Dickens. In vain, she returned to her starting point.

The section began: '"I wish to express my admiration and pleasure at the fine surroundings in which I find myself, and which have proved such an inspiration to both myself and my work."' The entry continued with Dickens holding forth on the fine atmosphere in Arcadia and remarking on what a wonderful place it was to stay.

There was no mention of any *other place*. No *creatures so unimaginably terrible*. Nothing that Jon had read out.

Anxiously, she checked the other entries. Conan Doyle's piece was similarly bland. There was no sign of anything by Barrie.

Lisa closed the book and laid it back on the sofa with a hollow feeling she thought would consume her.

'Oh, Jon,' she whispered.

The London Hospital in Whitechapel had been around for more than two hundred years, hanging on like a stubborn old man despite numerous politicians' attempts to turn off the financial machine. Jon approached it cautiously through the howling blizzard, warmed by his new found equilibrium that, despite everything, all was right in *his* world. The walk from Lisa's flat through the back streets of Spitalfields was short, though the snow had made it hard-going. It would have been easier to take a cab, but Jon didn't want to risk any questions about what he was doing visiting the hospital at that time of night.

A lone security guard sat behind the reception desk, but the area was too well-lit; there was little chance of sneaking by. He considered going through Accident and Emergency, but thought it wiser to avoid any place where there would be too many people. After minutes of prowling around the big old building, he found a door that looked promising and slipped into the maze of starkly lit corridors.

He wished he had some kind of plan, but the compulsion that drove him wouldn't allow him to pause. Taking the stairs to the first floor, he spotted a sister vacating her office to go about her rounds. When he was sure she wasn't returning, he darted inside, put the phone on the floor behind the desk and dialled zero. The switchboard operator answered.

'It's Detective Inspector Carlyle here,' he said confidently. 'I'm supposed to be relieving the officer guarding our high security patient. 'You know the one?'

''Course I do.'

'It's my first night and I've managed to get myself lost. The sister let me use her phone to call you for directions while she did her rounds.'

'I'm surprised the sister couldn't have told you herself. Everybody in the hospital knows . . .'

'She was in a rush.'

'Where are you?'

Jon told her while peeking over the top of the desk to check for any sign of the sister returning.

'Take the lift to the top floor, then follow the corridor right round to the back of the building. You'll see your man there.'

'Thanks.'

'You any closer to catching the nutter who did it?'

'We're getting closer all the time.'

Jon replaced the phone on the desk and eased out along the wall to the stairs where he relaxed a little. He checked his watch. 3.30 a.m. Anyone who stumbled across him wandering around the hospital at that time would be bound to challenge him. He could talk his way out of it – if there was anything the City had taught him it was how to lie effectively – but it would kill off any chance he had of getting to see Emma.

Anxiously, he ticked off the seconds waiting for the lift to come, then launched himself inside the moment the doors opened. But before they had a chance to close again, he heard a sound echoing around the stairwell that made his blood turn cold. It was the sound of metal scraping along a surface, like fingernails on a blackboard, mundane to anyone who had not heard it before – perhaps a porter dragging a trolley along a wall – but Jon recognized it instantly as the signature of a quick, brutal death.

He pressed the button to hold the doors open and hung out, listening, but the echoes made it impossible to tell where the sound had come from. With his heart pounding in his ears, he punched the button for the top floor.

There was an eternity of creaking cables and between-floor shudders as Jon held his breath, hoping that no one else would get in. When it finally reached its destination, he jumped out, ran to the stairwell and peered over the railing.

At first he saw nothing, but then a faint, fleeting movement caught his eye like a shaft of light reflected off a closing door. It was below him, and it was coming up.

He ran to the corridor and pushed through the swing doors. *I'm not going to let him finish the job*, he thought, but the notion was instantly wiped away by a more disturbing one: why was the Scissorman there, at that particular moment, when Jon was in the hospital? It was too much of a coincidence, but he couldn't think of anything that would explain it. Unless, of course, the Scissorman was coming after him. Hadn't Lisa said Velikovsky had warned that anyone who opposed the Scissorman became a target themselves?

As Jon hurried along the corridor, he was relieved to see they had isolated Emma away from the other patients. The rooms on either side seemed to be offices, out of use or for storage. It would minimize the chance of him being discovered before he reached her room. It also meant if the Scissorman did appear there would be no one to help him.

The thought had barely passed through his mind when he heard a burst of static and an urgent voice shouting into a radio from where the corridor took a turn to the left. He selected a room at random and threw himself inside. It was filled with medical supplies in boxes stacked from floor to ceiling. Jon pressed his ear against the door as two sets of feet sprinted down the corridor outside. As they passed, Jon heard one of them say, 'Highgate? Fucking hell, he's moving up in the world.'

As he waited for the footsteps to die away, he noticed the green of crisp new surgeon's gowns in one of the open boxes. At the same time he recalled one of the sayings bandied around the dealing room: *Big lies work best*.

All the time listening for any warning sound, he unfolded one of the gowns and put it on, located a surgeon's elasticated hat in one of the other boxes, then found a face mask and hung it loosely round his neck. If the balloon went up, there would be no going back after he had showed his face, but it was a risk he was prepared to take.

Psyching himself up to play the role, he stepped back into the corridor only to find it transformed. Ivy trailed across the walls and ceiling, while wildly flourishing sprigs of holly and mistletoe sprouted above his head. At the bend in the corridor, pressed into the crook where the two walls met, sat the elfin-faced boy from his dream. He was giggling quietly, with his knees tucked under his chin and his arms wrapped around his legs.

'He's com-ing,' he mocked in a sing-song voice.

Jon glanced back towards the stairwell. Through the glass in the doors he saw the light fizzing on and off, punctuated by bursts of blue sparks. A darkness seemed to be creeping upwards from the floor below like a veil being drawn over the scene.

Jon turned and ran, ignoring the whoops and giggles of the boy. But as Jon passed him, his hand snaked out and caught hold of Jon's trouser leg.

'He comes for *you* on Christmas Day,' he said with a grin that turned to a grimace.

Jon pulled himself free and ran on. Behind him, the boy called out, 'Blood and punishment, hearts reach out.'

Near the end of the stretch of corridor, Jon glanced back. The boy and the greenery were gone. As he watched, the light grew dimmer and tongues of shadow seemed to lick out hungrily from around the corner. Jon didn't wait to see what came in its wake.

Rounding the next corner, he slowed to a walk. Ahead a man sat on a chair outside a door, his head nodding. He looked up as Jon approached.

Before he could speak, Jon said, 'The nurse here yet?'

The detective shook his head.

'We need to change the patient's medication. She'll be up shortly.'

He made to walk into the room, but the detective stood up and held out his hand. 'Where's your card?'

'It's in my coat in my locker.' Jon protested. 'I've just dashed up from surgery in the scant few minutes I have between operations. Please don't make me waste my time by going back down.'

The detective looked him in the eye for a second, then nodded cautiously.

As Jon placed his fingers on the handle, he turned back and said, 'By the way, this might be nothing, but I thought I heard somebody prowling around on the stairs. There shouldn't be anybody there at this time of night.'

'I can't check it out. I'm not allowed to leave here, and the rest of the team have been called away.'

'Well, can you keep an eye out?'

'That's my job,' the detective replied sarcastically.

Jon hoped it would be enough; at least the detective could raise the alarm. With his stomach twisted in knots, he stepped into the room and closed the door behind him.

The room was too small for the bed and the machines desperately trying to keep Emma alive; that and the oppressive air of suffering made Jon feel like he was on the Underground during rush hour. He allowed his gaze to rest on Emma for barely a second before he was forced to snatch it away, but what he saw in that instant was enough to burn its way into his memory forever. Her right arm was missing at the shoulder. The fall of the bed clothes showed her right leg from the knee down was gone too. Jon couldn't see what other damage there was below the neck, but he guessed a great deal. Her face, though, was relatively untouched, apart from the patch on her cheek.

Forcing back the unfocused guilt and shock, he dropped down next to the head of the bed and whispered her name. There was no response. It was hard to tell her condition amid the tubes snaking into her nose and the corner of her mouth; if she was still in a coma he was wasting his time.

'Emma,' he whispered a little louder.

He could hear the guard shifting on his chair, but there was no other sound from outside.

Emma's eyelids fluttered.

'Can you hear me?'

A grunt slid up alongside the plastic tube down her throat.

'It's Summers, Emma. Remember, I was there when it happened, in St Paul's?'

A pathetic keening sound wheezed out of her mouth and her head and shoulders began to shake uncontrollably. Jon put a hand on her forehead to calm her.

'Don't worry. You're safe now,' he hissed insistently, then glanced at the door and thought: *I'm lying.*

'Everything OK in there?' the guard called out.

'Fine. She's woken up,' Jon replied. He turned back to Emma and whispered, 'I heard you call out in St Paul's. You recognized something about the person attacking you. You've got to try and tell me, Emma. We have to stop him before anyone else gets hurt.'

Her whole body was shaking so violently the bed was starting to rattle and Jon was caught between fears the guard was going to enter and she was going to have a heart attack. The keening sound rose and fell, but her eyes remained clamped shut.

'Emma, please calm down,' he urged. 'No one's going to hurt you.'

His words finally seemed to have some effect, for the violent shaking subsided to minor tremors rippling across her body.

'Good. That's good. Now try to remember what you saw.'

There was a moment of silence when Jon thought she had slipped back into sleep. Outside Jon heard the guard stand up suddenly and walk along the corridor.

'Emma?'

'Who's there?' The guard's voice was faintly irritated as if he felt someone was playing games with him.

'Emma, please.'

She mumbled something incoherent. Jon strained to hear.

'The tube's making it difficult for me to understand you. Can you say it again?' His eyes were fixed firmly on the door, every muscle held tense.

'Who's there?' the guard said again, outside the door, angrier this time.

Emma's mumbling continued, this time almost comprehensible, but Jon was no longer listening. He was acutely aware of a change in the atmosphere, like a pressure drop coupled with a taste in the air that made his lips tingle. He could almost feel the voracity of the darkness in the corridor radiating through the walls. He thought: *it's coming*.

He had a sudden urge to tell the guard to run away, but it was too late. There was the sound of blades being raked at speed along the corridor wall. The detective called out, 'Jesus—' but it was cut off in a snap. There was the crash of the chair tipping over, the thud of a dead weight hitting the floor and then a sickening silence that made Jon's head spin. He held his breath and watched the door handle.

A minute passed without a sound. Emma seemed oblivious to the disturbance; she was still trying to force out a word in a tearful struggle of grunts and moans.

It's waiting for me to come out, Jon thought. *Poised*

outside the door with its blades raised to slice me up with a single blow.

Emma muttered again and this time Jon heard.

He stared down at her closed eyes, not really believing. 'What did you say?'

Her lips moved slowly; there was no doubt. 'You.'

'I don't understand.'

'You.'

'What do you mean?'

'It was you!' A bubble of bloody saliva erupted from her lips as she burst into another bout of thrashing.

Jon stepped back from the bed until he felt the wall hard against his back. For a few seconds he couldn't think or speak or move as wild thoughts thundered around his head, but one by one they slowly fell into place and a creeping numbness spread through his body.

Gradually memories from the last few days surfaced, seen from a new, bleak perspective. He tried to focus on the book and what the great writers of the past had said, but it brought him no comfort. Emma's shaking subsided as if her unburdening had finally brought her peace. Jon's arms felt like lead, but somehow he managed to lift them so he could examine his hands, wondering who they really belonged to, of what atrocities they were capable. The journey to the door was like walking through mud; he knew what he would find when he opened it.

The detective was slumped on the floor. He appeared unconscious, a small mercy. The corridor was empty.

Richard stood on the doorstep, his face heavy with the effect of being woken from an alcohol-induced sleep. 'I have never been up at this time in my life,' he said wearily.

Sarah let him in. He was surprised to see her without glamour; she wore old leggings, a too-baggy jumper, no make-up, her hair tied up in an ungainly sprout.

'Jon didn't come home last night,' she said, wrapping her arms around her. She was edgy, chewing on her nails.

'Well, let's not jump to conclusions—'

'This is Jon we're talking about, Richard,' she snapped. 'He's *always* home. He loves this place more than . . .' She bit the words off and marched into the drawing room in search of her cigarettes. Richard followed, trying to kick-start his brain into life; Sarah was too sharp for him at the best of times.

'Yes, and he's also not the type to do anything stupid.'

'Well, where is he? Look at the weather! Do you think he might be sleeping out in that?'

'Jon's been keeping increasingly strange hours, as you well know. He's probably been sitting in an all-night café, brooding over his horrible life making pots of money.'

Sarah inhaled a deep breath of smoke, then let it out slowly as she clicked the nails of her little finger and thumb. 'I don't know,' she said eventually. 'I have a bad feeling . . .'

'It's just the pressure of everything that's been happening. It's understandable that you're worried.'

'He's been acting so strangely since he came out of that clinic, I can't predict what he's going to do any more. That's frightening. We've put in so much effort to sort things out, but he seems to be drifting further and further away.'

Richard took both her shoulders and gave them a squeeze. 'Let's not lose heart, old thing. It will all work out, you'll see.'

Sarah pulled away and turned her back to him. 'I wish I could believe that.'

'When he walks in that door in the next couple of hours—'

'And what if he doesn't?' She spun round, eyes blazing. Richard took a step back. 'What if he's run off with that stupid bimbo from the pub I caught him with? What if he's flipped his lid completely and he's stuck in some shelter somewhere not knowing who he is? What then?'

'Steady on, Sarah. We're on the same side here.'

She bit off a sliver of nail, then plucked it from her teeth. 'Sorry. I'm not being very cool, am I? What do you suggest if he doesn't come back?'

'I suppose we alert the police, although I have a natural aversion to involving the boys in blue.' He put both hands on her shoulders and pushed her down on to the sofa. 'Now you need to take it easy. You're going to burn yourself out getting so wound up about him.'

'It's the irrational things he does. It unnerves me,' she protested.

'Like what?'

'Like this.' She marched into the study and returned with an old book. 'I found it this morning in his drawer where he keeps that stupid journal.'

'Snooping again?' She didn't smile at his joke, and he took the book sheepishly.

'It's a first edition,' Sarah said incredulously. 'Probably worth a fortune.'

Richard shrugged, not really grasping her point. But as he flicked through it, the book fell open at various points where paragraphs had been neatly cut out. 'Oh, origami. I always told him to get a hobby.'

Sarah muttered darkly, and he made a mental note to curb his humour when she was in such a mood. He closed the book and examined the spine. '*Peter Pan*,' he noted thoughtfully. 'I used to have this read to me at bedtime when I was a boy.'

'That's fascinating, Richard,' she said sourly. 'Now tell me why Jon the book-lover is cutting out extracts from a rare print of a children's fairytale. And what the hell is he doing with them?'

*

270

Jon woke in the small storeroom that had been his refuge earlier. His watch said he'd been asleep for barely an hour. He had spent ten minutes wandering backwards and forwards along the corridor in shock, before sitting down to decide what he was going to do, and had obviously gone out like he'd been coshed.

In fact, his head *felt* like he'd been knocked unconscious. A headache thundered at the base of his skull and his face was filled with a hundred tiny pains centring on the wound in his cheek. *The self-inflicted wound*, he thought.

Gingerly, he stripped off the surgeon's gown, mask and hat and put on his jacket. His options were simple: give himself up or run. But could he really live with himself if he tried to carry on with his life, knowing the terrible things he had done?

With a bitterness he had never felt before, he wondered what had become of him, then set off to find the detective guarding Emma's room.

The policeman was still face down on the floor, but he seemed to be stirring. Jon bent down to help him to his feet and then noticed the blood seeping under Emma's door.

His breath seemed to clamp down somewhere deep in the pit of his stomach and darkness closed in around his vision. The door beckoned him and threatened him at the same time. With a hideous fascination, he grasped the handle and threw the door open.

The room was a charnel house, a vista into hell; blood streaked the walls, puddled the floor and dripped from the ceiling; it looked too much to belong to one person. And on the bed lay something that he couldn't identify; it spoke of no human shape.

Behind him, the detective cried out in horror. There was the crackle of a radio and an anguished cry for help. It seemed to be happening a million miles away. All Jon could think was: *too much blood*.

But then his consciousness came rushing back from some

distant place and he turned to see the detective scrambling to his feet. Animal instincts took over and Jon barrelled into him, knocking him back to the floor, and then Jon was away and running.

When he reached the stairwell, there were already angry voices rising from below and the thunder of insistent feet on the steps. He glanced at the lift, back along the corridor, and he realized there was nowhere else to go.

They found him waiting there a few seconds later, his shoulders hunched dejectedly, his stare blank, a hollow-eyed ghost of a man.

17

'The time is 6.35 a.m. Present are Detective Inspector Charles Culver and Detective Ryan Miles. We are interviewing . . . state your name.'

Jon looked the two detectives in the face, then lowered his eyes to the desk. He knew he couldn't remain silent forever, but he needed time to come to terms with what he had done. When it was straight in his head, then he would admit it and face his punishment.

'Let it be noted the interviewee refused to give his name and at this time he has waived his right to legal representation,' Culver said emotionlessly. 'What do we call you then?'

He stared until Jon felt he had to answer. 'Peter.'

'Well, *Peter*, as you had no ID on you at all, I suppose we'll have to settle for that. You realize you're not doing yourself any favours?'

Jon looked back at the desk.

'I presume you know what this is all about, so I'm not going to beat around the bush. Four murders—'

'Four?' Jon said in puzzlement.

Culver and Miles glanced at each other. 'Ronald Whittington. Miles Heath. Emma Rexe-Burke. And the one we found last night,' Culver said, trying to douse the spark of doubt that had suddenly ignited in him. 'Gary Finch.'

The look of shock on Jon's face was so honest that both Culver and Miles caught themselves.

'You know him?'

'Yes.'

'Did you work with him?'

Jon ignored them, lost in the memory of the last time he had spoken to Finch, in a champagne bar after work, a few weeks before his career had started to become a real problem. Finch was fiercely ambitious, even by the monstrous standards of the City. Desperate to escape his working class background at any cost, Finch had shucked off all ethics long before and was wading waist-deep in underhand activities to try to get ahead. At some point he had decided to cling on in Jon's wake, hoping, Jon guessed, that some of the money and glory would rub off. To curry favour, he had been giving Jon tips that had either paid off or that Jon had been able to pass on to others for the company's advantage. Jon had always had his suspicions about the source of the information, but he had never asked for the truth; it was a pathetic excuse to himself, but it allowed him to sleep at night.

Then, at the bar, Finch had slyly suggested interest rates would be rising the following day. Jon told him it was a ridiculous idea, but Finch insisted and Jon had already learned to trust his views. If they acted quickly first thing the next day, the information would make the company millions and Jon an excellent bonus. In return, Jon would guarantee Finch kudos and the first step on the ladder to success. But after another bottle of champagne, Finch drunkenly made the mistake of telling Jon his source, a government statistician who was a friend of Finch's family. Jon was furious his integrity had been compromised. But he used the information anyway, and from that moment he began to feel the job slowly killing him.

'Where did it happen?' Jon asked as the memory faded.

'Highgate. Late last night,' Culver said.

'As you bloody well know,' Miles sneered.

Jon felt the sucking vacuum return at the heart of him.

He could have done it on the way to Lisa's, blanked it out as he had obviously done so many times before, then pulled the skeins of fantasy around himself.

Culver was eyeing him so intently Jon couldn't hold his gaze. 'What were you doing at the hospital?' the detective asked.

'I went to see Emma.'

'You knew her well?'

'I was acquainted with her.'

'So you knew the two people who were murdered during the night,' Miles said, still sneering. 'It's not very lucky being your friend, is it?'

'No. It's not.'

'Where do you work?'

Anxiety twisted the knife in his guts. '"I have a terrible past. For three years now I've been living with a saxophone player."'

'It's obviously somewhere in the City. You know we're going to find out soon so you might as well tell us.'

'I will tell you, after I've had some time to myself.'

'Did you kill Emma Rexe-Burke?'

Jon had a sudden queasy flash of the blood and the shapeless thing on the bed.

'Where did you hide the weapon?' Miles said. 'And the clothes you were wearing? You must have been drenched in her blood.'

Culver looked in Jon's face one more time, then formally ended the interview for the benefit of the tape recorder.

'Don't you think we should plug on for a bit longer, boss?' Miles said with obvious irritation.

'No, we'll give Peter here his time alone. A few hours to collect his thoughts. Then we'll put a bit of steam behind it.' The last sentence carried an implicit threat.

After Jon had been taken down to the cells, Miles asked, 'What do you think?'

'I don't know,' Culver replied honestly. In truth Culver

didn't want to believe it was Jon. He wanted the murderer to be some hairy-knuckled low life with a body covered in tattoos and a history of mental illness, something he could understand.

'Poncy git. I reckon he did it.'

'You saw his face when we told him about Finch. He had no idea.'

'Maybe he's a good actor.'

Culver shook his head. 'And what about all the blood? Where could he have cleaned himself up after that fucking butchery?'

'Well, somebody did it, Charlie.' Miles thought for a minute. 'OK, say for a minute he is one of the fucking nuts we've had trooping through here pretending they've done it. What I want to know is how the sick bastard who did do it managed to surprise Deedes . . .'

'Deedes has got concussion. He can't remember anything.'

'. . . And how did he manage to cut up that body so quickly? There was barely an hour between the others leaving and Deedes calling in. They must have been going some to chop it up that quickly. And to do it so . . .'

'Efficiently?'

'Right. Reid said it's like a fucking master surgeon did it. And even then he'd have trouble in that time.'

Culver tried to look positive, but the bleakness that he felt at the onset was starting to consume him; there were moments when he felt they would never be able to explain it.

There was a knock at the door and a young detective burst in. 'Sorry to interrupt, Chief,' he said, 'but we've got something you might be interested in.'

'Tell me it's a signed confession, Burton,' Culver said dryly.

'Next best thing, Chief. A tape from somebody claiming

to be the killer. Calling himself Jack the Ripper. He even signs off with *from Hell*.'

Culver looked at Miles. 'Tenner says it's another nut.'

'I don't earn enough to give it away, Charlie.'

'Well, you never know, Miles,' Culver said hopefully. 'Jack the Ripper. That sounds promising.'

The sun came up on a Christmas Eve blanketed by snow across the length and breadth of the country. Lisa watched it rise above the rooftops, thinking she should feel hopeful and optimistic, not the emptiness that pushed her towards depression. Jamie still slept, but she had only snatched a couple of hours. Her thoughts had been turned towards Jon and his promise to return after his visit to the hospital; now she feared the worst.

The knock at the door was light and tentative, but she was there in seconds. Her disappointment at the sight of Velikovsky was palpable, but he didn't seem to mind. He stepped in without waiting to be invited.

'Time grows short,' he said coldly.

Lisa felt a surge of annoyance at the old man for the first time since she had known him. 'What do you want, Mr Velikovsky?' she said curtly.

He stared at her. 'Unless we find a solution, your friend dies tomorrow. Do you not recall?'

'I think we ought to stop this talk now. It's not doing anybody any good.'

Lisa caught herself before she blew up; the lack of sleep and the pressure had pushed her to the edge.

Velikovsky tried to read her face, then said, 'Tell me what has happened.'

As he removed his coat, Lisa noticed how awful he looked – thinner, if possible, his frame more bent. His skin had a faint yellow sheen and his cheeks seemed to be caving in. 'Are you all right?' She caught his elbow, afraid he would stumble.

Velikovsky passed a hand across his face. 'Tired. There has been some pain, but it will pass.'

Lisa sat him on the sofa. 'I should call the doctor.'

'No. There will be time to recover. This is the price that has to be paid.'

'For what?'

'For finding out the truth.'

'The truth!' Lisa laughed sadly. Then something he said connected. 'What have you been doing?'

'Knowledge ... true knowledge ... is not easy to come by. Those who have it will not relinquish it freely. It is rarely stored in books in libraries and, even when pressed, the keepers of such knowledge dissemble and obfuscate so that any meaning is lost. It can only be bought.'

While he was speaking, Lisa became aware that since he had entered the room he had kept his right hand hidden behind him. It had seemed natural at first, but the way he was sitting looked awkward and uncomfortable. She reached out and tugged at his jacket sleeve, and although he resisted at first he eventually gave in. His hand was bandaged tightly. The thumb was missing.

Lisa's stomach pitched and she thought she was going to be sick. 'Mother of God! What have you done?'

'I have bought the knowledge we need.'

'You've made yourself a cripple!' She stared at his hand in horror for a second and then burst into tears at the mindless stupidity of it.

Velikovsky allowed her to cry for a few minutes then put a hand on her shoulder. 'It was a price I was prepared to pay.'

'That makes it even worse, don't you see?' she sobbed. 'We've acted like children, indulging ourselves with all this stupid talk of the occult, demons and devils, and this is the result!'

'We talked about it. You believed—'

'I let myself be led! Why didn't I say something? God,

I'm so gullible!' She turned to Velikovsky, her eyes blazing. 'There is no supernatural! That's the simple option. We just couldn't face up to the fact that it's much more complex than that, that it's about life, real life, and people's minds and the things that can go on in there. You've cut off your thumb for *no reason*. And Jon has put himself at risk hunting shadows. For no reason!'

'I think you should tell me what has changed your mind.'

Fighting back the tears, she showed him the book and told him the things Jon had imagined he'd seen in there. 'Look for yourself. It was all in his mind. All of this stuff about the Scissorman was just something he dreamed up. Oh, I'm not saying he didn't believe it. That just makes it even worse.'

'It sounds like you have lost faith in your friend.'

'No, I haven't.' She paused. 'I love him. I'd do anything for him. I just think he needs help, not indulging in his fantasies.'

'You admit he was on the train when the second man was murdered?'

'Yes.'

'And in St Paul's when the girl was attacked?'

A pause. 'Yes.'

'Who, then, do you think committed those atrocities?'

'I don't want to think about that now. There are—'

'You cannot have it both ways, child. If some supernatural entity did not slay those poor people, then following your logic and your perception of reality, the only alternative is that your friend is the murderer.'

Lisa bit her lip and looked out at the cold, grey sky. 'I don't think he's capable. He's a good person.'

'Ah! A flaw in your argument!'

Lisa shook her head wearily. 'Mr Velikovsky—'

'If you accept the existence of the Invisible World, then the rules of this mundane world do not hold sway. An individual's perception is just that – one man's view.'

'No!' Lisa said vehemently. 'If you accepted that, it would drive you mad! You couldn't believe anything you saw or heard!'

'Exactly.'

'No.' Lisa stood up and marched to the window, then back; her head was spinning and she wanted Velikovsky away.

'If your friend saw something in that book and it is not there now, who is to say he is wrong? Perhaps you were not meant to see it.'

'No. That's ridiculous—'

'This evil exists. It is free, and it will not stop until the ritual is complete.'

Lisa dropped to the sofa and covered her face. 'I can't take any more of this.' She rested her eyes for a few moments, then said, 'Jon's gone to the hospital where the girl is recovering. He should have been back by now. I want to go and find out what's happened to him. Will you sit with Jamie?'

'You care for this man too much.'

'Will you?'

'Yes.'

After she had slipped on her coat and was about to step out, she turned back to Velikovsky and said, 'What did they tell you in return for your thumb?'

'They?'

'The people you went to.'

Velikovsky looked through her and shuddered. 'I was given the truth. Why this is happening. Why it needs to be ended.'

Lisa nodded. She glanced at his hand and thought what that senseless sacrifice would mean in the coming months and years; but he would find out soon enough. She didn't even want to know what stupid information had justified the decision in his mind. It was madness, and it was infectious. She stepped out, suddenly feeling very alone.

*

The cell was like a storage room for unwanted goods, filled with the smell of other people's sweat and urine. Jon sat on the hard bed, listening to the intermittent sound of a distant swing door opening and closing, trying to break through the sealed off sections of his mind where he believed the truth lay. He remembered the dream of Whittington's body, but for the life of him he couldn't recall the killing. There was no accessible memory of him plunging a knife into Miles Heath, of slicing Emma high up in St Paul's, of even meeting Gary Finch.

But Emma had said it was him with the conviction of someone close to death, and from a distance it all made a hideous kind of sense. A deranged mind blinking on and off like a faulty light was easier to accept than some supernatural entity. And although he didn't consciously believe he was capable of the Scissorman's atrocities, there was a hidden part of him convinced it was possible, the compartment where he had secreted all the self-loathing that had built up during his time at Steelguard. A man who could strip away his values with such disregard, well, he was capable of anything, wasn't he?

He glanced up from his ruminations and felt the black poison of despair seep into his heart; would it ever end? The cell had been transformed; luminescent, silvery trailings hung between ceiling and walls like moonlit Spanish moss, and the air was filled with the sweet, powerful fragrance of night-scented stock. In one corner, the Giant he had associated with the Ghost of Christmas Present lounged on a bier of yew and mistletoe. Standing pressed into another, the blinking man maintained his spasming expression. And in another was someone Jon had not seen before; a woman of remarkable beauty, her skin a translucent gold, alien and frightening, glowing like the sun.

He looked from one to the other and said despairingly, ' "I believe in God and mercy and all that, but the dead are happier dead. They don't miss much here, poor devils. What do you believe in?"'

'The time is drawing near,' the Giant rumbled.

'Leave me alone.'

'After the morrow we may never be apart,' the blinking man said.

'I know who you are. You're my conscience, trying to get me to stop the terrible things I'm doing.'

'You speak as if we have an interest in your welfare,' the Giant noted curiously. The woman gave a tinkling laugh that carried on too long.

Jon took a deep breath and, beneath the perfumed air, tasted something foul coming off the Giant. 'You don't care. My conscience doesn't care.'

The blinking man smacked his lips twice before he spoke. 'We have no interest in you at all. We enjoy the sport, as we always have, though it is harder to come by in these times.'

'That will change,' the woman interrupted.

'He will prevent it.' There was a dismissive lash to the Giant's tongue. 'They always have.'

The woman glided across the floor until she was at Jon's side. He felt his heart begin to pound. 'This has the reek of something different. I feel we may be at the threshold.' Jon noticed her lips never moved; the words seemed to appear in the air somewhere between them.

She reached out a hand and stroked his cheek, and for a brief moment a tingling sensation danced around his face. Then a thunderous rush surged through his system, like every gram of coke he had ever snorted. His penis engorged so rapidly his groin ached, and within seconds he had ejaculated into his trousers. There was a bolt of pain as if he had been kicked in his testicles, and as he doubled up, clutching himself, the woman withdrew in a bubble of chiming laughter.

'God!' Jon gasped, rolling on to the bed with his knees clutched to his chest.

The Giant and the blinking man seemed unaware of what had happened. 'He will prevent it,' the Giant repeated. 'Look at him, the pale, pathetic thing.'

'But if he did not . . .' For a second, the blinking man stopped blinking; there was a terrifying hunger in his voice.

'He will prevent it.'

Jon tried to comprehend what they were saying, but nothing made sense. Yet their presence in the room didn't seem to have the whiff of hallucination; it was as if his wildest imaginings had been made flesh.

'But don't you want to stop the Scissorman?' he asked, trying to exert his own will on the madness.

'His vengeance is without control. He acts for no one but himself. It irks me,' the Giant said. He ground his pointed teeth together.

'His loathsome presence may still reward us,' the woman said. 'Will we despise ourselves through him?'

Jon pulled himself into a sitting position. The vision was mesmerizing, dampening his anger and despair. As he looked around the room, he knew it would be so easy to give in to it and to shirk his responsibility for his actions. But if he did accept it, the price would be what remained of his sanity.

In one final act of defiance, he closed his eyes, put his head back and yelled, 'Go away!'

When the echoes had died, he heard insistent footsteps thundering along the corridor outside.

The policeman threw back the grille and peered in angrily. He had ginger hair and a moustache, and a florid complexion. 'Who are you talking to?'

The three figures looked at each other and smiled; he couldn't see them.

'Nobody.'

'Just shut it, you fucking nutter,' the policeman snarled.

'Keep it down, for fuck's sake.' He slammed the grille and marched away angrily.

The woman turned to Jon, her golden skin glowing brighter. 'A kiss,' she said, smiling cruelly, 'to keep you warm through the long day ahead.'

'Keep away.' Jon held up his hands and pressed himself into the wall at the head of the bed.

'He has a woman,' the Giant said.

'But for how much longer?' the blinking man added.

The words brought Jon's thoughts to a halt. 'What do you mean?' he snapped.

The three figures looked at each other once more; they were playing with him.

'Tell me!' Jon insisted.

'Four are gone, one more must fall.' The woman's smile seemed even more cruel.

'Sarah?' Jon felt his throat was closing.

The Giant continued his mockery. 'A woman,' he noted with a gleam in his eye.

'She will fall before the eve is gone,' the blinking man added. 'Her blood will nourish the garden of earthly delights.'

'The garden? At Arcadia?' Jon's thoughts were rushing out of control. He tried to read their mocking faces, but then something fell into place. 'No. Covent Garden. Where Sarah works.'

There was a moment in which he considered the future, and then he threw himself at the door, hammering madly. The guard stormed up within seconds.

'I thought I told you—'

'You've got to let me out! Or do something! My wife's going to be killed!'

'Oh, just remembered, have you?' he sneered.

'Listen—'

'No, *you* fucking listen. You're coming out when the

chief says so. And you'd better watch what you say to him – he's got a temper like a pit bull.'

He walked away and none of Jon's yelling or banging could bring him back. After a few minutes, he dropped to his knees and rested his head on the cool floor.

'Jesus, what am I doing? If I get out, I'm the one who's going to cause it. This is the best place for me.'

But it didn't calm him. Slowly he rolled on to his back and looked at the others looking at him. He examined their faces, their clothes, the streams of silver moss. Pulling himself to his feet, he walked over to the Giant and slowly reached out to touch his face. The Giant gnashed his hideous teeth an inch away from Jon's fingers and Jon snatched his hand away.

His head was spinning as if he was drunk. 'What can I do?' he pleaded. 'There's no way out of here.'

The Giant smiled horribly while the woman's tinkling laughter rose and rose. Jon turned from them and threw himself on the bed, burying his head in the pillow.

It was gone noon by the time Lisa returned to the house. She was cold and exhausted and feeling more down than she had done in months. She had wandered the hospital's corridors for two hours, and sat in the cafeteria for a third, but had seen no sign of Jon. Eventually she had found a friendly porter who told her of the *excitement* at the hospital early that morning. By the time she left, she was in no doubt that Jon had been arrested for the murder of the woman from the City. Someone on the WRVS stall even thought he had been charged, but the media hounds who had descended on reception throughout the morning seemed unaware of this 'fact'.

During her slog back through the snow, all she could think of was how terribly empty she felt. It made no sense, she convinced herself, but in her heart she knew why. And now it was over, in the worst possible way for everyone involved.

The house seemed grey and dismal as she trudged up the stairs. There was a depressing smell of cabbages, and it was uncannily quiet; not even Ralph's music was echoing through the walls.

She threw open the door to her flat wearily and called out, 'I'm home,' with as much enthusiasm as she could muster. It wasn't until she had removed her coat that she realized there had been no reply.

'Mr Velikovsky? Jamie?'

The flat was still, the bedroom empty, a game of draughts laid out, unfinished. She told herself they had gone to the park, or the shops, but it didn't feel convincing.

As she hurried to the window and looked out into the deserted street, she had the sudden, vertiginous feeling that her life was about to be torn apart. It wasn't over. The worst was still to come.

It was 12.30 p.m. and Culver's stomach was rumbling. The entire morning had been taken up analysing the Ripper tape without any firm conclusion being reached, but Culver felt in his gut that it wasn't true. There was a whiff of unreality about it, too many overwrought emotions, as if someone was living out a fantasy. And although the murders *seemed* unreal, there was no emotion in them at all, and it was that bitter pill that made them real.

Miles and some of the others weren't convinced, though, and he couldn't take a chance on being wrong, so he'd assigned one of the men to look into it. He certainly wouldn't pin his hopes on it; everyone remembered the Yorkshire Ripper case, when resources had been ploughed into a hoax tape and the real killer had slipped through the net.

'Ryan, how are you getting on with that Steelguard personnel search?' he called across the room.

Miles riffled through the papers on his desk until he found the one he wanted. 'Two current employees living in Highgate, Charlie, neither of them near the road where we found Finch, but I'm checking both of them out.'

'How about the messages? Have we located the book yet?'

'Not yet. Lehman's working on it. He's down at the British Library . . .'

Culver cursed. He had a gut feeling there would be another death, at least one, before Christmas was out. The crazies loved special occasions, loved imposing order on a mad world; this one wouldn't let Christmas go without forcing it to become part of their sick ritual. The clock on the wall was making him feel more tense with each hour of Christmas Eve that fell away, so he spun his chair around and looked out of the window at the London skyline, hoping inspiration would come like it always did in the movies.

'OK, Ryan, let's get that bastard from the hospital back in the interview room. He's had long enough to simmer,' he called out.

'You reckon he's ready to go for the limelight this time?'

'He hasn't got a choice. I've got a lot of anxiety to get out of my system and he's the designated whipping boy.'

Miles laughed and phoned the duty sergeant to get *Peter* brought from the cells.

Before they'd stepped out of the room, Reid burst in clutching a piece of paper, still wearing his white coat from the forensics lab.

'What's wrong?' Culver said warily.

'Don't always expect bad news, Charlie,' he said with a smile. 'While you were working on that obviously bogus Ripper tape,' he grinned, 'we found another book page at the hospital. A long one this time. And, guess what, it was *inside* the body this time.'

Or what was left of it, Culver thought.

'At the back of the throat. Do you want to read it?'

'You read it. You've got such a lovely speaking voice.'

Reid read carefully from the photocopy: '"Above, where all had been so still, the air was rent with shrieks and the clash of steel. Below, there was dead silence. Mouths opened and remained open. Wendy fell on her knees, but her arms were extended towards Peter. All arms were extended to him, as if suddenly blown in his direction; they were beseeching him mutely not to desert them. As for Peter he seized his sword, the same he thought he had slain Barbecue with; and the lust of the battle was in his eye."'

There was a moment of silence while Culver chewed over the words. 'Peter fucking Pan! Of course, the redskins!' Instantly the triggers started firing in his mind and he turned to Miles. 'Come on!'

'What is it?' Reid asked, hurrying in their wake.

'The bloke we picked up in the hospital chose an alias. *Peter.*'

'But how do you think he kept the blood off him? And where's the murder weapon?'

'I don't know, but it's too much of a bloody coincidence.'

'There's something else you should know,' Reid said as they chased down the corridors. 'Finch was missing a kidney. And Emma Rexe-Burke was missing an ear.'

Culver brought himself up sharp and Miles crashed into the back of him. 'So where's he hidden the organs, then?'

The team went over the whole top floor of the hospital with a fine-tooth comb,' Reid said. 'There's no way he could have stashed it there. So if this *Peter* is your man—'

'All right. We'll cross that bridge when we come to it. Let's just squeeze him and see what pops out.'

When they reached the interview room, the duty sergeant and two other uniformed men were already there. Culver saw bafflement, guilt and worry in their faces.

'I don't want any more bad news, Ron,' Culver snapped.

The duty sergeant flushed. 'He's gone, Charlie.'

'What do you mean, "He's gone"?'

'When we went to the cell it was empty.'

'You searched—'

'He didn't have anything on him, Charlie. You know those locks – they're unpickable. You can't get—'

'And how did he get out of the building?' Culver said incredulously, looking from one to the other. There was an air of incomprehension that made Culver feel uncomfortable. 'All right, check the cameras—'

'They went off-line, Mr Culver. Just for the time he was getting out of there. You know it's a closed circuit. There's no way—'

'I know, I know.' Culver waved them away and turned on his heel.

'Charlie?'

'Don't bother me now, Ryan. I've got to think.'

And that was the last thing he wanted to do. Because if he thought about it too closely, he would realize that none of it made sense. That the whole hideous business had finally crossed the line it had been threatening to step over since the beginning, into a place where all Culver's tightly held rules fell away, where anything could happen.

Covent Garden was filled with Christmas cheer, from the bars and restaurants packed to bursting, to the shops open late-night for last-minute presents, blasting out Wizzard, Slade and Crosby, to the streetsellers proffering hot chestnuts and the carollers in Victorian dress filling the night with the hopes of yesteryear. To add to the scene, the snow had started again, big flakes falling slowly, ideal for snowballs in the hands of children, rugby players and City workers finally realizing they could take at least one day's break from the pressures. Everyone agreed it was going to be a perfect Christmas.

Jon waited in the shadows under the piazza, lost in the crowds that surged by. He had called the house and left a message on the answerphone, he had called Steelguard, but Richard wasn't there, and he had called Sarah's office, but all they would say was that she was expected in later. And now there seemed to be police everywhere; walking across the square, questioning people by the Africa Centre, watching the drinkers in the Punch and Judy. His only option was to keep moving with the shoppers, darting in and out of stores so as not to look suspicious.

Gradually, he worked his way around to the south side of the piazza before slipping across the road to the entrance to Monkey Business. From there he could head quickly along the row of converted Georgian properties to the one which housed Sarah's office. Briefly he glimpsed someone he thought he recognized, passing in the crowd in the opposite direction. It was just a flash of fair hair, not enough to trigger a name or face, and then she was gone, swirling up towards the piazza and the tube station beyond.

At Sarah's building, he rode the lift to the top floor and was surprised to see the reception desk was empty. A new photo of Sarah looked down at him, replacing the one that had been slashed.

As he stepped into the deserted main office, his skin began to crawl and he had an urgent feeling that something was wrong. Sarah had probably let the staff go home early for Christmas Eve, but that didn't explain why the office was still open. When he was half-way across the room towards Sarah's office, he glimpsed her through the glass door. The high back of her chair was facing him and all he could see was her blonde hair peeking out over the top. She wasn't moving.

At that point he almost turned back. His mind was playing cruel tricks on him, offering quick flashes of what he would find when he spun the chair around, snapshots drenched in red, and he didn't think he would be able to live if he saw what he had seen in Emma's hospital room.

Moistening his lips, he rested his fingers on the handle for a few seconds, then swung the door open.

Sarah spun round, her face frozen in an instant of fear, but when she saw it was Jon it turned to a blaze of fury. 'You bastard! What are you doing? Where have you been?'

Jon's legs went weak at the relief and for a moment he couldn't force himself to speak.

'Well?' she raged. 'This had better be good. I've been worried sick!'

'I'm sorry.' It sounded weak and stupid, but it was all he could think of to say. He just wanted to hold her close, try to forget the scenes he had imagined, but the anger in her face kept him away.

'Is that all you can say? After I spent a whole day worrying—'

'You didn't call the police?' Jon had a sudden picture of Culver putting two and two together.

'No, I didn't call the police! I wanted to, but Richard told me you'd come walking through the door sooner or later. And he was right. It seems he knows you better than I do.'

Jon looked out of the window at the lights of Covent Garden. That's why she hadn't been moving; she'd been looking out at the Christmas scene, worrying about him, trapped in the bitter poignancy of it all. He felt a guilty shame for putting her through it.

'I'm sorry,' he said again.

'That's not good enough, Jon.' The heat of her anger subsided a little. 'Since you came out of the clinic, I've felt like I haven't known you at all. You've been going your own way in such a self-obsessed manner it's like you don't care about me any more.'

'That's not true.'

'Then how do you explain being out all night and all the next day without calling? That doesn't show much respect.'

What could he say: that he'd been arrested for murder?

It wasn't the right time; that moment would come. 'I've got myself in a bit of a mess.'

'What kind of mess?'

'I can't talk about it here.'

'Is there somebody else?'

'Of course there isn't! How could you suggest such a thing?'

'The way you've been acting—'

'Has been all about me. You were right. You know I've always been introspective, but the stress I was under made me go completely into my head.'

He saw his apology calm her, and seized the opportunity to round the desk and take her in his arms. She resisted at first, but then gradually he felt her muscles unknot and she relaxed against him. For a moment he was lost to the sensations that were more valuable to him than all the money he had made at Steelguard: the unique scent of Joseph perfume on her skin; the silkiness of her hair against his cheek; her warm breath at his throat. He wasn't going to let anything take it away from him.

After a moment she pulled back and looked searchingly into his face. 'If you're in trouble, you need to talk to me. I'm your wife. You know I'm not going to think badly of you, and I'll always try to help.'

Jon felt a pang of guilt for confiding in Lisa. 'I know I should have done. I'm sorry. I won't make that mistake again.'

She stood on her toes and kissed him gently. 'Let's go home. We always spend Christmas Eve together. Richard is waiting at the house in case you came back during the day, but we can get rid of him, have some mulled wine, settle down in front of the fire – just you and me, just like old times.'

'Sounds like heaven.' His relief after hours of unbroken tension made the emotion catch in his throat and for a while he couldn't speak, so he simply held her to him until it subsided.

'Come on,' she said eventually. 'Let's go home.'

They walked in silence across the office, holding hands like teenage lovers, but as they travelled down in the lift, Jon felt a creeping uneasiness. He had been told with certainty that Sarah would be the Scissorman's fifth and final victim, there in Covent Garden. He had seen no sign of a threat, and they could pick up a taxi outside and be at Arcadia within half an hour. Something was wrong.

As his nerves continued to jangle, he suddenly hit upon it. He was the one who had suggested Sarah would be the victim. The Giant had only said *a woman*. In a rush, it all fell into place. The woman he had glimpsed in the crowd outside had been Amanda Carlyle, formerly Steelguard's rising star, now a big shot at Treiner Brothers. Amanda was diamond-hard and just as bright. When she joined Steelguard, her sole ambition was to be best and within a few months that single-minded determination crushed all of the City's incipient chauvinism and had her nipping at Jon's heels for the top dog role. He should have stayed above it, but the culture had long since infected him. It was her competition that made him accept Gary Finch's corrupt information, his fears of being usurped that caused the numerous other minor retreats that left him a million miles away from the person he used to be.

It fitted the pattern exactly. All of the victims were people he had secretly blamed for the corruption of his values, his ethics, his soul. And they had all paid the price for him being unable to accept responsibility for his own actions.

Blood and punishment, hearts reach out . . .

His heart had reached out and they had been punished. In blood.

The lift touched down and the doors slid open. Jon hurried Sarah out into the street so quickly she gasped, and he hailed a cab before she could ask what he was doing.

'I'll see you back at the house,' he said, bundling her into the taxi.

The shock on her face quickly turned to irritation. 'Jon, don't do this to me—'

'There's someone I have to see.' He slammed the door. 'Don't worry. I'll be home soon.'

And then he was away and running, with an uncomfortable impression of Sarah's furious face staring at him from the rear window as the taxi pulled away.

He careered through the crowds to the piazza, desperately wondering how he would find Amanda in such a heavy mass of people. The snow was settling thickly, making it slick underfoot as he skidded past the choir who had just launched into 'While Shepherds Watched Their Flocks'. There were so many people he couldn't imagine how the Scissorman would be able to risk an attack, but his doubts didn't deter him. As he passed the Nag's Head's overflowing doors he suddenly knew where Amanda would be shopping. Just ahead was Floral Street with its high-class stores, and The Sanctuary, the exclusive women's fitness centre where Amanda was a member.

Jon sped down the centre of the street, diving into shops, crashing into passers-by who fired a hail of curses at his heels, but seeing no trace of Amanda anywhere. He'd reached the end of the street and had just about given up hope when he glanced back and saw her, in her Burberry overcoat, emerge from Paul Smith and head back towards the tube. He called her name, but the music and the crowds were too loud.

Jon barrelled down the street until his breath burned in his lungs. Hanging a left, he sprinted up to the junction with Long Acre, but there was no sign of her. She had to have gone into the tube. Looking at the crowds slamming into the ticket barriers from both directions, he cursed quietly to himself.

He bought a ticket and eased into the throng, fighting his

way forward with no thought for social graces, ignoring the elbows in his ribs and the furious glares. Due to the depth of the station, access to the platforms was granted by a series of lifts rather than escalators. They were laboriously slow and the passengers were already ten deep. The stairs were exhaustingly steep and slow in comparison, but the delay caused by the Christmas Eve throng made them a better prospect.

He dived into the dark stairwell and hurtled down the spiral so quickly he almost overbalanced. At the bottom, he sought out the southbound platform where Amanda would be waiting for the Leicester Square train and the change to the Northern Line for home in Wimbledon.

The platform was unbearably crowded with only a narrow space along the wall. He moved along it quickly, calling out her name.

When he was half-way along the platform, a sudden disturbance erupted at the far end. A woman was screaming hysterically and someone was shouting for help.

Jon thought: *I'm too late. It's got her.*

The cries were like a volcanic explosion on the ocean floor. There was a moment of silence when everything was held in stasis, then suddenly a wave of movement ran through the crowd towards him as people panicked and tried to force themselves away from any danger. Jon pinned himself against the wall until the crowd passed and then fought his way through the remaining gawkers to the end of the platform.

At the very end, a handful of people stood in a wide arc, staring into the dark tunnel. A woman with a shock-ghosted face pointed with a trembling hand while a man tried to comfort her. Whatever had happened, no one was trying to help.

'What is it?' Jon called out as he ran up.

The woman turned and stared, wide-eyed. 'She was standing there at the edge, in the corner. I was right next to her.' She caught her breath. 'Someone grabbed her coat and pulled her into the tunnel.'

'Are you sure she didn't jump?' the man next to her asked.

She shook her head vehemently. 'I saw something . . .' She swallowed. '. . . Someone . . . The look on her face . . . She didn't know what was happening.'

Jon looked into the sucking darkness of the tunnel and felt his bones grow cold. No sound emanated from the shadows.

He turned to the witnesses. 'Tell them to stop the trains.'

The man looked at him aghast. 'You're not going in?'

But Jon was already leaping on to the tracks and heading cautiously into the gloom.

As the sounds of the platform died behind him, Jon felt his heart go cold.

Tiny lights for maintenance workers winked at intervals along the wall, but there was a sea of darkness between each one, threatening to suck him under. Occasionally a blast of thick, hot air hit him, reeking of oil, and the rails sang with the threat of distant trains; he hoped the message had reached the control room.

Sixty feet into the tunnel, his foot kicked against something hard which jumped across the rails. He bent down and picked up a handbag, Italian, black leather, expensive. Amanda's. Jon held it tightly to his chest for a few more steps, as if that was enough to keep her alive, then threw it away in disgust.

The tunnel was the perfect place to kill in peace, full of little offshoots for maintenance, unused tunnels and long-abandoned stations, areas not seen by humans for decades. Here, beneath London, there was a darkness of years that had only recently spread to the surface.

The faint ringing in the rails was barely audible, but it sounded to Jon like the blaring of a siren and he threw himself against the wall with his eyes shut tight, praying the train would miss him. But after three minutes tensing his muscles as hard as the wall into which they were pressed, it gradually dawned on him that no train was coming. But the ringing continued, distant and intermittent. He kneeled on the wooden sleepers amid the stink of burnt rubber and grease and lowered his ear to the track.

Clang-clang-clang.

With a hollow feeling that threatened to consume him, he knew instantly what it was.

The sound of the Scissorman chopping.

After that his feet felt leaden as the adrenaline drained away, to be replaced by a sharp fatalism and a dull, unfocused anger. Whittington. Heath. Rexe-Burke. Finch. And now Carlyle. Five people who had contributed to the blackening of his soul, but none of them deserved to die. *He* had allowed it to happen and if anyone should be punished, it ought to be him. And the Scissorman. That vile spirit of vengeance and blind, uncaring evil. Jon might have pointed out the victims, but the Scissorman had condemned them to their fate. That thought gave him direction and renewed vigour, and with a slow, steady step, he followed the ringing in the rails to its source.

He didn't have far to travel. As he turned a corner where the tunnel swung round to the left, he saw an indistinct flurry of movement not far ahead in the oceanic darkness. Measuring every tread, holding his breath, he progressed cautiously as details slowly surfaced.

The Scissorman was kneeling over a vague shape with its back to Jon. The cruel, silvery blades were growing less frenzied in their movement as the task neared its completion. Jon could smell the cloying tang of blood in the air.

In a small alcove to his left, beneath one of the lights, an odd implement rested. It was like an iron hockey stick, but with a cleft in the curtailed business end; it looked like it was used for lifting the rails by workers repairing tracks.

His fingers closed around its hard, cold handle and it felt good.

The diving, blood-slick blades were growing slower, their business at an end. Jon would have to move quickly.

He grasped the tool and raised it high, holding it above his head with both hands, like Ahab preparing to plunge the harpoon into the great white whale. Then, with his heart ringing in his ears, he surged forward.

The tool came down with the force of a jackhammer. Although the Scissorman had seemed ephemeral in the past, at that moment it was solid, real. Jon felt the jarring impact through his arms and shoulders as the tool slammed into bone and muscle, bit deep, continued to delve. Jon leaned on it with all his weight, twisting and forcing, until he felt it burst free on the other side.

Only then did he stagger back, heaving gulps of air, horrified at what he had found in himself to complete the task.

No sound came from the Scissorman. Even at that final, awful moment, it still carried with it the heaving silence of night, and death. Nor were there any muscle spasms or wild thrashings. It simply fell forward slowly, coming to rest on the tip of the tool that protruded from its chest.

'Real,' Jon muttered in the voice of a man who had been given a reprieve from the death penalty.

Far away along the tunnels, raised voices echoed; the rescuers were finally coming, too late. What had been Amanda lay across the tracks, but Jon couldn't bear to look at her remains for more than the briefest moment.

But as he took a step back and prepared to walk away and lose himself in the crowd that waited on the platform, he caught a faint movement out of the corner of his eye. The Scissorman's tall hat was trembling gently as if the head beneath it was shaking with suppressed laughter.

Jon was caught between the desire to run as fast as he could and to watch the unfolding scene with a fatalistic horror. A sigh seemed to ripple through the hunched body, reaching out to the tips of its fingers and toes, and then the sigh became a tremor, and then a tensing of muscles as the Scissorman rose silently and easily to its feet. Jon caught his breath as it turned to face him, his rising fear matched by his knowledge that this was the first time he had had more than a lingering look at close proximity. He saw the gleam of its black leather shoes, the smart cut of its tightly buttoned Victorian suit, the white of its starched shirt collar, the gloves which seemed to have the suppleness of kid skin. He remembered the words in the book from the cellar and wondered what it *really* looked like when stripped of the perception he was enforcing upon it.

The face beneath the hat brim was still lost to the unshifting shadows as it stood and surveyed him carefully. And then the head shook again and this time Jon thought he could hear the faint rustle of a mocking laugh. Slowly it raised its hands to the tool which protruded from its chest; there was no blood around the wound. It grasped and tugged, and, with a nauseating sucking sound, drew the tool slowly through its body and was free. The weapon dropped to the rails with a clang.

Jon was mesmerized by the presence like a chicken before a fox. His every sense told him to flee, but there were too many questions tearing him apart.

'Why did you come to me?' His voice sounded insipid in the echoes of the tunnel.

The Scissorman raised its arms and the shears closed with a faint pinking sound.

'What are you trying to achieve?'

The voices in the tunnel were growing louder. If he could keep it there until someone else saw it, his problems would be over, but he knew it was a futile hope. As he watched, it slowly faded backwards along the tunnel without any movement of its legs, growing more insubstantial as it receded. And then, after a moment, the darkness seemed to fold around it and it was gone.

The spell disappeared instantly and Jon became aware of the urgency of his situation. If he was caught there alone with the body, it would all be over. Quickly he backed up the tunnel until he found an alcove in one of the darkened sections which would provide a hiding place until the rescue party had passed.

Pressed into the suffocating space in the gloom, Jon felt like he was standing on the edge of a precipice. Five deaths, Velikovsky had said, and now the Scissorman had completed the first part of his ritual. Jon felt the black mark on his arm begin to itch, the signature on his death warrant. Tomorrow, on Christmas Day, the Scissorman would come calling for him.

Lisa sat in the night-dark lounge, looking out at the familiar lights of the skyline. She was cold and hungry and more scared than she had ever been in her life. She had felt uneasy when she first returned to find Jamie and Mr Velikovsky missing, but had tried to tell herself it was nothing to be worried about.

But as the day progressed and each knock at the door and voice in the street proved to be nothing, her hopes began to flicker and fade with the light and she was overcome by a terrible, ominous gloom. She had tried Velikovsky's flat instantly, but the door was open and there was no sign that either of them had been there.

Fuelling her worries was the awful guilt a mother could feel: had she been remiss in her responsibilities in leaving Jamie with Velikovsky? Should she have left him with anyone at any time? Had all her work and studying been selfish when she should have been devoting herself to Jamie? But, like everyone else in the house, Mr Velikovsky had seemed worthy of her trust. He was a decent, honourable man, certainly not the kind who would abduct a child, not taking into account the numerous opportunities he had had in the past. So what was the alternative?

She shivered. The darkness in the room suddenly seemed too intense, a physical presence closing in around her. She thought of what Jon had said about the things that dwelled just a whisper away, that could break through at any time to steal people from their lives. And she thought about Velikovsky and his unshakeable belief in different realities, *different perceptions*.

And she thought of Jamie and wanted to cry, but held the tears back because they were useless; she needed to act, not mope.

Don't let superstition take you now, she thought.

So where could they have gone? She closed her eyes and forced herself to be rational. If Mr Velikovsky believed in the Scissorman and if he wanted to do something as badly as he seemed to, would he sit around the house? No. Where would he go? To the source of the problem, even if it meant taking Jamie with him.

She imagined Velikovsky in the flat, brooding, suddenly being taken by the desire to attack the threat, to do something, anything. Over the months, she had got to know Velikovsky well enough to realize he wouldn't just do nothing. But if he had harboured these thoughts, why hadn't he said anything to her before she left for the hospital?

The question echoed in her head, long after she had left the flat and set out for the tube station. She had rationalized well, but her fear still hadn't dissipated. Superstition, she thought, held a tighter grip on the human mind than she had ever realized.

But ahead lay Highgate, and Arcadia, and soon all those fears would be addressed.

18

Arcadia shone like a beacon in the street, though no light fell upon it; to Jon, as he trudged through the thickening snow, it was as if every brick emitted a radiance that the eye could not see, but the mind sensed fulsomely. The windows had a newly polished glint and the paint on the front door held a sheen that suggested it had only been applied that day. The brass knocker gleamed so brightly, that, from a distance, Jon thought it was a carriage lamp. In fact, the entire property seemed edged with charcoal which made it stand out solemnly and wonderfully more than all those around it. With the snow falling in big, dreamy flakes and the growing drifts keeping much of the passing traffic away, Jon knew instinctively he was witnessing something magical. The house had been transformed, ready to face that most magical of nights.

The effect did not diminish when he stepped through the front door. The hall was drenched in light, picking out starkly the black and white tiles, illuminating the majesty of the Christmas tree where numerous other lights twinkled with unusual power.

The moment the door closed behind him, Jon felt his muscles ease and loosen, his shoulders straightening as he shucked off all the fears that had been bearing down on him during the day. He had never felt such a sense of *home*; the security and wonder of being in the only place meant for him was almost palpable.

'Sarah?' he called out softly. His voice rippled along the hall and into the adjoining rooms with echoes of crystal clarity.

She was there somewhere, or had been recently; the scent of her perfume hung in the air with an unrivalled potency. And beneath it all the other subtle aromas of Arcadia that didn't seem to originate in that place: honey and lime, cardamom, thyme and woodsmoke, the scent of unknown and unknowable blooms.

Jon draped his coat over the coatstand and moved slowly down the hall, lost in the wild magic of the place. 'Sarah?' he called out again, almost unconsciously.

And then the blow slammed into the back of his knees with the force of a car, and the pain thundered through his body as his legs shot out in front of him and he crashed to the hard tiles with an impact that reverberated through his skeleton. For an instant he had an image of Sarah and Richard looking down at him with incomprehensible expressions and then he felt the power of another blow which stripped his consciousness away.

His first sensation, even before he opened his eyes, was of pain. Rivers of acid sizzled along his tendons and flared in his joints, and the back of his head was pounding so much he thought his skull was about to split. He woke to the stark light of the kitchen. He was tied to one of the chairs with an oily rope looped unnecessarily tightly around his chest, arms and shins. His arms had been yanked at an excruciating angle behind him, so that the wood of the chair bit painfully into the soft tissue of his triceps. His feet were pulled behind the chair's front legs and lashed there. The pain and disorientation made him nauseous and for a second he thought he was going to vomit.

'So, Little Boy Blue's finally awake.' Sarah's voice came from somewhere behind him. When he tried to turn his head to see her, the tendons in his neck burned with pain. She waited a cruel moment after his groan before walking into his line of vision.

'What's happening?' he said weakly, fighting against the crazy jumble of his thoughts. It almost seemed like another hallucination, but the pain told him otherwise.

She laughed. 'What's happening? Oh, Jon, sometimes I wonder if you're naïve or just stupid.'

Jon shook his head, trying to clear some of the cotton wool that was obscuring his thought processes. 'Did I see Richard—?'

'Hello, old chap.' Richard's voice boomed from behind, but his friend made no attempt to move where Jon could see him.

Jon flexed his muscles against the ropes, but they were bound so tight he had lost all feeling in his hands. He shook himself from side to side, but they didn't shift a millimetre. Sarah and Richard both laughed.

'This isn't funny!' Jon snapped.

Sarah gave a secretive smile, then turned to the cupboard and took out a jar of coffee. 'It's not meant to be funny, Jon. It's deadly serious.' She unscrewed the lid, then flicked on the kettle. She looked past Jon and asked, 'Do you want a coffee?'

'That would be nice,' Richard replied. A laugh. 'You know how I like it.'

'Stop this now,' Jon said. 'Come on. Who hit me? That was a bastard thing to do. Was it you, Richard? It was, wasn't it?'

Sarah finished making the coffee, then turned to Jon. 'We're going to have a chat. We'll see you later.'

'No! Let me free now!'

She laughed again, a tinkling, mocking sound, as she stepped around him in a wide arc.

'I said—!'

But they were already on their way to the drawing room, chatting and laughing together as if nothing was wrong.

Even when his head had cleared, Jon couldn't begin to grasp the game Richard and Sarah were playing. If Sarah wanted to punish him for abandoning her in Covent Garden, it was a cruel and heartless way to go about it. Or if they wanted to teach him a lesson for what they saw as his abandonment of his responsibilities, it was hopelessly unlikely to change his mind. What were they thinking? It made his head spin to consider it, and he was furious to think they had left him there trussed up and impotent, like some steer waiting to be broken. He called out to them a couple of times, but there was no response, and in his anger he decided the only way to get them back was to make so much noise they'd worry about it disturbing the neighbours.

He threw his head back and yelled until his throat was raw, caught his breath, then did it again. Just as he was about to bellow for a third time, a hand came out of nowhere and clamped around his jaw, the fingers digging into his cheeks so painfully he yelped and his mouth widened in an involuntary response. He caught a glimpse of a screwed-up handkerchief before it was rammed between his lips, then jabbed down until it was pressing at the back of his throat and he was choking and gagging. A second later he heard a ripping sound and then a strip of adhesive tape was plastered over his mouth. The sense of claustrophobia almost induced an anxiety attack and he had to force himself to calm down and breathe through his nose before he choked and died. There was a second or two of panic when the darkness seemed to be closing around his vision, and then his control reasserted itself.

They both stepped in front of him. Richard was angry, but Sarah was smiling, although he recognized the glint of irritation in her eyes; he'd always thought of it as her shark's smile.

'You noisy bastard,' she said lightly.

Jon glared at her until his attention was gradually pulled by something jarring on the periphery of his vision. Richard's arm was around Sarah's shoulders, at first sight a friendly gesture. But his fingers were stroking her neck sensitively, just a touch, a caress, but it was an intimate act that went several steps beyond friendship. Jon's stomach clenched and he couldn't tear his eyes away.

Richard followed Jon's stare to the stroking fingers and then he smiled knowingly. Slowly he brought his other hand up to Sarah's throat before lowering it to the top button of her blouse. He undid it with a deft flick of his fingers and moved on to the second. Sarah glanced at his hand, then at his face, and smiled back. Jon was transfixed in horror. She wasn't wearing a bra. He saw the delicacy of her breast bone, the smooth skin between her breasts where he would trace his tongue during their lovemaking. Richard slipped his fingertips under the material and gradually eased his hand over her breast. Her nipple was erect. Jon wanted to look away, but there was the same terrible fascination of watching a car crash. Richard kept his eyes firmly on Jon, mocking, challenging. His fingertips stroked the underside of her breast, then gently moved up over the curve until they reached her nipple where they circled once, twice, teasing her excitement. Finally he gave her nipple a gentle pinch. Sarah closed her eyes with a murmur of pleasure.

Lightning flashed across Jon's vision and he thought he was going to be sick. When his eyes cleared, Richard had pulled the blouse back over her breast and they were both grinning at him. There was something in their expressions – mockery, cruelty, a complete disregard for Jon or his feelings – that triggered a total collapse of his reason. He yelled and screamed, but it only came out as pathetic muffled yelps, and that simply made them laugh more, which drove him to greater excesses of fury. He threw himself from side to side with such wild rage the chair eventually tipped over on its side and he slammed his head on the cold floor. When the stars had cleared, they were still laughing.

'Well, that little episode has only served to make me horny,' Richard said in a matter of fact way. 'How about you, sweetness?'

Sarah hmmed her approval.

'I think we'll have to go and have a bit of nookie. Shame to leave you here like this, old chap – not very hospitable, I know – but one simply cannot think straight when one's got an erection.'

From his position Jon couldn't see their faces, but he no longer wanted to. Hot tears of frustration, betrayal and hurt welled up in his eyes and he blinked them tightly shut.

In that darkness, his sense of hearing was suddenly sharply defined. He heard the tramp of their feet as they left the kitchen, a giggle, and then, to his horror, he realized they were taking their sex no further than the hall. He wanted to cover his ears, but he couldn't, and every sound carried as if it was right next to him, every rustle of garments being removed, every smack of lips on flesh, every kiss, every suck, every moan, every thrust, until he prayed for the screams of anxiety in his mind to push him over into the uncomprehending peace of madness.

'They've found another body.' Miles looked pale and disorientated. 'Down in the tube, in a tunnel off Covent Garden.'

'Fucking hell, he doesn't waste any time, does he?' Culver yelled. 'I can see our jobs disappearing by the minute.'

'You think it's him, then?'

'Of course it's him! Why do you think he did a bunk?'

'But how—'

'I don't know how or why, he just did! How did he get out of the cell? I don't fucking know. How did he murder that poor bitch in the hospital without getting a speck of blood on him? I have no fucking idea. Where did he hide the murder weapon and her ear? Not even an inkling. But it was him, Ryan. It was fucking him and we had him!' Culver screwed up a piece of paper on his desk and hurled it at the bin with such force it flew across the room.

'We're going to get a right fucking rocket when the chief hears he got out of our so-called top security fucking cell and killed again,' Miles said glumly.

'You don't know the half of it, Ryan.'

Culver was feeling just as morose, but it wasn't for himself, it was for the poor sod they'd found in the tube. Another unnecessary death, and this time he felt a degree of responsibility. If he hadn't been sidetracked by that Ripper tape, if he'd questioned *Peter* more intensely first time round, they might have prevented any more bloodshed. But deep down he still couldn't believe the well-dressed, quietly spoken man *was* the killer. Culver instinctively sensed a harmlessness about him, maybe even a decency, that was in direct opposition to the vile acts that had been committed. He had trusted his feelings so much he hadn't followed up the line of enquiry with the required tenacity. How could his instincts have failed him so completely?

'Man or woman?' he blurted.

'What?'

'Victim number five.'

'A woman. They think.'

'Shit.' Culver blanched, checked his watch. Christmas Eve was getting on. He should be at home with Shirley, not dealing with things that made him sick to be alive. 'Come on. We'd better get down there,' he said wearily.

'You know Reid's cleared off to Scotland until fucking Hogmanay, the jammy bastard?' Miles said sourly. 'By the time we get the stand-in acquainted with the files and full autopsy, it'll mean a call-out on Christmas Day.'

'Par for the fucking course.'

The door opened and Detective Garner entered, carrying

a large folder. Culver turned to him warily; with his blond hair and pale complexion, he looked even younger than Miles, too innocent for the kind of work they were involved in. Culver took the folder from him with a grunt and opened it to reveal a pile of photocopies of the artist's impression of *Peter*.

'Here we are, Ryan. I've got something for you.' He dropped the folder on Miles' desk. 'Most of those dealing room types will be out and about getting pissed out of their heads. Get a team together and take these round every bar and restaurant in the Square Mile. Somebody will know him.'

'Right, Charlie.' Miles jumped up, eager to be doing something productive.

'I'll do my best not to get knocked down by a fucking tube train, then I'm heading home to try to forget all this ever happened. Give me a call first thing. By that, I mean after ten.'

When Miles left with Garner trailing behind, Culver stood alone in the incident room, trying to recall a treasured memory of a childhood Christmas with his parents in their Walthamstow semi. After five minutes, nothing had surfaced, and he had the terrible feeling it had been lost for good.

Jon was shocked alert by the sensation of rough hands grabbing his shoulders and hauling the chair into an upright position. He had been drifting in his own troubled thoughts since the sounds of lovemaking had died away, and he had lost all track of time. Sarah wandered in front of him and leaned against the units, her skin still flushed from the sex. Jon focused on a bead of perspiration on her top lip with a terrible fascination.

'Are you going to be a good boy now?' she asked.

Jon nodded, unable to look her in the face. He felt like something was broken inside him, that he would never be able to pull himself together again. Richard's huge hands snaked round and tore the tape painfully from his mouth before roughly wrenching out the handkerchief. Jon coughed and sucked in a gasp of clean air.

'That's better,' Sarah said. 'Do what you're told and you won't get punished.' His wallet lay on the floor where it had slipped from his pocket when the chair fell. She picked it up, examined it, then tossed it to Richard.

'What's this all about?' Jon asked breathlessly.

'What it's about is what a disappointment you've been to us,' Sarah sighed. Jon hated it when she used her manipulative little girl nuances; knowing her as well as he did, he knew how fake it was, and it was an insult she was using them with him.

'You and Richard . . .' he began, but he couldn't finish the sentence.

She nodded. He thought he caught a gleam of guilt in her eye, but if it was there at all, it vanished in a flash.

'How long?'

'Almost from the start.'

'The start?' Jon's head swam. 'From when we first met? Before we were married?'

'Before we were married, after we were married.' She wandered over to her handbag on the kitchen table and pulled out her cigarettes. She lit one with a flourish; it was a defence mechanism Jon recognized. 'Don't look so fucking hurt,' she snapped. 'You look like a pathetic puppy. Listen, it didn't get serious until you came out of the clinic and gave up on our life.'

'I didn't give up on us.'

'You think the life and us are separate?'

'But before we were married? How often—'

'Often enough.' She shifted uncomfortably and looked at Richard as if Jon had suddenly disappeared. 'I need a pee. I'll be back in a minute.' She almost skipped from the kitchen.

When Richard didn't take her place where Jon could see him, Jon snapped, 'Richard! Richard! Come here!'

Richard stepped in front of him with a sly grin. 'What is it, old chap?'

'*What is it?*' Jon exclaimed incredulously.

'I shagged Sarah the night after you did her. No one had any ties, there were a lot of drugs flying around—'

'But you carried on, even when you knew I was seeing her seriously?'

'It takes two to tango.' He paused thoughtfully. 'Bit of a cliché, but it's true. And you know Sarah has a bit of an appetite for all sorts of things. She doesn't like to be tied down if she's not getting what she wants. Or rather she does like to be tied down, eh?' He winked.

Jon looked away in disgust.

'It was a bit of fun between us. A quick shag here and there. You didn't have to find out.'

'We were friends!'

'Of course we were.'

'Didn't that mean anything?'

Richard shrugged. 'We had a laugh together, didn't we?' His eyes showed he would never grasp what Jon meant.

Jon closed his eyelids and sensed flashes of golden light sparking across his mind like meteor storms over a dead planet. His mouth was devoid of all moisture, his tongue swollen and impotent against his cheek. His back tingled from a trickle of sweat and an itch was developing beneath the rope over his right foot. He was aware of all the sensations in a heightened way because they drove everything else out of his head; living in the moment meant he didn't have to reflect on what he was hearing and kept the unbearable pain at bay. Even so, he couldn't stop himself probing at the wound.

'How did you manage to keep it a secret? Was I so stupid?'

'Well, to be honest, old chap, you were, though gullible is probably a better word. You're too smart to be stupid.'

'Trusting.'

'Exactly.' Richard nodded as if Jon had identified some particularly contemptuous character trait. 'How did we keep it a secret? Well, we didn't entirely. It was almost common knowledge around the office.'

'What?'

'You know how it is in an office. They love all that gossipy stuff. A few of the boys helped cover my tracks, came up with the occasional smokescreen to keep you happy. And then it just, you know, gets around.'

'They were all laughing at me?'

'There were a few jokes.'

The memory of being thrown out of the Christmas party loomed hideously in the light of a new perspective. The grins and secret winks as he stood drinking with Richard and Sarah. The mocking expressions on the faces of Bell, Rutherford and Smallthorn as the bouncers hauled him away. Bell sneering, 'Your wife and Mr Beeson are still welcome here.' And then other memories followed suit, a grim, speeding procession of nudges and laughter, sly jokes he had joined in with, but which he now saw had been directed at him.

'How could you do it?' he said pitifully. 'Morally—'

Richard sighed wearily. 'You've never really grasped it at all, have you? The fundamental lesson. I've said it before, but it still astonishes me that you can't even see it. Now that *is* stupid. Morals, ethics, values . . . all these words you keep dropping into your conversation. They mean nothing. They're from a different time. These days the rules of the City are the rules of the country: if it's possible to take something, you do; look after yourself because no one will look after you; everything counts in large amounts – that was the song, wasn't it? It's always amazed me that you did so well while being completely blind to the facts of life.

Still, God looks after children, drunks and idiots, I suppose – and you qualify for all three.'

'You really are an envious bastard, aren't you? I thought it was all part of this act you—'

'Sarah has always understood how it is,' he continued as if Jon hadn't spoken. 'She knows the score: look after yourself. It's a pity some of her didn't rub off on you.'

'How could you hang around with me if you found me so reprehensible?'

'It was particularly hard at the start.' Richard levered himself up on to the units which creaked under his weight. 'When I joined the company, the first thing I did was find out who was the top dog, the BSD. Then I made sure I got the desk next to yours so I could see how you were working, steal some of your tricks. And of course it didn't hurt for me to be seen around with you. Success by association and all that.'

In Richard's face, Jon saw reflected all the horrors he had projected upon himself. Richard was the culmination of the process which began in Jon when he joined Steelguard, a cautionary tale permanently at his side, but he had been too blind to see it. *Too trusting*, he thought with self-loathing.

'I pretty soon got the measure of you,' Richard continued. 'You're not exactly Machiavellian, after all. No deep, dark undercurrents in old Jonathan Summers. Sadly, what you see is what you get. Actually, I overestimated you in the first couple of days. I thought this thoughtful, caring persona was some kind of game you were playing. When I realized it was for real . . . !' He laughed heartily and shook his head. 'Remember old Smethwick and the red dye? I knew you'd fall for that! I could see the look of distaste on your face when he was slagging off that stupid bitch and it came to me in a flash what I could do to win you over. Then it was just a matter of feeding you treats like a dog.'

'You're so smart, aren't you, Richard,' Jon said coldly.

Richard's face darkened. 'Smarter than you, old chap. As you will soon see.'

Sarah marched in, rubbing her nose like she had an uncontrollable itch. Her eyes had a glittering, cold, coke-induced sheen as her gaze skittered contemptuously over everything she surveyed. It was a predictable response to the situation; Sarah had never been very good with emotions, so she had simply anaesthetized them. She looked at Jon, then looked away before he could speak.

'Everything under control?' she said to Richard.

'Yes. We've just been having a marvellous conversation about the facts of life.'

'When shall we start?'

Richard checked his watch. 'Oh, later. Let's crack open a bottle of wine. It is Christmas Eve, after all.'

Whatever they were saying was lost on Jon; his entire attention was drawn to Sarah. He couldn't help punishing himself with all the vibrant moments that had been the foundation of their relationship; standing at the top of the Empire State Building, surveying New York like they were rulers of the world; the two of them alone on the dance floor in St Lucia; kissing in the rain after Matthew Gold's wake. Fragments that gave his life meaning. When he thought how little he really had, it made his eyes sting.

'Why did you marry me?' he asked bluntly.

She glared at him. 'Why do you think? I loved you.'

'But you were having an affair. You—'

She waved her hand dismissively. 'Stop acting like a child. We got on well together. We liked the same things, we had the same aims. We complemented each other perfectly. You were the one who wrecked that – don't blame me.'

'But what about something deeper?'

'Pull yourself together. That's as deep as it gets.'

'I can't believe this.' Jon shook his head in dismay. 'That's your definition of love? What about the things we talked over after Matt's wake?'

She smiled and glanced slyly at Richard.

'What is it?' Jon asked.

'Funny you should mention that, old chap,' Richard said with a grin. 'That's when you came closest to catching us at it. We'd had enough of the wake – all those morbid people droning on about how decent the dearly departed was – so we thought we'd slip outside for a bit of nookie. Can't beat an open-air, backstreet knee-trembler for that surreptitious thrill.'

Jon stared at Sarah in disbelief. She shrugged, looked away.

Richard pulled a bottle of claret from the wine rack and opened it with a flourish. Sarah took two crystal glasses from the cupboard.

'We were going at it in the alley when we saw you wandering along like a lost puppy,' Richard continued. 'Talk about coitus interruptus! I almost had a heart attack. I dived back into the doorway while Sarah whipped up her knickers and went into her act. I must compliment her. She's bloody good when she turns it on.'

Jon couldn't tear his eyes from her face, praying she would deny it. She stared back unflinchingly with a faint sneer.

'I remember your heart beating against me so fast,' he said.

'The sex and the panic,' she replied. 'I was sure you'd seen us.'

'All those things you said—'

She shrugged again and sipped her wine. 'I think I overcompensated for my fear of being discovered.'

'Oscar material, eh?' Richard said with a wink.

Jon felt like his heart had been torn out, and his stomach was twisting painfully with an anxiety he hadn't felt for days. He had nothing. Nothing at all.

'"Fredo, you're my older brother and I love you. But don't ever take sides with anyone against the family again.

Ever."' The words rolled out, hard and dead like his emotions.

'You really should have spent longer in that clinic,' Richard said.

Jon took a deep breath to compose himself. 'OK, you've made your point. You took me for a real ride. You can untie me now. What's the matter – did you think I'd blow my top and go for you both with a kitchen knife? You didn't have to go to these lengths if you wanted a divorce.'

'I don't want a divorce,' Sarah said.

'No,' Richard continued. 'We just want to kill you.'

London swarmed with too many cars and too many people for that time on Christmas Eve. Every street in the West End seemed to have its own patrol car caught in the backed-up traffic, its flashing lights painting the buildings an apocalyptic red, a cold-hearted blue. The thick snow, still falling heavily, had obviously contributed something to bringing the capital to a grinding halt, as had some kind of obstruction at Covent Garden tube which had frozen a significant part of the Underground network. But as Lisa trudged through the drifts along Oxford Street, she was convinced it had more to do with the oppressive police presence, not just in the cars, but in the pubs and bars and on street corners; it seemed like every cop in London was out and about, holding up journeys home, even as the West End prepared to close up shop for the holidays. Something to do with the murders, she guessed, but the atmosphere of fear and oppression which it engendered only made her feel worse.

When the tubes were cancelled she thought the West End would be a good location to get a taxi to Highgate, but every cab seemed occupied, even the unlicensed ones that always hung around in Charing Cross Road. And now she was cold and exhausted and her only option seemed like walking the two or three miles to Arcadia.

She blinked away a few tears. She should have been taking it easy with a glass of wine, laying out Jamie's presents for the morning ahead, revelling in that rejuvenating Christmas happiness, not weighed down by a misery that almost paralysed her.

What if Jamie and Mr Velikovsky weren't at Jon's house? The answer lay in a gulf of shadows that threatened to suck her in. More tears. She wiped her eyes with the back of her hand, then bowed her head into the gale and turned off Oxford Street into the maze of side streets that led up to Regent's Park.

The crowds thinned and disappeared away from the main thoroughfare, and she soon found herself walking along pavements where the snow was undisturbed. Further on, in the shadows of a converted Victorian business block, was a minicab incongruously waiting for fares, its engine idling, occasionally coughing and spouting a gout of thick smoke into the cold air.

Her relief gave her energy and she ran to it and yanked open the passenger door. 'Can you take me to Highgate?' she asked breathlessly.

The driver was tall and thin with a bald head and the demeanour of an undertaker. 'Climb in,' he said with an accent which she couldn't quite place.

There was an odd aroma in the car, almost like frying bacon. 'I was lucky you were here,' she said, sliding across the back seat. 'To be honest, it's not the best spot to be waiting for a fare.'

'Perhaps I was waiting for you.'

'Another Christmas miracle?' she replied sardonically.

'This is the night when anything can happen.' He glanced at her in the rear view mirror and sniggered. As a passing streetlamp shed its light through the window, she had the disconcerting impression that his smile was made up of tiny pointed teeth like a piranha's, but before she could be certain it had fallen away and his waxy face was emotion-less again.

Lisa shivered and forced herself to look out of the passenger window. The cab wound its way through deserted streets, and she was amazed the driver knew so many short cuts and rat-runs to take them away from the main traffic-clogged avenues. She thought she knew London well, but there were many streets she didn't recognize at all, tiny, winding routes with overhanging houses, others with dark Gothic manses, oppressive and threatening. At times she thought they were no longer in the capital.

'How much longer?' she asked.

'As long as a laugh and as near as death,' the driver replied.

'I beg your pardon?'

'You will arrive in time. You will not miss the sacrifice.'

'What sacrifice?'

He was grinning in the rear view mirror once again, but this time she refused to look. Feeling increasingly unnerved, she pulled her coat tighter around her and pressed back into the seat, ready to kick open the door and flee at any sign of trouble.

Not a minute too soon for her, they turned into Jon's street, although she didn't recognize the approach. When the driver pulled up outside Arcadia, she dipped into her pocket for her purse, but he turned in his seat threateningly and snapped, 'No charge!'

Lisa bristled. 'I've never heard of a cabbie giving a ride for free.'

His lips spread slyly. 'The price asked of you is already high.'

His gaze made her squirm, and she flipped open the door and jumped out without another word. When she heard the car pull away to the end of the street, she glanced back briefly and had the oddest impression that it wasn't a car at all. In the flash between blinks, she saw something black and leathery, a shimmer of scales, a blazing red eye, and then it was gone in a flurry of snow.

Unnerved, she turned and ran through the thick drifts and up the steps to Arcadia's front door. She was surprised to find it ajar. Cautiously, she pushed it open a little wider, but before she could call out she heard the raised voices of Jon's wife and a man she didn't recognize coming from the kitchen. Her instincts told her to back away, but there was something in the tone that held her rapt. And then she heard Jon's voice, and a threat against him that made her blood run cold. Against her better judgment, she stepped in.

Before she could stop it, the door closed behind her with the faintest click. Anxiously, she tried the handle, but for some reason it wouldn't budge.

There was an atmosphere of violence flowing from the kitchen as the shouts and threats grew louder. Panicking now, Lisa hurried into the drawing room to try the window. But when she pulled back the curtains, she saw no view of a snow-covered street. Instead, the glass seemed black until she realized she was looking through it into impenetrable darkness. A burst of fire in the distance and another one much closer confirmed her fears. Half-heartedly, she rattled the lock, but it too seemed frozen.

The tightening in her chest heralded a fear quite different from what she had felt when she realized Jamie was missing; that was a fear of mortal things. What she experienced as she let the curtains fall back was something she hadn't tasted since she was a child in church with her mother, when the priest had delivered a fire and brimstone sermon addressing the damnation that awaited all sinners; spiritual fear, inexplicable, unattached to day-to-day reality.

Back in the hall, the voices had died down. With the only way being forward, Lisa crept up the stairs to see if she could get a better view of the kitchen through the banisters.

She felt like a child trying to sneak a glance at a troubling TV show after her parents had sent her to bed.

In the shadows near the top she had an unhindered view of a scene that made her head spin: Jon tied to a chair like some Nazi interrogation victim in an old war movie; his wife, whom she always thought of as *The Bitch*, looking on, grinning, not doing anything about it; and a big, red-haired man toying with a cut-throat razor. As she watched, the big man walked over and kissed The Bitch and then they both laughed.

Lisa's stomach turned. It was a hideous picture of cruelty. She couldn't see Jon's eyes, but she knew from the slump of his shoulders and the roll of his head that he was in torment. Why were they destroying him?

Oh, Jon, she thought, *I knew she was no good for you.*

Before she could work out all the complex possibilities that arose from the tableau, the big man suddenly raised the razor, glanced at its gleaming edge and nodded. Then he moved towards Jon's face.

Miles moved among the seething mass of drinkers at Portnoy's with a mixture of the contempt he felt for all people who didn't have his background and hope that they were finally on the verge of a breakthrough. There had already been several positive mumblings about the artist's impression, but nobody had yet come up with a name; it was only a matter of time.

Near the back of the bar the Christmas cheer was getting out of hand. Amid the smoke from the party poppers and the streamers and the bobbing party hats, some overweight drunk was dancing like a hippopotamus with gout while unbuttoning his trousers in front of a posse of screaming women. Miles eyed the scene with mild irritation, then thought better of telling them to calm down; it *was* Christmas.

Distracted, he failed to hear the first response from the smart-suited man examining the sketch.

'Oi! Are you listening?' Rodney Self said, tugging at Miles' arm. 'I said I know him.'

Miles noted Self's drunken glaze and mentally crossed his fingers. 'Well, who is it then?'

'It's old Jonny Summers. Poor bastard used to work for us.'

'Who's us?'

'Steelguard.'

Miles snapped alert. He tapped one of Self's party on the shoulder and took his chair, spinning it round so he could sit on it backwards. 'So why's he a poor bastard?'

'Got the bullet earlier in the year after tossing his terminal out of the window. Flipped his lid. Too much nose candy and booze, know what I mean? He got banged up in some clinic for a while. What's he done, then?'

'He's the Grinch that stole Christmas.'

'You what?'

'Nothing. Where's he living now?'

'Clapham. Got a place overlooking the common.'

'He's not there any more,' the drinker to Self's right interjected. 'Richard Beeson said he was renting some place in North London.'

'You know the address?' The drinker shrugged. Miles didn't mind. He flipped his notebook shut smugly and jumped to his feet. They'd find the place in Clapham easily and then it was just a matter of time to trace him back to his hide-out.

Outside in the car, he decided against calling Culver. The old man deserved some time with his wife and he would be busy enough on Christmas Day. He picked up the radio and called in the details, confident it would all be over by Boxing Day.

*

The razor shimmered in front of Jon's eyes, triggering memories of the Scissorman's blades poised to pierce into his brain, high up in the dome of St Paul's Cathedral. Sweat slicked his back and the anxiety knot in his stomach felt like someone had been hitting him with a hammer. He had finally accepted that they were really going to do it. Richard's face was set with determination; a muscle spasmed just beneath his eye. Sarah had the cold expression of someone about to perform a monstrous but absolutely necessary task. Jon's gaze was locked on her, searching for some sign of the person he thought he knew and loved, but deep down he knew it was the same old Sarah; he was the one who was guilty, of being blind and stupid.

The razor suddenly obscured his vision of her diamond stare, and he snapped his head as far away from it as he could, but that only bared the ripe curve of his throat.

'I really am sorry about this, old chap,' Richard said flatly, 'but it truly is necessary. It's the survival instinct, you see. Me or you. Us or you.'

'You've got to tell me why this is happening. You owe me that,' Jon pleaded with a bleak feeling that he was only prolonging the inevitable.

'No, I don't. There's no point in dragging this detestable business out. I'm finding it difficult enough as it is. I can't even cut up steak.'

Jon saw no emotion in Richard's face, nothing he could connect with; there was only the cold, blue glow of self-preservation.

'Just get on with it,' Sarah snapped, sucking hard on yet another cigarette, her eyes flitting in every direction but Jon's.

Richard drew back his arm and prepared to make a cutting swipe.

The knock at the door thundered along the hall. Sarah jumped like a startled rabbit, her eyes wide with terror. Richard clamped his huge hand over Jon's mouth and rested the razor against the pulse of Jon's jugular vein. Both of them were as rigid as statues, staring out into the hall; Jon knew his life hung by a thread.

There was a moment of tense silence and then the brass knocker hammered again.

'They're not going to go away. See who it is,' Richard hissed.

As Sarah's heels clattered along the hall, Richard's fingers bit deeply into Jon's cheeks. His impassive expression had been replaced by a murderous glare that left no doubt of his intentions. 'Don't fucking move,' he threatened.

From the muffled conversation at the end of the hall, Jon couldn't tell the identity of the visitor, but Sarah was cool and curt and the door slammed a moment later.

'It was just some old man and a young boy asking to see Jon!' she said incredulously when she returned to the kitchen. 'At this time!' She chain-lit another cigarette with a shaking hand and glared at Jon. 'I suppose you mad people flock together.'

'What did you tell him?' Richard asked, still refusing to remove his hand.

'I said Jon wasn't going to be back until the small hours and I was just off to spend the night with a friend so he couldn't wait. It kept the alibi intact.'

Richard nodded cautiously. 'Still, we could have done without it.'

'He was very persistent,' she added. 'We should put off doing anything for a while just in case he comes back.'

Richard sighed and snapped the razor shut. 'Please don't make a song and dance, old chap,' he said to Jon. 'I'll be forced to put the tape back on and it could get very uncomfortable. Especially, you know, at the end.'

Sarah glanced at the clock. 'Eleven-thirty.'

'What a way to spend Christmas Eve,' Richard moaned. 'I'll be glad when this is over.'

'I know!' Sarah exclaimed excitedly. 'We'll open the

Christmas presents. That will pass the time.' She hurried out to fetch them from under the tree.

'She's a live wire, isn't she?' Richard grinned.

'Are you going to tell me why you're doing this now?' Jon asked coldly.

'Oh Lord!' Richard threw his hands up in despair. 'Can't you work it out for yourself? I thought you were supposed to be the smart one.'

Jon waited patiently.

'Oh, all right. If it will make the next few minutes bearable. Steelguard's long-term strategic report leaked to our esteemed rival. You didn't do it.'

'No.'

'Because I did.'

'Why?'

'Why do you think? Big bucks, in the first instance. And then when the heat had died down, a new job with the buyer with a promotion and a significant increase in salary and bonuses. Then I'll be top dog.'

Jon sneered. 'Do you really think they'll give you a job? How will they ever be able to trust you?'

'Oh, get real. Everyone in the City knows how the business works. Initiative and success are rewarded. No one can be trusted. So it doesn't matter if they think I'm a scummy crook as long as I keep the coffers full.'

'I think you're wrong.'

'With your track record at reading the business, you're in no position to pass comment,' Richard said tartly.

'So you set me up?' Jon thought the dagger was up to its hilt, but it twisted a little more.

'Well, we tried to, we really did, but by some complete fluke you kept thwarting us. Of course, if you had stumbled there wouldn't be any need for this.'

Jon chewed on the inside of his lip until he tasted blood. 'How long have you been planning this?'

'Once we'd decided you were a lost cause, it all fell into

place. I was looking for a way out of my predicament – unfortunately I hadn't quite obscured the trail and fingers were starting to point in my direction. Sarah saw in me a partner who enjoyed the things she valued. The pay-off I got and the promise of the job sealed the bid. We could maintain a decent lifestyle rather than the horsehair-shirt existence you were proposing to her. You really didn't know her, did you?'

Sarah returned with an armful of presents and dumped them on the side. She tossed one to Richard, then said to Jon as an afterthought, 'Sorry, honey, I didn't get you anything.'

'We simply thought we could kill two birds with one stone,' Richard said, slitting wrapping paper with the razor. 'Get me off the hook and get your whingeing out of our lives. I planted enough seeds with Smallthorn and the directors to get you in the frame, but I could tell they still suspected me.'

'The Christmas party?' Jon asked.

'The state you were in we thought you'd hang yourself easily,' Richard sighed. He tore the wrapping paper off the box and held up a bespoke silk shirt from Jermyn Street. 'Look at that. Isn't it marvellous? You have excellent taste, old lump.' He blew a kiss to Sarah.

'So you really were trying to get me caught in Steelguard that night?' Jon wriggled his wrists against the ropes, but it was obvious they weren't going to budge.

'I certainly did my best. I even delayed my warning call to try to draw the guard towards you. God knows how you wriggled out of that one. You really do have the luck of the Irish. Of course, I can't believe you fell for my flannel and went in the first place.'

'I trusted you.'

'There's that word again.'

Sarah unwrapped a box of Joseph perfume, obviously

from Richard, and sprayed some on to her wrists before smelling it. 'My favourite,' she said with a smile.

'Sarah and I were already celebrating your incarceration when you walked through the door,' Richard continued. 'That called for another spot of fine acting from your darling wife. Of course, after that, with your refusal to listen to any more of my words of wisdom, the situation got rather desperate.'

'So who's idea was it to kill me?'

Richard glanced at Sarah and smiled; she looked away uncomfortably. Jon felt the final twist of the knife in his heart.

'There was no other option,' Richard said. 'You weren't going to go down obligingly which meant my neck was firmly on the block, and that didn't benefit anybody. So we came up with a little scenario: a Christmas Eve burglary by some chancers. You, unfortunately, tortured and killed for the location of your non-existent valuables. Sarah and I with rock-solid alibis elsewhere – I won't bore you with the details. And then the dramatic discovery of some Steelguard papers on the premises which pointed to you having access to the leaked strategic report. And everything works out swimmingly. I've already started planning for my new job. I've convinced that eager young chap Gary Finch to join me with his inexhaustible source of contacts. You should have looked after your resources, Jon.'

Jon smiled. 'You were going to meet him here last night, weren't you?'

Richard's eyes narrowed. 'Yes. Didn't turn up for some reason. Must have a word with him about that. How did you know?'

Sarah had picked up the present from Jon. She glanced at him oddly before beginning to unwrap it. When the silver mirror emerged, Sarah turned it over in her hands, then laughed.

'I saw you admiring it in Selfridges,' Jon said icily.

Sarah examined her reflection carefully, dabbing at the edge of her lipstick, brushing a stray hair from her brow. 'Yes, I remember.' She smiled at him pityingly. 'You really are a soppy fool, aren't you? But on this occasion you misread the situation.'

'What do you mean?'

'I wasn't admiring this little thing. I was using it to look at Richard so you wouldn't see.'

'She was giving me the eye, old boy.' Richard laughed. 'The Sarah Summers come-on.'

Jon stared at the floor desolately; there was nothing left within him.

After their laughter had died down, Richard said, 'Now I think it really is time.'

As Jon looked up, Richard's oversized fist slammed into his face. Light exploded behind his eyes and his nose gouted blood. Before he could yell out, Richard hit him again, bursting his lips against his teeth.

'Sorry I can't do this quickly, old boy, but you have to look the part.' Richard cracked his knuckles, then turned to retrieve the razor from the side where he had left it after opening the present.

At that moment, the cat jumped on to the table and padded over to sit near Jon. Both Sarah and Richard seemed oblivious to its presence. Through the pain and his hazy vision, Jon was drawn by its swimming green eyes flecked with gold. It was staring directly at him, hinting at a deep, alien intelligence. Its pink tongue flicked out over needle-teeth.

'Blood and punishment,' it rasped. 'Hearts reach out . . .'

Yes, Jon thought. *Yes!*

Richard clicked open the razor and held it aloft, but he was already too late. He looked at Jon in horror and it slipped from his slack fingers to clatter on the tiles. Sarah was frozen in shock, her mouth an O which emitted a faint, strangled cry. The hand mirror followed the razor down, exploding in a burst of glittering shards.

Jon could see both of them, but his vision was fragmented, distorted. Deep within him, an odd sensation wriggled frantically like a snake working its way past his organs. He knew instantly he had felt it several times before, but it had been forgotten like the pain of an operation. Glancing down, he obliquely realized his skin had burst, his shirt torn open, and twin blades were protruding from his ribcage. The wriggling became wilder, now like a rat in his intestine; arms followed the blades, and then a body heaved itself out of him. Thoughts burst like flares in the dark night of his ignorance and he suddenly saw everything with startling clarity.

Jon's bonds fell away at the touch of the Scissorman's blades and he stumbled off the chair, his limbs sparking with pain as the blood rushed back into them. And then the Scissorman was out, the first time he had set it free willingly.

Richard split open like a ripe fruit. The scream that tore from his throat was agonizing to hear, like a soul suffering hell's torment. The Scissorman was an artist, creating a masterpiece of blood and flesh, dismantling and rearranging in new and wonderful shapes. A cut that could be measured in microns, another that missed the bone by a hair's breadth. His creation was pain undreamed of, each little agony a payment for one of life's failings.

The fear that gripped Sarah was swept aside by a rush of self-preservation. She thrust Jon to one side and bolted from the kitchen, her heels skidding on the floor. Frantically, she yanked at the front door, then gave a shriek of frustration when it wouldn't open.

Jon scrambled out into the hall to see her dart into the drawing room before emerging a second later looking bewildered.

The house isn't letting you go, he thought deliriously.

She launched herself up the stairs, hoping to find somewhere to barricade herself in, only to stumble across Lisa rigid with terror near the top. Sarah's surprise was momentary. Snarling like an animal, she lashed out with her elbow, catching Lisa full on the temple.

If Lisa felt any pain, she didn't show it. She swung up a leg sharply and planted a boot at the back of Sarah's knees. With a cry of pain, Sarah went down hard on the stairs. Lisa managed to land three more punches of anger before Sarah wriggled free and disappeared along the landing.

'Bitch!' Lisa yelled after her.

Jon hauled himself to her side, almost teetering backwards until Lisa caught hold of his belt.

'I'm so sorry,' she said with her arms tight around him.

'No time,' he gasped. The disorientation and pain he had suffered had left him on the brink of blacking out.

In the kitchen, the sickening chopping sounds began to subside.

Lisa helped Jon to the top of the stairs and together they moved swiftly down the landing to the nursery. There was no sign of Sarah. In the middle of the floor, the saucer contained an ear, a kidney and a liver. The ritual was complete.

'That man downstairs . . . Is he dead?' Lisa wrapped her arms around her body to stop herself from shaking.

'I doubt it. Five deaths, that was all it was supposed to be.' Jon paused. 'Until mine.'

'Mr Velikovsky was right.' Lisa's eyes grew wide and unfocused; Jon grabbed her before the shock took hold. 'I saw him!' she added suddenly. 'At the door, with Jamie! I wanted to call out, but I was afraid of what they'd do to you.'

Jon led her across the room. Lisa looked around in terror as if she had seen where they were for the first time. 'What are we doing here? We're trapped!'

'There are doors,' Jon said hazily.

Lisa grabbed hold of his shoulders and shook him. 'Jon! Pull yourself together! We've got to get out of here!'

'Everything has changed,' he said. 'We've been flipping in and out.'

The sound of blades being scraped along a wall advanced towards them.

Jon checked his watch: midnight. 'We've crossed over,' he said.

Then he grabbed her by the shoulders, yanked open the wardrobe door and bundled them both inside.

19

Among clustering trees crusted with rime and snow, they wandered, adrift in their own thoughts. Darkness lay everywhere, on the edges of their vision, between the trees, pressing close upon their every movement. There was a sense of being not quite there, as if it was a drug trip or a hallucination.

'Where is this place?' Lisa asked dreamily.

Jon looked up at the towering sky, unpolluted by sodium glare, where a thousand, thousand stars glittered, more than he had ever seen in his life. He listened as the distant, intermittent cries of unknown animals echoed through the night. And he breathed in the rich aroma of complex scents he couldn't begin to describe. Then he said simply, 'The garden.'

Lisa put a supportive arm around his shoulder. 'This isn't the garden,' she stated defiantly.

'It is, sometimes. It's just a different way of seeing it.'

'Is this their place?'

Jon didn't need to answer.

Beneath their feet were uneven, flagged stones, heavily worn by age. 'Don't stray from the path,' he whispered.

Gradually, memories of the other place surfaced and Lisa stifled a sob. A tremor ran through her as if she was afflicted by some tropical fever. Jon knew she couldn't reconcile what was happening to her, and he was surprised he was coping himself, but then nothing really mattered any more;

everything he had experienced since the clinic had been a long, slow process of self-destruction. He would be glad when it was all over.

'Is it here?' she asked.

'The Scissorman? Yes. It's all been building towards this.'

'What does it want? I mean . . .' Another sob caught in her throat. 'There has to be a reason for all this suffering.'

'Does there? You think there's a reason for all the suffering that goes on around the world every day?'

'There has to be.'

She was right; there was too much intelligence behind it all. Why have such a complex ritual if it wasn't leading towards an end?

'It's not just the Scissorman,' Jon said. 'I'm responsible too.'

'How?'

'I let it out. I provided a refuge for it. It burrowed into my mind like a worm in a corpse, and there it discovered all the people I despised most, the ones I felt had stripped my life from me, and it made them its victims. I gave it direction.'

'You're talking about a subconscious act. You can't blame yourself.'

'I have to take responsibility for my own life. I was the one who made all those terrible decisions. Nobody forced me. But the Scissorman punished them anyway.'

'It's not that simple, Jon. That's a black and white child's view of the world.' She took his hand, calmer now she was thinking about someone else. 'You trust people, Jon. And they betrayed you.'

Away in the trees he heard a snort and a stamp of hooves. For an instant he glimpsed something that looked like a fiery ember burning in the shadows. He wondered if the Palatin was hungry.

'When the Scissorman was inside my mind, it controlled

me,' Jon continued. 'I wrote the note to Emma. I was its hands.'

'But *it* killed. Not you,' Lisa said forcefully. 'You could never do that.'

'I could. Anyone could, if they had a good enough reason.'

Her words did little to comfort him because beneath it all he couldn't shake the suspicion that he had allowed the Scissorman in willingly. That he had *wanted* those people to be punished.

Lisa's nails dug into his ribs, snatching him back from his introspection. 'Jon, I can see things among the trees,' she said. 'People.'

'Don't look at them. Just stay on the path and keep your eyes ahead.'

'But they could—'

'They won't bother us on the path.'

'Says who?'

'I dreamed it.'

He could see them too, silhouettes darker than the shadows that seemed at times animals, at other times men, sometimes both at once.

'Where are we going?'

'We'll get where we have to go. We don't have any choice in it any more. This has to be played out.'

'I'm scared,' she said tremulously.

Before he could reply, a piercing shriek split the silent night. They turned to see a shape hurtling towards them along the path, billowing like fog, but with what looked like the head of a vulture. And within the thunderous cloud things appeared to take shape, then disappear, like the leathern wings of a bat, claws and scales and bursts of fire, and before it, the cruel, snapping blades of the Scissorman. As its shriek rose up deafeningly, Jon knew they were seeing, if not its true shape, its truer shape.

A wave of terror flooded him. It was past midnight,

Christmas Day. After days of feeling secure in the knowledge that the Scissorman was hunting other victims, suddenly *he* was the target. And in that instant he knew what all the others had felt in the moment they looked into the Scissorman's face: hopelessness. There was no way to fight it.

Desperately, he hoped the path would protect them. He reached out to grab Lisa's hand and hold her fast, but she was already gone, bolting through the trees.

'No!' he yelled. 'Stay here!' He had a second to decide whether to save himself and then he launched after her, crashing through the grasping branches, feeling the razored brambles tear at his skin, but the moment he was past the treeline, she was nowhere to be seen.

With the shrieks growing louder, he ran aimlessly, yelling Lisa's name until his throat burned, stumbling numerous times until he winded himself so much he could barely breathe. And then suddenly he realized he could hear the shrieks no more. The forest was silent apart from the moan of the wind through the branches far above his head. He slowed to a walk and as he did so large flakes of snow began to drift down all around him, glowing with an extraordinary luminescence. Ahead of him he could see another light, golden and flickering; there was nothing to do but walk towards it.

What could have been five minutes or an hour later, he broke through into a clearing. On the far side, the Giant sat on a throne of heads, showing his pointed teeth in a cruel smile. Above him there was a crashing in the branches and the giggle of the flying boy.

'Nearly over now,' the Giant said with mock-comfort.

'You warned me about the Scissorman right at the beginning,' Jon said. 'Could I have stopped it?'

The Giant merely smiled. The giggling above turned into a screech of glee. 'The vile spirit of retribution forever punishes,' he said. 'It is the black smear on the heart, the cancer in the brain. When it is out, it dances to its own tune.'

'Where is this place, really?'

'It is in your head,' the Giant replied.

'In a dream,' the boy called out from above, still laughing.

'It does not exist,' the Giant continued. 'You are sitting in a room with blood on your hands after slaughtering your best friend. You despatched the five in blood and vengeance.' He raised his hands and gestured around him. 'This is how you see it, but it is not how it is.'

'Nothing is real,' the boy yelled.

Jon shook his head. 'I can't believe anything you say. You play games. You deceive.'

'Then why ask questions of me?'

The wind caught the stench of the heads that made up the throne, and Jon took a step back, trying not to gag.

The Giant leaned forward in response and stared with his piercing black eyes. 'Which is better – your cruel world or this cruel world? Dreariness or wonder? That is your choice.'

His face still had the waxy appearance of a mask; Jon wondered what lay beneath.

'See here,' the Giant added. 'I have something to show you.'

He pulled from the side of the throne a crystal bottle containing the golden light Jon had seen through the trees earlier. As the Giant held it out, Jon saw the light was flowing like liquid and within it things appeared to be moving. He looked closer. Suddenly screaming faces surfaced, Miles Heath, Emma, the others, all twisted in torment.

Jon took a step back. 'What is that?'

The Giant thrust it behind the throne before Jon could look again. The flying boy's laughter rose to a hysterical whine and then abruptly snapped off.

'Look!' the Giant said, raising his huge arm to point through the trees. 'Illumination!'

Far away, Jon thought he could see some kind of movement. When he looked back the Giant was gone.

Cautiously he set off in the direction the Giant had indicated. The snow was still falling heavily, but somehow he wasn't cold, nor did his broken nose or split lip ache any more. He realized unnervingly that he felt more alive in that moment than at any point since he was a child.

As he squeezed between the trunks and forced his way through the vegetation, he heard a strange burbling sound that slipped in and out of the wind. Moving closer, he identified it as the croaking of toads, hundreds of them gathered in one spot. With an anxious feeling growing in his stomach, he curbed his speed and tried to peer through the gloom.

On his hands and knees in the snow, retching like a cat with a furball, was the boy Jon had seen frozen in the pond. He was wearing the same quaint Victorian suit, but his flesh had the ochre tinge of nausea, and his shining black hair fell lankly across his sweat-slicked forehead.

Without a thought, Jon ran forward to help. He crouched down and put his arms across the boy's shoulders where muscles as taut as cables jerked under the skin. 'Are you OK?' Jon asked.

The boy looked up with wide staring eyes and in them Jon saw madness, desperation and years of suffering. The boy retched again and a globule of bright green mucus spewed from the corner of his mouth and fell to the ground, where it sizzled like acid. Then he turned and retched into the snow, only instead of vomit, a large, mucus-covered toad dropped from his mouth and hopped away to join the multitude nearby.

The boy looked back at Jon with tears in his eyes. 'They filled me with toads,' he said.

Jon lifted the boy into a sitting position and the boy

folded into Jon's arms with a hunger for human contact that was almost voracious. 'How long have you been here?' Jon asked.

'An eternity.' The boy's voice was like an old man's.

At the sound of him, Jon felt the years fold back. 'When I was a boy I heard you calling out for help.'

'Many times I pleaded for my mother and father to bring me home.' A shadow passed across his face and when he looked at Jon the madness was back in his eyes. 'The things they do! Like the torments in the Bible my father used to read aloud on Sunday evenings. It hurt, it hurt, it hurt! And as one ended, they would find another way to make me cry, another game to play. They like to play!' He grabbed Jon's sleeve anxiously. 'And you can never die! They keep you quick so you endure more, and they can enjoy more.' He closed his eyes. 'They filled me with toads.'

'What are they?' Jon asked queasily.

'Fairies and elves and dwarfs and giants and dragons and creatures from every story you heard in the nursery. But not really. Behind the glamour they are terrible to see.'

He was shivering more from shock than the icy chill that had suddenly descended on the spot as if a door had been opened, so Jon held him as tightly as he could and stroked his head, trying not to think of the terrible suffering the boy endured.

'What's your name?' Jon whispered after a time.

'David Saul Cartwright.' It was the boy from the article he had found in the ledger, as he had suspected. He had been in that forsaken place since 1888.

'How were you taken?'

'My father gave me up freely.'

'Your father?'

'I don't recall . . . so long . . . so much. I remember him crying. He loved me, he said. Then why did he do it? I think . . . yes, I think it was because of Jack of Knives.'

Jon's muscles tightened at the image the name suggested.

'There had been blood, hadn't there? Lots of it. In the East End. Poor women, my father said. Poor, poor women.' His voice trailed off. Jon brushed the snowflakes from his head, thinking of the long, dark history of the Scissorman and his world, and its intersections with our own, never seen for what it really was, so people could never prepare, or defend.

The black sigil on his forearm was starting to burn, and he rubbed it aimlessly until the skin around it was raw. There was little left for him now, but he could try to make it easier for others. If only he could see how it was supposed to pan out. The aims of the Scissorman were as obscure as when it first crossed over.

'I'll try to get you home,' Jon whispered in the boy's ear.

'They'll never let me go,' the boy said in a cracked voice. Then he added, 'I'm not fit. I'm like them now.'

'Hush. Of course you're not.'

'See,' he quavered, pointing in the direction of the croaking toads. 'See what I've done.' And then again, almost a whisper, 'See what I've done.'

An inexplicable feeling of dread swept through Jon and he laid the boy to one side and made his way towards the noise. The croaking grew louder and then louder still as he progressed until he couldn't begin to imagine how many toads there were.

He'd gone thirty feet when he saw the ground falling away into a pit. The croaking was coming from within. Cautiously, he peered over the edge.

Sarah was looking up at him with wild eyes, the toads filling the pit up to her neck. She had the same patina of madness he had glimpsed on the boy, only it had not yet taken an absolute grip. The toads wriggled and hopped around her, nuzzling at her ear, trying to force their way into her mouth. From the spasms of pain across her face, he could tell they were doing something else to her, but he had no idea what until she managed to force one hand free from the surging mass. The skin was melting away where the acidic slime from the toads touched it. They were eating her alive.

Suddenly she broke through her insanity and her eyes locked on Jon. 'Please!' she screeched. 'You've got to help me!'

He looked around for a branch or something he could use to help drag her from the pit, but he feared it was already too late.

'Please!' she screamed again so loudly he thought her throat would tear. 'Plea—!' Her cry was cut off as a large toad wriggled into her mouth. In her panic she tried to bite it in half, but somehow it resisted her and disappeared within.

Jon took a step back so he didn't have to see her suffering. The boy had arrived silently at his side.

'They will come for her in a while,' he said. 'They have new games to play.'

Jon remembered his dream, the journey across the strange land, what he saw among the trees and the creature saying, 'This *will* happen.' He shuddered and turned away.

Her cries suddenly returned with a fearful intensity – 'Jon! Jon! Jon!' over and over again – but they gradually diminished the further he walked from the pit, until he could hear them no more.

They walked through the eternal forest for what seemed like hours, but Jon guessed his only progress in time or space was towards his death. He glimpsed many strange and fearful things hidden among the trees, but, despite not being on the path, nothing bothered them. They were untouchable, already dead and taken. At one point he came across the garden pond and fountain, larger and more ornate than they had ever appeared in Arcadia's garden, oddly out of place in the wild wood; the boy shied away from it as if it would consume him.

As they were working their way through an area of

uncommonly thick vegetation, Jon heard strange noises emanating from a wild mass of briars. He was tempted to ignore it, as he had all the other odd, inhuman voices he had heard calling his name from the dark, but there was something in the faint, desperate sounds that he recognized. He told the boy to wait and attempted to peer into the tangled bank.

The first thing he saw was a pair of piercing eyes staring at him, and then he heard a strangled plea. 'Help me.'

The voice was familiar. 'Velikovsky?' he ventured.

Jon called to David for help and soon they were pulling the briars free from the old man. Their wicked barbs encircled his limbs and chest, biting into his flesh; there was a coil around his throat that was almost choking him. The boy tore at the briars in a frenzy, oblivious to the way they raked his skin, and soon Velikovsky was free. He collapsed into Jon's arms, red with blood.

'I climbed into the garden with the boy,' he gasped. 'Jamie. You must find him.'

'He's here?'

'They will not hurt him. At least, not yet.'

'We'll look,' Jon said, 'but you've got to rest for a while. You've lost a lot of blood.'

'There is no time! I know!' He closed his eyes and steadied himself against Jon to prevent a faint. 'I know what all this is for.'

Jon supported him as he staggered away from the briars and they slumped down at the foot of a gnarled oak. The boy stood a few feet away, watching them as if they were an alien species.

Velikovsky took a deep breath and then looked at Jon with watering eyes. 'The ritual, the five deaths, the placement of the bodies, it was all designed for one end – to open the door between this world and ours permanently.' A cough rattled in his throat, then became a fit that left him wheezing. When he recovered, he continued in a thin voice,

'At present, their access is confined to specific times and places. That is not enough. In the past, many centuries ago, they came and went as they pleased, although the place of their crossing was proscribed. Something changed that—'

'How do you know all this?'

Velikovsky held up his right hand where the bandage over his missing thumb was now dirty and torn. 'I paid my price for knowledge,' he said. 'If the ritual is not halted, they will cross freely. Not just the Scissorman, all of them. Can you imagine the terrors which would be inflicted on our rational world? When they last had access, the world was thinly populated. Now there is no space in our land for their wild magic. They would destroy everything.'

'It can still be stopped? At this late stage?'

Velikovsky searched Jon's face. 'It will cost you your life.'

'I haven't got anything to live for.'

'And more—'

His voice was cut off by a distant droning away in the night. They all looked round, feeling it in the pits of their stomachs as well as hearing it.

'It comes,' the boy said with a blank, white face. 'Jack of Knives, the Spirit of Vengeance.'

His cry was echoed by others nearby, rippling through the trees in a wave of fearful anticipation. Jon started and looked round, unaware that there could have been so many things so close.

The droning grew louder, like an angry cloud of bees, and after a few seconds Jon saw a speck of light in the trees, twisting and turning in on itself as it drew closer. Soon it became the billowing cloud with the head that resembled a vulture that he had seen earlier, rushing voraciously towards them, its blades clashing hideously.

The boy threw himself behind the tree and Jon found himself pressing hard against the oak as if he hoped it would swallow him up. The sigil on his forearm was on fire.

As it hurtled in their direction, tiny lights sprang up among the trees all around, like candles to show it the way. Out of the gloom, a dark shape emerged and struggled awkwardly among the trunks. As it drew closer, Jon saw it was Lisa, carrying Jamie in her arms. She looked dazed as if she had emerged from a heavy anaesthetic, but as her eyes fell on Jon connections sparked and she called out his name in relief. He ran towards her and pulled them both back to the foot of the tree; Jamie was whimpering as if he had been whipped.

Jon stroked his head. 'Hush!' he whispered. 'Don't worry.'

The Scissorman came upon them like a storm in the tropics, raging and vengeful. Jon could barely bring himself to look upon its terrible presence as it halted a few feet away, constantly shifting through a myriad of hideous shapes.

'Oh God!' Lisa sobbed. 'Is this hell?'

Jon put his arms around her and hugged her tightly.

'The time has come.' The Giant was standing nearby. Behind him, emerging from the shadows, came the blinking man, the golden woman from the police cell, the flying boy trailing a spark of light, and others, wonderful and terrible to look upon.

Before anything else could be said, Velikovsky moved with surprising animation. He snatched Jamie from Lisa's arms and threw himself forward until he was right in front of the Scissorman. Jamie howled and stretched out his arms to Lisa, but Velikovsky held him tight.

'Take him!' he said.

'No!' Lisa screamed. She tried to run forward, but thick grass had wrapped itself securely round her ankles. 'No!' she sobbed again.

'What are you doing?' Jon yelled.

The Giant smiled. 'The sacrifice. There is always a price to pay.'

Jon's mouth gaped as he struggled to comprehend what was happening.

'You cannot offer him up,' the Giant said to Velikovsky in a voice like thunder in the mountains. He pointed to Jon. '*He* must make the choice.'

Lisa grabbed Jon's shirt and thrust her face into his. Her eyes were wide and filled with terror as she pleaded, 'Jon! You can't do this! Not Jamie!'

'I don't understand—'

Velikovsky turned to him and shouted, 'It is the only way to end the ritual! A gift of innocence. They will take the boy back with them in return for giving up their claim on the passover. Your life will close the gate.'

Until the next time the Scissorman is freed, Jon thought. He experienced a sudden startling moment when everything around him seemed a façade, which peeled back to reveal him sitting in Arcadia's kitchen, clutching the razor with Richard and Sarah dead before him and Lisa and Jamie whimpering in a corner. But the vision faded in an instant and he was back staring at the Scissorman.

'Jon, listen to me,' Lisa pleaded.

He looked down at David, no longer human because of his suffering, who had emerged from behind the oak and was clutching Jon's trouser leg tightly. Jon understood why his father had given him up freely. The choice must have destroyed him.

'Help me, Jon! Help me!' Jamie called out. Jon tried not to hear.

Then Jon looked into the endlessly shifting cloud of the Scissorman. It had been a part of him for so long, dominating his thoughts, prevailing over every hour of his waking life, he almost felt a bond. It was his dark brother, the other side of him. He watched the shapes come and go, examined the hideous turn of its beaked head. He hated it. In an ideal world, he would have faced up to it and destroyed it with his own hands. But there was no hope of that. The evil

343

power that radiated from it dwarfed him so completely he felt he was shouting at a hurricane. He closed his eyes and sensed its hunger. It wanted him. It wanted to finish the ritual, one way or another.

'No, Jon.' Lisa was crying now as she saw the doubts crossing his face. 'Please, not my boy!'

The look in her eyes cut him in two. He was going to destroy a woman he loved for the sake of everything else. It wasn't fair, not to her, not to him, not after all the pain they had suffered in their lives. But it had to be done, as it had been done so many times in the past. The life of one boy to prevent untold horror.

He pulled her hands free from his shirt and stepped away, closing his eyes so he didn't have to see her face. But he couldn't block out her cries, each one a razor-sharp blade slashing through his flesh as he stumbled towards the sound of Jamie's tormented sobbing.

His own sacrifice would not be one at all. Death would be a merciful release after such an act of damnation.

With shaking hands, he wrenched Jamie from Velikovsky's grasp and held him up to the terrible face of the Scissorman.

Prologue: Boxing Day and Beyond

I

Culver rubbed his stinging eyes. It was 11.30 p.m. and away in the cold heart of the building he could hear the night shift shuffling through their rituals. There's no rest for any of us, he thought.

He packed up the five victim files containing the autopsy reports and other pertinent personal details and slipped them into his top drawer; he couldn't bear to look at the snapshots pinned to each of the covers any longer, smiling faces, hopeful eyes, people surprised to be caught in life; they made him uncomfortable.

He rested his hands on the cover of Summers' journal for the briefest instant as if there was a chance all the missing information would leap into his fingers from wherever it had been written in invisible ink. Perhaps if Summers had kept writing until the bitter end it might have made some kind of sense, but as it was, the book only provided an inconsequential glimpse at his motivations. A man bitter at what he saw as the waste of a life, seduced by money and power, torn from his hopes of more innocent concerns. A mind fractured by drink and drug abuse, lost in childhood fantasies, hiding the true brutality of his solutions. It was too pat and, as he knew from experience, life was never like that.

Miles had done a bloody good job tracking the house down so quickly, but if only they could have got there sooner. They might have had some idea of exactly what had happened to Summers. An accomplice turned nemesis? He had his suspicions about the wife who was still missing. Or self-inflicted? Hard to believe he could have survived so much pain and blood loss to keep hacking away at himself – they would have had trouble IDing him if not for his wallet – but there had been so many other inexplicable things about the case, he was prepared to accept anything, whatever the medical experts said. He obviously *did* have anatomical knowledge – he missed all the major arteries and that couldn't be luck alone. And with a razor . . . Culver's stomach clenched.

And what was that odd child doing wandering around in all the carnage? When Miles had first called in the early hours of Christmas Day to say they had Summers in custody in the ICU, he had felt a relief that had brought him to the verge of tears. But as the day progressed, he found he couldn't concentrate on the turkey or the TV, or even Shirley. Doubts and fears began crawling into the back of his mind, pointing out all the niggling details, refusing to let him rest. By evening he knew his decision to take a relaxing day off had been wrong.

Now he had the feeling the only way he was going to find out the truth was from Summers' own lips. He had to question Summers one more time before he died, just in case he could squeeze out that crucial droplet of information which would make everything blossom. He had to go the extra mile for his own peace of mind.

Lansing's number was in his Rolodex and he dialled her pager. It was unfair to call her at such a late hour after she had worked a long day at the hospital, but time was running out.

'What is it, Mr Culver?' she asked wearily when she checked in five minutes later. 'I was in bed.'

'Sorry to disturb you, Doctor, but it is important. I need to talk to your man—'

'Out of the question.'

'Doctor, this is my only chance—'

'Mr Culver, he'll be lucky if he survives the night. He's not in a state to be of any use to you. Let him have peace.'

'Summers has slaughtered five innocent people, Dr Lansing. He doesn't deserve any peace.'

The silence that followed his words was so sudden he thought Lansing had hung up.

'Doctor?'

'Didn't you get the message?'

'What message?'

She sighed. 'I got the medical and dental records through before I left for the night. I couldn't get you on the phone so I asked the night team to give you a call.'

'Nobody's called me.' The tension that had been growing through the conversation turned to sudden alarm; he no longer wanted to hear what she had to say.

'It's not Summers, Mr Culver. The records don't match. Patient X is taller, bigger-boned, he's got ginger hair—'

'Well, who the fuck is it then?' Culver exploded. He calmed himself instantly and apologized before hurriedly taking his leave.

Another stupid mistake, he thought bleakly. Summers was still out there.

Arcadia. The fields of heaven. Culver considered the irony of the name as he worked the lock until he heard a successful click. He swung open the door and stepped into the black and white hallway illuminated by the moon shining through the window over the entrance. He had hoped the unnerving sensation of being watched from the inky windows would dissipate the moment he was over the threshold, but if anything, it was worse. There was a sticky feeling of some hidden figure observing him from nearby, and odd scents in the air as if someone had passed through the space only moments before.

'Miles?' he called out hopefully. His voice rang from the

walls. It was too much to hope Ryan would still be lurking there, however keen or tenacious he was. When Culver had called his home before leaving the office, his girlfriend had answered anxiously; she had thought he was working late again. Culver felt guilty about worrying her, but by then he was concerned himself; Ryan was *always* only a phone call away. Although he hated the thought of it, at that point he had no option but to return to Arcadia. It was the last place he had seen Ryan, and also, in those instinctive scramblings at the back of his head, he felt it still harboured secrets, however closely the forensics team had scoured it.

He flicked the light switch, but it failed to dispel the pervading atmosphere of foreboding. He had felt it many times before in houses where there had been violent death, as if the walls had soaked up the suffering; Arcadia's walls must have been saturated. He could understand how houses became haunted.

With a cold weight in his heart, he wandered from room to room, searching for what his instincts told him was there. The drawing room smelled oddly of honey and spices, the study of woodsmoke, ghost aromas that had no business being there. Culver ploughed on regardless, scanning walls, floors and furniture until he reached the spot in the kitchen where they had found Summers' latest victim; his blood still left a dark stain on the cement between the floor tiles that no scrubbing would ever get out.

He began a minute search of the area; it would be there somewhere. Like all psychotics, Summers would be unable to break the bonds of his ritual. After fifteen minutes, he dragged the fridge out of the space in the fitted units and located the wad of paper that had been wedged under the front. Culver slipped on the translucent plastic gloves he had brought with him and unfolded it keenly.

And there it was: one last message to the world, one final chance for Summers to hang himself.

II

And we end with visions of sugar plums dancing before our eyes. The wicked witch has paid the ultimate price. The beautiful princess has been rescued. And the hero returns to society with a magic gift. Not a goose that lays golden eggs or a talking harp. A magic gift to dwarf all others, a trophy of monumental alchemical abilities. But I'll get to that in a while . . .

I should have guessed at the start how it would end; there are some patterns in life that never change, rituals stitched too deeply into the fabric. Five deaths and the sacrifice of an innocent to put the monster back in the box. Five, that mystical number of ill-fortune and mortality.

The Scissorman is real. It's there in all of us to some extent, that destructive, antisocial force that our moral education forces us to keep locked up. Secretly, though, we want to let it out so it can punish all those who make our own personal reality a darker place. That makes the Scissorman seem like a metaphor, which it is, but it's also much more than that.

There's another reality that impinges on our own. Maybe in the dim past it was *part* of our own, responsible for all our race memories and ferocious archetypes. It's a place where all the metaphors live, where the symbols wait to be empowered. Somewhere so alien that we could never see its true form; we shape it, and whatever lives there, to fit our own perception. Fairyland. Neverland. Narnia. The Elysian Fields. All our greatest dreamers have glimpsed some aspect of it.

The Scissorman is vengeance, an abstract given solid form, but it needed a human intellect to give it direction so it could complete its ritual. The Scissorman took root within me, deep in my subconscious, and blindly I showed it the way. It needed five victims and there they were, laid out side by side in my head, and it manipulated me to get what it wanted. That's by way of an explanation, not to absolve me of any guilt. We are all responsible for our actions, even our subconscious ones; that guilt is the price I have to pay for corrupting my own nature.

I'm not leaving this as a warning to posterity; there's nothing anyone could do anyway. But somehow it seemed right to close the circle. Ritual and symbolism *are* important, and from this day on, more than ever.

I wonder how all the humanists and rationalists will feel, all those apologists for the Age of Reason? Really, it's not all it's cracked up to be. I'd go so far as to say the Age of Reason is a misnomer. Yes, we have open-heart surgery and gene therapy. We also have lab-constructed diseases poised to kill whole populations and more land mines than there are people in the world. We have an infant mortality rate that's almost negligible – in the West. And the exact opposite in the Third World. But no sense of wonder or faith or hope or trust or love. The Age of Reason is just an excuse for scientists to build better video recorders and businessmen to make more cash. And what have we lost, what have we lost? We live in a world where profit stands over people, where the human element is stripped from the equation. Where a woman believes love is an alignment of interests and ambitions, where a best friend will cheat, steal and kill for a bigger house, a nicer car. It's a virus that started small, but has infected the world. And there's no cure.

Except one.

I had an opportunity to maintain the status quo. But then I looked in the faces of a boy and a woman who meant more to me than anything in the world, and I looked into my own heart, and I thought, *Is the world I'm fighting for the best that there is? If so, what's the point?*

I don't know how it happened, but since the Dark Ages the creatures of myth and our own land have been pretty much separated. Oh, they could dip into our world and whip some poor unfortunate back to their own; lots of people *have* gone missing. But very rarely could they cross over. And that was right – the Age of Reason could not exist in the face of such unreason. But we paid a big price to keep things that way: all those devalued qualities I mentioned earlier, that sense of wonder, our soaring imagination. Let's face it, science hasn't made us better people, it's simply given us better things.

That big price also included the life of a child and the heart and mind of his mother. That's what those creatures demanded to give up their claim on our world, for a few years at least, just a twinkling of an eye in the great scheme of things. And for a long time people thought that was a reasonable price to pay. No longer.

Sometimes a grand gesture is the only thing that can be done. Sometimes you have to tear it all down to start again. And 'Some day a real rain'll come and wash all the scum off the streets'. I offered up a little boy, and then I took him back and gave him to his mother and together the three of us turned our backs on it all and returned to our lives. I gave them what they wanted, so they had no need for any of us, you see. With the barriers permanently fluid, we found our way back to the house and this world, and by the time you read this, whoever you are, we'll be away somewhere, discovering what life *really* has to offer. The police might try to find us, I suppose, but my betting is that pretty soon they'll have other things on their minds.

Soon, maybe today, maybe next month or next year, Black Annis, the devourer of children, may be spotted in the Leicestershire countryside. The Wild Hunt could tear across East Anglia in search of lost souls. Bloodless bodies may be found in a churchyard in Whitby or lone travellers might go missing on Dartmoor near the old places. And let's not forget the Scissorman – its blades will be forever crimson.

They're coming back.

That's what they always wanted, and the Scissorman was the ritual key to make it happen, but I don't think any of them really believed it would. They were simply running through the habitual game they had been playing for centuries. Still, life's full of surprises.

But it's not all going to be death and suffering and ancient horror. I would never have done it if that was the case – I want the world to be better. There'll be mermaids off the coast of Cornwall, wild magic on Salisbury Plain, satyrs in Sydenham and centaurs in Sunderland. Wonder. Breathtaking new vistas. A chance for us all to grow again.

So bring on the new Dark Age. Say farewell to the old certainties, forget the office politics and the commuting and all the myriad blows that destroy life. This is going to be horrible . . . and this is going to be fun.

'I love the smell of napalm in the morning.'

You don't have to believe this, of course. It could all be the ramblings of a deranged mind. Just keep your eyes open, and listen, and smell the wind. You'll soon know the truth. In the words of Walt Disney's Peter Pan, 'All of this has happened before . . .

And it will all happen again.'